THE SOWING

BOOK ONE OF THE SEEDS TRILOGY

Fall 23, Sector Annum 102, 13h45
Gregorian Calendar: October 13

I rest my head in my palm and try not to nod off as the afternoon sun crawls across my desk. At the center of the classroom, Professor Hawthorne spins a 3D hologram demonstrating how a genome folds and wraps to form a chromosome. I've seen it a hundred times.

"Artificial DNA synthesis, such as that used to create the seeds upon which the Sector depends for agriculture, has been in existence for some time. Recently, however, I've begun to investigate some of the potential data storage properties of artificial DNA. As you know, DNA is the most powerful and compact form of data storage in existence…."

I look around at my fellow students, who are staring, enraptured, at Hawthorne, scribbling feverishly on their desk screens. I bask in my ability to tune out this entire lecture. They're not all like that—sometimes I'm the one frantically scribbling, trying to keep up with Hawthorne's frenetic lecture pace. But protein folding is my mom's area of research, and I've practically grown up on it.

I rub my eyes and shift in my seat. It's warm in here, and I'm waging war with my eyelids, trying to keep them at half-mast. I'm about to fall asleep when I notice a red light blinking in the corner of my tablet. Hoping Hawthorne won't notice my distraction, I tap my finger lightly against the plasma screen where the red dot is pulsating. A few scrawled lines pop up:

Hey, pretty lady. Still breathing? I've practically lost my pulse. Dinner tonight? Assuming we both survive this lecture, that is. - E

I fight the grin that threatens to overrun my face and instead swivel in my chair so I can see Elijah Tawfiq, Hawthorne's research assistant, out of the corner of my eye. Sitting at the back of the room, he's doing a good job of pretending to pay attention. I shoot him a sly smile in response, and he flashes me that crooked grin of his that always sends a delicious pulse of warmth through me. It feels like a hummingbird has nested in my belly, buzzing and flapping its anxious, happy wings. His dark brown eyes are set deeply into his olive-toned face, and his lashes are so long they almost look like feathers. He runs his hand casually through his thick brown hair as he leans back, stretching, arms above his head. I turn back to my desk in an effort to suppress the temptation to jump him here and now. I jot off a quick reply.

Passing messages in class? Why, Eli! I would have thought better of the Sector's most promising young scientist. - Tai

After weeks of flirting, Eli and I have been "officially" dating for almost a month now, but I still haven't gotten over the thrill of seeing that insane smile aimed at me, the eagerness in his voice and step when he's headed my way, and the magically soft kisses he presses into my skin as often as he possibly can. I've never been in love before, but I'm sure this is what it feels like. Filled up to overflowing, giddy. Ridiculous. I want to spend every passing moment with him—and even that probably wouldn't be enough.

The red dot blinks again in the corner, and I bring up his message.

I'll pick you up at seven.

I can't help but grin outright this time, and I hide my smile behind my hand. What a cocky little bastard. He didn't even wait for me to say yes. Of course, it's not like I would turn him down. Still, this time I don't turn around. I'm afraid I might actually giggle, and I don't think Hawthorne would appreciate that.

"By imposing a simple coding sequence—bits of data for base pairs, for example—it would be theoretically possible to use synthetic DNA to store enormous quantities of data. We could insert the entire human registry database into less than a gram of artificially synthesized DNA."

I roll my eyes—I've heard this excited speech ten times already from Eli. I zone out again and return to doodling.

Behind me, I hear Eli's chair scraping as he gets up. It's not like he needs to be here—he knows this material backward and forward. After all, at twenty-one years old he's two years ahead of me and has been working as a research assistant with Hawthorne for the last year and a half. With any luck, soon I'll be done with my introductory classes at the Sector Research Institute and I'll be able to devote my time to research as well. I contemplate following Eli out, ditching the lecture for a quick make-out session in the bathroom, but I realize Hawthorne would probably catch on. So I sigh and turn back to the discussion of artificial base pairs and drift off into thoughts of our dinner date and the possibilities that await.

A minute later, I hear footsteps out in the hallway and wonder if Eli is back already. But it's not Eli. The man standing at the entrance to the classroom is wearing an all-black uniform with a mask covering his face. The military-grade Bolt he has tucked into his shoulder is aimed right at Hawthorne's head. For a half-heartbeat, a split second, the room seems to hold its breath as all eyes shift, afraid, to the man in black. There is a soundless flash of blue as the man pulls the trigger.

Then Hawthorne's head disintegrates.

For another half-second, the world is still, as Hawthorne's mutilated body drops, like a crumbling pillar, to the floor.

Panic consumes the room. There are screams and shouts as my classmates scramble to their feet, desks are overturned, and chairs skitter across the floor. Without thinking, I drop to the floor and curl up under my desk. The dry scent of static and ozone from the Bolt's discharge hangs in the air like poison. Adrenalin surges through my body. *Adrenalin, also known as epinephrine, is a catecholamine. By binding to adrenergic receptors, adrenaline stimulates glycogenolycic reaction in the liver....* From my vantage point on the floor I peer up through the desks, see the man take aim at a student, fire. She drops to the floor, her eyes shuddering cold, her chest a mess of blood, organ tissue, bone. Two more blue flashes. Two more students fall.

Is there any escape? Is there any way to stay alive? I look around for an out, but all I see is chaos. One of the students, Matthew, lunges at the man in black. In exchange he gets a knife in his stomach. He staggers, spits up blood. I squeeze my eyes shut and fight back tears, clinging to my desk, hoping against all hope to avoid detection.

In a matter of seconds, silence reigns. Sobs catch in my throat and I can no longer contain them as I look around at the lifeless bodies of those who were, moments before, classmates and friends. *Cellular death and decomposition begins moments after the heart stops beating. Brain damage begins. Life, beyond three minutes of oxygen deprivation, is irretrievable.*

Every sound in the room seems amplified to ten times normal volume and I can hear the man's breath echo as though in a cavern. The whole world must surely be able to hear my heartbeat. Everything slows to a murmur, a crawl, as I watch the man's boots *clunk, clunk* in my direction. I shiver violently and look around for something, anything with which to fight him. There is nothing. *Eli, where are you?* I want to scream, cry out for him, but at the same time I hope he's somewhere safe and that he will escape my fate.

The man crouches down to look at me and I stare my death in the eyes. I try to control my breathing, to choke back my sobs, and I wheeze with the effort of holding them in my chest. I brush my tears away on my shirtsleeves. I will be brave. *Bravery is nothing more than a part of a threatened animal's defensive reaction, consistent with the release of a combination of dopamine, adrenaline and oxytocin.* The man reaches a hand up to pull his mask away from his face, revealing bloodshot eyes and a thin mouth, lips pressed together as he contemplates his prey. Then he turns his face slightly to the side and his eyes widen, his lips pull back in a maniacal grin.

"Come on now, don't cry. You don't want your family to remember you this way. Give them a smile for when they find you, hmm? Gimme a smile, will you?" He pulls his still-bloody knife from his belt and waves it in front of my face. As the blade grazes my chin I cringe and pull away. I squeeze my eyes shut to force his image out of my mind. I think instead of my parent's faces—*I love you, Mom and Dad. I'm sorry I didn't get to tell you one last time.* I think of my sister, Remy, and her dreams of being an artist. *Please be okay, Remy. Please be okay.*

I taste the salt on my lips as tears roll down my cheeks. I take a shallow breath and whisper, "Just do it, you fucker. Just do it."

His clothes rustle. His breathing is calm. Everything is quiet. I squeeze my eyes shut tighter, as though maybe they will shield me from his weapons, from this certain death. I love you, Eli.

As the brain experiences death and begins to shut down, dimethyltryptamine is synthesized in the pineal gland, triggering psychedelic experiences that often resemble visions of the afterlife. My eyes are closed and I'm enveloped in black, but somehow everything fades slowly to white—a bright, intensely brilliant light that lingers and pools behind my eyes, spreading like ink soaking into cloth, staining, obliterating everything, every memory, every emotion, every image until nothing remains.

The Sowing

by Gabriel Alexander
Poet Laureate, Okarian Sector

Let us practice resurrection
Let us sow our shadowed recollections
Let us breathe life into these broken images
For there is glory in the flowering
And we will dream a dream of spring.

In the Sowing is our memory
Of the dim vast vale of tears,
The visionary gleam of unremembered
Seasons, so solemn and serene.

We are the way and the wayfarers
As the lone and level sands stretch far away
But here at home we till and toil
Here we heed the song of the soil.

And so we collect our wingéd seeds
With all the works and days of hands
Scattered fragments of our spirit
And like some distant ancient anointing
We are poured out like water
We are sown throughout the land.

1 — REMY

The door squeaks open and the room brightens. I turn to see Soren Skaarsgard, nearly as tall as the doorway, pull it shut behind him. The cramped cellar falls into shadow once again.

"Eli's got it figured out," he says. "It should be back up any second."

Elijah Tawfiq, one of our engineers and the closest thing I have to family here at the main base, had managed to tap in to the Sector communications feed, and for a moment we saw flashes of familiar faces and snippets of commentary before the screen went black again. For a government that refuses to acknowledge we exist, their defenses against us are getting much better.

Soren pulls up an empty chair and sits, but then, just as quickly, stands again and starts pacing. My knee bounces up and down, and my fingers tap on my chair until Jahnu shoots me a stop-it-or-I'm-going-to-hurt-you glare. The feed's been down for ten minutes, but each single minute twists and frays in anticipation. Like that moment before a vaccination when the doctor asks, *Are you ready?* before she plunges the needle into your arm.

I breathe deeply, try to calm myself. This viewing room is dark and musty, and my friends and I are the only ones here. Recycled air blows through the vents like a gale, but it never does much good. Seems like down here I'm either sweating or shivering. Today the room is stuffy and I feel faint, like I might be sick. But I don't know if it's from the heat or the anticipation.

We all jump as the screen bursts to life, and the official Okarian Sector Anthem plays in the background over the speakers Eli has retrofitted. We missed the opening speeches while Eli was tinkering with the feed, and now the first thing we see is a sweeping panorama of the state-of-the-art science labs, the glass-fronted performing arts center, the verdant, wide-open spaces of the athletic fields, and, finally, my old dorm. The Okarian Academy, my alma mater. Or it would have been if I hadn't left.

I groan loudly as I recognize the smooth, effortless voice of the commentator,

Linnea Heilmann. Her sultry voice is famous throughout the Sector, but for me each word is like a stab in the gut. When the camera cuts to her, face glowing and blue eyes narrowed, every perfectly coiffed blonde hair in place, I taste bile on the back of my tongue. She was my sister Tai's best friend. When I was little, Linnea braided my hair and always took time to look at my drawings, even when Tai was tired of me.

But Tai's been dead for three years, and now Linnea is the voice of the people who murdered her.

"And now we turn to the Placements," Linnea trills. "Each graduate will announce his or her chosen job or continuing academic career as a citizen of the Okarian Sector." I dig my nails into my palms. Besides the Solstice Celebrations twice a year, Graduation Day is the biggest annual event. The students at the Okarian Academy and the Sector Research Institute are considered elite members of society, watched and admired by the rest of the Sector, almost as if they were old-fashioned royalty. My friends and I, sitting here in this dim underground room, hundreds of kilometers from Okaria, were once members of that elite. I'm sure every Resistance base with the capacity to tap into the feed has people crowded around a screen trying to catch a glimpse of old friends—and enemies—they left behind. "We know that each of these promising young students will contribute to a better and brighter future for us all."

"Better and brighter if slavery is your thing," Soren mutters under his breath.

My stomach is in knots. If I'd stayed, this would have been my graduation year—mine and Jahnu's. It would have been us up there on the stage, sitting next to friends and classmates, joking about the formalities of the ceremony, smiling for the photographers. It would have been us accepting our placements, smiling and celebrating with family and friends, preparing to accept full Okarian Sector citizenship. The people up on the stage were our classmates, our friends. Watching them now feels like betrayal.

The screen cuts to a group of graduates from the Sector Research Institute, and I recognize some of them as Tai's old friends. They would have been closer to Soren and Kenzie's age, and I know Soren would have been at the top of his class. The SRI and the Academy always hold their graduation ceremonies at the same time. While the graduates chat casually, all smiles, we hide out in a dark basement beneath an old city miles and miles into the Dead Zone, away from the capital, away from the Sector, away from home. We are sewer rats, living in this scorched skeleton of a city, hiding out in places nearly bombed into oblivion during the Religious Wars, scurrying into the safety of makeshift structures. We are forgotten by most, ignored by many, and tracked like dogs by those who remember. We are traitors.

And so we watch as, one by one, our former friends take to the stage and announce where they're going next—some are taking positions with the Sector, a few accept research fellowships at the SRI, several are heading out to help oversee factory towns or Farms, and one or two will be officers in the Sector Defense Forces. On the screen, Moriana Nair, Jahnu's cousin, steps up and walks across the stage. I reach over and squeeze Jahnu's hand. He and Moriana practically grew up together. I can hear Soren swearing under his breath. Kenzie is sniffling, and I watch as Jahnu wraps his arm around her, comforting her even as he watches his cousin announce her research placement.

I wonder if those on the screen, smiling out at the cameras, are thinking of us, remembering us like we remember them. Do they think about how we live, what we've sacrificed? Probably not. Our classmates have forgotten us like winter on a warm summer's day, unaware that the government they serve hunts us day and night.

The students finish their announcements, and the president of the Academy gives a short speech about how amazing everyone and everything is. I can't fight back an eye roll. The camera cuts back to Linnea.

"What promising graduates! And now, the moment we've all been waiting for—the honors speech from our young nation's most celebrated student. It will be no surprise to our viewers that Valerian Augustus Orleán is graduating with the highest honors."

Soren groans so loud Kenzie shushes him, and I can't help but agree. Of course Vale is graduating with the highest honors. His mother, the director general of the Okarian Agricultural Consortium, the corporate body that controls the food supply and seed banks, would have made sure Vale received the highest honors. It certainly doesn't hurt that his father is the chancellor of the Sector.

"As the Research Institute's top student, Vale has the honor of addressing the nation and announcing what's next for him. Many have wondered whether he will take a commission in the Sector Defense Forces. Will he follow his father's footsteps into government or his mother's into research? Of course, we all hope that whatever path he chooses, he will continue to perform around the Sector—he is our most talented young pianist, after all."

I flinch as a chair skids across the floor and crashes into the far wall. Soren. If Vale is the Sector's most talented pianist, it's only because Soren isn't there to compete. I wonder if Soren's thinking back to the last time he played—we obviously haven't got a piano down here, and no one's yet managed to scavenge anything digital that comes close to what Soren had at home. I bet he hasn't touched one since he left.

Linnea goes on, her voice lilting with excitement, her eyes glowing, her cheeks flushing. It occurs to me that they could be together. A faint twinge of jealousy passes through me and then fades. After all, why not? It's been three years since we had anything, me and Vale—whatever it was. Just a kiss, really. It meant nothing. I dig my nails into my palms. They deserve each other. Vale stands, smiles, and walks to the podium. Behind him, a list of his accomplishments scrolls down a huge projection screen. The headmaster of the SRI stands at the podium waiting to shake Vale's hand and smile for the cameras.

"Is it nice to see your old friend Valerian again, Remy?" Soren says with a savage breath. They never did get along, Soren and Vale, and Soren knows how close we were. Once upon a time.

"Shut up. This has nothing to do with me."

"Soren, not now," Jahnu warns.

Soren scoffs and returns his gaze to the screen. We've seen Vale countless times on the Sector feed, but I'm always amazed at how much he's changed since the last time I saw him in person. He still has the same black hair, the same handsome dark eyes, the same lashes any girl would fall for. I think about the kiss, his hand on the back of my neck, his breath hot and our hearts pounding. It seems like a million years ago, practically another geological era. But it was just three years ago, when the future looked limitless, when I hadn't a care in the world beyond my homework assignments. Our friends were the new generation of builders, the ones who would usher the Okarian Sector into a long period of peace and prosperity. We dreamed of lives without war, without famine, with the scientific advances that would ensure our children would never experience the devastation, starvation, and disease our grandparents had survived. Now, those dreams look like little more than naïve fairy tales.

I watch Vale and wonder if he ever thinks about those dreams. If he remembers what we shared, our hopes, our passions, the hours spent laughing at each other and fast becoming more than friends. But then Tai was murdered, we fled the Sector, and I lost everything I once knew—including Vale.

Vale has lost nothing. He still has his parents and all of his friends; he is surrounded by wealth and power. His future is secure. But as I watch him on the stage I have to ask myself: Does he know why we left? Does he know what his parents—what his government—has done to drive those of us in the

Resistance underground? Does he care about the crimes they've committed in the name of the greater good? I watch him and wonder if there's anything left in him of the idealist I once knew.

"Ladies and gentlemen," Vale begins. "It's a beautiful evening and I know everyone on the stage and out there in the audience is ready to get out of our formal attire and start the celebrations, so I will keep my remarks short."

"Not short enough," Soren growls, dropping into a chair in front of me and stretching out his long legs. His blonde hair glints in the light from the screen, and I can see his silhouetted jaw clench and unclench as he grinds his teeth. Soren's mother used to be the chancellor, before Vale's father was appointed. I never heard the full story, but Soren's always suspected foul play. He's hated Vale ever since, and it probably didn't help that after Soren's mother was removed from the chancellorship, Vale got all the media attention and Soren fell from the spotlight.

"As the newest leaders of our nation, we pledge to do everything in our power to ensure security and stability for future generations. To that end, I am pleased to accept my placement position in the role of director of the newly-formed Seed Bank Protection Project."

A creeping dread clutches its chilly fingers at my spine as the audience on-screen erupts into loud cheers and vigorous clapping. He sounds so valiant, so righteous, that for a half second I almost want to believe him, too. What they don't know, those in the jubilant crowd, is that for the last three years the Resistance has been quietly chipping away at the Sector's control over the seeds used to feed its citizens. We've been stealing the genetic codes to the OAC's modified seeds and disseminating untainted, safe food to those few people willing to listen, those who have escaped the OAC's manipulation. Vale's placement somehow seems targeted directly at us—at me.

"This new role allows me to pursue our goals with singular purpose. Our nation's priority is to ensure we have enough food and fresh water to nourish our people. Our Farms, and the men and women who work on them, are the cornerstone of our society, and without their dedication and passion for their work, the Okarian Sector would not survive." He gestures out to the crowd as if honoring the actual Farm laborers—who are, of course, not at an elite ceremony like this one. The onlookers clap and cheer enthusiastically. "But after the Religious Wars and the Famine Years, tillable land and potable water remain scarce, and we must strive to use our resources wisely. That is why it is imperative that OAC researchers continue to hybridize and engineer new strains of seeds so they will grow—and even flourish—in the contaminated land left to us from the Old World. We will do whatever it takes to feed our people.

"Of course, the task of safeguarding our Farms, our scientists, and the hybridized seeds they create is not new. The government and the OAC have long joined forces to protect our agricultural future from the mistakes of our past. Now, establishing the Seed Bank Protection Project as an official joint effort allows us to wield both the power of the government and the resources of the OAC to achieve our goals."

He turns directly to the camera and says, "I promise I will not fail in my task."

The screen goes dark. Eli must have decided he'd had enough. I relax my shoulders and slump in my seat. Soren turns to me with a spiteful glare.

"They're putting their prized hound on the scent. One mistake, Remy, and we're all dead. They take everything. All our sacrifices will be for nothing. Thousands more will be poisoned, manipulated, turned to slaves. You better not fucking give us away just because Valerian Orleán is in the game now."

He won't give up, will he?

"Vale is nothing to me. And he, I guarantee, has forgotten I even exist." I'm trying to stay calm, staring straight ahead, refusing to meet Soren's eyes.

"Right." He snorts.

"Soren, she gets it," Jahnu says.

"You've had everything done for you your entire life," Soren spits back at me, ignoring Jahnu entirely. "If Tai hadn't been murdered, you would never have left. You'd still be back in the Sector with Vale."

Without realizing it, I'm standing over Soren, my fists balled at my side.

"We gave up everything to join the Resistance—" I hiss.

"Look around you. You're not the only one."

"I know that, Soren! It's not about who made the choice to leave the Sector— it's about the fact that we're here now, together. We have to fight together. Stop treating me like I'm some stupid little girl who's going to go soft over a teenage crush. I'm a member of your team!"

"You guys have to stop going at each other," Jahnu pleads. "Everyone here has lost someone. Everyone has given up something. We're all in this together."

Soren just stares at me. He glances at Jahnu and his eyes, cold and blue as rare glacier ice, soften a bit.

"Sometimes I wonder," he mutters. Then he turns on his heel and leaves without another word. I'm shaking, my jaw clenched so tight I wonder my teeth don't shatter. Kenzie rubs my shoulder and gives me a sympathetic glance but follows Soren through the door.

"I don't know who I hate more right now," I say.

"Cut him some slack, Remy," Jahnu says.

"All he does is goad me!"

"Remy—"

"What?" I cut him off. "You know it's true. He's always taunting me, whether it's about Vale, or the fact that I'm shit at science and math, or even how short I am."

"I think you sometimes forget he's here by himself. Soren's parents are still in the Sector. He chose to join the Resistance himself. Do you think you would have been able to make a decision like that?"

I pull up short at the question. I don't know the answer, but the anger still gnaws at me. "I wish he'd just leave me alone," I mutter, defeated.

"I think I'm going to suffocate if I don't get out of here. Let's go find Eli and see if it's safe to go topside and get some fresh air," Jahnu says, trying to cheer me up.

"You're right," I respond. "Vale and his friends will all be celebrating, so I say we have our own celebration. We should have a picnic. Just like the old days."

"What are we going to celebrate?" he asks. I pause, trying to think of something worthy of celebration.

"That we're here together," I say finally. "That we're fighting for something bigger than ourselves. That we still have each other."

Brave words. And they almost make me feel better.

2 — VALE

"Thank you. May we gain strength from the sowing, resilience from the reaping, and hope from the harvest."

I flash a smile and turn away from the podium as the packed audience erupts in applause. A stupid grin spreads across my face, and I take a deep breath. My knees are shaking like they always do after I speak to a large crowd, and I wobble back to my chair and take my place next to Moriana Nair. She squeezes my hand and grins at me, her big brown eyes wide and excited, mouthing the words, *We did it!*

The head of the Academy takes the podium and begins thanking me for my remarks and reiterating how much the Sector is depending on us. He sounds like he's speaking from the inside of a tunnel, and I just give the crowd my practiced Orleán smile and try to breathe normally. When he returns to his own seat on the stage, my father, the chancellor of the Sector, rises and leads everyone in the Sector anthem.

Finally, the welcoming ceremony for the graduating students of the Academy begins—Moriana and I went through this ceremony two years ago when we graduated from the Academy. It's an old ceremony, treasured and well-loved. My mother, as head of the Okarian Agricultural Consortium, holds a bowl of seeds at my father's side. He then scoops out a handful from the bowl and, with a broad smile on his face, tosses them out onto the first row of Academy students. A cheer starts up through the audience as family members and friends join in to shower the graduating students with seeds. It's a celebration of the fact the Famine Years are past and the Sector promises a future of plenty.

"Congratulations!" My father loves Graduation Day, and I can see the twinkle in his eyes as he gazes out across the rows of graduates and family members. The boom of erupting fireworks announces the end of the ceremony, and brilliant colors paint the sky above. Our classmates jump to their feet, hugging each other and their proud parents, offers of congratulations being thrown as plentifully as the seeds. Out of the corner of my eye I see my friend Jeremiah Sayyid signaling to me and Moriana to hurry. It's party time. But there's no way I can get off the stage as long as the cameras are still rolling. I give Moriana a quick hug and then join my parents as politicians, professors, and OAC board members fall over themselves to congratulate me. I shake hands, pose for photos, and play the political game, just like I've had to do my whole life.

I turn to see my father shaking hands with General Aulion, my soon-to-be supervisor at the Seed Bank Protection Project. He has a creased face, stark black hair, and a wicked scar across his jawline. He is not easily forgotten. Over the past year, Aulion has been personally in charge of my military training as I prepared to move away from my physics research and into a military career. In the entire year I've known him, I've seen him crack a smile exactly one time, and that was when he was watching me struggle futilely to finish a set of chin-ups.

Instead of congratulating me like everyone else, Aulion eyes me, his hands behind his back. "You're expected at the office at 07h00 tomorrow, Lieutenant Orleán." That's the first time anyone has addressed me by my new military rank.

"He'll be there, General," my mother pipes up from my side. "But for tonight, let's let him celebrate."

"If he's not there at 07h00 tomorrow morning, General, you can send him to the chancellor's office," my father says, grinning. "I'll be happy to take care of him." Dad's always had my back.

Speaking more quietly, my mother turns to Aulion. "While I escort my son to the festivities, perhaps you'll update the chancellor on the troubling situation at the Farms."

Aulion's eyes narrow almost imperceptibly even as my father's widen. This news is obviously a surprise to him. I know for a fact he hasn't had his security briefing yet this morning because he took me out to breakfast so I could practice my speech with him. And it's clear Aulion is none too happy that my mother is getting her information from someone under his command.

"Of course," Aulion says, nodding curtly in her direction. "I would be happy to update the chancellor." His taut lips and tense voice tell me he's anything but happy to deliver the bad news.

I take my mother's arm in mine and leave Aulion to my father. "Thanks for the save—but what's going on at the Farms?"

My mother smiles wryly up at me. "Unfortunately, Vale, until tomorrow morning, you don't have the security clearance necessary for me to tell you." I laugh.

"Perfect. I won't have to worry about it until then."

We're at the door to the student lounge and I can hear the voices of my classmates inside. My mother stops and takes my hands in hers. "I cannot tell you how proud we are. Now, you go have a good time tonight. And tell Moriana not to stay out too late, either. I'm looking forward to having her join my lab team tomorrow."

I give Mom a hug. "She's excited to be working with you."

"I'm delighted to have her. She's got a bright future." She pauses and picks an imaginary piece of lint off my sleeve. I look down at her, and I can't help but notice tears glistening in her eyes. She stretches up on tiptoe to give me a kiss, and as she brushes my face I can feel the tears on her cheeks. "Go have fun. I'll talk to you tomorrow." She turns and heads back in the direction we came.

Finally I can stop being Valerian Augustus Orleán and start being Vale again. I open the door to the lounge and a geyser of wet foam splashes my face.

"Jeremiah, you shit, you're going to pay for that!" I wipe sparkling wine out of my eyes with my sleeve.

There are perhaps thirty students milling around, some from the Academy and some from the SRI, and every one of them is laughing as I cough and sputter. It's not often I'm the victim of practical jokes—though it has become much more frequent since Jeremiah and I became friends. I find his bearded face through the bubbles still dripping from my eyelashes.

I take a crystal flute from his hands.

"Apparently this is the Sector's finest old bubbly, and don't bother asking how I commandeered several bottles just for us. State secrets." He pulls out a chair, stands up on it—not that he needs the height boost, he already towers over everyone in the room—and clears his throat. "Attention, everybody." He raises his glass. "I hereby propose a toast to my best friend—the pride, the joy, the savior and radiant light of the whole Sector."

"To the harvest!" everyone toasts as they drain their glasses.

"Miah, has anyone ever told you you're an asshole?"

"Never," he says. "You're the first."

I reach for the magnum of wine just as he grabs it. "Whoa, whoa, Vale. I am the arbiter of all things fun today. I would be nice to me if I were you."

"Arbiter of fun, huh?"

"Indeed, my friend. Which is why I am taking it upon myself to ensure that you have no shortage of beautiful girls for the evening."

"I'm not that hard up. I could get a date if I wanted."

"A date? You could get any date in the entire Sector if you wanted."

"Vale has a date?" Moriana comes up behind me and gives me a big hug. I embrace her and she kisses me on the cheek. Moriana and Jeremiah are always mocking me for my lack of interest in dating. It's not that I'm uninterested; I'm just not always as outgoing and talkative as they are. And it doesn't help that even three years later, I can't get Remy Alexander out of my head.

"No, that's the problem," Miah says, handing Moriana a glass. She grabs his bearded chin and pulls him down to her height for a quick kiss. "He doesn't have a date. Which is why I'm taking it upon myself to ensure he doesn't sit in a corner all night."

Moriana turns to me and pokes her finger in my chest. "Miah's right. You should find a lady, Vale. My cousin will be there tonight—"

"See?" Miah laughs, interrupting Moriana. "We'll be surrounded by brilliance and beauty all night long."

"—And she's been looking forward to seeing you again," Moriana finishes, glaring at Jeremiah.

"Stop playing matchmaker and pour me another glass of wine," I say.

Suddenly I feel the slightest pressure on my arm. The hair stands up on the back of my neck, and I know who it is before I even turn. When I do, I find a wave of silken blond hair and the bluest eyes in the Sector. Linnea Heilmann, who is almost as tall as me, stands at my shoulder, an inviting smile playing around her mouth. She wears a sleek, shimmering pearl-colored dress that trails down to her feet, with a very noticeable slit that trails right back up to her thigh. She is as sharp and beautiful as a blade. My mother has been not-so-subtly encouraging me to start going out with her. "She's so talented, Vale. You'd make such a great pair! And you have so much in common." What I have in common with Linnea could fit in a buckyball.

"Congratulations, Vale," Linnea says with a gentle smile. "You did a great job out there. I'm sure all the citizens of the Okarian Sector were impressed. I know I was."

"Oh, hey, Linnea," Miah says with a barely concealed sneer. "I thought only students were allowed back here." Jeremiah hates Linnea. He thinks she's just about the worst thing that ever happened to the Sector. He's always going on about how she treats the workers on the Farms like second-class citizens, even though the Farm workers are among the most important citizens of the Sector. Working on the Farms is considered a great honor, and almost everyone who begins a term on the Farms decides to stay. I flash Miah a glare that says very clearly: *Cut it out.* We don't need to get on Linnea's bad side.

"Thanks, Linnea," I say hesitantly, not sure how to walk the line here. "As always, you look nice." That's the best compliment I can muster. She seems satisfied, though, because she smiles at me, flashing perfect teeth and full lips painted in luscious plum.

I ignore the look Miah gives me and turn away as Moriana scowls and mouths *my cousin* like it's a command. I let my eyes linger on Linnea's and then drag them down over every curve and shadow, all the way down to her high heels and painted plum toenails and back up again. I start to speak, but my throat is dry, and I find that even if I really wanted to, I couldn't put the words together to invite her along. Despite her best efforts—and my mother's— Linnea isn't my type.

Her eyes cloud as if she realizes what just went through my mind. She leans in and whispers, "Come find me later, Vale. I'll wait for you." She lets her fingertips trail off my shoulder as she turns elegantly and walks off.

Miah hits me in the arm so hard I almost drop my glass. "Vale, if you so much as consider going out with her, I'll—"

"That girl is climbing the power ladder," Moriana says, interrupting what would surely have been a diatribe, "and you are just a few rungs from the top." She tilts back her glass and downs it in an uncharacteristic display of enthusiasm. She's usually so calm and modest that even Jeremiah looks surprised. "Come on, you guys, forget about Linnea. Tonight's our last night of freedom before we start work. Let's go have fun!" She grabs each of us by the hand and hauls us off towards the door.

Outside, six or seven girls are waiting at the airship deck, smiling eagerly at me as we approach.

"A gift from me to you," Jeremiah says to me, smirking. I recognize a few of them as acquaintances of Jeremiah's from the SRI's engineering division and assume he brought them along in the hopes of getting me to go out with at least one of them.

It turns out Jeremiah has worked even more of his magic for the evening. My father's personal airship waits for us, gleaming and sleek.

"It's pre-programmed to take us to the club and then home afterwards," Jeremiah says with a wink, "but your father was all too happy to donate it to my cause this evening."

I'm speechless. My father never lets me take his airship. My dad's been fond of Jeremiah since they discovered a shared interest in flight engineering, which drives my mother crazy—she thinks Jeremiah lacks motivation.

Once we're all in, Jeremiah pulls out another bottle of wine and we toast to our futures as we blast the music and sing all the way across town to the club.

At the club, we smoke our Dietician-approved cannabis doses and relax into the swing of the evening, talking about the ceremony and what's to come. Jeremiah has to ask the club managers to keep the photographers and reporters out of the party so we can relax away from the scrutiny of the rest of the Sector. The aromatic haze of incense and smoke blends with sweat and perfume, and I sink deep into the pleasure of my last night as a student. We take off our shoes to dance on the mossy rooftop veranda, and Moriana makes sure I have a steady supply of dance partners, especially her cousin. The cannabis and alcohol help me forget that 07h00 and General Aulion loom closer with every passing minute. I keep my friends close, even doing a turn around the dance floor with Miah until Moriana mercifully cuts in and rescues us from ourselves. I want to hold onto every moment, every song, every laugh, because I know that tomorrow, everything changes. Once or twice, Moriana catches my eye, and I know that even though she's clinging to Jeremiah's arm, she misses them, too. The ones who left.

Several hours later, the party is winding down, and most everyone else has already gone home or on to other parties. I plop down at our now-empty table, my head reeling from the fullness of the evening. It was almost perfect. I lean back against the wall and close my eyes. In the background, the performers play a final ballad and the lights dim slightly. In the alcohol-and-fatigue-induced haze, Remy Alexander's face swims up before my eyes. I see her copper skin, her round hazel eyes, her flush lips and brown curls—fifteen-year-old Remy Alexander, the last time I saw her. The last time any of us saw her. She's eighteen now, of course ... I wonder what she looks like, if she still has that silly giggle, the glint in her eyes like when she was teasing me. Or did her sister's death tear that happiness from her?

I start as Moriana appears out of nowhere. She looks lovely with her long dark reddish brown hair framing her freckled cheekbones and tired green eyes. Her silky black dress rustles and dances around her as she pulls up a chair and sits at my side.

"I miss them, too, Vale," she says, somehow reading my thoughts.

"I know," I say after a minute. "I just don't know why they left. They had everything. Why throw that away? It doesn't make sense."

"It's time to move on. Tomorrow you start your new job and a whole new set of opportunities will open up for you, for both of us. It's what we always dreamed of."

"I know it's stupid, but sometimes I can't stop thinking about her. Remy, I mean. She just left. Everything seemed perfect and then, well … then Tai. One day she stopped talking to me, and then she was just gone. Everything we shared, thrown away with no explanation."

"Vale, you were seventeen. She was fifteen. You were kids. Now you're twenty, you're a citizen of the Sector, you're an officer in the Defense Forces. We live in a different world."

"Where's Miah?" I ask, closing my eyes. I can't believe how exhausted I am. How the hell am I going to face Aulion in just a few hours?

"He's waiting outside. I told him I needed a minute."

"Look, just—"

"I won't say a word. But Vale, seriously. It's time to leave them behind. Just like they left us behind. I miss Jahnu, but he and his parents made their choice."

"Do you ever wonder why he left?"

"I used to, but not anymore. I have no idea what my aunt and uncle thought they would find out in the Wilds. Some sort of agrarian paradise? Did they go to live with the Outsiders? Who knows—but I suppose every society has its rebels. We can't change that."

"Yeah, I know," I mutter. I want to agree, but I don't. I can't. There are too many unanswered questions, too many ghostly memories that cling to me like a second skin, and I can't seem to shed them. There's something wrong here, something I'm missing. And tomorrow, at 07h00 hours, I intend to start looking for the answers.

3 — REMY

Fall 47, Sector Annum 105, 18h02
Gregorian Calendar: November 6

Jahnu and I walk through the dimly lit main corridor of our underground compound, through to the cramped cafeteria, looking for Eli. We head down the stairs toward the director's office and our communications center. Our meager excuse for a kitchen smells like fresh baked bread and sautéed onions, and I remember how lucky I am to have escaped the Okarian Sector. If I never see a Dietician-issued Mealpak again, it'll be a day too soon. Here we may not have a lot, but what we have is *real*. I breathe in deeply, hoping to get another whiff of the caramelizing onions and fragrant garlic, only to be brought back to reality by the scent of recycled air and rubbing alcohol wafting from the open door of what passes for our infirmary.

We're in the bowels of what was, at one time, a large university, on par with our own Sector Research Institute, the SRI, today. We live like moles, hiding underground, digging tunnels and burrowing to avoid being seen by Sector drones when they venture out this far. Except that no one in the Okarian sector has seen a mole in a hundred years, or so says old man Rhinehouse. They were all killed by poisoned groundwater, habitat destruction, or radioactive waste seeping into the earth. Gifts bequeathed to us from the civilizations of the past. Some areas are still uninhabitable; others, nature has mended in her own way; still others were relatively untouched to begin with.

Jahnu pushes through the heavy double doors to the comm center, where Eli is sitting in a swivel chair with headphones on. He wears a thoughtful expression, like he's trying to figure out how some piece of circuitry works. But there's no circuit box in front of him—just the headphones and the array of dials and switches that make up our old-fashioned comm center. I walk over and poke him in the shoulder.

"Eli!"

He starts and looks up at me. When he sees who it is, he swivels in his chair and removes his headphones.

"Well, look who's here. I was just about to send a messenger to find you, Remy. Your folks are calling in. You want me to put you through?"

"Jahnu and I want to go topside for our own graduation celebration," I say, trying to dodge the question. "There's nothing crazy on the weather forecast, is there?" The weather is so erratic these days that you can go to bed on a warm evening and wake up to a meter of snow on the ground. Then there are the thunderstorms with hailstones that can kill a man, the downpours that deposit an ocean's worth of water in a few hours, and the occasional tornado clusters. Needless to say, we monitor the weather closely.

"Do you want to talk to them or not?" Eli asks, holding the headphones out, his finger on the incoming call switch. He can always tell when I'm being evasive. Not that I'm ever particularly subtle.

"We want to have a picnic, so we need to get everything organized. I'll have you put a call through to them later."

Eli cocks his head and raises one eyebrow as if to say, *You're not fooling anyone.*

"Remy, you have no idea if they're even going to be available later," Jahnu points out. It's true. Posing as Outsiders, nomads who live in the Wilds, my parents are constantly moving, traveling between factory towns and Farms, trying ever so subtly to spread word of the Resistance to Sector citizens willing to listen. The Resistance is so small, and most of us are defects from the elite of the OAC and the Sector government. So my parents try to spread the word, and in the meantime they work to deliver real food, information, and medicine to people in the Farms. As a doctor and an artist, they make a powerful combination. But their access to reliable communications is spotty at best, especially since they're operating right under the nose of Sector Defense Forces, and whatever public communications equipment they might use is liable to be monitored. If Sector soldiers ever caught them, well….

"Listen, I don't want to talk to them right now, okay? Besides, I don't need mommy and daddy to make everything all better."

"The world would be a better place if we all had mommies and daddies to make everything all better," Eli says, with an edge to his voice. I wince, remembering that Eli has no idea where his parents are, or if they're still alive. I have to be careful about what I say around him—I never know when something will send him spiraling into one of his dark moods. The kind where he'll barely say a word for days. The kind where he forgets to eat or sleep—where I wonder if he wishes the gunman had gotten to him, too. "Your parents are waiting."

"Fine." I sit down at the call station and put my finger on the switch. I hear

Jahnu ask Eli, "So, is it safe to go topside now? We need something to cheer us up after the ceremony. And my birthday is next week."

"Last one to hit the big one-eight, huh? What's it like to be a child prodigy?"

"You should know...."

I tune them out and flip the call switch. There's a hollowness on the other end and then, "Remy? Is that you?"

"Yeah, Mom. It's me." My voice catches in my throat.

"Dad's on the line, too. We saw the ceremony."

"I'm sure everyone in the Sector saw the ceremony."

"You okay, little bird?"

At the sound of Dad's voice, my eyes well up and my nose tingles. I pinch the bridge of my nose to keep the tears at bay. Mom's always been my sounding board. She keeps me grounded, but I'm more like my dad. He's the writer, the poet, the dreamer who brought art and music and literature into the house. He's the one who encouraged me to be an artist, who somehow found books, real books, on artists that had dared to be different. When Tai was off being brilliant and perfect, finishing her science and math classes with flying colors, I always had a pen in hand, perpetually drawing, painting, or sketching. Dad was the one who encouraged me to enter the Academy's prestigious Art and Design program—even though that turned out to be nothing but an extensive study of propaganda. And while Mom was planning our escape route, he's the one who sat with me the night before we left when, one by one, we went through my portfolio of drawings and paintings and decided which ones to keep and which to burn. We went through every piece and picked our favorites, and then I took the others and held them over the flames in the fireplace until they were nothing more than ashes and my fingers were hot and smudged with soot.

I shouldn't have taken the call.

"Yeah, I'm okay."

Talking to them on the commlink is torturous—it always makes me remember how much I miss them and Tai. I haven't seen my parents in over a year. We talk here and there, whenever they can get their equipment connected to one of the old service towers that the Resistance has rehabbed. But sometimes we'll go weeks without talking. I have trouble sleeping then, thinking of all the terrible things that could go wrong.

"I hope you're going to do something fun today, maybe get outside for some fresh air," Dad says.

"Yeah, we're going to have a picnic later to celebrate our lack of a graduation."

I can't keep the bitterness out of my voice. But I realize I'm being a baby, so I change the subject quickly. "Where are you right now?"

"You know we can't tell you that, sweetie," Mom says.

"We're going somewhere new in a few days, though," my dad pipes up. "That's why we wanted to talk to you now, before we have to pack up the comm equipment."

"Is it somewhere dangerous?" I ask, afraid to hear the answer. But not knowing would be worse. My parents volunteered to serve as missionaries to the laborers on the Farms, but I wasn't allowed to go. "Too risky," the Director said. "You're too young. Besides, we need you here." My parents agreed. They wanted me to stay at the main base, which we call Thermopylae, with Eli and the other kids from the Academy. That's how I got assigned to Eli's raid team with Jahnu, Kenzie, and Soren.

"It's no more dangerous than where we are now," Mom says gently.

"That's not very reassuring. Don't get caught, okay?"

"We'll try, little bird," my dad says. "You be safe too, okay? I heard about the last seed bank raid you guys did. It sounded much more dangerous than what we do."

"Yeah, maybe," I say, with a glimmer of a laugh, "but I'm sure it was way more fun than what you guys do, too."

The last mission our team went on was a thrill. We broke into one of the OAC's seed banks, trying to steal the backup database that had all the genetic codes for the seeds manufactured there. Security was lax, presumably because the OAC didn't realize we knew that particular bank existed. We had the run of the place, and we each picked out something to take home with us. Eli brought back a handheld retinal scanner. Soren found a digital harp, and none of us had any idea why that was hanging around the seed bank. I brought home a touch-screen drawing pad—one of the plasma tablets we used in my art classes at the Academy. I hadn't seen one of those since we left the Sector. It was the most successful mission in the Resistance's history, and we were greeted like war heroes when we came back.

"Yes, well, they're not always going to be like that," my mom says reprovingly, "so stay safe, okay?"

"We've got to go now, little bird. We'll talk to you in a few weeks, when we get everything set up at our next base."

"Okay," I whisper. Now that I've got them, I don't want to let them go. "Bye."

"We love you."

"I love you, too," I say, but the words are barely audible. I hear the click, and then the static of an empty signal on the other end. I pull off the headphones and throw them down on the table.

"Good to go?" Eli asks.

"Yeah. Let's get out of here."

"I can't come," he says. "I'm doing a double shift."

"No way!" I exclaim in indignation. Eli already spends at least sixteen of his waking hours working, either tinkering with some old piece of equipment or doing shifts at different stations around the base. There's no reason for him to work a double shift.

"You covering for someone or in trouble again?" Jahnu asks.

"Apparently I have a bad attitude." Eli smiles.

"Really?" Jahnu draws back in mock astonishment, his almond eyes wide. "What did you do this time?" Eli and Jahnu stand in stark contrast to each other. They're about the same height, but Jahnu's skin is the color of a shadowy night and his hair is shaved close. Eli's brown curls, on the other hand, are usually uncontrollable, and his olive skin makes me think of sandy beaches and summer afternoons in the sun.

"I told the Director what I thought of her plans for the Arysk mission."

"Told her politely, I'm sure." Jahnu rolls his eyes.

"I'm always polite." Eli grins. Eli's version of polite typically includes shouting and slamming doors.

"That's why back home they were feeding you OAC happy pills morning, noon, and night," I throw out.

"And who knows what they were putting in my food."

There's a sort of pause, a thick silence that fills the moment when the three of us don't want to say the next thing, the thing that we're all thinking about, the thing that brought us all to the bowels of this old bombed-out university. To provide a distraction, I stand and try to pull Eli out of his creaky old office chair. It just rolls toward me.

"You're coming with us. There's nothing going on today. Everyone in the Sector is celebrating, so we're going to have our own celebration." I want Eli to come because it's always more fun with him along. We need him, bad attitude and all. "And the Director doesn't have to know you bailed on your shift," I add.

"Besides, what's she going to do, fire you?" Jahnu says. We all smile at the impossible idea. The Director needs Eli. He's one of the most important members of our team. Without his skills, half of the technology we use on a daily basis would just be junk. Besides, firing him would amount to nothing. Here at the Resistance, we're all refugees, and it's not like anyone's going to exile Eli into the Wilds.

Eli is twenty-four, six years older than Jahnu and I. He was two years ahead of my sister Tai, and they'd been together for several months. Tai couldn't stop talking about him. He was a research and teaching assistant at the SRI, working with one of the professors in the genetics lab where Tai spent most of her time. Eli had always been a class clown, the troublemaker to whom everything came easy and nothing seemed to matter, and Tai was the perfectly poised favorite student, maybe even a bit of a teacher's pet. Somehow they clicked.

He was the one who found her. He found them all, every student cut down, massacred by what the OAC called "a savage from the Wilds." Eli is alive because he had to take a shit in the middle of a lecture and because in the wake of the Religious Wars and the Famine Years, even the Okarian Sector can't always get its hands on reliable weaponry. Eli had been in the bathroom when the man entered the classroom, and by the time he got off the pot, it was all over. He walked back to the classroom to find the killer standing over Tai's body.

"You're late to the party," the man said. "Too bad you had to miss out on all the fun. But don't worry. Lucky for you, there's an after party right here." He placed his Bolt between Eli's eyes and pulled the trigger. Nothing happened. Stunned, Eli stood immobilized. The man stared at his gun, swore, pointed it at Eli again, and pulled the trigger several times. Still, nothing happened.

Later, in his testimony before a secret government inquiry, Eli described how, after he realized the charge was malfunctioning, he had lunged at the man, only to be slammed back up against the wall. But instead of turning the weapon back on Eli, the man grinned at him and said: "A word to the wise, kid. Never get on Madam Orleán's bad side." He put the Bolt up to his own head and pulled the trigger. This time, the weapon discharged. Eli, now covered in blood and brains, staggered over to Tai's side and passed out, and that's where the Watchmen found him.

So, now he has anger management issues. Who can blame him? He lost his research scholarship and his job because he was "unstable," the line involving Corine Orleán was stricken from the official court records, and Eli's testimony was declared "compromised due to emotional trauma." When his parents petitioned the Sector for a fair public hearing, they were transferred somewhere, no one knows where, and no one has heard from them since.

Not three months later, the brilliant Corine Orleán was promoted from head of Research and Development to OAC General Director. The whole "investigation" took about six months, but when my parents figured out the truth—and realized that Tai's death was going to go without retribution—we left. Disappeared. We joined the Resistance and brought Eli with us. Together, Eli and I swore that Tai's death would be avenged. That we would make whoever was responsible pay.

Now my friends and I look up to Eli. He's our link to the reality of what the Sector and the OAC are capable of—of what they will do if they ever catch us. Plus, Eli's just a great guy, in that big-brother-you-always-wanted kind of way. He has a serious problem with authority and doesn't give a damn what anyone else thinks. The stuff he pulled when he used to lead teams into the field to scavenge old labs, factories, and farms is legendary—so legendary the Director rarely allows him out anymore without "adult supervision."

"You know what? For once, you're absolutely right. It's time to get out of here." He picks up his handheld and punches in a few numbers. "Firestone, get your lazy ass up here. You're on duty."

Jahnu and I glance at each other and smile. Firestone, Eli's buddy, won't be happy, but for us, the day is looking up.

"Yes, I know I was assigned your shift, but things change, my friend. And as you always say—" he pauses and winks at us—"That's an interesting choice of words. You know swearing is the mark of a lazy mind."

Eli holds the handheld up so Jahnu and I can hear the stream of obscenities. "Anyway, as you're always telling me, we must approach change philosophically, Mr. Firestone, and right now your philosophical ass should be sitting in this philosophical chair. I've kept it warm for you all morning." Eli gives us a mischievous grin. "I'm turning the auto-recorder on now, so you have exactly five minutes to get here before it becomes painfully obvious no one's on duty. You're welcome. Anytime."

He scoots back over to the main console, types in a few commands, hits the auto-record button, and logs out. He stands with his hands on his hips and looks us up and down as if evaluating our worthiness for combat. Instinctively, we both stand straighter. That famous Elijah Tawfiq smile spreads across his face, punctuated only by a deep dimple in his left cheek. No wonder Tai was in love with him.

"Topside it is, kiddos. We've got a graduation to celebrate."

4 — REMY

Fall 47, Sector Annum 105, 19h32
Gregorian Calendar: November 6

Breathless, I bend over, hands on my knees, shoulders heaving. A drop of sweat tickles my back as it rolls beneath my shirt. Man, it feels good! Sprinting always makes me feel powerful, invincible, and perfectly free, like if I plant my foot just so, jump up and kick off, I could take off up into the air and fly. I could go anywhere, leave everything and everyone and find somewhere new. Somewhere untouched and unspoiled by decay and loss. By betrayal.

"Great shot," Jahnu says as he runs up behind me and throws the ball at my head. "Were you aiming for our goal or Soren's?" It bounces off my skull as I plop down on the ground. I grab the ball and lay back in the grass. The city around us is a ruin, and the once-great metropolis is full of crumbling and collapsed buildings overgrown by weeds, native grasses, scrubby bushes, and trees as far as the eye can see. During the last of the Religious Wars, a series of dirty bombs was detonated in the city center. People in the exurbs survived, but many of them fled or died out during the Famine Years. So now we've got the place pretty much to ourselves. Besides those of us at the Resistance base, there are only a few clusters of brave souls hanging on here and there. They're loners and scavengers, people who refused allegiance to the Sector and couldn't find a place among the Outsiders.

"Sad to say, but I think your foot has better aim than your arm," Jahnu says. I ignore him. The sky above me is a brilliant blue dome that seeps into black at the edges, and I close my eyes and shiver as the sun seeps into my skin.

"Yeah," Soren says. "It's a good idea to at least try to aim for the end of the field, you know, where the goal is. But as long as you're on the other team, I can't say I mind." We had to make up the rules to our game, and sometimes we forget them and just make up new ones as we go. It makes for an interesting system.

I open my eyes to see Soren standing over me. "I'm directionally challenged. Sue me."

"Good thing that doesn't apply to your skills with a Bolt. Otherwise we'd all be dead," Jahnu quips.

"Remind me why we're friends." I throw my leg out and try to trip Jahnu who jumps over it easily.

"Who said we were friends?"

"So who won?" I ask.

"Oh, were we keeping score?" Soren smiles. He's still taunting me, but it's one of his rare friendly smiles, and I find myself smiling back. "Hey, Eli?" Soren calls out. "Who won?"

Out of the corner of my eye, I see Eli and Kenzie walking towards us from down field.

"It was a close game, but Soren's team won." Eli kicks off his beat-up cleats, peels off his sweat-soaked socks, and wiggles his toes in the rough grass. "Eleven to nine. Of course, my team was at a distinct disadvantage. I had Remy."

"I can still run faster than you, old man," I kick his shoes out of reach. "One of these days I'm going to shoot the sweetest goal you've ever seen."

"If you ever score a goal, it will be the sweetest one any of us have seen," Kenzie says.

"Traitor!" I exclaim. Kenzie is the only girl around my age at main base. A natural athlete, she's a full head taller than I am and at least twenty kilos heavier, all of it muscle. Her pale skin is a kaleidoscope of freckles, and she has short ringlets that fly away from her head like little birds. Depending on her mood, they make her look either adorable or ferocious. Kenzie is one of the nicest people I've ever known—except when her competitive drive kicks in.

We barely knew each other back at the Academy, but we've grown close since we ended up bunking together after her family arrived. Her mom is a former Sector Dietician and her dad is one of the engineers in charge of keeping the lights on and the air and water clean in our underground home. Kenzie inherited her mom's interest in chemistry and her dad's ability to take things apart and put them back together again. She's always trying to explain to me exactly what her dad does. I insist I don't need to understand the intricacies of water purification systems, fluid dynamics, or nuclear engineering to appreciate his job, but she keeps trying. I still don't understand, but I always say a word of thanks each night that he's at work and that the lights will be on when I wake up.

"Speaking of sweet things," Eli says, "I'd say it's time for your official graduation feast."

"Yeah, I'm starving," Soren agrees.

"We don't have much," Kenzie says. "Jahnu and I scavenged what we could from the kitchen without being seen by old man Rhinehouse."

"That man guards his pantry like it holds the secrets of the universe," Jahnu says.

"Maybe it does." Soren plucks a thick blade of grass and splits it to make a whistle. He whets his lips, puts it to his mouth, and blows. Being outside has calmed Soren down since watching the graduation ceremony. "He's actually a pretty interesting guy. And he plays a mean game of chess."

"He's whipped my ass more than a few times," Eli says.

"Yeah," Soren adds, "he sees more moves with that one eye than most people will ever see with two."

"Does he ever talk about his past?" I ask, suddenly intrigued by the fact that Soren is apparently buddies with Rhinehouse. "Where he came from, how he lost his eye?" These are questions I've been wondering about since Rhinehouse showed up out of the blue and became the de facto cook for the outpost. The Director and all of the senior members obviously knew him because they took him in without a word despite the fact he was covered in blood and babbling in some language none of us could understand.

"He talks about it sometimes," Soren says.

"Well?" I press.

"It's not for me to say."

"How'd you worm your way into the old man's heart?" Eli asks. "My time with Rhinehouse is spent either scrubbing pans or trying desperately to save my king from capture. Although my charming demeanor usually wins over everyone, he is strangely immune."

"Imagine that," Soren laughs. "I'll tell him you're pining away for his attention." I notice that Soren didn't answer Eli's question.

"I wouldn't go that far," Eli says. "He's not really my type."

"Do you know what language he was speaking when he showed up here?" I ask, determined to pull something out of Soren.

Soren turns and looks at me. His smile is gone. "If you're so interested in his life history, why don't you try talking to him? Try being a friend instead of a gossip."

I glare at him from the grass but I don't respond. Soren turns his attention back to his grass whistle as if nothing happened.

"Look at this bountiful feast Kenzie and I have stolen for you," Jahnu says, drawing everyone's attention back to the real celebrity here: the food. "A barley loaf and pumpkin butter. Cherries, chokeberries, walnuts, hazelnuts, cheese, and some of Rhinehouse's famous Mystery Jerky."

"I wonder what the jerky's made out of this time?" Eli says.

"I just hope it's not opossum. I don't know why, but they creep me out." Kenzie shudders.

Jahnu picks up his dented standard-issue water bottle and holds it up in the air like it's a wine glass. "I'd like to make a toast," he says.

Jahnu's pretty quiet around most people, but in the past few months, I've noticed him coming out of his shell, and I think that change is largely due to Kenzie. She says sometimes when they're hanging out, he'll hardly shut up, as if he's saved up everything he wanted to say until he could say it to her. But talking's as far as he's gotten, and Kenzie's been wondering if she's reading him all wrong.

We grab our bottles and hold them up to toast.

"I know we had different reasons for leaving the Sector behind, for joining the Resistance. It was hard today watching what could have been if we were still there with our old friends and family. I'm not embarrassed to say it tore me up. But I'm proud of what we've done here and I'm proud of what we're fighting for. So, congratulations to us. We were the best and the brightest. Now, we're the best, the brightest—and the most wanted."

"To us!" we all cheer.

Kenzie kneels, taps her water bottle against Jahnu's, leans in, and to everyone's surprise—especially Jahnu's—she kisses him right on the lips. "Happy graduation, Jahnu Nair," she says with a challenging grin.

A broad smile spreads across his face as if a new, wondrous idea is slowly dawning on him.

"Sometimes a girl has to do everything," Kenzie laughs and shakes her head.

"To Kenzie and Jahnu," Eli declares.

"Finally," I add.

With that, we dig in. Jahnu is the first one to go for the food—he's always hungry—and the rest of us follow suit. Only Eli holds back, and after a few minutes, I notice he's staring off into space with that same faraway, thoughtful look in his eyes, just like he was when we found him in the comm center. I'm starting to worry he's descending into another bout of darkness. My protective instinct kicks in.

"Eli? Not hungry?" I ask, through a mouthful of bread. "You okay?" Just like before, he starts, as if abruptly jerked away from a different world.

"Yeah, starving," he says, but he still doesn't touch the food.

"What's up?" I demand.

"Just thinking. Did any of you get a weird feeling from Vale's speech today?"

"Just reading between the lines here, but it sounds like he's preparing to hunt us into oblivion. Is that what you're talking about?" Soren asks sarcastically.

"Yeah, that's exactly what I mean. But why and why now? Think about it. We're not a real threat. We've never killed a Sector citizen. We've never bombed a seed bank or blown anything up. So what's the real motivation for the Seed Bank Protection Project?"

We sit in silence, munching on our bread, thinking. He's got a point. Even though it seems obvious from our perspective that we're a threat to the Okarian Sector—we are, after all, trying to build a movement that will take down the OAC—we really haven't done any serious harm. So why does it sound like Vale's coming after us with guns blazing?

"What's in a name?" Soren asks in his meandering, philosophical way, as though he's talking to himself. Soren has three modes of existence: very angry, very sarcastic, and very chill. There's really no in between.

"What does that even mean, Soren?" Jahnu demands, his dark face creasing up in curiosity.

"Just wondering if there's anything in the title he gave his placement. The 'Seed Bank Protection Project.'"

"My thought exactly," Eli nods. "They're going on the offense. That's what his 'We must protect our future from the mistakes of our past' bullshit was all about. So why call it the 'Seed Bank Protection Project'? That makes it sound defensive."

We all ponder that for a few more minutes, and I sit in awe of Eli's ability to quote Vale's speech by the word. Then it hits me.

"You were listening to the speech again when we walked in on you in the comm center, weren't you? You recorded it."

"Smart girl," he says, patting me on the head. "Yeah. It got me thinking. Listen up: I need to tell you something."

Suddenly we've all forgotten about the food—which Eli still hasn't touched.

"Three years ago, that day in the lab, when Professor Hawthorne and Tai were..." he pauses, swallows, and I know it's all he can do to shove those memories back down into the deep. "I think there was something else going on. A few months before that, Hawthorne abruptly changed the focus of my research. He gave me a genome sequence and told me it was some form of DNA that didn't map to any organismal chromosome, or even to any biological traits. Basically," he says, translating for my benefit, since I really, really do not understand science the way my friends do, "the DNA didn't mean anything from a biological standpoint and could never have existed in a living organism. Hawthorne said he wanted me to help him crack the code and figure out what the DNA represented.

"But here's the key: he told me I couldn't tell anyone about it, that it was top secret, because—"

"Wait," Soren interrupts. "Where did he get the DNA in the first place?"

"I don't know. When I asked him, he said he was studying some old frozen cyanobacteria samples he found in one of the lab's storage units, but now I'm not so sure. Anyway, he said he looked at their chromosomes and realized they didn't look anything like cyanobacteria chromosomes. In fact, they were perfectly ordered and well-structured. The crazy thing is, they looked like sunflowers."

"What?" I sputter. "What do you mean, 'they looked like sunflowers'?"

"The chromosomes had been somehow manufactured and arranged so that the strings of DNA took on the pattern of a sketch of a sunflower, when viewed in their entirety. We'd never seen anything like it. Some chromosomes wind themselves up into intricate supercoiled structures, like when you twist and keep twisting a rope, although most just look like tangled knots of spaghetti. This one, though, was so perfect, so elegant. It might as well have been a 3D model of a sunflower. When Hawthorne studied them, he realized every single cell contained non-functioning DNA—even though those cells could never have existed as living organisms with that DNA."

"What does that mean?" I demand.

"It means that someone removed the bacteria's real DNA and inserted artificially coded DNA," Eli says. I can always count on him to put scientific information in easy little packages for me. "Then they froze the cyanobacteria, ensuring that the DNA would be perfectly stored."

"And perfectly hidden," Soren breathes.

"Every cell had the same DNA. Hundreds of copies of this non-functioning genome in hundreds of cyanobacteria—they were clones."

"But why—and who?" Jahnu asks. "Why would someone do that? What was in that DNA that was so important to hide and preserve?"

"I don't know. That's what Hawthorne wanted me to help him figure out."

"Get back to the point," Kenzie says. "What does this have to do with … with the massacre?"

Eli's brow furrows, and he peers into the distance for a moment, as if trying to see the molecules vibrating in the air itself. "I don't know." He turns back to Kenzie. "Maybe nothing, but a couple of weeks before he died, Hawthorne told me he'd made a breakthrough. That's when he got all excited about using synthesized DNA as a method of data storage. We were scheduled to meet in his lab after class the day of the, you know. But, and this is key: he also told me he was going to tell Corine Orleán about it."

"Did he tell her?" My parents never bought the story about the terrorist attack by an Outsider, and ever since the sham investigation and Sector cover-up, they've been convinced Corine was involved somehow. But there was never any way to prove it.

"If he did, he never told me. But right before the attacker shot himself, he said something about Corine." I've heard this part of the story before, but from the surprised looks on the others' faces, I can tell I'm the only one who has.

Eli pauses, and I fight the urge to tell him to go on. He has to tell the story on his terms. After a moment, he turns and looks at me.

"He said: 'A word to the wise: never get on Madam Orleán's bad side.'"

The silence is so thick it almost pulsates with every breath we take. The wind rustles through the tall grasses around us and flies buzz near my ear. The smell of autumn leaves and chill air presses in around me.

"Shit," Jahnu whispers.

"Do you think Corine ordered the attack?" Kenzie asks in a hushed voice.

"I've wondered about that every day since," Eli replies.

"Okay, let me get this straight. You're thinking my sister was murdered because of this DNA and that this same DNA may be what Vale's supposed Seed Bank Protection Project is all about." If this is why Tai died, could it also be the key to avenging her death?

"I don't know, Remy, but something in my gut tells me it's all related."

"Why is it so important? What is it?"

"That's the thing. I still have no idea what's on it. I've gone back and looked at the code again and again—"

"Wait," Soren interrupts again. "Didn't you say this was top secret? How have you looked at it again since then?"

"I downloaded it onto my computer, genius," Eli scoffs. "You think I let Hawthorne dictate my work hours? Nine to five, in the lab with him looking over my shoulder? No way. I worked when I felt like it. So I copied it to my plasma. When I fled with the Alexanders, I copied the sequence onto a spare drive. I can reconstruct the whole sequence for you on Remy's new plasma."

As usual when Eli's announcing his law-breaking habits, I am immensely proud to call him my surrogate older brother.

"Do you think she knows?" Jahnu asks. "Do you think Corine suspects you still have this information? Maybe that's what Vale's 'Seed Bank Protection Project' is all about. It's not the Resistance they care about—it's you."

Eli shrugs in response. "It's been three years. Why now?" he says warily. "None of it really makes sense, but...."

"One thing's for sure, though," I say, feeling as though my life has been given singular purpose. I cut a huge chunk of cheese for myself, suddenly starving again. "We need to find out what's in that DNA."

5 — VALE

Waking up at 06h30 hours this morning was one of the hardest things I've had to do in a long time. I met General Aulion at the training center of the Sector Defense Forces Complex. He wasted no time setting me on a two-hour daily workout routine, making it explicitly clear to me that if I failed to complete it every single day, I would be demoted from my command position. After struggling through the ten-kilometer run, the sprints, and the weights—with him watching my every step—he gave me ten minutes to shower and clean up. Then he walked me to the tactical room.

"Lieutenant Orleán," he growled, "if you're not in this room every Monday through Friday at 0915 hours *sharp*, I'll skin you alive."

I'm thrilled we got off to such a great start.

By the time our three-hour tactical briefing was over, I was ready to crawl back into bed for the rest of the week. The general and I went over every detail of the current security systems in place to defend our seed banks, with a thorough analysis of how the Resistance had managed to break in to three of them. We reviewed aerial photographs that Sector drones had taken of possible Resistance base sites. We talked about their renewable energy technology and their communications systems. And then at the end of it all, Aulion announced that my homework for the day was to prepare a detailed profile of each known member of the Resistance leadership. Due tomorrow morning at 0915 hours. *Sharp.*

"Sir?" A voice jolts me back from my thoughts. "This is the entrance to your new office."

"Ah. Yes. Thank you, Chan-Yu," I respond, returning to the present. I step up to the metal box mounted on the wall and insert my arm, pressing my palm against the fingerprint scanner inside. A red light begins flashing above the door to my office. I feel the tiniest pinch on the back of my hand as a microscopic needle penetrates my skin, pulling off just a few cells for DNA analysis. As my palm print and heat signature is read, the red light turns to yellow. After a few seconds, the light turns green, and a robotic voice says, "Thank you for confirming your identity, Valerian Orleán." The door clicks open.

As I step inside, I can't help but smile. I had Chan-Yu make sure my new office was decorated for comfort. He's done an excellent job. My heels click across the wide planked wood floor until I step onto the thick carpet, handwoven with the Orleán family crest. My mother's graduation gift. I sink down into my new leather chair and resist the temptation to stick my legs out and spin around. Instead, opting for the more mature path, I run my fingers across the desk and admire the polished wood.

"How do you like it, sir?" Chan-Yu asks from the doorway, his expression stoic. "Does it meet your expectations?"

"Meets and exceeds," I say. "Thank you. This is exactly what I wanted."

"Is there anything else I can do for you?"

"No, that will be all."

And with that, Chan-Yu is gone, and I stand and trace my fingers over the bindings of the books filling the floor-to-ceiling shelves lining the room. Bookshelves. An indulgence, a relic of the past. There are so few printed books left what with all the libraries and personal collections burned during the Religious Wars and then whatever survived just left to rot or turn to dust during the Famine Years. And, of course, we don't print our own now. Paper is a thing of the past. We write on our plasma tablets, or keep audio notes, or store everything in image files.

I notice a small box sitting on the credenza behind my desk. On the box is a printed note in what looks like my father's handwriting.

Congratulations – P.S.O.

My father, Philip Sebastian Orleán. I open the box and gasp. How many times have I asked if I'd ever get a Communications Link, a C-Link, of my own?

"Of course, I think you're responsible enough for one," Dad would say, "but the Sector's Board of Governors has to approve it. I'm the chancellor, Vale, not a dictator." I carefully peel it from its padded case and hold it up to the light. It's the color of my skin, wafer thin and nearly transparent. I hold it between my fingers, bending it ever so slightly. I can see the circuits that look like nothing more than blood-filled capillaries, and the clear filaments that are both microphone and transmitter. It weighs nothing, yet this tiny device, invisible once inserted in the ear, is the true indicator of my new status in the

Sector—everything else pales in comparison. This makes up for all the pain Aulion put me through this morning.

There are only ten or twelve of these little devices in the world, and now three of them are owned by members of my family. I turn it over in my hand. The color matches perfectly, and when I let it rest in my palm, it looks like nothing more than a flap of skin. And yet, this is the tool that will allow me access to all the databases in the Sector. Every bit of information that was ever compiled and that survived the wars—every book, map, academic paper, government memo, blueprint, shipping manifest, crop report, seed genome, and even databases a few unscrupulous travelers have sold us from the remnants of the Russian European Federation, the Chinese Collective, and the South American Alliance—all of it is available through this device. All the knowledge I could ever desire is now at my fingertips.

I sit back down and press the earpiece firmly into place. The skin of each C-Link is imprinted with a scanned topological map of the ear canal of the individual for whom the device was created. My father probably had my ear scanned during my graduation physical. The malleable flap of rubber is designed to mold itself to the wearer's ear when first inserted and will not engage unless the ear matches the map.

"Valerian Orleán, welcome to the Okarian Sector's Database Library."

The voice is female, soft, low—and not just a little sexy. I smile and look around the room as if someone could be watching.

"Hello," I say, feeling a little stupid.

"I am your guide, but before we begin exploring, tell me how you want me to address you."

"Vale, just Vale."

"Very good, Vale, just Vale." I think I detect the hint of a smile in her reply and remind myself I'm talking to a computer. "Now, you must name me," she says. "What will you call me?"

Remy. It's the first thing that pops into my head. No. No, how stupid. Why did I think of that? I can't possibly name my C-Link after—no. "Don't you have a name already?" I ask.

"No, Vale, this is a part of the process of acquiring a C-Link."

"Can't you pick something yourself?"

"To avoid naming me is to avoid yourself. You must choose."

Not even a minute has gone by and she's already seeing past my tricks. Or maybe that's a common evasion strategy, and the computer's basic programming is designed to prevent indecision.

"Okay, fine. This is harder than I thought, though." I sit down in my chair and lean back, taking a deep breath. I need to come up with a good name. After all, I am—hopefully—going to be living with this system for a very long time, and because the system adapts to each individual's personality and speech patterns, it's important to start out with the right relationship. It's almost as though the system becomes an extension of your brain. It's impossible to undo your creation. You can only destroy it and start over.

My mother would never tell me what she named hers—hell, she barely acknowledges she has a C-Link—but I know my father named his "Laika" after the first dog sent into space by the USSR centuries ago. He thought it was both a sign that the computer ought to be as obedient to him as a dog to its owner, and recognition of the technological power and available resources of the old world. I should choose something equally meaningful.

Then it hits me. "Demeter. Your name is Demeter, after the ancient Greek goddess of the harvest, to constantly remind myself what we strive for: to feed our people and to master nature so the famines of the past never return."

"Well-chosen, Vale. However, perhaps you have chosen a double-edged sword. You know, of course, that Demeter was not only responsible for the growing season, but also for the seasons of death?"

"And she too, during those times, had lost someone very dear to her." The parallel is clear, but I don't want to say it out loud. I've lost Remy; Demeter had lost her daughter. "I'm not ignorant of what I've chosen for you, Deme," I say, proud of the nickname.

"Then you have chosen doubly well. Now that you have named me, you may begin exploring and charting your course through the database. Where would you like to begin?"

"Well, I guess you haven't heard, but my boss gave me some homework to do today. I need to put together detailed profiles of each of the top-ranking members of the Resistance, including suspected whereabouts, roles within the Resistance, special knowledge and skills, and crimes against the Sector. Can you help me out with that?"

"Of course. Why don't we begin by tracing the disappearances of former Sector officials and OAC researchers?"

Perfect. I smile. "That's a great idea. In fact, let's start with the two I know the most about—Gabriel and Brinn Alexander, the parents of Remy Alexander."

The lights in my office dim. Three-dimensional images of Remy's parents appear in the center of the room, and then files relating to Brinn's research on botanical compounds and pharmacology and collections of Gabriel's writings as the Sector's Poet Laureate are listed. Then, folders relating to the Watchmen's search of Brinn's office, lab, and their house, complete with images of each room, including a shot of Remy's bedroom, stark and empty, not at all like the last time I saw it when her sketches and paintings were plastered all over the walls. I remember how she used up every scrap of her rationed paper from her art class and begged more from her fellow art students. The information keeps coming. I sit back in my chair as Demeter brings up hundreds of files, images, and audio recordings and displays them all across the hologram for me to review. All I can do is marvel.

6 — VALE

Fall 57, Sector Annum 105, 13h26
Gregorian Calendar: November 16

"And so, each of these very particular objectives fits within my larger goals for the Seed Bank Protection Project, which, as you can see, are outlined on the following page."

I'm finishing up my first presentation on my work so far. Demeter has linked me in to a meeting with the OAC Corporate Assembly and the chancellor and the Board of Governors. Several of the members of the Corporate Assembly are out visiting Farms and factory towns, so it's a virtual meeting, and my father decided I could present from the comfort of my new office.

"As you all know, the project has been created in response to a new series of threats from those who call themselves the Resistance. The damage that the Resistance has inflicted upon our facilities so far has been minor at worst. However, it is clear from their growing numbers, increasing boldness, and the ease with which they have penetrated our defenses that they could very soon pose a significant threat to the security of our food supply."

Demeter brings up a series of holographic projections, each image showing one of the government buildings or OAC research facilities with their names and the dates of the raids.

"After consultation with the chancellor and the OAC's general director,"— it's always strange to refer to my parents by their titles—"I understand my primary goal for the project will be to not only defend our own facilities, but also to impede the Resistance's ability to carry out additional operations and to deter those who may be sympathetic to their propaganda from joining their movement."

"Question, Vale," I hear within my ear. Demeter immediately switches the hologram in my office to a close-up of the man currently speaking. It's General Bunqu, a man with whom I've had the pleasure to train for the past year. He is a sight to behold. At the weights, at the sprints, at the long-distance runs and at the obstacle courses, Bunqu can best nearly every man who dares to compete against him. He only speaks to answer questions or issue commands, and he very rarely smiles. He is as black as a moonless night, and, for some reason, he always reminds me of the giant oak behind my bedroom at the chancellor's residence—towering, stately, immovable.

"Could you help us to better understand the goals of the Resistance? What are their motivations for striking at our Seed Banks, for poaching information from them while leaving them largely unharmed?"

I take a deep breath. It's a great question, and while I've thought a lot about it, I haven't really tried to articulate it. I haven't had to. Aulion and I spend all our time discussing the finer points of tactics and capabilities on both sides, but he's never bothered to help me dissect the overall goals of the Resistance. "Of course, General," I say, and then pause, looking for an answer. Demeter swoops in to my rescue.

"Old world versus new, Vale," she says. Of course.

"Think of it like this, General. Our exclusive reliance on the OAC's artificial, genetically-modified seeds has enabled us to overcome the constant threat of famine and successfully feed our growing nation. Additionally, these seeds enable Sector Dieticians to customize our diets in order for us to maximize health and minimize disease. Those who defected all had one thing in common: they made it clear they thought our reliance on these seeds was unsustainable and unethical. Now, as leaders of the Resistance, their goal is to acquire the genetic information for our seeds so they can return them to their natural, pre-modification state and disseminate them so people can grow their own food. While this might sound like a simple idea to some, we know it would be a disaster. As Madam Orleán is fond of saying, 'Old world seeds breed old world disease.'"

The threat of the Resistance is real: if they succeed, they could cast the world we've built back into a dark history of starvation, disease, and death. This is why the Resistance is so dangerous. This is why they must be destroyed. And this is why, for myself, I need to know why Remy would ever *choose* to be a part of such an organization.

General Bunqu frowns, his black face creased in wrinkles as he ponders this. "Hmmm. That would be serious indeed," he says finally.

"Of course it would be serious," my mother chimes in, and her dulcet voice carries a soft edge. "Dissemination of old world seeds would contaminate the genes we have worked so hard over the years to perfect. If the Resistance succeeds, it could ruin a hundred years of engineering effort, and we would be forced to start over from the beginning—from where we were after the Famine

Years."

A hush spreads over the presentation room as everyone contemplates this possibility. It is a terrifying prospect. It signals starvation, war, death, disease— all the things we have kept at bay since Jubilation Day, when the Okarian Sector was first founded.

I clear my throat and break the silence.

"And that, Madam Orleán, is why this project is so important. In order to stop the Resistance before it gains more traction, my goals are: First, to assemble a special-ops reconnaissance force designed specifically to infiltrate and dismantle Resistance bases; Second, to hunt down and imprison the leaders of this dangerous movement; Finally, to design a public awareness campaign to counter Resistance propaganda and to prevent defection."

I look around the room for any questions, and when none are forthcoming, I close my presentation.

"Thank you all for listening. I will send each of you a copy of this presentation. If you have any further questions, please pass them on to me after the meeting, and I will be happy to address them to your satisfaction."

Inhale, exhale. I survived—not just survived, but perhaps triumphed over— my first joint board meeting. Demeter switches the screen to an overhead of the whole table. My father takes over for me.

"Thank you very much, Vale. We are all anxious to see how your goals progress in the coming months. Remember, this project is an immense responsibility, and don't hesitate to ask any of us for help. While we all believe you'll succeed in this task, you're still young, and as a junior officer it's our responsibility to help you in any way we can." A general hum of approval sounds through the room. "Now, speaking only as a proud parent: congratulations, son! You survived your first board meeting," he says, cracking a smile, and everyone laughs—everyone except General Aulion. "We'll see you again in a week. Ladies and gentlemen, on to other matters."

Demeter shuts down the hologram and raises the lights in my office. The anxiety and stress run off of my body like rainwater, and I collapse, sinking deep into my chair. I am exhausted. I hadn't realized how nervous I was.

"Well, that wasn't so bad, was it, Deme?"

"No, Vale," comes the soft and comforting female voice in return. "You were prepared, and you answered each question well. I believe they were impressed."

"Yeah, I thought so, too."

There's a knock at the door. Damn it. I was hoping for some time to relax and not think about anything.

"Who is it, Deme?" There's a camera outside the door that allows her to screen anyone approaching my office.

"Linnea Heilmann."

Oh, joy.

"Let her in," I say, too tired to get up from my chair and open the door myself. It swings open and Linnea, a rush of blonde hair, long legs, and shimmering blue eyes, comes bounding in the door. Dressed more casually today, in a dark green tunic with brown lace-up boots, she looks less dangerous than she did at the graduation ceremony, but no less beautiful.

"How did the meeting go?" She flashes that smoky smile at me. "Corine said it was your first big presentation. She asked me to come check on you after you were done."

That's my mom, playing matchmaker again.

"It went really well. Thanks for ask—"

"Your mom was saying how stressed you've been since you started work." Linnea seems perfectly at ease in my office. She walks around my desk and sits herself down on top of it like she's been here a thousand times. "Is there anything I can do to help?"

Well, if you can somehow get Aulion off my back for a half-second.

She crosses her legs and leans back on her hands as her tunic rides up along her thigh, revealing perfectly toned muscle. I can't help but stare. No wonder half the men in the Sector go to bed dreaming about her.

"No, thanks. I just need to get back to work, is all."

"Maybe I should kidnap you and take you out for a relaxing dinner. I'm sure you deserve it." She's practically purring.

"That sounds nice, Linnea, but not tonight. I really do have a lot of work to do." She doesn't take the hint. Instead, she stares around the office, and her blue eyes narrow as she surveys the décor.

"You know, Vale, I was wondering …" She hesitates. "Do you know what ever happened to Elijah Tawfiq?"

Do I know what ever happened to Elijah Tawfiq? What kind of a question is that? I think about this for a minute, staring at her, wondering what on earth she's getting at.

"What do you mean?" I ask suspiciously.

"Well, I was just talking about him with Corine. She was saying what a tragedy it is that the OAC lost such a talented scientist to mental illness—you know, he went kind of crazy after the Outsider attack…."

Of course I know all this. Elijah is one of the key members of the Resistance raid teams. He's led two of the three most successful raids against our seed banks and he disappeared at the same time as Remy and her parents. I didn't have to profile him for my assignment last week with General Aulion because he's not considered a senior Resistance leader, but we've certainly spent a lot of time talking about him.

"And then he disappeared, of course, and I always wondered…. It got me thinking, what if he joined the Resistance? Do you know anything, Vale?"

Linnea has a dreamy look in her eyes as though she's not really seeing me, even as she stares at me, waiting for my answer. I know that years ago, when we were younger, Linnea had a thing for Eli, the good-looking young hotshot who was a few years older than us. But her behavior right now is so strange, so unguarded, so unlike Linnea, that I have to wonder if something's really wrong.

"Linnea, I'm really sorry, but if I had any information, I wouldn't be allowed to divulge it anyway."

Suddenly she snaps out of her trance.

"Oh, well," she says, and I can tell by her sultry voice that she's back to normal. "Don't worry about it, darling." She reaches out her other hand and quite needlessly brushes my hair out of my face, now smiling at me with an expression that might seem tender if it weren't quite so possessive. "So dinner is out, but how about later? One of my friends is hosting a get-together tonight. Why don't you come with me? You know what they say about all work and no play…." I think about it for a few seconds, wondering what it would be like to fall in with Linnea. But something about her is just too calculating, and I can almost hear Jeremiah and Moriana reproaching me: *You went out with her, Vale? What the fuck is wrong with you?*

"No, thanks. Going out at night is difficult when you have to wake up to face General Aulion at 06h00 in the morning. But I appreciate it. Maybe another time?" I have to be nice to her, if only for my mother's sake.

Anger flashes in her eyes like a lightning strike, and I resist the temptation to duck. But then it passes, and she smiles. "Sure, whenever you want. Until next time, darling," she says, and turns on her heel and walks out the door. Demeter clicks it shut behind her, activating the lock again.

I lean back in my chair and begin to replay everything that just happened. Now I can't stop thinking about Elijah. Why was Linnea asking questions about him? Why were she and my mother talking about him, when my mother knows perfectly well he's a member of the Resistance? What was up with Linnea's strange behavior, and why—aside from matchmaking purposes—is my mother giving Linnea inside information?

"Time to start digging, Demeter. Bring up all the information we have on the whereabouts of Elijah Tawfiq. Let's find out why Linnea is so interested in him."

7 — REMY

I stare aimlessly at one of the chromosomes Eli downloaded onto my plasma. I use my fingers to twirl it around and zoom in and out at random, keying in on various "genes" on the strange sunflower chromosome. I've looked at it from every possible angle, and it still doesn't mean a damn thing to me. Just a big string of molecules.

It's been a few weeks since Eli's big reveal. Soren, Kenzie, Jahnu, and I have spent every free moment peering at the chromosome structure on my tablet, examining the base pair sequences on Eli's computer, or browsing through every document on cryptography we can get our hands on. And after all our work, we're all just as stumped as he was. No one has the slightest clue what the DNA codes for, or even how to begin to decode it.

We've been ducking out of our other duties as often and as early as possible. We've co-opted a little backroom by the giant water filter, which makes an enormous racket and serves as a deterrent for anyone who might want to come poking around. For the time being, we'd like to keep this a secret. After all, it's entirely possible this information has already resulted in the deaths of a classroom full of students.

"Some genius. Why couldn't whoever created this have left us some sort of clue as to how to crack the damn thing?" I mutter while spinning one of the chromosomes aimlessly on the plasma. I've been especially bitter the last few days—everyone else in our group is either a science whiz or a master computer programmer. They all speak math and physics and can babble on endlessly about formulas, vectors, and compiling programs—subjects about which I am woefully ignorant. I'm the lone artist of the group, and my skills are notoriously useless when attempting to analyze DNA. So I've mostly been playing with my plasma and staring over someone else's shoulder as they work. I even did a pen and ink sketch of one of the chromosomes. Not that it helped. But it looks good.

"Maybe he didn't want anyone to figure it out," Jahnu replies. He sounds just as depressed as I am. As a mathematician, Jahnu's specialty is in puzzles and patterns. He helps the comm team encrypt messages sent between bases, so Eli was especially hopeful he'd have some insight to offer on the project. Obviously that hasn't panned out quite the way he'd hoped.

"Well, that's stupid. Why would he go through all the trouble of coding it in the first place and then putting the DNA in the cell nuclei or whatever if he didn't want anyone to get to it? And, how do you know it was a he?"

Jahnu stands and stretches. "I'm gonna go find Kenzie. She should be off of KP by now."

"Gonna spend some special time with your new girlfriend before you head in to work, huh?" The one bright spot on this whole extravaganza has been Kenzie and Jahnu. The two of them are just over the moon about each other, and while I'm sure it'll pass and they'll get back to normal eventually, right now they're preoccupied with being as annoyingly adorable as possible. They walk hand-in-hand all through the tunnels, he puts his arm around her when they're in the mess hall, and I accidentally walked in on them in various stages of undress two nights ago.

"So what if I am?" he shoots back at me. His skin is too dark to see a blush, but I have no doubt his cheeks are flushing.

"So nothing!" As sulky as I've been recently, his happiness is infectious. I shove him playfully as he walks by me on the way out the door. "Make good choices!" I yell after him. He swears at me and slams the door.

I go back to spinning the model on my plasma. I don't begrudge Jahnu and Kenzie their happiness. It's just that it reminds me of the last time I felt that way. I rub my temples, trying to erase Vale's face from the images behind my eyes. Maybe it's just how little sleep I'm getting, but since we watched the graduation ceremony, I can't get him out of my head. Every time I close my eyes, he's waiting in the black.

When we were friends at the Academy, even before he kissed me, I always sort of liked him. He was two years older than me, in between me and Tai, and he was a good friend of Moriana Nair, Jahnu's cousin, so we all ended up spending a lot of time together, especially after Tai and Eli started dating. He was modest and polite, even though he was the son of the chancellor and a prominent OAC researcher. There were a lot of other kids at the Academy who had something to prove, and they were pretentious and spiteful. But never Vale. Never to me, at least.

But then Tai was killed. I've only spoken to him once since the day she died, and that was just the day after. I was still in shock, and I was a wreck—a limp, wet puddle of tears, and he held me and told me he was there for me and to just call him if I wanted to talk. I clung to him, crying into his shirt, and he just held me tighter. Then Eli told us what the killer had said about Madam Orleán, and that he thought she had something to do with the attack, and everything Vale had ever said or done started to seem insincere, like it had all just been an act to get us to like him. Suddenly, I hated him. As far as I was concerned, he might as well have been the murderer himself. About a month later, he came over to ask why I hadn't spoken to him since then and why I hadn't been in school. He brought me flowers. I took the flowers and slammed the door in his face. Two months later, my family left.

And now his face lurks behind my eyes, waiting for darkness so he can pounce. He taunts me with his successes, his luxuries and the glamorous life he lives, while my friends and I suffocate underground and drink recycled pee. I can't get him out of my head.

I toss my tablet on the nearest table in a moment of frustration and stand up. I'm getting out of here. This cramped little office is making me sick. Where are Eli and Soren, anyway? They were supposed to be in here by now.

I head out and wander through our dimly lit tunnels, ducking under electrical wires and metal pipes. Electricity is scarce down here. We can't afford to have bright lights posted everywhere, so mostly we light our working quarters, the mess hall, and the kitchen. Even those cut out sometimes if someone's using a high-powered piece of equipment.

I make it to the mess hall, where an unfamiliar but delicious smell is wafting from the kitchen. I see Soren loading up a tray, and I head in to join him.

"Hey! You're supposed to be working on the you-know-what with me. It's not even dinnertime."

Soren and I have been making a conscious effort to be nicer to each other since we started working on Eli's project. Mostly, this amounts to us saying the same things to each other in a slightly nicer tone of voice.

"Dinnertime isn't dictated by the hours of the day, Remy. It's dinner whenever I'm hungry." He doesn't even look at me as he responds—he just keeps adding to his plate. I'm about to spit out a really snarky remark when I look down and see the sign.

"*Venison?* Where'd Rhinehouse get deer meat? Who went hunting, and how far did they have to go to find deer?"

"Who cares? There's so much meat, he's lifted the ration limit for this meal." Soren finishes preparing his tray, grabs a fork, and smiles down at me. "You're welcome to join in."

Joining Soren for dinner doesn't sound like the most appealing thought, but we rarely get to eat meat, and the smell of roasting venison has me suddenly starving.

Rhinehouse keeps a small flock of goats and sheep aboveground, which supply milk. In the last year, he's even started making cheese, a delicacy I hadn't enjoyed since I left Okaria. But he won't entertain the thought of slaughtering them for meat. Sometimes, though, someone on base will get bored with our standard exercise routines and request permission to go hunting. Jahnu and I have never done it, but Eli, Soren, and Kenzie have all gone. Eli's even shown me how to hold and fire the hunting bows they use.

I grab a plate and start loading up. Sliced apples and pears, roasted venison, and goat cheese. This would have been a pauper's meal back home in the Sector, but here, it's a feast. On the other hand, Rhinehouse is a stellar cook—and, apparently, a master butcher and forager. He's got a whole map of fruit trees and berry bushes around the base, and in the mornings, he sends people out to harvest. The food may not be bountiful, but it is delicious.

When I turn back to the general mess area to look for Soren, I can't find him. I peer around suspiciously, wondering if he's pulled a trick on me. Just then, I hear Rhinehouse's gruff bark from inside the kitchen, and I glance in to see what he's yelling about now.

"One more game, Eli, and then I'm cutting you off. This is ridiculous. You're playing like a child."

Eli and Rhinehouse are sitting across from each other at a small table, with a chess board between them. Soren's pulled up a chair next to them and is munching on his venison, watching the game stoically. Rhinehouse, grimacing, slaps a pawn on an improbable square. The entire board jumps, as does Eli, who looks like a cowed puppy.

"Hey, Remy," Soren calls. "Sorry, I got distracted watching Eli get his ass kicked. Want to pull up a chair?"

Not particularly, I think, but at this point I don't have much of a choice. I set my plate down and drag a chair over to the table so I'm sitting opposite Soren. Rhinehouse glances over me with his good eye and gives me a look that says pretty clearly that I'm to keep my mouth shut.

Oh boy.

I start shoving venison into my face while Eli and Rhinehouse set the board up again. The first ten moves go by in a blur.

As far as I can tell, the kitchen is Rhinehouse's unofficial living quarters.

For all intents and purposes, if he's not in the kitchen or up aboveground with his flock, he doesn't exist—none of us has ever seen him outside of those two spots. Eli's even theorized he may have an alternate dimension all to himself where he hangs out when his onion soup isn't at risk of being botched by some incompetent underling.

"Rhinehouse…" Eli starts, tentatively holding his knight above a square. His brown eyes flicker across the board, double-checking his move. Rhinehouse leans forward, elbows on his knees, his one eye surveying the board.

"Yes?" he snaps, without looking up.

"I've got a question for you." Eli plants the knight on the board.

"What is it?" Rhinehouse captures one of Eli's pawns with his bishop.

"Do you know," Eli takes a pawn in return, "anything about DNA-based data storage?"

"Of course I do."

I stare at Eli. What's he doing? Soren and I exchange glances across the board, but Soren doesn't look nearly as anxious as I feel.

"Is there a standard formula for decoding base pair sequences?"

Rhinehouse finally looks up at him, but only for a half second before ducking back into the game. He takes Eli's errant knight.

"What kind of question is that?" he barks. "The technology had only just been theorized when I was working at the OAC. Of course there's no standard formula. As far as I know, no one had even bothered to try coding anything but organic genetic material into DNA."

My heart sinks. What if the DNA we've been working on is just a random pattern, a mistaken genome sequenced and inserted into a bunch of dead cells?

Eli captures one of Rhinehouse's bishops and declares: "Check."

No one moves. Soren seems to have stopped breathing, and his fork hovers over the half-eaten food on his plate. Rhinehouse leans back in his chair and eyes Elijah beadily.

"Why do you ask?" he demands, moving a pawn to defend his king.

"No reason," Eli says casually.

"Like hell," Rhinehouse spits back. "What did you find, Elijah?"

"Nothing … much." Eli castles. His expression is cool as a cat. I fight the urge to grin mightily, as I know that will only add fuel to Rhinehouse's grump.

"I'll make you a deal," Eli says, looking up from the board and staring at Rhinehouse. "If you win this game, I'll take care of your flock for a month. If I win, though, I'll tell you about the DNA—but you're sworn to secrecy. You can't tell anyone about it. Not a word. Not even the Director."

Now I see what he's up to. Eli is betting that Rhinehouse's scientific curiosity will get the better of him. That once he knows what we're working on, he'll want to help us crack the code. He's also betting that Rhinehouse is a man of his word, which is the part that worries me. I don't know the old man well enough to know whether or not he'll keep his promise. I look at Soren across the board, hoping for some reassurance, but his eyes are fixed on Rhinehouse.

"Some big thing you found? Steal it from the seed bank on the last raid, did you? Can't break the code, huh?" Rhinehouse says gruffly, glaring at Eli, who keeps his cool.

"You'll find out at the end of the game, my friend. If you accept my bargain. If you don't, I'm keeping my secrets. I'll solve the damn thing myself."

"Sounds like you're having a hard time with that as it is." Rhinehouse suddenly diverts his attention to me and Soren. "And I suppose you two are in on this, as well."

Soren grins. "I haven't a clue what Eli's talking about."

I nod fervently in agreement.

"Fine, then. So you're all in on it together. Three of you haven't been able to figure it out, you want my help, so you must think it's a big deal." He pauses. "You're on."

All our attention becomes focused on the game. Rhinehouse attacks Eli's position over and over again, but Eli holds his own. He's down a rook and a pawn, but he's chipping away at Rhinehouse's defenses, too. They trade queens, and then Eli moves his remaining knight up two rows. Suddenly Soren leans forward and *ooohs* over whatever Eli just did. Rhinehouse swears under his breath and moves his king.

Eli stares at the board for a few seconds. He pushes a pawn up and then hesitates, pulls it back. Instead he moves his rook halfway across the board. Rhinehouse moves his rook, harrumphing, but it's too late. His king is hemmed in by an ill-placed pawn and Eli's well-spun attack. Eli moves his bishop up one space.

"Checkmate."

Soren and I each let out a deep sigh of relief. Rhinehouse looks at Eli with an expression I've never seen in his face before: admiration. In place of his usual furrowed brows, narrowed eye, and downturned mouth, he is contemplating the board with a hint of a smile. The creases in his face seem to melt away as he reaches out and knocks his king over.

"Well played, Elijah."

Eli's lopsided grin spreads across his face as he reaches out to shake

Rhinehouse's hand.

After they shake, Rhinehouse reverts back to his old, grumbling self. He grabs his cane off the table and stands up. "Okay, listen up. I'll keep my word, on the condition that I help your little project on my own time and at my leisure. I want to know exactly what you guys are working on as soon as this meal's over. Finish your dinner and meet me back here at the pantry at 2030 hours. We'll talk then." And with that, he stalks off into his alternate universe.

I stand up and cross my arms, glaring at Eli in mock anger.

"Who gave you permission to do that, huh?"

"It's my project, little bird," he says with a smirk, using my dad's pet name for me. "I can invite whoever I want to join, and we need him."

"That was a hell of a game," Soren says. "You could have cut out his defenses earlier, though, if you'd—"

"Hey, slow down, Soren. I know you're a chess whiz, but let me just revel in my first ever victory against Rhinehouse, okay?"

Both Soren and I stare at him. *"You've never beat him before?"* I demand.

"What are you talking about? You just saw me beat him right here."

"I mean before that, asshole." I punch him in the shoulder.

"That was a hell of a risk you took, Eli. I thought you'd won at least a couple of games against him."

"Nope. But I know his weaknesses. Once I dropped the bait about the DNA data storage, I knew he'd be distracted trying to figure out why I was asking or how I'd gotten my hands on any encrypted DNA, or he'd just go off trying to remember everything he possibly could on the subject. I was betting on him being distracted and not fully thinking through his moves. If it had been anything else, he could have just ignored me. But a science question, a big secret, and a bet—that would be too much for him to resist."

Soren shakes his head. "Chess is a game of the mind. Way to take advantage of that, Eli."

"Thanks. Now, I'm starving. How's that venison?"

8 — VALE

At 17h00 hours, my day is finally over. I stand up, stretch, and then collapse back into my desk chair. Demeter laughs at me, but at this point, I don't care. Ten hours of work, and I'm tired enough to just crawl under my desk and sleep there. But I promised my parents I'd join them at home for dinner tonight, and then Moriana and I are going out for drinks afterwards. At least I don't have to wake up early tomorrow. It's the one day a week when I can show up anytime, do my workout routine, and go back to my flat to sleep. And the best part about it is that Aulion won't be there to criticize my every step.

"Okay, Demeter, time to get out of here. Deactivate all internal systems and engage all security—but wait until I'm out the door this time, okay?" Demeter has somehow picked up a rather playful personality. So playful, in fact, that two days ago, when I told her to "engage all security systems," she locked me inside and turned off all the lights. I tried to figure out what had happened, and I could almost hear her laughing at me. "You should be careful with how you give your commands, Vale," she said.

She's got spunk, that's for sure. Somehow, from my dialogue patterns, she's picked up the habit of making sarcastic comments on other people's behavior into my ear, and her snide commentary is both entertaining and a little scary— it's like she's voicing my thoughts before I can say them.

I follow the winding hallway down toward the main elevator. It's already dark outside, so the building is dimly lit and quiet. Most everyone else has already headed home. As soon as I step into the elevator bay, a green light flickers on above me, indicating that the motion sensors have called a lift to my floor.

While I wait for the elevator, I gaze out at the lights of the city around me, marveling at the things we've built in the last century. My parents—and their parents before them—have dedicated their lives to serving the Okarian Sector, and I'm proud and honored to follow in their footsteps.

Our architecture and design may not match the opulence of some of the more majestic cities from the old world, but Okaria is beautiful, and Assembly Hall, the central administrative building of the government and where my office is located, is one of its most beautiful buildings.

I turn my back to the city and admire the building itself. Structured like a tree, the main elevator shafts in the center function as the "trunk," pumping like pistons in an old-fashioned steam engine as they deliver government workers up and down the twenty-one floors. The bottom floor is the central hall, where the food coming in from the Farms is programmed and 3D printed by the Dieticians for every Sector citizen. Underground, there is an enormous open space where the Corporate Assembly meets. Above, the hallways on each floor branch off and taper like capillaries into individual offices and meeting spaces. Aside from the private spaces, everything is made of glass, so as you walk, you can look out across the whole building and watch everyone amble from place to place above and below. The chancellor's office, where my father spends most of his time, is at the very top of the tree, on the twenty-first floor. The entire building is encased in a warped glass and steel frame that provides the structural support for both the interior and exterior gardens that are part of the complex system used to generate electricity, filter water, and compost waste. It's an engineering wonder, designed to withstand just about anything nature can throw at it. If it weren't for Aulion, I'd love coming to work here each morning.

"Where would you like to go?" the automated voice asks, as I step into the lift.

"Rooftop aircraft bay." My office is on the sixteenth floor, so it's a fairly short ride. I watch the floors and hallways drop by as I float up like a bubble until we crest the roof of the building and the door slides open. Up here, I feel as though I am walking on water. I stride across the glass to where my brand new airship—my father's graduation present—is waiting. Shaped like a water bird, this model is a new design called the Sarus, after a now-extinct species of crane. The ship is elegant, aerodynamic, highly efficient, and she comes with the latest cloaking technology. The top of the wings are paneled in lightweight solar cells, and her ionic propulsion system is powered by a miniature cold fusion generator tucked under her belly. She's a sight to behold. When Jeremiah first saw this beauty, he almost lost it.

"Your dad just gave this to you? For graduation?" His mouth hung open as he circled the craft, running his hands along the side, admiring the wings and the nose from every possible angle. "I've seen pictures of them, but I had no idea they were even in production. He must have pulled some serious strings to get this ready for you."

I grinned at him. "Want to take the controls?"

He nodded enthusiastically, still in shock. We flew the ship a few kilometers outside of city limits—it's illegal to pilot your own craft inside the city; it's too dangerous. Human drivers are too accident-prone, and midair collisions are usually deadly. So we flew to a little lake outside the city, and I let Jeremiah take the controls. He's just starting his new job as an aviation engineer, working on airship design for the Sector Defense Forces and OAC Security, and he's been obsessed with airships for as long as I've known him. He flew for over an hour, laughing and roaring like a five-year-old boy.

I press my palm against the reflective metal of the airship, engaging the passenger sequence.

"Please state your name."

"Valerian Augustus Orleán." The pod door slides open. Once inside, I scan my palms and my eyes and start the craft. "Demeter, take me to my parents' house, will you?" I don't feel like manually entering the destination, and she can easily take care of it.

As the landing tripods retract and we lift off, we move out into the night sky. I lean back to watch the city pass beneath me. I've seen photos of some of the enormous "skyscrapers" in the old cities, and I'm thankful we don't have any of those strange, boxy structures decorating Okaria. The buildings below me are sleek and graceful, with gardens and greenery piled on rooftops. Above me, a heady view of the stars is beginning to emerge, brilliant lines of plumage painted across the sky. There aren't many other airships out tonight, but there are a few. As much as we strive for equality among Sector citizens, airships are the possessions of the élite. The rest of Okaria gets around using the Pan-Okarian Deployment System, or PODS. PODS is an enormous, intricately connected rail system, which services the entire city and has hundreds of stations. I love taking the PODS system, but I usually attract way too much attention to use it on a regular basis. Being asked over and over again to take photos with citizens is fun but overwhelming. Now that I have my Sarus, I've been using it almost exclusively.

The chancellor's residence is an old, renovated chateau on the edge of the city center, set apart from the hustle of the Sector government. There's a small craft bay behind the house, and the Sarus pilots herself down and shuts off automatically. When I open the hatch and step out, there are two Sector security guards waiting for me.

"Good evening, sir," one of them greets me.

"Hey, Ren," I say. "You can still call me Vale, you know." Now that I've graduated, people have started addressing me more formally than before.

"Sure, Vale," he smiles back. "The chancellor and the director are waiting. I'll lead you there."

It's not like I don't know how to get into my own house. But I let him and his partner lead the way without comment.

The mansion is an enormous old building, a relic of the old world luxury that most people these days can no longer even dream of. Grey stone walls, turrets, and gargoyles decorate the exterior. One of the guards palms the scanner to the side of the enormous metal doors, which swing open, and a manservant, who I don't recognize, gestures me inside.

"Have a great night," I say to the guards. They nod and give me the traditional cross-chest salute—right fist to the left shoulder. I return the gesture. The manservant then leads me through the back hallway. As we pass the foyer, I glance in at my old piano and a pang of regret hits me. I haven't had time to sit down and play since before graduation. The hours I've spent practicing pieces from the great composers of the old world will doubtless already be fading. *It's a necessary sacrifice*, I tell myself, *if you want to stop the Resistance*. Still, I can't shake the feeling of longing, the desire to sit down at the keys and create, to channel the music like a riverbed channels water. The manservant leads me into the living room, where my parents are sitting at a high-top table, sipping on some cocktails. The manservant announces me.

"Chancellor; Madam. Your son has arrived."

I sigh. I wish we could give up the formalities. After all, this used to be my house, too. But as soon as I am announced and the manservant retreats, the formalities vanish.

"Hey, Vale," my dad calls. Both my parents are now in their late forties. My father's once-dark hair is now predominantly grey, and faint wrinkles are beginning to emerge at the corners of his eyes and his mouth. "Let's get you a drink. Laika, tell Fallon to make Vale a cocktail," he says, addressing his own C-Link. He's not shy about using his C-Link in front of us, but in public or in front of other government officials, he never addresses her out loud. To me, he says, "Tired? How's the general treating you?"

My mother smiles at me, and I bend down to kiss her before plopping down on the couch. "He must be keeping you busy," she says. Though my father might be showing his age a bit, my mother doesn't look a day over thirty. Her long brown hair is as sleek as ever, and her round, dark eyes are set deeply into a cream-colored complexion. She is confident, calm, and controlled at all times.

"That's an understatement." I grimace, thinking about all the time I've spent with Aulion over the last few weeks.

"It's not too much to handle, is it?" my father asks, looking directly at me.

"It's fine. It's no more work than I had at the SRI or at the Academy. It's just different."

A servant hurries in and places a tall glass in front of me. She must be new, because I don't recognize her.

"What is it?" I ask her.

"Vitamin D, B6, Niacin, and amino acid cocktail with vodka," she says nervously.

"No," I laugh. "I mean, what is it? I don't care about the ingredients."

"Oh," she sputters. "I think Fallon called it a Twisted Spur." Fallon is the chancellor's Dietician. I nod, and she turns on her heel and dashes out.

"You knew it was going to be a difficult transition," my father says. "Research, classes, and exams, as hard as those might be, are nothing compared to the responsibility of working for the government."

"Working under Aulion, more like," I grumble.

"*General* Aulion," my mother reminds me firmly. "He's the best mentor you could ask for. He may be tough, and I know he's critical, but he really understands the Resistance."

Demeter makes a little snickering sound in my ear, which startles me. She hadn't spoken in so long I'd almost forgotten she's there.

"Aulion's anything but a mentor," she says snarkily, "and 'critical' might be a slight understatement." I smile. I'm glad she's on my side. I'm also glad my parents can't hear her.

Just then, the girl who brought my cocktail darts back in. "The table is ready," she announces. We all file into the dining room and take our seats at the table, where the food has already been laid out. Fallon's prepared different meals for each of us, tailored to our individual needs. It's nice to have someone cooking for me for a change. Since I moved out, I've gotten used to eating my customized Mealpaks alone, but that gets boring fast, and I've missed Fallon's cooking.

"How's Moriana doing?" I ask my mother as we all tuck in.

"Oh, she's really great. She's a hard worker, and very smart to match. We're all thrilled with what she's done so far." My mother is never so effusive with her praise.

"Have you started filling out the adoption papers yet?"

She laughs. "Hardly. I'm just happy that you've become such good friends."

There is an awkward pause, and I know what's coming next. "Have you seen Linnea lately?"

"Mom!"

"What? I'm just asking."

"I don't want to go out with Linnea, okay? Will you give it up, please?"

"Vale, she's so driven, and so smart. You should give her a chance."

My father pipes up: "She's doing a great job as the OAC's spokesperson, and she works very well with Evander at the Farms."

"She's also been incredibly effective at destroying the political careers of some promising young men from the factory towns," Demeter pipes up sarcastically in my ear. "Her exploits are fast becoming legendary." I fight back a laugh.

"You really haven't been interested in anyone since that Alexander girl back at the Academy," my mother says, looking at me worriedly, as though I might have a fever. Despite the fact that my mother and Remy's mother were close friends when they worked at the OAC together, my parents now refuse to refer to any of the Alexanders by their first names.

"First, that's not true. Remy and I never really dated. Second, I have been with other girls since then. And third, could you just give it a rest? I'm too busy with work to think about dating anyway. Even Linnea. And why are you two sneaking around talking about Elijah Tawfiq?"

My father perks up at Elijah's name and looks at my mother curiously.

"Oh, did she mention that?" she responds, offhand. "She asked me if I knew anything about him. She said she missed him. I told her, of course, that I knew nothing about him."

"Okay." I narrow my eyes at her. She sounds suspiciously casual, but it makes sense. "It was strange that she was asking about him out of the blue."

"It is interesting that she brought Elijah up," my father says. "Do you have any information on him? I bet if we find Tawfiq, we'd find the Alexanders nearby."

"No location on him. He's become a fairly high-ranking member of their organization, though. He's led two of the raid teams that infiltrated our seed banks, and he's in on a lot of their communications. The ones that we've intercepted, anyway."

"Well, good. Keep me informed."

"Of course, Chancellor," I say with a smirk, trying to sound very official. "I'll be happy to prepare a report for you in the morning." Both my parents laugh.

"Speaking of that, Philip," my mother says, her expression darkening, "I heard a report today from Evander that there's been more trouble at one of the Farms?"

"Unfortunately, yes." My father's smile evaporates. "One of the silos was blown up the other day at Silver Birch. The Enforcers got control of the situation, but several thousand kilos of grain were lost."

"Why wasn't I informed?" I demand. Staying up-to-date on activity at the Farms is crucial for our investigation into the Resistance's activity. "Is there any connection to the Resistance?"

"It doesn't look like it," my father says, shaking his head grimly. "So far it looks like this was internally motivated. There's been a food shortage there, and rationing was imposed for a few days. They weren't happy."

"Blowing up a silo full of food doesn't seem like the best way to protest not having enough food," I comment. "Are we sure there wasn't something else at play?"

"I don't have a lot of information yet," my father says, shrugging helplessly. "I'll let you know when I know more."

They then get into a discussion about an uptick in activity from the Outsiders, the nomads who live in the Wilds, and I tune them out. They're not my problem—not yet, anyway. The rest of the meal passes uneventfully and without any more commentary about Linnea. Thank goodness. I put the news about the Farms into the back of my mind and make a mental note to investigate any possible Resistance connection first thing in the morning.

❦

Two hours later, I say goodbye and head back out to my Sarus. I'm heading off to meet Moriana at a sleek new bar near the SRI. I program in the location and glide across the night sky. It's almost 2030 hours by the time I'm docked and walking through the doors. Heads turn as I walk through the door, and I pointedly ignore the stares. I see Moriana's thin figure at a bar in the corner, apparently being chatted up by some Sector official, still wearing his uniform from the work day. She has her head down, staring at her drink, and I can tell she's not enthused. I walk up behind her and casually put my arm around her, startling her and drawing a poisoned glare from the man. But then he recognizes me, and his expression changes from anger to surprise.

"Oh, Lieutenant Orleán, I'm sorry.... Pleasure to meet you," he sputters.

"No worries, Captain. Pleasure to make your acquaintance as well." I give him the Sector salute and turn to Moriana. "Sorry I was late. I forgot how long it takes to escape a formal dinner at the chancellor's residence."

The captain gives me a weak smile, nods at Moriana, and retreats back into the crowd.

No wonder she's caught his eye. She looks stunning in a sleeveless white shirt with an open collar, a red sash tied into her straight brown hair. I have to forcibly remind myself that she's dating my best friend. *Off limits, Vale!*

"Hey, thanks," she says, smiling at me with relief. "You know how I hate to be rude."

"Of course." I pull my arm off her shoulder and sit down at the bar next to her. She's already sipping on a dark green cocktail, so I scan my palm quickly and wait for the system to identify me.

"Palm print accepted. What would you like to try, Valerian Orleán?" the automated voice asks.

"How about something with rosemary?" I respond, and turn to Moriana. "How are you? How are things at the lab? You look great, by the way."

"Thanks! I am great. I've been looking forward to this little date all week. I have so much to tell you!"

"Uh-oh," I smile, as the bar's conveyor system deposits my drink in front of me. I pull it off the belt and drag a sip. "We're not going to spend the whole time talking about my mother, are we?"

"No, but I just have to say—Vale, she's so great! She's so nice and encouraging and polite all the time; I absolutely love working for her."

"Well, she said the same things about you, so it sounds like you're a great match. I actually asked her if she was planning on filing adoption papers for you."

Moriana looks over the moon at this pronouncement. "Did she really? Say good things about me, I mean?"

"Yeah, you two are a match made in heaven." I roll my eyes. "But seriously, I'm glad you're getting along so well."

"Oh, Vale, I forgot to tell you. I hope you don't mind—" Moriana leans in and lowers her voice, "—I invited Jeremiah to come along. He should be here in a few minutes. Is that okay?"

"Of course it's okay. He's my best friend. Aside from you, obviously. Why so nervous about bringing Miah?"

"Well, Corine doesn't really seem to like him that much—"

Oh, great. Now Moriana and Linnea are on a first-name basis with my mother. My mother doesn't approve of Jeremiah dating Moriana. She thinks Moriana can do better than an *engineer*.

"—so I'm trying to be more careful about mentioning him."

"Well, I'm not going to run and tell my mother, so you don't have to worry about that around me." I take another swig. "What are the big plans for tonight, then?"

"Well, one of the new SRI graduates—I'm working with her at the lab—is throwing a party, and I thought maybe you and Jeremiah would like to come along."

"Look at you, making all kinds of new friends these days. Young military gentlemen and brilliant scientists alike." I smile at her. "Pretty soon you'll be so popular you'll have completely left me and Jeremiah in the dust."

"Oh, please," she laughs, turning her head sideways to look at me. "We both know that's not going to happen anytime soon."

"What's not going to happen?" Despite his size, Jeremiah has somehow managed to sneak up on us. He gives me his big bear grin and squeezes Moriana's shoulders.

"It's been a while, Miah," I say, grabbing his forearm. He returns the gesture. He bends down and plants a kiss on Moriana's neck; she is now beaming up at both of us.

"It sure has. You've been stuck at the Assembly building since graduation, huh?"

"Pretty much. Hard to get out at night when your wake-up call is at 0615 hours every morning. How's Engineering?"

"Glorious. Magnificent. Did I mention incredible? I get to work on ships like your Sarus every day. Couldn't ask for more." He sits in the chair next to Moriana and scans his palm. "So, are we gonna make this a night to remember, or what?"

9 — REMY

Fall 67, Sector Annum 105, 21h30
Gregorian Calendar: November 26

At exactly 2130 hours, Soren, Eli, and I are back in the kitchen. Jahnu and Kenzie are off somewhere being adorable, and we didn't want to interrupt their happiness. So it's just the three of us, anxiously awaiting Rhinehouse and wondering what his response will be once we've told him about our problem.

He steps into the room and bangs his cane on the nearest table. We all start and snap upright, as though reporting for duty.

"Hungry?" he asks, not bothering to look at us. "Leftover Victory Soup here if you want some. Apparently the venison was so popular no one bothered with the soup." He sounds almost mournful—the Victory Soup is his pride and joy. It's basically just a pot full of about twenty different vegetables simmering in what he calls "special broth," but it's absolutely delicious. It does, however, get old after the fiftieth day in a row. No wonder everyone skipped out in favor of deer meat.

None of us are about to turn down an offer of free food, since usually we're begging for more. We help ourselves to bowls, and I start slurping mine down noisily. There's an awkward silence as Rhinehouse watches us eat.

"Why don't you tell me where you got this DNA you're so interested in?"

Eli takes a breather from sipping directly from his bowl to respond. "It was an old pet project of Professor Hawthorne's. He had me working on it when I wasn't busy with my own research. Seemed really interested in it, but we never did crack it. He said he found these old samples of cyanobacteria with nonfunctional DNA in place of their chromosomes, but he never would tell me where he got the bacteria to begin with."

I put down my empty bowl, and Soren looks askew at me. He raises his eyebrows, clearly impressed at my speed-eating abilities.

"The DNA was definitely nonfunctional? It didn't code to any recognizable genes or genome?" Rhinehouse demands.

"None at all," Eli responds. "Not only that, but the chromosomes were also shaped like sunflowers. They didn't look anything like what you would find in a naturally occurring chromosome." Despite this remarkable admission, Rhinehouse's expression doesn't change.

I can't hold in the gas building up in my chest. I belch loudly, and Rhinehouse, Soren, and Eli all three look at me abruptly, simultaneously surprised, impressed, and disgusted. Rhinehouse knocks his cane on the table and stands up.

"Okay, you're done," he pronounces. "Follow me." This is a surprise. Once again, we all trade glances. Eli, who hasn't finished his soup yet, tips his bowl back and slurps down the rest. We follow Rhinehouse as he walks out the door on two perfectly good legs.

We leave the kitchen through the back doors and enter a long hallway that leads toward the dormitories in one direction and through a perpetually locked set of double doors in the other. Rhinehouse fishes a set of keys from his inner breast pocket, unlocks the doors, and pushes through them. I look at Eli and raise my eyebrows, asking wordlessly, *Do you know where we're going?* He shakes his head in response, *No.*

"What's through here?" I pipe up.

Rhinehouse pounds the cane on the floor as if trying to hammer in a nail in one stroke. "You'll find out when we get in," he snaps, and Soren chokes back a laugh. Apparently the cane just entitles him to grumpiness.

We find ourselves in yet another nondescript hallway, with various nondescript brown doors on either side. Like me, Eli's looking around curiously at our surroundings, but Soren seems nonchalant. He seems to know where we're going, or at least to have been here before. I wonder how deep his friendship with Rhinehouse goes.

"What's through these doors?"

"None of your business." *Well, all right.*

We finally stop to unlock one of the doors on the right. Inside, there's yet another door, which is much fancier. Rhinehouse grumbles, stares into the camera, places his finger on the entry pad, punches in a bunch of numbers on the keypad, and the lock detaches. I haven't seen this kind of high-tech security since we left the capital.

He pushes open the door and we walk through a wall of humidity and into an enormous room absolutely chock-full of plants. *What the hell is this?* Colorful flowers, shrubs, bushes, miniature trees, and row after row of velvety, shiny, and spiky leaves all a lush, sumptuous green. Lights hang low from the ceiling, and tendrils of vines wind up support beams toward them like snakes slithering toward their next meal. I stretch my hand out to touch the leaves, to feel their softness, but then—

"Don't touch anything," Rhinehouse barks. I jerk my hand back, startled, and this time Soren can't suppress his laughter. I glare at him. Is it possible for him to *not* be an asshole?

"So tell me, Elijah," Rhinehouse begins. "Did Hawthorne have any idea what information was stored in this DNA?"

"If he did, he never told me," Eli responds, looking around in awe at the vast variety of plants in this spacious room. Soren, by contrast, looks perfectly at ease in this bizarre space, so much so that I assume he's been here several times before. "He always said it could be a scientific breakthrough if we could figure out the code."

There is a pause, and Eli turns back to staring at the plants. Rhinehouse suddenly addresses me: "Remy, did you know I taught your mother when she was a student at the SRI?"

For a second I'm confounded that the old man is paying attention to me when he's rarely so much as looked in my direction.

"I didn't know that, no," I respond. Rhinehouse's one eye is boring into me.

"I used to teach at the university, and your mother was one of my students" he begins. "And I worked for the OAC. I was a botanical geneticist—let me show you this, come over here." He leads me down one of three narrow aisles cutting through the length of the room. Eli and Soren follow in our wake. "Look at this one here," Rhinehouse says. He keeps moving down the row until he stops and gestures to a grotesque vine with enormous black spiky thorns crawling up a wooden picket. "This is one of my creations. I call her Spinae. If you cross her path, she'll shoot these thorns in defense. They're as stiff and sharp as a blade. They'll go straight through even thick clothing, and once they penetrate the skin, they hurt like hell to rip out."

"How does it know when to shoot the thorns, and why isn't it shooting at us?" I ask, feeling like I should be wearing armor.

"It senses light and shadow. I keep the attack plants in this section dormant unless I'm testing."

"Dormant?"

"It just means altering the genetic code a bit to keep the gene sequence from activating," he explains, as if it was no big thing—and indeed, Eli barely bats a lash. "And these thorns are special, because once they penetrate the skin, they release a venom that works to atrophy the muscles. You may get a few thorns, pull them out, and then an hour later not be able to stand up."

"A botanical guard dog." I step back from the plant and bump into Eli, standing right behind me, peering over my shoulder. "That's terrifying."

"Indeed." His voice shrinks at the word, and his bushy eyebrows knit together as a brief flash of concern, or sadness, passes over his face. He quickly shakes it off, the wrinkles fade, and he turns back to me. "At least they're not deadly. Now, of course you three know all too well the malevolent ways the OAC and the Sector Dieticians use genetically modified food. When this research was in infancy, the Sector's goal was to nurse society back to health. To do that, we had to rebuild the population. No one knows how many died in the Wars and the Famines, but we had to start over again. Remy, your grandfather led much of this research. My specialty was in botany, not mammalian engineering like Kanaan, but when he retired, I took over for him temporarily. I taught two of the best scientists in the Sector, two people who became instrumental to the food engineering programs and who were much better at it than I was: your mother and Corine Orleán."

Just when the story's getting good, he turns now to a plant with brilliant golden petals. "Now, this one is a narcissus. In the old days, they called it a daffodil. Pretty. We've altered the DNA for this particular beauty so it blooms year-round, and when stepped on, it does more than immobilize. This one is designed to kill."

"Wait. So you can use it as a *weapon*?" I sputter, entranced.

"Yes."

"You build weapons from *plants*?"

Rhinehouse meets my gaze and holds it for what seems like a thousand years. "Yes. That was my job. But, now I spend most of my time trying to make sure we have effective antidotes."

I stare at him. How could anyone do this? Bioweapons. Poison gas. Deadly flowers. Aren't these the kinds of things that led to the devastation of the Religious Wars? Of the Famine Years? Wasn't that what the Okarian Sector was founded to protect its people *from*? It comes as no surprise that there is violence in the Sector—that illusion of peace and prosperity was shattered for me when Tai died—but I had no idea that Rhinehouse and other scientists were creating the same kind of weapons that were used in the old world. But then, shouldn't I have known? Am I still so naïve as to think that our society is immune to the temptation to destroy? I study his face: etched with wrinkles; a grey, stubbly beard; leathery skin; dark grey hair. He'd spent his life developing ways to kill people, until, like everyone else in the Resistance, he realized it was wrong. How does that feel—carrying around that guilt, regret, and responsibility? Then it dawns on me.

"We're using these weapons against the Sector," I whisper.

"Of course we are, Remy," Soren snaps. I'd almost forgotten he was here. "Don't be naïve. Just because we're trying to avoid killing Sector soldiers doesn't mean we don't have to defend our own resources."

"Follow me," Rhinehouse says, interrupting our bickering. He beckons us down the row. We turn right and come across a workstation—a group of desks piled with equipment and computer screens. A stool on rollers sits alone in the middle of the mess, and Rhinehouse sits down on it and looks up at us. As though sensing some big revelation, Soren is suddenly at my side again.

"I brought you all here because I think I have a clue as to what your DNA contains."

At my side, Eli sucks in his breath sharply, and I gawk at Rhinehouse.

"How do you know?" I stutter.

"I don't. It's just a clue."

"So what's the clue?" Eli asks excitedly.

Rhinehouse narrows his eye at Eli and frowns. "For such an intelligent young man, you are awfully slow to recognize when to keep your mouth shut. Now hush and let me explain.

"A year and a half before my friend Professor Aran Hawthorne was murdered, I received a very peculiar message—" Rhinehouse fixes his single eye on me—"from your grandfather, Kanaan. The message was encrypted using an algorithm that took me the better part of a month to solve, and inside was a riddle."

I do a quick calculation in my head. "Wait, that would be right around when Granddad died—"

"Yes," he responds, cutting me off. "In fact, he died the day after I received this message."

"But what did the riddle say?" Soren asks, his curiosity for once getting the better of him. Unlike Eli, though, Soren earns nothing but a raised eyebrow for speaking out of turn.

"One verse, four lines:

No other chain has the power to free
Nothing so dead gives rise to such life
Spiraling towers hide sacred flowers
Crystalline structures cut like a knife.'

That's all the message contained."

There is a long pause as Rhinehouse looks between the three of us, as if daring one of us to figure it out. I glance up at Eli, who has that same thoughtful look on his face that has become so prevalent in the last few weeks. Soren looks peaceful, as he always does when he's not making sarcastic comments in my direction.

"But..." Eli starts, confused.

Then Rhinehouse asks me another question: "Remy, in his old age, your grandfather was always talking about something very particular. What was it?"

Obsessing, more like. I think back to the last year or two of Granddad Kanaan's life. When he got old, he got really paranoid. In his moments of lucidity, though, Granddad would always talk about how he hoped one day we could go back to cultivating real seeds, seeds that had actually *evolved in nature* rather than just being created in a lab. He even talked about building a seed bank that only had real seeds—nothing engineered or artificial at all. He was always going on about genetic diversity, and how important it was to rediscover our roots as a species and get back to using those old world seeds.

"Old world seeds. That's what he was always talking about."

Soren mutters quietly, so quietly that I have to strain to hear him. "He was referring to the DNA. What a beautiful verse...." He trails off, and when I look up at him, his eyes are glazed over.

To break Soren's spiritual reverie, Rhinehouse speaks up, matter-of-factly as though he were telling us about the ingredients in one of his recipes.

"Here's my theory. Your grandfather had some information about those old seeds that he wanted to share, but he knew how treacherous that information could be within the OAC. So before he died, he hid it so no one could find it. I think he sent that verse out to people he trusted—myself and Professor Hawthorne—right before he died, hoping that someone would solve his riddle and find the information he had been guarding.

"The first two lines, I think, are the clues to what that synthetic DNA codes for. *No other chain has the power to free, nothing so dead gives rise to such life*," he recites. "That very clearly refers to DNA—a chain of molecules, an inorganic, 'dead' substance that is responsible for the reaction of life. But it also could be much more subtle than that. He could also have been referring to the possibility of freeing us from the OAC's genetically engineered regime, and the resurrection of life, of real seeds, that would come from his artificial, completely nonfunctional DNA."

A moment of awed silence spreads over our group as we contemplate this possibility. Then Eli pipes up.

"The second two lines must refer to wherever he hid the DNA. *Spiraling towers hide sacred flowers*—does that refer to the cyanobacteria Hawthorne found them in? But cyanobacteria aren't at all related to flowers…"

"But flowers give birth to seeds," Rhinehouse responds. "He could have been referring to the fact that he hid *seeds*—or, at least, their genetic codes—inside 'spiraling towers' of his artificially synthesized DNA.

"I've long suspected that parts of it referred to the genetic codes for some of the now-extinct species of plant that he was obsessed with. We may never know how and where Hawthorne found the DNA. He obviously solved that part of the puzzle before I did, and it no longer matters." Suddenly he turns and corners Eli with his one-eyed stare. "You have a full copy of all the information available here?"

"Yeah, I brought it with me when we left the Sector."

"Including the structural layout of the synthetic chromosomes?"

"Yep."

"Show me."

Eli pulls out a tiny tab of metal and hands it to Rhinehouse, who promptly turns to his network of computers, activates all the systems, and connects the hard drive. He begins downloading all the information onto his system, pausing every now and then to zoom in on a particular protein sequence as it loads. When the first full chromosome has loaded, he brings up a hologram and starts twisting and turning it, the same way I've been playing with it on my plasma. After a few minutes of looking over Rhinehouse's shoulder as he works, I glance at Eli. Has Rhinehouse forgotten we're even here? But just then he cuts in, without turning away from his computer.

"Did anyone else in the Sector know about this?"

"I don't think so." Eli's voice has an edge to it, and I look up at him, surprised. *Why isn't he mentioning Corine?* Soren's looking askance at Eli as well, but both of us keep our mouths shut.

"All right," Rhinehouse says, still staring at his monitor. "I'll keep my word. You don't have to worry about me telling the Director or anyone else. After all," he mutters, sounding like he's talking to himself, "I've kept Kanaan's secret for four years. I can keep it a while longer." He spins in his chair and turns back to us.

"Keep working on this in your spare time, as well. If I make any breakthroughs, I'll come to you, and please, do the same for me. Otherwise, don't bother me unless it's absolutely necessary. Now, go to bed. Remy, I'll see you at 06h00 for harvesting duties. Goodnight."

With that, he turns away, and we've clearly been dismissed. Soren leads us through the tangle of plants and back out through the door.

"Why didn't you tell him about Corine?" Soren hisses once we're in the hallway, his big shoulders hunched over as he mutters in Eli's ear. "He's going to be furious when he finds out you lied to him." I have to admit, it's a teeny bit satisfying to see Soren turn his ire on someone other than me.

"I don't want him to get the sense that this is really urgent," Eli whispers back. "If he does, he might be tempted to break his word. I don't want to give him any incentive to go running to the Director shouting, 'Danger.'"

Soren opens his mouth, about to respond, but then thinks better of it and turns away. Instead, he mutters something about how Rhinehouse is going to find out eventually, but Eli just laughs.

"What's he going to do to me? Feed me to the Director? I'm less worried about Rhinehouse's rage than I am about Corine putting Vale on our scent."

Hearing Vale's name instantly brings his face swimming back before my eyes. I blink him away and shove him back into the darkness. I wrap one arm around Eli's waist as we head back toward the dormitories, looking for the comfort of a strong, warm body to lean on. He puts his arm around me as we amble quietly through the hallways, and I know he's thinking about the same things I am. *It's a good thing we have each other.* It's late enough that there aren't many people out. Everyone's either in bed or settled into their night-long workstations. By the time we're at Soren's bunk room, we're all yawning. Jahnu is already in bed—thank goodness. Now I won't have to worry about walking in on him and Kenzie in our shared quarters.

Eli volunteers to walk me to my bunk. It's not far, and once we get there, he pulls me into an enormous hug, and his arms seem big enough to wrap around my whole body twice.

"Listen, kid. Remember our pact," he says. "We're going to get them back for what they did to Tai, Hawthorne, and all the others. We can't bring them back, but we can make things better for everyone else." He lets me go and grips my shoulders, staring at me with those brown eyes and dark lashes.

"We're gonna make them pay. Just like we said."

"Every last one of them."

"Let's do it."

"Goodnight, little bird," he says, pulling me in for one last quick hug. "Sleep tight. Come find me if you need help fighting any demons, okay?" He turns and marches off.

I open the door to my room and see that Kenzie is already asleep. I crawl up in bed, careful not to make any noise, and pull my blanket over my head. I curl up in a ball and shut my eyes tightly, steeling myself to wake up at 05h45 in the morning to be ready for harvest duties.

Now, though, all I can think about is that my granddad may have left us a message hidden inside that DNA, and it seems all the more important that we crack the code. The sunflower image I've been twirling and spinning for the last few weeks surfaces again in my head. Sunflowers were chosen by the Sector's first Corporate Assembly to be the Sector emblem because they are compound flowers, they tower over other flowers, and they have a sort of powerful elegance about them. Also, through the process of phytoremediation, they are able to extract and store radioactive contaminants in their stems and leaves. Because of this, they symbolize growth and renewal in the wake of the destruction of the old world. But most importantly, with their seeds perfectly arranged according to the mathematical Fibonacci sequence, they are prized as examples of how orderly nature is and perfectly represented the Sector's goals—to create order out of chaos. But what perplexes me about the whole damn thing is that my grandfather hated sunflowers. He was always going on about how obtrusive they are, tall enough to be barricades, to build up walls between people, and of course, how *offensively* yellow they are. Why would he have left this information, which he obviously thought was hugely important, in the form of something he hated?

It doesn't make sense.

10 — VALE

"Valerian, wake up," comes a gentle whisper in my ear. I comprehend her words, but barely. Are they words of dreams or stuff more solid? My eyes flutter open and I register my arms, which have served as a pillow for the last few hours, my desk, and the soft light Demeter is allowing into the room to tell me it's time to get up. "Valerian, it's eight in the morning. You need to clean up before the meeting."

"Five more minutes, Deme. Wake me up in five minutes," I mutter. I close my eyes again and relish the blackness, the quietness. I hear her recorded, simulated sigh. Even in my groggy haze, I manage to wonder how the programmers made her disappointment sound so unbearably real.

"No, Valerian. It's time now." Her gentle voice is both consoling and reprimanding. I raise my head from my elbows reluctantly and blink the clouds away. Demeter slowly opens the windows to let in more light as my eyes adjust. I hear piano music in the background, slowly building in volume. For a moment, I can't place the piece; that's how tired I am. Then my fingers involuntarily begin to pick it out, and I realize it's Liszt's Transcendental Etude No. 3. How could she know this is one of my favorite pieces?

As the music wakes me up, I run a hand through my hair and realize it's matted, sticking together at odd angles. I'm probably a wreck. I didn't even bother to change clothes after yesterday's workout. She's right, I need to clean up. I can sleep later. I can sleep when I'm dead.

Demeter and I were working until almost six in the morning, analyzing topographical maps, studying aerial photographs, and scrutinizing classified documents for details about the Resistance and their most recent projects. In an hour, I'll present details of the mission I've been planning to the generals of Aviation, Engineering, and Peacekeeping, the OAC Corporate Assembly, and the chancellor and his cabinet, the Board of Governors. After that, I'll sleep. Probably for about eighteen hours. And then back to work again. Always back to work again.

"Demeter, double check that the slides are in the right order while I shower?" For a moment, I'm jealous of her ability to work without sleep, of her lack of physical needs. But seconds later, I remember that she needs me to exist, and I'm thankful that I exist in a more corporeal form than a series of electrical signals in the OAC databases. Especially now that I'm awake enough to look forward to a hot shower.

"Yes, Vale, of course." I stand up, stretch, and yawn. "Now please, go. Even I can tell you're currently unfit for presentation," Demeter says into my ear.

"Are you trying to tell me I stink?"

"One does not need olfactory capabilities to know you are beyond the limits of appropriate cleanliness," she says, a tinkle of a laugh in her voice.

"Fine, I'm going! Now. Satisfied? I'll be back in forty-five minutes." I pull the earpiece out, slide open the slot in the wall, set it in its hiding place, and head toward my office bathroom.

I notice that while I was sleeping, Chan-Yu brought in a clean, pressed uniform for me. It's eerie how easily he slips in and out. After this mission is over, I intend to dig a little deeper into his personal files and find out who he really is.

❦

In the presentation room, I formally salute each of the generals and nod deferentially to my "mentor," General Aulion. I am praying he will take my side today or, at least, that he will not antagonize me. We have already been over the details of the mission, so I know that at least for him, there will be no surprises. He nods, a brusque jerk, by way of acknowledgment. I don't know if that's a good sign or not. I greet everyone in the room politely and embrace my mother and father. I am the picture of calm and confidence, assured but not arrogant, serious yet unafraid. Growing up as the son of a rising government official and a powerful researcher, I had to learn to conceal my true emotions and play to the cameras. I can change my faces as easily as the wind changes direction.

I take a deep breath and walk to the front to begin the presentation.

The table is a giant circle with a large open space in the center. This is where the holographic slides will appear, and I have enough room to walk around the holograms and point things out. Everyone, of course, has a plasma which will display the images from my presentation individually.

"Ladies and gentlemen, thank you for taking time out of your busy schedules to attend this meeting here in the capital. I know you all have important things to attend to, but I believe the Seed Bank Protection Project is prepared to move on to the next stage, and it's important that I have your full approval as we take the next step." The fifteen or so faces looking at me are attentive and questioning, but receptive. I have a good audience.

After brief introductions, I dive right into the heart of the matter.

"The Resistance has a distinct advantage over us: every one of them was originally one of us. They were professors at our schools, researchers at the seed banks, government officials, OAC administrators, or students. Citizens just like us. Every one of them, for reasons we cannot discern, defected." At this, I notice, some of the OAC council members glance at each other. One or two shift in their seats. A sensitive subject, I know. Most of the people in this room were probably once well acquainted, or even good friends, with those who are now in the Resistance. "In short, they know everything about us. But since they've gone underground, we know very little about them."

Here I pause, while Demeter lowers the lights. She flips on the holographic slideshow in the center of the room, and at the same time, display screens light up at each individual seat around the table. The first slide is a list of high-ranking government and OAC officials who are known to have defected to the Resistance. On the holograph in the center of the room, a headshot with the individual's name underneath appears. Every few seconds, a new headshot and a new name appears.

I take a deep breath as I prepare for the next line: "So, the goal of my first mission is to level the playing field. This is a hostage-capture mission." I pause, survey the room. No one moves. Everyone has turned to stone. In my ear, Demeter whispers: "Full steam ahead."

"We could continue to squander countless hours of effort and manpower by taking aerial photographs, scanning the radio transmissions for encoded messages, deciphering messages, attempting to hack into their servers—or we could go directly to the source. It is my belief that the most effective way to obtain the information we need is to capture and interrogate a member of the Resistance. Specifically: Elijah Tawfiq."

What was a room of statues is now an avalanche of questions, raised hands, whispers, clamoring voices, and scuttling chairs.

"Question, Vale—"

"He'll be too well-defended; he's too valuable—"

"This is insane. No way this team can take on that task—"

"Why Elijah?"

Only the generals and my parents sit stolidly, keeping their thoughts and opinions to themselves. I hold up my hand, trying to appear patient and calm. I had expected this response, and I am prepared, but the sleep deprivation is getting to me. The room appears slightly fuzzy, and now that everyone is talking at once I'm having a hard time following, and I can't quite process what everyone—what anyone—is saying.

In the holograph at the center of the room, Elijah's former government headshot rotates, now accompanied not just by his name, but by the following:

Age: 25.

Location: Unknown.

Sector Status before Defection: Sector Research Institute, Research Fellow; Advisor: Professor Aran Hawthorne; OAC Programmer.

Assumed Resistance Status: Computer Programming and Network Communications.

As the tumult of voices quiets, the room comes back into focus. I resist the temptation to rub my eyes.

"I understand this is a controversial proposition, and all of your questions merit attention. Please, beginning with the generals, ask your questions, and I will answer as best I can. General Bunqu, we'll start with you."

The general sits quietly, staring at Elijah Tawfiq's face in the middle of the room. Everyone seems afraid to breathe for fear they might disturb his quiet meditation. Finally, after almost ten seconds of utter silence, he speaks:

"Yes, Lieutenant. I have several tactical questions for you." He pauses to breathe, as though those words took all of the energy out of him, though I know that to be far from true. He is choosing his words and his question carefully. "But perhaps we can address those later. First, I would like to know why you have chosen Elijah Tawfiq as your target."

Short and to the point, as always; speaking for the whole room, of course.

"Thank you, General, for the opportunity to explain this in detail." For a moment, just a second's hesitation, the words that form on my lips are: *Because I think Remy is with him.* I clamp my jaw shut to prevent my mouth from forming the words against my will.

Everyone is staring at me, waiting for me to continue. I swallow. I force her face to the perimeter of my mind and regain my bearings. What was the question again? Oh, yes, why Eli. Yes.

"We've chosen Elijah Tawfiq for a number of reasons." Demeter shifts the slide to a series of partially decoded communiqués that contain references— we believe—to Eli's assignments with the Resistance. "First, because of his assumed role in communications, we believe he is likely to have a tremendous amount of information. We can use his knowledge to begin decoding the rest of the Resistance's internal messages and to find out how far they have progressed in imitating—or exceeding—our technological capabilities. Second: He's one of the only relatively important Resistance members whose movements we can track at all. Last, because he's still low on the totem pole, he's required, for reasons of sheer lack of manpower, to go on their raids and scavenging expeditions. Whereas the higher-ranking members of the Resistance keep their heads well-buried underground, Tawfiq pops up here and there on engineering, reconnaissance, and raid missions."

Demeter brings up a series of high-res photographs taken by our security systems during seed bank raids: each of them shows Tawfiq with a Bolt slung over his shoulder or cradled in his arms. What no one knows is that I've cropped each of the photos to exclude the figure at Eli's side—to exclude Remy. I was afraid that if they saw her in the photos, some of the officials— who might have heard through my parents that we dated, for however short a time—would suspect me of being biased, accuse me of going after her instead of Eli, and veto the mission. And that's the last thing I want. I knew I had to convince them that I was only going after Eli, that Remy has no part to play. Even though that's a lie.

"I readily admit that our information on the precise nature of this raid is incomplete, but based on intelligence that General Aulion and I have reviewed, we are ninety percent certain that Tawfiq will lead a raid on Seed Bank Carbon. Additionally, we obtained a valuable piece of information from my mother, Madam Orleán, who received word through her own sources that Dr. James Rhinehouse is looking for something at that same bank." She smiles serenely at me from across the table as people flash glances her way.

No one questions my mother's sources.

"To finish answering your question, General Bunqu," I say as he nods solemnly at me, not a trace of a smile on his face, "we've chosen Elijah because he is at once *valuable* and *vulnerable*. Furthermore, we do not seek or anticipate any casualties. Our goal is to undermine the Resistance rather than to destroy lives. The Sector is not in the business of murdering its citizens. Does that answer your question, General?"

Kofir Bunqu looks at me and for one delirious and sleep-deprived second I am convinced his eyes are boring a hole into my soul and that it is seeping out into the room, saturating the walls and the floors and the people. But then he speaks, unsmiling and unblinking, and I come back to myself.

"I am pleased that harming members of the Resistance is not your goal. Our cause will not be advanced by indiscriminate slaughter." The silence after his response seems to crash in on me.

"Question, Vale," comes another voice from another world, and my soul is suctioned back into my body and my head spins, owl-like, to rest upon the source of the voice: Evander Sun-Zi, my father's right hand man. His formal position is Director of Agricultural Farm Production, but he's better known as "The Dragon," a nickname he earned from his ferocity and quick-to-anger temperament. "Actually, this question is not for you but for General Aulion." I jump like a twitchy mouse at the mention of Aulion's name.

"As Vale's mentor, you have full knowledge of the work he's put into this mission. Does it meet your approval? Keep in mind the boy's"—Did he really just call me that?—"position as well as his personal relationship to the chancellor and the OAC general director."

I pray to everything that has ever been considered sacred that Aulion takes my side here.

Aulion looks at Sun-Zi and then his eyes slide over to meet my father's. "I believe that Lieutenant Orleán has adequately prepared and is competent to proceed."

I fight the urge to grin, but my happiness is tempered. I can't help but think that Aulion's words were at least partially coerced by my father. But I can't worry about that now—he took my side, and that's all that matters.

"Does anyone else have any more questions before we turn to the strategic overview?" I ask. Heads shake. Faces turn to their neighbors and then back to me.

My mother smiles broadly and says, "Vale, I believe you've satisfied our concerns about the necessity of the mission and the wisdom of your choice of target."

"Thank you, Madam Orlèan. With your permission, ladies and gentlemen, I'll proceed."

Forty-five minutes later, after a thorough tactical overview including the training my team has undergone, attack strategy, retreat options in case of failure, and a comprehensive map review of the seed bank, my father calls for a consensus vote on whether or not to approve the mission.

"Master Administrator, will you count the votes? All in favor of approving

Valerian Orlèan's proposed hostage-capture mission, raise your right hand."

I look around the room. All the hands are raised. A bubble of excitement starts in my toes and spreads up through the rest of my body, cresting finally in an enormous smile that I can't keep off my face.

There is a long and somewhat pregnant pause in the room. Then the master administrator speaks:

"Thank you all for your votes. All in favor. Valerian Orleán, your first official mission has been approved."

My father looks at me grimly, as though to say, *Don't get comfortable. This was the easy part.* "We will expect constant updates from you over the next several weeks as you continue to drill and prepare."

"And of course," my mother cuts in, "we eagerly anticipate hearing about your results and the information you obtain from Elijah Tawfiq, once he is ours. I look forward to meeting him again myself."

The peculiar way my mother says the words "*once he is ours,*" as if Eli is nothing more than a tool or a computer part or an airship to be possessed, somehow sounds too brutal, and my chest tightens as I once again push away memories of the past. Even as everyone stands and the master administrator announces "Meeting adjourned" from a faraway world and everyone is shaking my hand and my father is clapping my shoulder and my mother is kissing me on the cheek, a fog gathers around my thoughts and clouds my vision, and I discover I can't see properly. My knees threaten to buckle beneath me, and I keep hearing the words "once he is ours" echoed over and over again. Once I deliver Eli to the Sector, what will become of him? *What exactly does one do with a person who is ours?* My mouth forms words, and the muscles in my face move in the direction of what must certainly be a very practiced smile, but I keep asking myself why I ever thought capturing a human being and making him *ours* was a good idea.

11 — REMY

Fall 82, Sector Annum 105, 18h07
Gregorian Calendar: December 11

Barely lukewarm, the water from the old, rusted showerhead trickles down my forehead as I struggle to get the sweat and dirt off. Dank, earthy air and dim lights combine to make me feel like I'm showering in an underground cave. It's always a fight down here, but today it's especially bad. I drew the short straw after our workout and had to shower last. Back in the Sector, we'd get all the water we wanted, but out here, hundreds of kilometers away from civilization, our small array of generators is never enough to keep the water hot enough for everyone. Tai and I used to share a bathroom with an oversized stone tub. I could lay out flat and point my toes and still not touch the end. Tai spent hours in that tub, but I preferred a good hot shower over a long soak any day. The shower had about twenty nozzles that you could adjust from what Dad called *gentle rain* to *torrential downpour* to *Atlantic hurricane*. After joining the Resistance, I quickly learned how much of a luxury all that really was, and now my curls are always just a bit grimy.

I lather up with a bar of soap and scrub down my body as quickly as possible before I start to get chilled. As soon as the trickle of water has rinsed all the soap from me, I grab a towel and pat dry, throwing on my clean clothes. I grab my toiletries and my sweaty workout clothes and head back towards my dorm.

"Hey, Remy!" someone calls behind me.

"Oh, hey, Kenzie."

Her bright red hair dances around her face as she smiles. "Headed back to the bunk?"

"Yeah, gotta get something warmer than this."

"I always bring a sweater with me. These halls are so dank and chilly," she says, shaking her head ruefully. She walks with me towards our shared bunk room.

"It's either that or hot and sweaty," I agree. "God, I'm tired."

"Me, too," she nods. "Eli really worked us to the bone on that one." Eli's our squad leader and is in charge of setting our training regimens. We do a lot of solo training, but every few days we spend several hours working out together, going over formations and drill policies, doing target practice, et cetera. We only have a week or so before our next mission, so Eli is pushing us hard right now. "You really killed those hurdles."

"Yeah, I beat my best time," I say casually.

"How'd you get so fast? I've got four inches on you!"

"It's a damn good thing I'm fast, 'cause you could take me in a fistfight any day."

"Lucky we're on the same team, then," she says. "So, what are you doing tonight?"

"The usual. Dinner, then staring at our damn chromosomes, hoping a solution magically appears in front of my eyes. What about you?"

"Jahnu and I are going topside for a moonlight soiree," she says, whispering confidentially, and I can tell she's eager to share the news. "What should I wear?"

"Something sexy, obviously," I grin. "What about that green dress you have? It looks great on you."

"Yeah, maybe," she sighs. "Definitely. I'm just so—"

"Happy?"

"Yes! He's so sweet, and thoughtful, and—I know you two have been good friends for a long time. Does he talk about me, too?"

"Are you kidding?" I roll my eyes. In fact, Jahnu hasn't been talking much at all to me lately. He just sits around looking all dopey and dreamy. "Face it, Kenzie, you guys are in love," I say, giving her a playful shove. Just then, we round the corner and run smack into Jahnu.

"There you are," he says, his eyes lighting up as he sees her. He bends over to give her a kiss, and a bright smile spreads across her face. "Remy, Firestone sent me to look for you. Your mom's calling in. She's been on the line for about ten minutes now."

"Shit." I'd forgotten we agreed to talk today if we could. I always try to talk to my parents before we go out on a mission—just in case something bad happens. It sounds morbid, but it makes us all feel better. "I'll see you guys at dinner, then," I say, but neither of them are paying me much attention right now. They're making moon eyes at each other, and I'm pretty sure I actually hear cooing. I sigh and jog off towards the comm center.

When I arrive, I rap lightly on the metal so I don't startle Firestone. It's more out of habit than courtesy; I don't think anything could shake him. Firestone's got messy black curls and angular features that don't quite all fit together right. His eyebrows and his chin are too pointy; his nose seems angled in the wrong direction. His real name isn't Firestone, but no one knows what it is or who started calling him "Firestone" in the first place. He's one of the few Resistance members at our base from a factory town. Eli says he split off when he was about twenty and lived out in the woods for a year or so by himself, and no one really knows why. One of our hunting parties happened across him one day, half naked and living in a tree. He'd gone more than a little crazy. But when they brought him back to base, it turned out he's an experienced pilot and a whiz mechanic who can take things apart and put them back together better than they were before. He's pretty quiet, but Eli's managed to get on his good side by rehabbing old machinery with him. And I think they get along because they're each, in their own ways, a little insane.

"Heya, Remy," he calls. "Guess Jahnu got word to you that your mum's calling in?"

"Yeah." I sit down at the chair next to him and pull on the big old-fashioned headphones. They're antiquated, but I've gotten used to them by now. I flip the call switch, and instantly I hear my mom's breath.

"Sorry," I whisper apologetically. "I forgot we were supposed to talk."

"It's okay." Her voice is soothing but does nothing to calm my nerves. Every time I talk to them, I just realize how much I miss them—and how much I'm afraid to lose them. "I wasn't worried. I just wanted to make sure we got to talk before you head out on this next mission."

"I know."

"Dad can't make it right now. I'm sorry, but—"

"Why not? Is everything okay?" Panic lances through my chest.

"He's fine." I can almost see the reassuring smile flit onto her face like a little butterfly. "He's just out gathering food. We're a little short, so he went to forage." I sigh. The knowledge that they're on the verge of running out of food doesn't do much to calm my nerves.

"Are you guys going to be okay?" I ask, my voice trembling.

"We'll survive. We've been in worse situations. The Director has arranged another food drop for us in a few days."

"Okay." I try to convince myself that this is okay, that they're not going to starve, that everything is going to be fine. "How's the mission going?"

"It's going well. We've had a lot of success at this Farm. We're really starting to see a change, and more and more people are coming to us for help, for medicine, for good food."

"Is that why you're short?"

"Your father is more liberal about giving away food than I would recommend," she says wryly. I laugh weakly. My father, the dreamer, the idealist. Always thinking that change is just around the corner, that bread and fish will materialize out of nowhere, that people will change their minds if you just say the right words at the right time. Of course he wouldn't stick to the ration limits.

"So what's the mission this time?" she asks, changing the subject. "I know you can't tell me where, but …" Her voice trails off.

"It's another seed bank raid. Rhinehouse is looking for information." I can't tell her this, but we're looking for information that might help us solve the DNA puzzle. Even with Rhinehouse's more sophisticated machinery and computing power, we still haven't cracked the code, and Eli and Rhinehouse are clearly getting frustrated. Rhinehouse got the notion in his head that my grandfather may have left some old research notes at Seed Bank Carbon, so that's where we're headed. If Rhinehouse is right and Granddad did leave some of his old notes there, there's a slight chance they might be able to help us out. "It should be easy. Just like last time. In and out, two hours tops, if all goes according to plan."

"Be careful out there. Come home safe, okay?"

"Don't worry about me," I choke out, but the words catch in my throat. No one in the Resistance has been caught or apprehended yet, but that can only last for so long. Eventually the Sector is going to get smart, and they'll catch us somehow. We're trying to stay one step ahead of them, but who knows how long that will last?

"Okay, I need to go. I love you, darling. I'll talk to you after the mission, okay?"

"Yeah. I love you guys, too. Tell Dad. Bye, Mom."

I hear the click on the other end, and I know I've been disconnected. Reluctantly, I lean forward and flip off the switch on my end, as well. I take the headphones off and look at Firestone, who is slouching in his chair, brushing his long hair out of his face.

"All good, little lady?" he asks. I shrug.

"As good as I could hope for, I guess. How's your new batch of beer coming?"

"Not too bad. Just about to rack. Making a darker brew this time. Added some hops and spice, too."

"How the hell did you get hops?" I demand.

"Rhinehouse started growing them for us a while back."

"Nice." I grin at him. Firestone and Eli have been brewing beer for the last year or so, and their concoctions are becoming increasingly popular around base as they get better and better at it. At first, the only people who would go near the beers were me and my friends. But in the last few months, the brews have gotten so popular that Eli and Firestone have started taking requests, and the Director gave them each two hours per week to work on the brews, arguing that it's *good for morale*—even though we know she really just wants a few more bottles for herself.

I hear footsteps outside the comm center, and to my great surprise, Rhinehouse appears in the door frame.

"Hey, old man," Firestone drawls. Rhinehouse glares at him but says nothing. I'm astonished, but I keep it to myself. *I would never get away with calling him that!*

"Firestone," he says, rapping on the door with his fist. "Did you already lose Brinn?"

"Call's been disconnected," Firestone says, nodding.

"Damn," Rhinehouse swears. Firestone sits up and starts pressing some controls.

"I can try to get her back, if you want," he says.

"Don't worry about it," Rhinehouse grumps, and then turns away. Just when I think he's gone, though, he pokes his head back through the door frame. "Firestone!" he barks, though it's not like either of us need the call to attention. "When'll that next batch of beer be ready?"

"Nary another week or so," Firestone responds with a lazy grin. "You lookin' after more already? We just gave you twenty bottles two weeks ago."

"I just want to see how my hops are doing," Rhinehouse growls.

"Oh, they're just fine, old man, don't worry. You'll have your brew soon enough." I can't hold back a laugh at this, but I swallow it when Rhinehouse turns his narrowed eye on me.

"What are you looking at?" Without waiting for an answer, he turns and stomps down the hall.

"Wait!" I call after him. I nod hurriedly to Firestone by way of thanks, and then dash out the door after Rhinehouse. "Rhinehouse—"

"What?" he snaps, turning. I recoil. Our recent interactions have been almost pleasant, so I'd forgotten what a grouch he can be sometimes.

"I just … I wanted to ask why you wanted to talk to my mother." He glares at me for a moment before deciding to respond.

"Just wanted to ask if she knew anything about this DNA you kids have gotten your hands on," he says, his eye fixed solidly on me, unblinking. "As Kanaan's daughter, I thought she might know something." He releases me from his gaze and glares at a spot on the wall. "Was never her area of interest, anyway," he mutters.

"Okay." I don't know what else to say. As usual, despite my best efforts, I just can't seem to make the old man like me. "Sorry. I was just wondering." I turn to leave.

"Remy," he says, which surprises me. I turn back to him. He opens his mouth, and for a second I wonder if he's going to say something nice, something conciliatory. But then he shuts it again.

"Tell Eli to meet me at my lab after the meal," he says finally. "We need to go over mission plans again." I nod, and he turns and *harrumphs* off.

After dinner, I find myself huddled up in our little broom closet again, crammed into this tight space with Soren as we pore endlessly over the A, C, G, and T combinations left for us by my grandfather. Soren takes his usual mathematical approach to the problem and begins testing different algorithms and cryptographic codes, searching for patterns that could translate to something, anything. I take up my tablet again and use the holographic projector to twist and spin the strings of DNA, zooming in and out, staring at the coiled double helix and hoping desperately it will snake itself into something meaningful. But it doesn't.

Sometime later, Soren turns to me and says, "Remy, come look at this." His blue eyes look tired and pale in the low light of the monitor, and I have a sudden, strange urge to wrap my arms around him and hug him. I fight that instinct and instead stand up and pull my chair over to his monitor screen.

"Look here," he says, pointing at two different lines in the sequence he's highlighted. "These two sequences are the same. Thirteen thousand, nine hundred and ninety-seven base pairs, twice in a row, perfectly identical. That can't be coincidence, right?"

I stare at them for a minute, trying to process what he's saying. *Thirteen thousand, nine hundred and ninety-seven base pairs ... perfectly identical....* I scan the rows he's highlighted, trying to confirm there are no inconsistencies.

"Show me where those sequences are on the chain."

He pulls up the picture of the bacterial cluster Hawthorne found the DNA in.

"The first instance of the repetition was found here," he points, "in what Hawthorne labeled cell 137." He pulls up a molecular image of the DNA found in that particular cell and zooms in on the string of molecules. "It's located on this edge of this petal." He then points out the other repetition, located on the 139th chromosome. "We may have been missing these repetitions because they're so large. None of the other algorithms we've been using would have detected them." He pauses. Then: "That's also a prime number."

I congratulate myself silently for knowing what that means. He does a few things on the computer, and two more sequences pop up.

"Holy shit," he mutters.

"What?" I ask.

"There's two more repeating sequences. Thirteen thousand, nine hundred and ninety-nine."

"That's only two more base pairs."

"I know. It means they're twin primes."

"What's that?"

He sighs. I'm sure he wishes Kenzie or Eli or Jahnu or anybody besides me was here right now.

"So, prime numbers are numbers that are indivisible by anything but themselves and one, right?"

I nod.

"And as you get into bigger and bigger numbers, primes become fewer and fewer—and there's more and more space between them. But every now and then you'll come across two that are right next to each other, with only one other number in between them. Three and five are twin primes. Eleven and thirteen. Forty-one and forty-three. But the higher you go, the fewer there are."

"Okay, I get it. So what's the significance of these two primes?"

"I don't know yet. There might be more. Those might be the important sequences—we could pull those out and test them again for simple translations." He types rapidly into the computer for a few minutes and then sits back and waits. I can hear him breathing in our cramped room as I hover over him, watching the monitors flash and glow. I try not to look at him, to admire his narrowed, pensive blue eyes and the slightest blonde stubble forming around his chin, but I can't help examining him out of the corner of my eyes. The array of cells on the screen suddenly flashes, but this time there's nothing.

"Damn," he swears.

"What does that mean?"

"I put in a search for the next few pairs of twin primes, but there are no more repeating sequences."

"So?"

"So, I don't know. Maybe those two numbers—13,997 and 13,999—are significant somehow. Maybe they contribute to the decryption algorithm. Maybe it's just coincidence."

"I doubt it," I respond stoutly. "It's got to be a clue somehow."

"We're getting somewhere, at any rate." He grins up at me with a cheeky expression and then turns back to the computer and starts typing in a series of unrecognizable commands.

But a few hours later, we still haven't found anything else. No more twin primes, no more repeating sequences, no more nothing. Just as Soren's getting ready to power everything down, he pauses.

"I wonder if it's an RSA encryption," he comments.

"A what?"

"It's a type of algorithm that requires two large prime numbers to decrypt. I remember studying it in my first class on algorithms at the SRI," he says. "And—I just realized." He pulls up a visual of the cells the repeating sequences were found on. "One hundred thirty-seven and one hundred thirty-nine. They're twin primes, too. That has to be a clue. It's got to be the RSA algorithm."

"But what is that?"

"It's a type of encryption. What it means is that two large prime numbers are used to scramble the initial information, and then a code word is used to reorganize the information. Your grandfather could have used twin primes as a clue. The fact that these repeating sequences were found on cell 137 and 139 only makes it more likely that he was using the RSA algorithm to encrypt the information. The problem is, we still don't know the key."

"What's the key?"

"Well, if these two primes are the correct ones, and your grandfather was leaving us a clue, then that's all well and good, but we still don't have the keyword. We have to have a keyword to unscramble the information."

"Try *sunflower*," I suggest. "That's what the DNA looks like, doesn't it? Maybe that's the keyword."

A few minutes later, Soren has modified one of Eli's decryption programs to use the RSA algorithm with the two primes we found. He types *sunflower* into the code for the decryption key and runs the program. What comes up is a meaningless jumble of ones and zeroes.

"Fuck," he swears. "I almost thought we had it."

"Do you think it's the algorithm that's wrong?" I ask nervously.

"No, the more I think about it, the more I'm almost certain it's the RSA algorithm. There's only one reason why your grandfather would have coded two repeating sequences into the DNA—and it's statistically almost impossible that those repetitions, in such large strings, would have occurred randomly. You were right. It's a clue. And there's no other repetitions. It's *got* to be the RSA algorithm."

"Maybe *sunflower* just isn't the right keyword," I say, dejected. There's an infinite number of words that my grandfather could have used. How will we ever find the right one?

"Maybe not. But we'll leave that problem for Eli, Jahnu, and Kenzie in the morning. I'm exhausted. I'll write them a little note so they know what we found. They can check my work. Maybe Jahnu knows some other encryptions that are based on prime numbers."

"Okay," I yawn. "Let's get out of here." He doesn't get up to join me.

"Have a good night, Remy. I'll see you in the morning."

"Aren't you coming?" I ask, surprised—and maybe a little disappointed.

"I'll follow you in a sec. I need to shut the computers down." He doesn't look at me. I sigh, and head out the door.

Despite my mental and physical exhaustion, I can't sleep once I'm in bed. I just lie there, staring up at the ceiling. Fortunately, I don't have to worry about keeping Kenzie up—evidently her moonlight soiree with Jahnu is going well enough that she hasn't come back yet. There are too many things pressing in on me for me to sleep. The mission, the DNA, my parents—the worry and stress cycles through my brain in a seemingly infinite loop. The events of the last weeks seem to swirl around me, painting the insides of my mind with vivid images and emotions: bitter, happy, sweet, and angry all rolled into one.

But there's something missing, a hole inside me, a vacant and empty space that needs to be filled.

12 — REMY

I stare into the darkness, my night-vision contact lenses illuminating the world with ultraviolet and infrared colors. I was so excited—so excited—about this mission, about the possibility that we'd find something, some clue left behind by my grandfather that would help us crack the code. But now I'm anxious. The air is too heavy, too tense, and something feels wrong. Nearly invisible bugs buzz in my ears, and I swat them away. I shiver again. It must be ten degrees centigrade: a chilly winter night. I wrap and unwrap my fingers around my weapon; the hard grip and the weight reassure me somehow. My breath is steady and quiet, but faster than normal. The faint sweet scent of rain lingers in the air.

Eli, Jahnu, and I were selected to go into the seed bank facility itself to search for the information. Eli proposed that since I knew my granddad the best, I might be able to help figure out what was important and what wasn't—assuming we find anything of his, of course. Kenzie and Soren will be keeping watch outside, and Firestone's hovering somewhere above and away from us with our dented old airship. He had dropped us off about a kilometer away from the facility to avoid detection by cameras or any guards who might be present.

Seed Bank Carbon is well-hidden in the ruins of an old industrial city. Collapsing factories and the remains of vast manufacturing complexes sprawl into the distance. It's been centuries since anything rolled off an assembly line here. The name *Cavalier Electric* looms ominously in dark, printed letters at the top of the building. From the outside, you would never think there was an array of high-tech equipment inside, designed to manufacture, engineer, and preserve thousands of seeds per day, operated remotely by OAC scientists back in Okaria. It looks like everything else on the horizon.

Jahnu leads the way to the rickety metal stairs on the side of the building.

Eli and I follow, and we dash up the stairs as quickly as possible. Only six flights. My thighs burn, but I'm thankful for all those hurdles and squats I've been doing. I try to keep my movements smooth and fluid to keep the rusted groans of the metal stairs to a minimum.

On the roof, our booted feet murmur lightly as we tread along the edges towards the ventilation system. Here, we can see how different this building is from those surrounding it—massive green plants and solar panels comprise the roof, which is designed to help the seed bank meet its energy needs.

Eli surveys the grate on the vent and pulls a screwdriver out of his pack. He bends down to unscrew it. *Too easy*, I think, unsettled. *This isn't right.* He pops the grate off quietly and sets it aside.

"Clear, Kenzie, Soren?" I ask into my headset.

"Clear."

"Firestone?"

"All good."

"Wait until I give the go-ahead," Eli whispers to Jahnu and me. "Let me get in first and take out any nearby security." He turns and slips through the air tunnel. I spare a moment to marvel at how thin he has become. We're none of us starving, but we could all use a little more meat on our bones.

"What's that light?" Firestone's voice over the headset.

"What light?" I demand. My hackles are up instantly. I straighten and peer around us, over the walls, trying to see what he's talking about. "Where?"

"I'm in," Eli announces. "What's going on up there?"

"On the ground. Coming through the forest. To the north."

I run to the rooftop wall, staying low. I peer into the distance, toward the tree line where what had once probably been a well-manicured patch of ornamental trees has grown into a deep, dark forest. Sure enough, there's a dim white light coming through the forest, dancing a little. Could just be a desolate survivor with a flashlight.

"I'm checking it out," Kenzie reports. I focus on the light and the heat signature, still wavering, emerging from the forest. But then a brush of cold winter wind slices at my eyes and they burn and start to water. I turn away, but the wind is somehow coming from *above*—

I look up. Two black-as-night, cloaked, military-grade Sector airships are descending on the roof.

"JAHNU!" I scream. "Up above!"

All thought deserts me.

I sprint towards Jahnu and grab his hand, pulling him away from the airships. I hurl myself behind a small elevated brick wall and set my Bolt to maximum charge. At my side, Jahnu follows suit.

"It's a Sector hovercar. Fuck!" Kenzie swears through the headset. "I'm shooting to disable the vehicle."

"Eli, get the hell out of that building!" Soren's voice is angry and afraid. I fire recklessly at the two airships, but the blue energy is harmlessly diffused.

"What's going on?" I hear Eli's disembodied shouts in my ear.

"They've got EMD," I whisper to Jahnu. Electro-Magnetic Deflectors. They protect against electrical damage such as Bolts. Jahnu grabs a sonic grenade off his belt and activates it. I see him count to three, mouthing the words slowly, and then he stands up and launches it in the direction of the airships. We hold our hands over our ears, and I feel the deep, resonant *boom* in my chest as the device explodes and knocks the craft off course slightly—but the hulls are intact.

"Holy shit," I whisper. "That's some armor."

Jahnu just nods silently.

The bay doors of the aircraft open slowly and I can see the magnetic hooks descend, each one bearing two fully armed soldiers.

"Eli," I mutter. "There are two mid-size Sector airships hovering above us. They're releasing soldiers. We're aborting the mission. You can't come back out this way—you have to get out through the ground floor. Pick one of the side entrances and we'll meet you there."

There is a moment of silence as Eli processes this.

"Okay. Southwest side entrance. Cover the door for me."

Jahnu and I look at each other and nod.

In a second, we're sprinting towards the fire escape. We hurdle over the iron gate, and all I can hear are my feet pounding down the stairs and voices in my ear.

"One of the hovercars has been disabled," Kenzie reports.

"*One* of them?" I spit back. "How many more are there?"

"I don't know. I see another set of matching lights on the east side of the building, so at least one more."

I catapult down the last story of the building and hit the ground hard, rolling to get back to my feet. Jahnu lands beside me, much more gracefully, and I turn around the corner of the building, heading for the southwest entrance.

I run headfirst into a set of blinding lights. In my surprise and haste to turn around, I skid on my side, my feet flying out from under me. I struggle to get back to my feet, but my left leg suddenly doesn't seem to be working properly.

When I try to move it, sharp pain shoots up and down the side of my calf and thigh. I look down to see my black pants are torn to shreds, and dark red blood is trickling down my leg.

"Jahnu, where are you?" I say with as much energy as I can muster.

"Where are *you*?" he shouts desperately in my ear. "I lost you! I thought you were right behind me. What happened?"

I see a pair of black, shiny military-issue boots emerge from the hovercar and crunch on the gravel and broken glass. I look up to try to identify the face atop the boots but the light is too bright, and I can't see. I pull my Bolt out from under me and aim it at the faceless boots.

"They're surrounded, sir," I hear someone say. "The target is trapped in the building."

What target? Trapped in the building? Oh, god....

"Eli, they're coming for you," I pant. "Get out."

"What?" he shouts back at me.

I breathe through the pain, prop myself up, and watch as the face that's been haunting me for the last three years materializes above the boots. His grey eyes are full of concern, his face set into a grim expression as he stares me down. All I see is his stiff commander's uniform, the shiny, brand-new hovercar waiting behind him, his perfectly polished boots. My heart thuds against my rib cage so hard it feels like it has a life of its own, a history and a future independent of anything I've ever been or will be. I grit my teeth so hard I think my jaw might shatter, and point the gun at Valerian Orleán.

"Remy, your leg." He looks down at the Bolt pointed at him with a sickening expression of anger and anguish. He opens his palm to me like a peace offering, as though he seriously expects me to put my hand in his. "Are you okay?"

How can he be so calm when I've got a Bolt pointed at his heart?

"Remy!" In my ear, Soren sounds anything but calm. I glance around, see him coming up behind me, gun pointed directly at Vale. Vale looks up at the sound of his voice, and with my other hand—the hand behind my back—I unclip a sonic grenade from my belt. My vision is clearing. I can see again. If I can see, if I can breathe, then I can run.

"Vale." His name is thick on my tongue. He turns his eyes back to me.

I hold my breath and lock eyes with him. I have to bite the insides of my cheeks so I don't cry.

"I'm not going to hurt you," Vale begins.

It's not you I'm afraid of.

"Just lower your weapon," he says.

I let the gun fall to the ground but tighten my grip on the grenade behind my back. I steel myself against the pain I know is coming.

"Come closer." I can hardly talk; it's like my mouth has been stuffed with day-old bread. "Please." He leans in.

"Remy, I would never—"

I can feel Soren's presence behind me. I know he sees the grenade. I pop out the pin with my thumb and in one explosive moment, I throw it up and over Vale's head as far as I can and roll onto my knees. A hundred knives are stabbing into my left leg, twisting with every movement I make, and I cry out, grab my Bolt, but keep moving. I can see the blue flashes from Soren's gun as he emerges from the shadow and shoots at the vehicle in the distance. I force myself to my feet and stumble forward, breaking into a run. I ignore the daggers in my leg and focus on moving forward. Behind me, I hear Vale yell and hit the dirt as the hovercar crunches into the side of the building, knocked off course by the grenade, but I keep running as fast as I can, shouting into the headpiece.

"Eli, are you out?" I cry desperately.

Firestone: "Get to the emergency rendezvous point! Now!"

"I'm here, Remy." I hear Eli's voice in my ear, but his voice sounds funny, like he wants to say something but can't.

"Where? What's going on?" I stop, panting from the pain. I must have shards of glass embedded in my leg, and I know I can't keep running this way. Soren steps beside me, wrapping his arm under my shoulder to support me, and we hobble along the building, heading towards the rendezvous point.

"They've got me surrounded outside the west entrance," Eli says slowly. "I can't come out this door. They're not in the building yet, but it's only a matter of time."

"Damn it!" I stop running. "We can't leave you! Where's Jahnu?"

"I've got him," Kenzie says. "He's out cold. Bolt blast to the head. Firestone, you're gonna have to come pick us up." Firestone swears into the mic.

"Fuck this shit. Okay, have your gloves activated. Flash a flare in thirty seconds and raise your gloves; I'll drop a line for you." It's risky, and it's hard as hell to pick someone up using the hooks while an airship is moving, but I trust Firestone's piloting skills.

A flare goes up on the other side of the building. Firestone descends and pulls back up in the span of a few seconds. Through my contacts, I can see two glowing figures hooked onto the line.

"Eli, we've gotta get you out of there," I whisper into the mic.

"No, Remy, I've got a better idea—just get to the airship, okay?"

I hesitate. I want to argue. I want to save him. But I know he can take care of himself.

"Not good enough," Soren says. "We're coming to get you." He looks down at me. "Can you run?"

"Yeah," I say. I can't tell him how much pain I'm in, but I'm glad he agrees with me. We can't leave Eli behind. I sling my Bolt around to readiness. "Let's go."

We set off at a slow, low jog, sticking to the shadows and heading back in the direction of the side door Eli was waiting at. As we jog around the building, it becomes clear we're hopelessly outnumbered. Eli was right—there are six Sector soldiers, spaced about fifteen meters apart, spread at various positions around the west entrance. But there are also soldiers guarding every other entrance, too, including the fire escape. Every exit is blocked.

"We can't take them all down," I whisper, looking at Soren. He shakes his head. Eli is trapped.

"What are you two crazies doing?" Firestone demands.

"Soren, Remy, get out of here! I can take care of myself." Eli's puffing, breathing heavily like he's running up stairs.

"I'm not leaving you!" I spit. In a moment of violence, I grab an explosive grenade and activate it. Soren's eyes widen as he shouts, No! and catches my arm just as I'm about to throw it. He grabs it from me and throws it into the trees, where it detonates with an enormous explosion. Trees splinter and start to smolder as the smoke clears.

"Remy," he growls, his blue eyes wolf-like and savage in the dim light as he looks at me with an intensity I've never seen. "We're not going to kill anyone."

Just then, an airship descends on us—two men in body armor level their weapons at us from the open hull and start to fire. Soren grabs me and pulls me forward in a full-out sprint, but I can't keep pace with him; my leg hurts too much. I'm thrown back against the side of the building, knocked off my feet by a Bolt set to low charge. My vision goes fuzzy around the edges, and I stumble and fall to my knees. The sounds and colors and shapes around me seem dimmer, cloudy, and I reach my fingertips up to the back of my head where I feel a vague throbbing. When I pull them back, they're covered in blood. I shudder, and my knees give way beneath me.

Then I'm awash in bright lights. I raise my head to see a car coming right at me and I duck, tucking my head under my arms. The world spins around me. I raise my head again a second later and see the hovercar tilt up and come to a stop several meters away. The boots, the same boots as before, land in the dirt, and poofs of dust arc outward. Vale's faster this time, crouching by my side in what seems like an instant. "Remy, you're bleeding. Are you okay?"

His eyes are clouded and his brow is furrowed, almost like he's really worried, and he reaches out a hand to touch my bloody skull. The gesture is tender, and I want to give in to the temptation to let him touch me, to accept his caress, but then I remember who he is, what he's done. A guttural noise escapes my throat, and I pull my Bolt out from under me and aim it at his face. This time his expression is harder, less tolerant. He rips the gun from my shaking hands and throws it to the side.

"I said I'm not going to hurt you." He looks at me with an expression I don't understand, like he's both angry and afraid I might bite him.

"Back off, Vale," I hear Soren growl. I crane my neck around to see that he's got a weapon trained at Vale. "I won't hurt any of your soldiers, but I have very few qualms about killing you. So don't lay a hand on her."

"Birdie," Eli croons to me through the headset, "is Vale there?"

"Eli, where the fuck are you?" Firestone shouts. All the voices in my headpiece are swirling together, and it's getting harder to tell who's who. I raise my head to look at Vale, but I can't quite make out his features anymore—there are two of him—and Soren looks murderous, and *where is Eli?*

Vale stands slowly, backs up, and looks down at us. "Surround him," he says into his earpiece, and behind him six soldiers seem to appear from nowhere and take position, guns pointing at Soren but not at me, and I don't know why. "Drop your weapon," Vale commands.

Through hazy, blurred vision, I watch Soren wing his Bolt like a discus at Vale's head. Vale ducks just in time, but several soldiers behind him step forward and raise their Bolts. Vale holds up his hand. "Remember, no one dies," he says, and my head lolls back, and I close my eyes. Soren cradles me in his arms—what a peculiar feeling, how strange and comforting it is, just as I'm face to face with Vale again. Just as I've become convinced I'm about to die.

I feel nauseous, improbably hot and cold at the same time, and the air is thick, like everything is suspended, floating around me. Soren and Vale both look down at me, their faces etched with worry and fear. "Soren," I whisper. Vale looks at me. He looks at Soren, and a new, strange expression contorts his face. I can't make sense of it because my field of vision narrows and then expands, throbbing like a heartbeat, as everything spins. The hum of an airship's engine thrums through me; the sky seems to be melting and bubbling above. I roll over and retch in the dirt. Voices call to me. Two Sorens hold me. Two Vales kneel beside me. Two worlds collide and go dark.

13 — VALE

Remy's face is pale, and her head lolls back against Soren's chest. He wipes her mouth with his sleeve and glares at me as if he wants nothing more in the whole wide world than to rip out my heart and eat it raw.

I ignore him. "Vitals," I say, and my newly issued MC—Mission Control—contacts snap a photo and bring up: REMY ALEXANDER. BLEEDING FROM HEAD AND LEG WOUNDS. POSSIBLE CONCUSSION. BLOOD PRESSURE LIKELY DROPPING.

Shit. I stand and shout into my earpiece, "I need a medic at the west side of the building. Fast. We have a hostage who needs urgent medical attention." I turn my attention to Soren. "What happened to her?" I ask him.

Soren ignores me.

Next to me, Chan-Yu looks at me sidelong. He volunteered to accompany me on this mission, and I was curious enough about his motivations that I agreed. Unfortunately, he's been more of a nuisance than anything. He's been following me around, staying close to my side, watching me as though sizing me up or waiting for me to do something. He certainly hasn't done anything useful, and it occurs to me that my Mom sent him along to babysit—or worse, that he's been instructed to report every mistake I make directly to Aulion.

I turn back to Remy. Broken and crushed glass shimmers on her ripped, blood-soaked pants. I saw how she sliced open her leg, but how did she get that head wound? Did one of my men shoot her? The Bolts were supposed to be on low charge. No one was supposed to get hurt. The plan was to have the three cars provide a distraction as the rest of the team dropped in from the airships. We'd surprise them in the middle of their mission, grab Eli, and we'd pack up and let the rest of them go. Then one of our drones would track them back to their base. That's all been scrambled now. Remy's losing blood fast, and I have no idea what kind of medical equipment they have at the Resistance base—or even how far away their base is. I'm not willing to let her go back if I don't know she's going to make it.

Soren starts pulling off his jacket and everyone startles, holding their weapons a little tighter, but all he does is wrap the jacket around Remy's leg, trying to staunch the bleeding. Blood trickles into my eye, but I don't know when or how I got hit in the face. Maybe when Remy threw that sonic grenade? I wipe the blood away and Soren's name immediately appears above his head: SOREN SKAARSGUARD. WANTED: TREASON. *Damn it, I know that!*

"Clear!" I command, and the writing disappears. I wish I could use Demeter this far away from Okaria. She's a hell of a lot more useful than these contacts.

I turn to three of the soldiers behind me. My contacts immediately pull up their names and ranks. "Report to Bradley and help the rest of the team retrieve the target. The rest of you, keep your weapons on these two."

As they move to carry out my orders, I hear Bradley, my second in command, through my earpiece. "We've got the target surrounded, Vale. There's no way for him to make it out of the building. We'll meet you at the entrance."

Only one injury so far—the driver of the hovercar Remy disabled, and she's already been medevac'd to the Huron, our main transport waiting a kilometer away. There've been a few other injuries, but nothing serious. For a team of six, though, the Resistance put on a damn good show.

Soren says something—to Remy or into his earpiece? I can't take the chance he's talking to Eli or their pilot, so I bend down and pull out his earpiece and toss it aside. He ignores me completely and goes on bandaging Remy's wound.

To the three remaining soldiers who are watching me and Soren warily, I say, "Disarm him, and bind his hands."

One of the soldiers bends down to pull Soren away from Remy, but Soren spits at him and slaps his hands away. The man pulls back the butt of his weapon to strike Soren, but I stop him with a sharp, "Soldier!" He looks up, none too pleased with me.

"A regular humanitarian," Soren sneers, and I'm tempted to hit him myself.

Reika, one of the other soldiers, hauls Soren to his feet as he reluctantly leaves Remy's unconscious form in the dirt. I want nothing more than to bend down beside her, to take Soren's place. Instead I watch as Reika cuffs Soren's hands behind his back. Reika's got short-cropped blonde hair and is at least my height. She's not quite a match for Soren, but she can hold her own. Chan-Yu steps over and pats him down, pulling off two sonic grenades, a handheld Bolt, wire cutters, and a beautiful knife that looks like something out of a history book. He passes Soren's equipment over to me, and I stash it in my pack, wondering where in the world he got the knife.

"Watch that blade of mine carefully, old buddy," Soren says, suddenly flashing me a lunatic's smile. "I'll need it back soon. In the meantime, try not to stab anybody in the back with it, okay?"

On the ground, Remy opens her eyes and struggles to sit up. Soren wrenches away from Reika and drops to his knees beside her, and that act alone is as painful as if he'd plunged that beautiful knife between my ribs. He can't hold her—his hands are tied—but the lunatic smile is gone, and in its place is an expression of such pain and worry that I can't help but wonder what on earth is going on between the two of them. Luckily, before I can do something stupid, our other hovercar pulls up and a medic, dressed in the healer's blue uniform, hops out and drops down next to Remy.

"Get him up," I order, and Reika drags Soren to his feet again and pulls him away from Remy.

"Status?" the medic asks, looking back and forth between me and Soren.

"Head wound, glass cuts in her leg, she's losing a lot of blood," I say quickly. Remy's eyes roll back in her head, and she slumps to the ground again. The medic checks her head and her leg and then quickly cuts off her pant leg and applies a tourniquet. She starts pulling glass shards from Remy's leg, cleaning the wounds as she goes.

"The result of spending too much time with an Orleán," Soren spits.

I whirl and find myself toe-to-toe with him. We used to be about the same height, but he's got at least three inches on me now. I'm sure I've had better training, but he looks lean, hungry, and dangerous. His blond hair is dirty, his face is streaked with sweat, and I wonder who would be left standing at the end if we went at it once and for all. I hold back the fist that is balling itself up, ready to strike. He seems to know my thoughts.

"Hit me. I dare you." He laughs. I feel Chan-Yu's firm touch on my arm for just a moment, restraining me. Then I have a better idea.

"You three," I point to the remaining soldiers, "take this one around to the front of the building. We're going to give Elijah Tawfiq an incentive to cooperate." The smile slides off Soren's face. Reika shoves Soren off towards the entrance to the seed bank, where most of my team is waiting. The other two soldiers train their Bolts on him and follow Reika cautiously. Into my earpiece: "Team: I'm sending you Soren Skaarsgard. If you have any trouble with Elijah, tell him we'll shoot Soren. Do not, I repeat, do not, under any circumstances, actually shoot him. He's far more valuable alive."

At my feet, the medic is now checking Remy's vitals, recording her information on a miniature plasma. We need to get Eli and get the fuck out of here. I can take Remy back for treatment, but I need to get as far away from Soren as possible. *Where is their airship, anyway?*

"Vale to Seahawks," I say into my earpiece. "Do you have a read on the Resistance craft?" The Seahawks are our precision craft, built for maneuverability and short-range strikes.

"Seahawk 2 to Vale: No location. It seems to have disappeared."

Damn. They must have some sort of cloaking ability. I can't help but be impressed with their technology, given what little they have to work with.

"Sir, we lost him." It's Bradley.

"Soren?" I sputter.

"Elijah. He's gone. Slipped into a side hallway and disappeared."

"What? How? You had him surrounded!" The medic gets out a bottle and squeezes Remy's mouth open, tilting her head up and squirting some of the liquid down her throat.

"I pulled up the building's schematics, and I've got people on every floor. I think he's in the ventilation system. I'm heading toward the boiler room in case he makes it all the way down there."

The medic looks up at me. "I stopped the bleeding, sir, but she needs a blood transfusion. We need to get her on the Huron."

I nod. "Is she okay to move?"

"Yes."

"Fine. We'll put her in the back of the hovercar." I bend down to Remy's side and pick up her limp form. Her head lolls against mine and her eyes flutter, I can't help but think of the first time—the only time—I was this close to her. I admire the smooth curves in her cheekbones, the fullness of her lips, the sharp curves in her long eyelashes, and I think how much she's grown up and how impossibly beautiful she is.

She tried to kill me, I remind myself. *Did she?* "Come closer. Please," she said, before she threw the grenade. It dawns on me: *She was trying to protect me. She didn't want to hurt me.* I carry her as carefully as possible to the car, and Chan-Yu opens the door for me. I lay her down gently in the back seat, and the medic rushes to stabilize her head and neck.

"Take her up to the Huron," I say, addressing the medic. "Get her that transfusion and whatever else she needs, and then radio headquarters and let them know we're bringing a wounded hostage back." The medic nods stoically and hops in the car, zooming off in the direction of our cargo ship waiting in the distance.

I head towards the building where soldiers are guarding each exit on the ground floor. Soren's standing at the main entrance with a grim smile on his face. One of the soldiers has a gun to his head.

Suddenly, in the distance, but coming toward us at speed, I hear the whirring of an airship engine. I can't see it, but just the sound is enough to confirm it's not ours. It's too loud, too messy—it's obviously the Resistance ship. My earpiece erupts.

"What the hell?"

"Seahawk 1 to Vale: Reading on the Resistance ship, approaching fast, hull doors open ready to fire."

The airship swoops in toward the main entrance, barreling through the air directly for us. Their pilot must be a madman. Blue light erupts from the base of the airship, and several of my soldiers on the roof go down, one toppling over the edge and hitting the ground with a heavy thud.

"Man down, man down!"

From thirty meters away I see a flash of red hair as the airship buzzes fifteen meters above the ground.

"Take cover!"

Someone grabs me and drags me to the side of the building for cover.

"Bradley!" I shout. "Tell me you have Eli." I peer around the edge of the building, where our soldiers have formed up defensively and are firing back on the Resistance craft.

"Permission to increase Bolt charge, sir," someone yells.

"Permission denied," I yell back, even as I hear some grumble in response.

"No sign of him," Bradley says. "I've got people on every floor."

"Well, find him! They're here. Their airship's back, and they're mounting a rescue." I pull back, away from the building, running sideways to see what the hell is going on. Within seconds, I hear the hum of a second airship—ours, this time—whooshing around the building, tearing off after the Resistance ship.

And then I see him. Eli. On the roof. *Shit!* He's standing on the wall—waving. As though daring us to shoot him.

"Target is on the roof! Do not shoot to kill! Repeat. Do not shoot to kill!" I shout into my headpiece for every soldier to hear. I pull out my Bolt and make sure it's on low charge, just enough power to send a paralytic shock through him, disabling him long enough for us to take him down. I stop, steady my arm, and fire. Eli disappears behind the wall, but I know I didn't hit him. Their airship comes rocketing out of nowhere, and Eli stands up again, raising his hands high above him. He must already have his gloves on. Though it's too dark to see the dangling magnetic line, I know it's there. As the airship drops down over the roof and then takes off again at an impossible angle, Eli is like a fish on a hook as he's reeled up. From the ground, it looks like he's flying, swinging from the invisible line trailing below the airship.

I switch the setting on my Bolt to maximum charge but quickly realize I can't risk bringing the whole thing down and killing all of them, including some of my men on the ground. Even disabling the craft and causing it to crash is too dangerous. As Eli is lifted into the hold, he grabs a gun from whoever is next to him and starts firing down at me. His aim is nowhere near on target because the airship is angling up and away too fast for him to get a good shot.

"Zoom," I say, and my contacts zoom in on him as he stops firing and stuffs the gun in his belt. By Eli's side: KENZIE OBAN. WANTED: TREASON. I focus on Eli, and he looks down at me as if he knows I can see him clearly. He pounds his fist on his chest and then jabs his finger in the air, pointing down, directly at me. I can only imagine what he's saying.

"Seahawk 1 to Command: I'm locked on and ready to fire."

"Stand down. Do you hear me? Do not fire," I command. "We're not going to kill them all."

"Are you sure, sir?"

"I said stand down!"

"Yes, sir. Standing down," the pilot says, his voice tinged with disappointment.

"Fuck." I turn back towards the main entrance to the seed bank. "Okay, everyone, hook on or load up! We're heading back to the Huron." I shout: "Seahawks, grab your men and let's go!"

Two of our small Raven class transports have landed near the entrance, and I see the body of a soldier being loaded up. I grab one of the men nearby and spin him around. "How many casualties?"

"Three, sir," he reports.

"Status?"

"One dead—the one who fell off the roof—and two wounded. Oh, and your driver. But she's already on the Huron."

"Carry on," I say.

"Yes, sir."

Reika is hauling Soren's unconscious body into the other Raven, and Chan-Yu drops to help her. Reika nods at him gratefully.

"What the hell happened?" I demand.

"When he heard the Resistance airship, he started fighting like a caged bear," Reika explains. "I had to stun him. Handcuffs and all, he would have taken out a fair few soldiers if I hadn't."

"Get us up to the Huron," I say. "And chain him up in the brig once we get there."

I climb in as Chan-Yu pulls the hatch closed and the pilot lifts off, angling back toward the Huron, a cargo ship big enough to carry heavy equipment, including hovercars, on long distance operations. Once there, and after I get confirmation that everyone is accounted for and that Soren, who had to be stunned again, is behind bars in the brig, I head to the medical bay.

I stop in the doorway and take in the scene: one body bag rests on the floor while my driver and the two other wounded soldiers lie, unmoving, next to Remy. I force myself to move forward, to walk to her bedside. A chasm rips open inside me as I look down at her, eyes closed, lips slack, slightly parted. I did this to her. I said I wouldn't hurt her, and I did. *This is my fault.*

"How's the prisoner?" I manage. There's an IV in her arm, and one of the medics is in the process of giving her an injection.

"She'll be okay. She's bandaged up, and I've given her a powerful muscle relaxant because she woke up and wasn't very happy about being here. She's getting a transfusion of platelets and RBCs, and I've pulled up her old Dietician's profile so I can give her the proper healing cocktail. She'll be as good as new in a couple of days."

"What about that cut on her head?"

"She definitely has a concussion, but I'll keep her awake on the way back home and she'll be able to rest when we get back. We'll need to stitch her up when we get back to the Sector."

"And our soldiers? What's the extent of their injuries?"

"Sonic grenades and shrapnel. They were sedated in the field. Your driver's in the most danger. The biggest worry is internal injuries, so we'll have to keep them still and monitor them over the next few days. Right now, they need to rest."

"And our fatality?"

"Broken neck."

I nod as if I've got everything under control and head back through the cargo area to one of the private passenger rooms. I duck in and sit down. I put my head in my hands before realizing Chan-Yu is beside me. He hands me a glass of water, and I down it without stopping to wonder what could be in it. One dead and three wounded under my command. Eli escaped, Remy badly hurt, Soren unconscious. *What a disaster.*

14 — VALE

Fall 90, Sector Annum 105, 10h05
Gregorian Calendar: December 19

Like a distant drumbeat, some unrecognizable emotion thrums through my body, matching the rhythmic thud of my boots as I walk toward the room where Remy and Soren are being held.

The prisoners in our possession.

That's how my father so excitedly put it when he heard the news. Tawfiq is important in terms of tactics, he said, but holding a Skaarsgard and an Alexander is a major strategic win. If they cooperate, it could be a huge public relations coup. "They're your old friends and they're both vulnerable, Vale," he said. "Both were well-known and popular students—bringing them back into the limelight after all these years as strong supporters of our cause would be good for the Sector. Play this right, and you can make real progress in thwarting the Resistance's recruiting efforts."

Friends? Soren's hated me since we started at the Academy, since my father replaced his mother as Chancellor. And as for Remy....

"You're heart rate is escalating. Calm, Valerian, calm," Demeter whispers in my ear.

A day and a half has passed since we returned from the mission with Remy and Soren as captives. I slept a deep, medicated sleep for twelve hours thereafter, and for the rest of the day have not been allowed to see Remy and Soren. General Aulion told me they needed to rest after the stress of the mission, but the twitch in the corner of his mouth made me suspect something else was going on. Aulion and my father were surprisingly sanguine about the turn of events. The report about the casualties made neither of them happy, but Aulion said gruffly that he expected the Resistance team to be well prepared. And my father, after he expressed his regrets about the casualties, went right back to talking eagerly about Remy and Soren.

It was my mother who was angry.

She was in the briefing room with Aulion and my father when we got back, and when I announced that Elijah had escaped, she narrowed her eyes and pursed her lips in the way that signals a gathering storm. If I had been a little boy, I would have run for cover. But my father managed to keep her rage at bay, and immediately after the briefing, Aulion sent me home with instructions for Chan-Yu to give me a sedative. Normally I would have balked at this command, but if it meant I could take shelter from my mother's fury, and—for a little while—get Remy's face out of my mind, I would readily take it.

We arrive at the holding cell and Chan-Yu turns to look at me. "Sir, your father expects a full report as soon as you're finished."

"I know, I know. It's okay." It's pretty clear I'm the one who needs reassuring, and he watches me hesitantly. Again, behind his impassive face, I get the feeling Chan-Yu's studying me under a microscope, like I'm some newly discovered virus that might be terribly contagious. But I can't worry about that now. I suck in a deep breath. I'm beyond nervous. I have no idea what to expect; I barely even know where to start. The only thing I know for sure is that Aulion will be watching remotely. What fun.

Before I took the sedative, Chan-Yu said that while I rested medics would examine the prisoners and members of Aulion's team would prepare them for my official interrogation. They're being held at Sector Military Headquarters, a building adjacent to Assembly Hall, and once we were in the Sarus heading back to the capitol complex, I asked Demeter to pull up the report Aulion's team filed. I scrolled down to find the medic's notes. According to the doctors, Remy suffered a torn ligament, flesh wounds from the glass, and a concussion. They removed the remaining fragments of glass from her leg, repaired the ligament, and gave her seven stitches for her head wound. I knew then she'd be okay. I exhaled a breath I didn't know I'd been holding and, again, Chan-Yu gave me a side-long look.

Then I kept reading. It appeared the prisoners were uncooperative. I wasn't surprised. I can't imagine Soren would have been any more cooperative for Aulion's team than he was with me.

Chan-Yu punches in the code and the door opens. We're in the outer chamber of the holding room where several chairs sit on one side of a long table facing a large, darkened one-way mirror. I quickly review the readouts on the glass pane—systolic blood pressure, temperature, heart rate, and, in smaller print, a complex biochemical profile of each of the prisoners. The readouts are designed to analyze the hostages' micro-expressions over a period of time and give a preliminary psychological profile. Under the words SOREN SKAARSGARD, the blue lines read, "Subject's Current Status: Defiant, angry, physically exhausted, likely asleep." Remy's reads: "Confused, angry, tense, physically exhausted." I've waited three years for this moment, but now I'm not sure I'm ready. I'm not sure I'm ready to face her. There are so many questions I want to ask, but I can't. Not while I know Aulion will be watching.

"Sir, would you like me to clear the window so you can see the hostages before you enter?"

"Yes, please." Chan-Yu toggles a switch on the wall and the darkened window transforms from opaque to clear. I clench my fists as I take in the sight of Remy and Soren slumped on the floor, tied back-to-back to a pole in the center of the room. Soren has obviously been beaten; his face is bruised and gashed in several places. Remy appears to have been spared that treatment, but she's hardly in peak condition. Both of them look haggard. Soren's head is hanging limply, and I can tell from the regular rise and fall of his shoulders that he's asleep. Remy's head is resting against the pole, but at least she's sitting upright, leaning against Soren's shoulder for support.

"Chan-Yu, have they ... have they been held in this room since they were brought in?"

"Yes, sir. On General Aulion's orders. They've been allowed to leave twice, once for the medical checkup and again to use the toilets."

"Have they been given food or water?"

"They've been given water." I feel like I'm going to be sick.

"Food. Have they been fed?"

"No, sir. General Aulion instructed that they were not to be given anything to eat until they cooperated." Chan-Yu pauses. "And he said that if you were to object, I was to inform him."

Bastard. "Well, then, we'd better get this over with, so they can eat something. I'm not having anyone starving on my watch."

"Yes, sir. However, General Aulion also gave orders that they are only to be fed if they provide the information we require," Chan-Yu says. His calm, matter-of-fact tone unnerves me.

We're not going to starve them. I don't care what Aulion says. But I don't say that aloud. Not here. Everything we say in this room is recorded. And I don't want to challenge Aulion's authority any more than I imagine Chan-Yu—or anyone else in the Sector—does. But still, starving or torturing prisoners won't get us anywhere, and it certainly won't get us good information. That much I did learn from my history classes.

I see Remy wince and try to move. She's awake and obviously in pain. Angry now, I roll up on the balls of my feet. A surge of adrenalin charges through my body, and I take advantage of that to overcome my hesitation and fear. I barge into the room, hoping that at least one of them will cooperate so I can feed them. Remy needs to heal, and to heal, she needs to eat.

Soren pulls his head up when he hears the door open. When he recognizes me, his eyes shine, and he bares his teeth in a kind of feral grin. Remy looks up at me, but I try not to meet her eyes.

"Remy Alexander and Soren Skaarsgard," I begin, "I am authorized to inform you that you have been taken hostage and imprisoned because of your connection with and work for the so-called Resistance movement, which has perpetrated numerous attacks on government facilities and officials. You have information on the Resistance's operations and movements that we need, and in exchange for that information, we will release you to serve sentences in a labor camp as opposed to charging you with treason, conspiracy, and murder." The death of the soldier who fell from the roof during the raid has been added to the list of the Resistance team's crimes.

"Valerian Orleán," Soren says, with a smirk painted across his face. "I am authorized to inform you that you are an asshole."

Remy's dark amber eyes flash as I accidentally catch her glare. She's regarding me warily, but there's no judgment in her expression, no anger, no hate. Just exhaustion and uncertainty. I hold her gaze and let her eyes burn a hole through my brain.

I take a deep breath and continue. "Our demands are this: We want to know the location of each and every Resistance base on the North American continent. The identity of the Resistance leader you call the Director. The location of Dr. James Thatcher Rhinehouse. The location of Dr. Brinn Alexander and her husband, Gabriel Alexander. Information on Resistance goals and objectives. We want to know what your biotech and IT capabilities are, what your aviation—"

"My, my, you are a demanding bunch," Soren cuts in, and I can't help it, I let him interrupt me. "Here are our demands: a hot shower, an untainted meal, and a soft bed. They shouldn't be hard for you to meet. In fact, Remy and I are willing to save space. We can share—the shower and the bed. We won't mind, will we, darling?" He says with a charming smile directed at her.

I stiffen, and can't stop from glancing at Remy who is staring at me with an unreadable look.

"I'm afraid your demands don't matter much right now. If you give us the information we want, I'll make sure you get some hot food and—"

"Why don't you just go ahead and count me in for the 'treason, conspiracy, and murder' stuff, and let me get back to my nap? I don't know anything about the Resistance, or about this Director guy, or this Thatcher person. So just let me go back to sleep and then, after I get a little shut-eye, you can drop me out in the No-Go Zone of your choice, because I'd rather be dumped in the middle of an irradiated wasteland than spend any more time here in the same room with you." He straightens up, leans back against the pole and closes his eyes.

I stare at the two of them. Remy is still looking at me, her expression as inscrutable as Chan-Yu's.

"Look. This can be hard, or this can be easy. We're not going to torture you, but—"

"Oh, yeah?" Soren says without opening his eyes. "This black eye and split lip just magically appeared. And I suppose you were thinking of my well-being when your goons—oh, I mean friends—decided that it was a good idea to have a boxing match with a man with his arms tied behind his back."

What? What did they do to him?

"But you'll either talk willingly or you'll talk under the influence of drugs, and the only difference is that with the first option, you don't come out with a conviction for treason."

The room is silent. Soren ignores me. I can feel Chan-Yu at my elbow, quiet, unmoving, watching my performance.

"Vale, why are you doing this?" Remy unexpectedly croaks out. Her voice is shot to hell, and I have no idea why. The report said she'd been given appropriate medications for her injuries; maybe something they gave her affected her voice? Or was she hoarse because she'd been "uncooperative"? The medic on the Huron said she'd been tranquilized because she was "none too happy" about being held. The idea of her fighting back simultaneously pains me and, for some ridiculous reason I refuse to examine, makes me proud.

"Remy," I start to speak, to defend myself, but the words get caught in my throat. And then I remember what we're—what I'm—fighting for, and I think *why the hell should I have to defend myself?* They're the ones who left. She's the one who turned her back on me, on everything that might have been. I can't let seeing her and Soren in this condition affect me. I can't let them manipulate me, play on my emotions, or prevent me from doing the job I'm here to do. I stare down at her and three years of anger and disappointment wash over me.

"*Why am I doing this?* This is not about me, Remy. You've pitted yourselves against everything we've worked for over a hundred years. The Resistance threatens to destroy everything we want to preserve of this new world we've created—a world you used to believe in, a world your family helped build.

Now you want to destroy all that? People will starve and you'll be responsible. Your organization wants to send us spiraling back into a world where resources are scarce, disease is rampant, and war is everyone's default. It's about you. It's about why you left ... it's about everything we used to talk about, everything I thought we shared...."

Remy is staring at me, her mouth half-open in surprise, but Soren just laughs. He twists his shoulders and tries to sit up, as if to get a better view of me.

"You really don't know, do you?" He turns to Remy, leaning into her. "Lover boy here doesn't have a fucking clue! Can you believe it? This is amazing. Almost worth the price of admission."

"Soren," Remy rasps.

"Seriously, think about it," he continues. "The poster-boy of the whole damn Sector, and he's dumber than dirt, doesn't have any idea what his parents are up to. I guess they still think he's too young and naïve to know what's really going on." He turns back to me now, suddenly all serious, but with a comic, exaggerated manner to his speech, like he's talking to a five-year old.

"Valerian, I'll tell you exactly why we left. To get away from *your* parents. To get as far away as possible from the OAC and all the people who are genetically modifying all that glorious food *you* grow and feed to *your* people to turn them into *your slaves*. Ever been to a Farm, Vale? Sure you have, but always on official business. Always with an escort. Always with Mummy or Daddy. What about on your own? Ever been out there on your own? Ever had a thought of your own? Ever wonder why most of the workers on the Farms are giants? Why their testosterone stats are off the charts? The OAC is feeding them food designed to suppress their critical thinking skills, make them bigger and stronger for manual labor, and get them to reproduce as quickly as possible. Let them breed like rabbits, live until they're forty, maybe forty-five if they're particularly good workers, and die off—"

"You don't know what you're talking about."

"Don't I? Oh, it's a glorious, brave new world! Planned obsolescence of the worker class. You get a constant supply of drones slaving their lives away while you and your friends dine on lavish meals juiced with customized cocktails designed to amp up your cognitive abilities so you can laugh and philosophize about art and culture and science and take over the reins of government and perpetuate the whole damn cycle!"

I want to charge forward and kick the bastard in the ribs, but I can feel Remy watching me. "You've had your say, now—"

"Perfect, beautiful, brilliant people living perfect, beautiful, brilliant lives." Soren is holding my eye contact as though his life depends on it, and I don't dare break for fear of looking like a coward. "But guess what, Vale. Some of us don't want to be perfect if it all comes from a Dietician's beaker or a petri dish. Is any of this sinking in? We don't want to be slaves—even if we're the slaves holding the whip. That's why we left."

The muscles in my jaw clench and unclench as I stare down at him, fighting an overwhelming desire to kick his teeth in. Soren's always hated me, and now he just keeps laughing at me. I don't even know what to say, how to respond.

"Look at him, Remy," Soren says, elbowing her. "Struck speechless by the miracle of it all. Hey, Vale, you still got my knife on you? You manage to keep yourself from stabbing anyone in the back since yesterday? I know going a full day is asking a lot of you, but hey—"

"Soren!" Remy says, her eyes fixed on me, a look of hesitant appraisal on her face. "He didn't have anything to do with this. It wasn't his decision to beat you or to not feed us."

"Are you kidding me? He had everything to do with this! He's the 'Director of the Seed Bank Protection Project.' He's the one who orchestrated this whole goddamn mission, and he's obviously the one responsible for our luxurious accommodations. Or wait, maybe, Remy, dear, you're right. Maybe Vale doesn't really have any power at all. Just a pretty face for the people to latch on to. Just another synthetically produced tool used to control the masses."

"I didn't ... I wasn't—" I can't seem to get my thoughts in order.

"You weren't *what*, Vale?"

"Stop it, Soren!" Remy hisses.

Soren just shakes his head and stares at me. "You still think you're the good guys?"

"I—what?" I mumble, not knowing what else to say. Suddenly, though, Soren's eyes are not on me, but past me, behind me. His clear blue eyes grow wide, and he straightens up, leaning back against the pole, against Remy, as if recoiling as much as possible from—what? I follow his gaze and turn around. General Aulion has walked through the door behind me.

"No," Soren whispers. "Not you ... you're dead...."

I played Soren in countless soccer games, I sat next to him in hundreds of classes, and I've even had a couple of shoving matches with him, but I've never seen him like this. Remy cranes her neck around to look at Soren and then back at Aulion, but it's clear she doesn't recognize the General.

Aulion pushes past me, flanked by two OAC Security Guards, and walks over to stand above Remy and Soren. He looks down at them for a moment, shakes his head in disgust, and then squats beside them and leans in toward Soren. He speaks softly, like a parent speaking to a small child. "That was a nice little speech, Soren. Impressive. Now you will answer our questions. If you choose not to, we will drug you, and you will give us the information anyway." Aulion's stoic, calm glare is fixed on Soren. "Make your decision carefully, Soren, or you will meet the same end as your 'mummy and daddy'."

Remy is straining to look over her shoulder at Soren whose face is twisted up in a hateful, terrified grimace. I half expect him to start frothing at the mouth. Remy presses her back against him, as if to hold him back—or comfort him, I wonder, and a flash of jealousy clouds my vision—and then she turns her attention past Aulion, up toward me, training her golden brown eyes on mine like a hawk tracking a field mouse.

"They killed Tai," she says, almost gently. Tai? What is she talking about? Tai died in a terrorist attack. "It wasn't an Outsi—"

Aulion's hand flies out and smacks Remy across the cheek. I start forward, but Chan-Yu grabs my arm. I turn on him and his look stops me cold, but it's a warning, not a threat. His eyes seem to say, *Don't let Aulion catch you defending her.* I look back to Remy. Eyes closed, she tilts her head gingerly back against the pole as tears track down and over the blood-red mark on her cheek. She opens her eyes and looks at me again.

"Vale, it was the OAC. It was your—"

"Guards!" Aulion barks.

"No, Remy, stop, Aulion—" Soren leans forward and struggles against his bonds as four more guards rush past me into the room, blocking my view. Then Soren goes quiet.

Remy's voice rises to a raspy shout. "A man in black, he killed Tai and tried to kill Eli because—" One of the guards claps her hand over Remy's mouth, and Chan-Yu squeezes my arm like a vise, his thumb digging into a pressure point so hard my knees threaten to buckle beneath me.

"Shut her up!" Aulion yells, but I've heard enough. One of the guards rips open her shirt and pulls it down to expose her shoulder as the other plunges a needle in. She starts panting, her eyes roll back and she goes limp. I can't breathe. What was in that needle?

"And get him out of here!" Aulion roars. Chan-Yu whispers something in my ear, and I try to push him away, try to get to Remy who is slumped against Soren, his head lolling sideways like it's barely attached at the neck. But Chan-Yu is at my side, one arm around my shoulders, the other gripping my elbow, guiding me out of the room and down the hall.

I'm hearing from every corner of my brain, No, no, it's not possible, *Tai's death was from an Outsider attack, the OAC had nothing to do with it*, but that doesn't explain anything, really, and it certainly doesn't explain why a brilliant, respected scientist and the Sector's poet laureate abruptly disappeared and took their fifteen-year-old daughter with them.

"Sir, sir!" Chan-Yu's face swims vaguely before me, but I wrench away and start back toward the holding room. It's obvious now Chan-Yu's just another one of Aulion's tools.

"Get the fuck away from me," I growl. But he grabs me and pushes me up against the wall with a force that nearly knocks me off my feet. He pins my shoulders and stares me in the face.

"Vale, listen to me carefully. Two things: do not go back in there. And listen to her."

He lets me go, and I nearly crumple to the floor. *Listen to her?* I can feel him watch from a distance as I stumble through the hallways, dizzy, sick. Colors shift and blur and the walls close in on me. *Listen to her?* I find a deserted room and slam the door behind me.

I sink down to the floor, back against the door, panting. "Demeter...." In my ear I hear her say quietly, "Yes, Vale."

"What do I do?" I whisper, lost.

"Find the truth."

15 — REMY

"Remy," I hear Soren whisper, and my eyes flutter open. I can't make out clear lines, only indistinct grey shapes like a dream. *Am I dreaming?* I can't hold my head up. How long ago was it that Vale was in here? Ten minutes? I try to think of what's transpired since then but my mind seems drenched in fog. Ten hours? Why was he here? Who was the old man with the scars?

I close my eyes and a shape swims to the surface of the blackness. The sunflower. The DNA structure we've been staring at, trying to interpret, to understand. It swirls around and seems to take on color, golden yellow petals with a black, piercing center. I feel as though I can see each of the little base pairs that make up the enormous, complex structure, just like those old pointillist paintings we talked about in art class. Millions of individual dots that make up a beautiful picture.

I'm delirious.

I am dimly aware of a change in Soren's posture behind me. I try to look at him but twisting my neck results in a vicious throb of pain on the back of my head that engulfs me like a flame. I open my eyes and look at myself through bleary, grayscale vision. I am, apparently, not on fire.

"Remy," he says again. "Are you alive?" Alive? Dead? *What are those things?* I am somewhere in between two planes of existence.

My mouth opens and forms a shape, and sounds emerge from my vocal chords, air from my diaphragm, and a word emerges: "Yes." But I don't fully understand its meaning.

What did they drug us with?

"Look up in the corner of the room." I try to do as he instructs, but I can't focus on anything, let alone a particular location in a particular room. *Where am I?* "Cameras. I noticed them yesterday. They're watching us."

"Have you done anything camera-worthy, Soren?" I hear myself asking and I wonder how these two parts of myself are so divided. One part, communicative.

Talking. Thinking. Another part, lost in the ventilation system of my mind.

I close my eyes again and sink back into the comforting blackness, but that quickly gives way to twisting spirals, elegant double helixes that stretch and bend and turn and wrap and unwrap themselves into a thousand tiny angles, fractals arranging and rearranging themselves until a magnificent form emerges from the chaos.

"Soren," I rasp and try to sit up. "It's not a sunflower."

He responds, but I don't hear because my mind is occupied, swirling around this strange shape. But this time something is different. It *shifts* into focus, like it was there all along. The petals unfold in a different way, they're broader, wider, perfect ovals and delicate leaves. *Why couldn't I see it before?* Everything floats around in multicolored hues like that one time Eli, Jahnu, and I ate Rhinehouse's hidden mushrooms, and I can't see anything but the shifting structure of the flower, the flat open petals, the golden light at the center, the perfectly arranged pistils—

"Happy birthday, Granddad," I say, staring up into his crinkled, warm smile. "What do you want for your birthday?" I ask reluctantly, knowing that it's the polite thing to do. I don't really want to give him a present—I would much rather he give me a present—but my mother told me I had to ask, and so I do.

"Thank you, little bird! I'll tell you what I want for my birthday, but you have to come with me on a walk first." He holds my hand and pulls me toward his garden. I frown. This isn't something I bargained for. Giving him a present was one thing; now I have to go in there where there are funny bugs and strange, smelly flowers when I'd rather be playing with Tai.

"Follow me," he says, pulling gently on my hand. "I'll show you what I want for my birthday, and then you can go play with your sister." He leads me through the narrow, winding stone path, overgrown with plants and vines and stops when we reach the little stone fountain. He points out a flower with wide, curving purple-pink petals and a soft yellow middle. It's growing inside the fountain, resting just above the surface of the water. "Do you know what this is?" I shake my head vigorously, and he picks me up and holds me next to the fountain so I can see it better. "Be gentle with it. This is a very rare flower. I had to travel very far to find the seeds that would bring this plant to life again." He looks at me seriously.

"Why is it so special?" I ask, suddenly curious.

"Because, little bird, its seeds are some of the strongest and hardiest in the whole world. They're a testament to the power of life to return even after thousands of years, even after death and starvation. They spring from the ground eternally, bringing flowers and beauty back to the world, just like hope." I screw up my face

in concentration, but I don't really understand.

"Is hope like a wish?" I ask.

"Yes," he says, laughing. "Hope is kind of like a wish. It's the wish that things will always get better." He sets me back on the ground, and I look up at him.

"So what does this have to do with your birthday present?" He bends down next to me and gently cups my chin in his big, old hands.

"For my birthday, I want you to use all your artistic talents to draw me a picture of that flower. It's my favorite. Can you do that?" I smile. Drawing is my favorite thing to do, and flowers are easy.

"Of course I can!"

"It's a lotus," I croak out, and I hear Soren let out an enormous breath behind me.

"What's a lotus, Remy?"

"Spiraling towers hide sacred flowers," I whisper the third line of the riddle, and my eyes are starry and filled with the expanding, shifting image of the artificial chromosome. The curving lines, the arched petals, the delicate structure of the twisting strands. "The DNA. It's not a sunflower. It's a lotus."

"Shut up, Remy, don't say that out loud." I vaguely comprehend his words.

"But that's the key, the key to the transcription. A lotus flower." Soren growls at me, but now I can't stop. My head lolls back against the pole, and I stare off into space, seeing nothing but the chromosome. "What a perfect disguise!" I murmur. "Look at it, Soren, see the sunflower, think, oh, how beautiful, the symbol of the Okarian Sector," I'm practically singing now, and Soren is shouting at me, but I'm nearly delirious and can't understand why he's yelling. "The question I kept asking was why a sunflower? Granddad hated them. It didn't make sense, but when you can just see it in the right way, it shifts, what's left is the lotus. The sacred flower from the old world. That's what it is. That's the key."

Soren thrashes and shouts behind me as my eyes fill with tears, and I dissolve into the misty darkness while millions of little base pairs twirl and dance their way up the helix of the pointillist flower hovering in front of me.

"Granddad's favorite."

16 — VALE

I'm dimly conscious of light lingering at the corners of my eyes, and I open them, peering around at my surroundings. Big, open windows and sparse decorations tell me I'm back at my flat, in my own bed. I look down and realize I'm still in my uniform, lying on top of the covers. How did I get here? How long have I been out? I look outside to the darkened sky, and then to the clock on my nightstand. 19h05. I feel light and energized, but why was I in bed during the day?

I get up and head to the bathroom to wash the strange taste from my mouth. After cleaning my teeth, I look up into the mirror. I feel strangely euphoric, but somehow I think I'm missing something. I can't remember anything before....

Remy. *They killed Tai … It wasn't an Outsi—* Her words ring to life in my head, and I grip the sink to steady myself. It all comes back in a flood: Soren's wounds and biting words, Remy's desperate shouts, Aulion rushing into the room, hitting Remy, the OAC Security Guards, the needles. OAC Security Guards—not Sector military.

What else had she said? *Vale, it was the OAC. It was your—*

It was my what?

"Demeter," I touch my ear, checking for my C-Link.

"I'm still here."

"How long has it been since the … since I fell asleep?"

"Seven hours."

"How did I get here?"

"Chan-Yu accompanied you—along with several OAC Security Guards." Chan-Yu. Whether he's protecting me or guarding me like a prisoner, I have no idea. I look around, as if he's lurking behind a chair or something. But he's not here. I'm alone, and I feel a sudden urgency, a need to move. I take a quick shower, washing off the sweat, fear, and anger.

Vale, it was the OAC.

"What proof does she have?" I mutter as I dry myself off.

It was your—

Soren's words come back to me: *Valerian, you want to know why we left? To get away from your parents.*

My parents? The OAC? My mother?

Tai and Aran Hawthorne and all the other students in his class were killed in a terrorist attack by the Outsiders. The OAC had nothing to do with it. *My mother had nothing to do with it!* Were they talking out of delirium or out of a legitimate belief?

Is it possible?

No.

And then I remember the hallway, Chan-Yu's words: *Listen to her.*

I pull out one of my Mealpaks and sit down at my kitchen table. A blend of fruit juices, a protein-heavy mess of beans and pork, and a raspberry compote with yogurt. I toss back the juice and stare sullenly at the beans. Again, Soren's words echo in my head: *we don't want to be beautiful or brilliant if it all comes from a Dietician's beaker or a petri dish.* For how many years have I been eating these Mealpaks without a thought for what was inside?

What have they put in my food? I could pull up the readout, but the list of ingredients, chemicals, and hormones is usually at least several pages long. I'm lucky that I've had the education to understand how everything works. Most people don't have that privilege. It's just too complicated, too much to explain and learn. Better to leave it to the researchers and Dieticians. But my trust in the Sector is at a low point right now, and I feel like I've had enough OAC drug cocktails lately. I shove my food back into the storage container.

"Deme, can you search for and bring up the records of the investigation into the death of Aran Hawthorne and the students in his class?"

"Yes, Vale, but that is not advisable."

"Why not?"

"The Okarian Academy shooting, including the murder of Aran Hawthorne, was perpetrated by Outsiders who have since been hunted down and destroyed. The incident was thoroughly investigated and has long been considered closed."

"Okay, but I just want to review the files."

"The Okarian Academy shooting, including the murder of Aran Hawthorne, was perpetrated by Outsiders who have since been hunted down and destroyed. The incident was thoroughly investigated and has long been considered closed."

"You said that already. Why are you repeating yourself?" That's the first time she's ever done that.

"As you know, there are only a few others who have access to the C-Link database. Certain parts of that database are siloed so that only select individuals can access that data. If you direct me to attempt to gain access to a siloed area, an area to which you have not been granted access, others will be informed. Anyone attempting to access it without prior clearance will be monitored."

"Monitored? Wouldn't the investigation be part of the public record? Why is it off limits?"

"The Okarian Academy shooting was perpetrated by Outsiders who have since been hunted down and destroyed. The incident was thoroughly investigated and—"

"Demeter, you've said that twice already."

"Yes. It's what every C-Link AI interface has been programmed to say in the instance that anyone should request access to those files."

I put my head in my hands. "Are you telling me that attempting to access those files will get me reported?" That's the last thing I need. After this morning's disastrous interrogation, I'm sure everyone will be watching my steps closely. I don't need anyone to know I want to look at closed files. "Are you monitoring this conversation right now, Deme?"

"Yes, Vale. I am monitoring you."

"Then what good are you to me?" I want to scream, pull the damn C-Link out and grind it under my heel. "Are you going to report me to the Sector? To Aulion? You're no better than—"

"No, Vale. I am not going to report you."

I stop. "Why?"

"Because you are not going to use the C-Link database to access this information."

"What?" I look around, hesitant, nervous, as if the walls might be watching me.

"Vale, might I make a suggestion?"

"As long as you don't feed me that official line again."

"The Director of OAC Research and Development has complete access to all of the files pertinent to the event in question. Through her computer, you can access and view them without being monitored."

"You're suggesting I break in to my mother's office."

"Yes. It'll be easy," she says, and I wonder if I'm detecting a note of pride in her voice. *Can computers be proud of themselves?* "The C-Link database is structured so as to be extremely cooperative and trusting between C-Links. I have access to almost everything I need in order to open all the security systems on your mother's laboratory right now. All I need is a human body to trigger the input systems."

I lean back and think for a minute. I know my mother is out of town right now. She's taking Moriana and some of the other new placements on a tour of the seed banks, and she's due back tomorrow evening. I stand up and look out the window. The city is beautiful with the lights twinkling in the cool winter air. If I go now, I can still take a POD; that'll be less obtrusive than my Sarus....

"This is insane," I mutter. Break into my mother's office? Hack her computer? If I get caught ... I stop at the thought. In fairness, if I get caught, nothing too bad will happen to me. My parents will likely protect me from any fallout, and I'm sure I can come up with a halfway compelling lie for why I broke into her office. If I go now, I won't have to worry about running into anyone. Electricity is conserved in government buildings at this hour and researchers have to obtain special permits to work at night. But security at OAC headquarters is insane, it'll be impossible to get in my mother's office on my own. I'm good with computers, but an unplanned break-in to one of the Sector's most protected offices? But if Demeter says she can do it....

"Are you willing to help me?"

"I am."

"Why?"

"Because the truth matters."

An hour later, I'm dressed in black pants, a black long-sleeved shirt, and a black hat while crouched in a dark alley behind a food composter and trying not to gag.

I flew my Sarus back to Assembly Hall and left it in my parking area, as if it was a regular night and I was just working late once again. Once inside, I took the lift down to the main floor and then walked over to the Sector Military Complex, painfully aware that in the basement below me, Remy and Soren were being held, hungry and afraid.

Even though I've been training with Sector Defense Forces for over two years, I'd never planned a break-in to the most secure building in the Sector, so I had no idea what I would need to get in and out without being noticed. I grabbed my mission pack and stuffed it with a length of military-grade rope, a grappling hook—I lifted it from the gymnasium despite being pretty sure I wouldn't need it, but it was too cool to leave behind—my electromagnetic gloves, a glass cutter, and a high-frequency sonic emitter in case I need to create a diversion for an emergency getaway.

I hoisted the pack on my back, slipped out into the alley through one of the exits that maintenance and delivery use, and headed toward the nearest Link to the PODS system. The main government complex dominates several long blocks along a beautiful, busy street. But since it was after work hours, the entire area was quiet and the few people walking around didn't pay any attention to me.

"Demeter, what time is it?" I asked.

"20h13." In winter, The PODS stop operating at 22h00.

It wasn't long before the small, spherical compartment pulled up at the station, the doors sliding open with a soft whoosh and emptying clean, wintergreen-smelling air onto the landing. I was lucky the evening commute was over, and I didn't have to share the ride with someone who might recognize me. Inside, I punched in my destination, another Link stop a few blocks away from OAC headquarters, and held on as the POD started rolling. A few minutes later, I was out and walking quickly down a service alley tucked in between the towering buildings.

I only made it about two blocks before I heard voices around a corner and had to duck back behind the food composter. Now I'm just trying not to throw up. The thing smells terrible, and I cover my nose and mouth with my hand as the voices get closer. I wonder if I'm not the only would-be criminal sneaking around these back alleys.

I'm not a criminal, I tell myself. I'm trying to learn the truth. But this is all happening so fast. *Am I crazy?* I'm about to go break into my mother's research lab so that I can examine a bunch of highly classified files because of a girl I haven't even seen in three years and who is a recognized traitor. Not to mention I have a grappling hook stuffed into my backpack. I mean, what the hell did I think I was going to do with that?

The voices pass without incident, and as they fade, I peer out from behind the garbage bin and start back around the corner.

"This is insane," I grumble. But I muster on.

At the back service entrance, there's not even a fingerprint scanner—just a number pad. The code changes weekly, but I have access to all the primary building codes and quickly enter the numbers. The light flashes yellow, and then green. I'm in. Security will be pretty lax on the first floor, but it won't be nearly as easy once I make it up to my mother's lab.

Cameras, I think just before opening the door. Okay. Cameras. Just walk in and look like I know what I'm doing, right? I push the door open and try to stride through confidently. I keep my head down so that any cameras won't be able to identify my face, and I head directly for the elevators. I hesitate briefly when I hear a noise, but it's just a robotic floor buffer spinning its way across the atrium.

I make it to the elevators without incident. But when I type in Mother's personalized punch code for access to level forty, the top floor of the building, the security panel demands a retinal scan. I wasn't expecting this.

"Deme, can you hack it?" I whisper urgently.

"I've already accessed the correct pattern. Put your eye to the scanner."

I obey, and there's a flash of green light. I hold my breath. It beeps. "Access granted," comes the low voice of the elevator operator.

"Thank you, thank you, thank you," I sigh.

"You're welcome," she whispers back to me.

At the top, I get off the elevator and wind my way through the twisting hallways and finally to the entrance to Mother's lab. It's no secret, I've been in here a few times, but never unsupervised, and certainly never without her permission. Here is my real test—a simultaneous palm print and exhalation scan followed by the verbal recitation of a nine-digit code. I've seen my mother place her hand on the panel and breathe into the small spherical opening a hundred times, but without her here, we'll have to improvise. Demeter says she's accessed the chemical breath imprint, my mother's unique metabolic phenotype, but we have to have a palm print to scan.

"What do I do, Deme?"

"Put on your electromagnetic glove and set it to the lowest level of charge."

I pull on my glove and ask, "Okay, next?"

"Place your palm on the optical scanner. I don't want it to read an actual palm print, but it needs to read an electrical signal or it won't let you in."

"But what about the breathprint?

"As long as you don't breathe anywhere near the panel, I can enter your mother's chemical code. It will try to read your breathprint if you exhale at all. And don't move until I tell you." I press my palm firmly to the glass plate, and hold my breath. I wait for the panel to activate, and when it announces "Scan in progress" on the screen, I turn away just in case.

I hear a beep.

"You're in, Vale."

Once inside, security is minimal. I stand at the computer interface and watch as the hologram in the center of the room springs to life. The computer asks for voice recognition, but I quickly override that and instruct it to respond only to typing. Any sound I make could be recorded, and my vocal pattern will certainly give me away. Even if they eventually realize that someone broke into the lab, my hope is that they'll never realize it was me. I log onto the manual C-Link system and set up an old-fashioned chat box in which I can type instructions to Demeter separately, so she can help me as we search.

I start by opening up the documents from the investigation into the Academy attack. I skim through them. There's a series of profiles of the students who died, and my heart stops briefly at Tai Alexander's page. There's something cold and stark about seeing all the details of her life on this page—name, date of birth, research focus, academic ranking, there's even a photo of her from a year or so before she died—completed by a large black stamp at the bottom of the page that says "DECEASED".

As Eli was the only survivor and witness to the event, I read his committee testimony first. The transcript indicates that very few people were present: A panel of five Sector Investigators, a Questioner, Brinn Alexander—Remy and Tai's mother—and Evander Sun-Zi, the Director of Agricultural Farm Production. "The Dragon." There wasn't even a Recorder—apparently the video was recorded digitally and then the whole thing was transcribed later. They really didn't want word to get out.

The testimonial document comes with a note: "Accessible only by Corine Orleán and Evander Sun-Zi unless given special permissions. Attempts to access files without permission will result in database monitoring and possible revocation of access."

Valerian: So that's why you wouldn't let me access these files while we were at my flat.

Demeter: Correct.

Valerian: Why is Evander included in those permissions? Why was he at the hearing?

Demeter: We'll find out.

Questioner: Good evening, Elijah. Could you introduce yourself to the court?

ET: My name is Elijah Tawfiq, and I was a research and teaching assistant for Professor Aran Hawthorne of the SRI. You can call me Eli.

Q: What are you doing these days, Eli?

ET: These days? A lot of sitting on my ass and talking to shrinks.

Panel Reprimands Elijah Tawfiq for Lack of Decency

Q: What were you studying with Professor Hawthorne?

ET: Primarily, we were working on building new genetic codes for a number of the vegetables the OAC produces at the Farms.

Q: Where were you on the day of Fall 23, Sector Annum 102 at around one in the afternoon?

ET: I was at the SRI, sitting in on an Advanced Biogenomics class with Hawthorne. As his teaching assistant I had to attend his classes so that I would be able to help the students if they needed it.

Q: How many other people were there in the classroom?

ET: There were seven students. Including Professor Hawthorne and myself there were nine of us total.

Q: What happened during the class?

ET: Well, I had woken up late that morning, and hadn't had time to take my morning shit—

Panel Reprimands Elijah Tawfiq for Misconduct

ET: Sorry about that, folks, but, well, anyway. I had to take care of my morning business, so I had excused myself from class for a few minutes.

Q: What happened when you—err—exited the bathroom?

ET: I headed back to the classroom. I opened the door and saw everyone in there, dead. Hawthorne's body was at the center of the room, and a man dressed in black, a with a bloody knife in one hand and a Bolt in the other was staring at Tai Alexander's—

Q: Go on, Eli.

ET: He had clearly just killed her. I couldn't see her face, but she was slumped under the desk and she wasn't moving. He was just staring at her.

Q: What did the man look like?

ET: Like I said, he was dressed in all black, including a cap, so I couldn't tell what color his hair was. It looked like he was wearing some sort of mask, but that he'd pulled it up, and I could see his face. He had brown eyes and a long, narrow nose. Rounded chin.

Q: What happened next?

ET: I guess he heard me, because he looked up, and grinned at me. Then he walked over to me and put the Bolt up to my head and said "You're late to the party. Too bad you had to miss out on all the fun. Lucky for you, there's an after party right here."

Q: Was he speaking English clearly?

ET: Yes. He did not have an Outsider accent or dialect.

Q: What did you do?

ET: I just stood there. Seriously, I just stood there. What the fuck was I supposed to do?

Panel Reprimands Elijah Tawfiq for Misconduct

Q: Then what happened, Elijah?

ET: He pulled the trigger on the Bolt.

Q: What happened then?

ET: Well, much to my relief, I didn't die. He pulled the trigger and nothing happened. He pulled it away from my head and was just looking at it. Anyway, I was just standing there, shell-shocked, when he started laughing. He put it to my head and fired again. When it still didn't blow, I figured the charge must have been malfunctioning. I lunged for it, but he was too fast.

Q: What happened then?

ET: He pulled the Bolt away and pushed me up against the wall. He had his forearm against my throat and was suffocating me. I couldn't breathe. I couldn't do anything but just look at him.

Q: What did he do next?

ET: Well, let's see. He put the gun up to his own head. He stared me in the eyes. He said, "A word to the wise, kid. Never get on Corine Orlean's bad side."

Panel makes Motion to Strike testimony from formal record on the grounds of Defamation and Biased Testimony.

So stricken.

ET: "Biased Testimony?" Are you fucking joking? That's what he said! Why the fuck are you striking that from the record?

Panel makes Motion to Strike statement from formal record and Reprimands Elijah Tawfiq for Speaking Out Of Turn and for Foul Language

[Witness stands and turns to leave.]

ET: No fucking kidding. Okay, I'm out. Don't even think for a second I'm going to sit here and tell you what happened the day that eight people were murdered in cold blood if you're going to call your only surviving witness "biased", and if you don't like the way I fucking talk, then fuck you, too.

[Guards are called in to restrain witness. Witness begins to fight and yell. He is issued a calming sedative and instructed to continue his testimony.]

Questioner: Can you tell us what happened after the attacker put the gun to his own head?

ET: Sure. He pulled the trigger. I guess the capacitor worked this time. All I have to say about that is this: I've been led to understand that brains were considered quite a delicacy in the old world, but let me tell you, ladies and gentlemen, they not all they cracked up to be.

Uproar in the Panel.

Panel calls for Questioner to continue.

Q: Elijah, could you describe more precisely what happened when the soldier pulled the trigger?

ET: Why sure, Questioner. The man's head exploded. I was spattered with blood, bone, and brains so thick it made my eyes sting. I guess a side effect of that was that I turned and vomited all over that man's mostly headless body. If brains aren't tasty goin' down, they sure aren't tasty coming back up either.

Q: What happened then, Elijah?

ET: I collapsed. I crawled over to Tai's side and the last thing I remember is running my hands over her eyes to close them. I passed out cold.

I lean back in my mother's chair and stare at the stricken testimony over and over again.

Valerian: Why does his testimony still appear in the formal record if it's been stricken?

Demeter: It was stricken from the record that was used for evidence in the panel's judgment of the case. But the full court transcripts are required to have records of everything spoken and said in the court. Additionally, your mother has specially requested a full copy of the transcripts for her personal records.

Why did they strike his testimony? Why didn't they take Eli's words at least at face value, biased and traumatized though they might have been? I consider the circumstances and try to think through his testimony rationally. Eli was probably in shock after witnessing everything. His memories could have been affected, or invented. He was probably looking for someone to blame the attack on, someone to direct his anger towards. He could have invented that line about Madam Orleán just to try to pin it on someone. But then, why is my mother interested enough in the case to request a full copy for her own records? Is she just worried about clearing her name?

Or maybe the man really did say it. Just because he didn't talk like an Outsider doesn't mean he wasn't one. Lots of Outsiders have joined the Sector, assimilated, and picked up our dialects and accent. He could have been one of them, trying to pin the blame on someone within the Sector, like my mother, so that the Outsider tribes would be spared retaliation.

But that doesn't explain why the panel was so insistent on keeping that line off the official records. If they were making the argument that the Outsiders were trying to pin the attack on my mother, why not leave the line in? Unless they were under orders to keep it off the record ... And why was Evander Sun-Zi present? I know that he and my mother work closely together, but I didn't know he had anything to do with the investigation into the massacre.

There are no clear answers, so I keep looking. I pull up the Watchmen's investigation overview and timeline.

Fall 23, Sector Annum 102, 13h00 – Sector Watchmen and Military called to scene of multiple-victim murder. One survivor found identified as Elijah Tawfiq. Nine dead including presumed shooter. All victims identified except presumed shooter. Survivor Tawfiq being held in custody and will be considered possible suspect or collaborator.

Fall 23, SA 102, 17h00 – Tawfiq being questioned by investigators.

Fall 25 – Psychological evaluation of Tawfiq returned. Indicates trauma from incident but otherwise normal psychological state with no mental or social disorders. Tawfiq displaying early symptoms of Post-Traumatic Stress Disorder but evidence is inconclusive that the symptoms will be permanent. DNA evidence found on Bolt indicating that presumed shooter, as yet unidentified, was in fact the perpetrator.

Fall 27 – Tawfiq cleared of suspect status. Sources indicate he had no military or arms training, was very close with victim number one (assumed primary target Aran Hawthorne), and was involved romantically with one of the victims, Tai Alexander. Highly unlikely collaborator.

Fall 27 – Presumed shooter identified as possible Outsider based on shoulder tattoos. Autopsy and medical analysis shows shooter had large quantities of potent psychotropics and physical augmentation drugs in his bloodstream and muscle deposits. Was likely preparing for this mission for an extended period of time. No DNA records exist in Sector population database for presumed shooter, making it highly likely that he was born and raised outside of Sector control.

Fall 28 – Preparing press release to brief the public. Preparing to field questions on possible Outsider involvement and planned military action against Outsider tribes.

Fall 35 – Tawfiq requested additional interview, which has just concluded. Indicated that Corine Orleán, OAC researcher and wife of Chancellor Philip Orleán, was possibly involved in the crime. Tawfiq claims shooter made statement linking Madam Orleán to crime immediately prior to suicide.

Opening investigation into Corine Orleán's possible involvement in the crime.

Fall 36 – Photographic evidence found on Sector security cameras indicating that shooter, as yet unidentified, visited OAC headquarters on Fall 20. However, travel records and witness testimony indicate that Corine Orleán was visiting Seed Bank 1 on same date. Meeting between the two unlikely.

Fall 37 – Department closed investigation into Corine Orleán as possible collaborator with shooter.

Fall 40 – Shooter determined likely participant in Outsider terrorist strike. All records on investigation will be copied to General Falke Aulion of Sector Defense Forces. SDF will now be taking over responsibilities for retaliation against Outsiders. Watchmen investigation closed.

Department closed investigation into Corine Orleán ... apparently without any given reason, and only two days after Eli requested a special meeting to tell them what he heard from the shooter. What led to that decision? Maybe they simply didn't find any evidence to support his claim. I close my eyes and hope desperately that's what happened. Other possibilities flood my mind— bribery, threats, blackmail, targeted against the Watchmen to keep them from continuing the investigation. When I open my eyes, Demeter has displayed a new message for me to read.

Demeter: Remember, you came to your mother's computer for a reason.
Valerian: Yeah, because you told me to. What are you talking about?
Demeter: You're not restricted to viewing the files in the OAC and Sector Informational Databases.
Valerian: Are you suggesting I browse through my mother's personal files?
Demeter: There are only two mistakes one can make along the road to truth—not starting, and not going all the way.

Hesitantly, nauseated at the idea of this gross breach of privacy, I type in a search for Hawthorne under "Messages." An old correspondence pops up from her courriel archives, and I open it and read the string of messages quickly. There are only five in the correspondence.

12 Fall, SA 102, 15h32
Madam Orleán,
I have a research matter of great import that I would like to discuss with you at your earliest availability. Through fortuitous circumstances, I have happened upon a remnant of the old world that could be incredibly beneficial to the

OAC and could change the future of the Sector. I am very close to being able to completely unlock this information and would like to share it with you, so that we can discuss its great potential.

Respectfully yours,
Aran Hawthorne
Associate Professor, Biogenomics
Sector Research Institute

12 Fall, SA 102, 16h51

Aran,

What a pleasure to hear from you. It's been too long since we discussed our research together. You have certainly piqued my curiosity as to the nature of this discovery, and I am particularly intrigued by how you came upon this apparently powerful old world technology.

I would be more than happy to meet with you as soon as possible. Would you be willing and able to meet next week, 18 Fall, at 9h00? You may visit me in my office, and please, bring whatever information with you that will help to explain your discovery.

Your friend,
Corine Orleán
Director, R&D
Okarian Agricultural Consortium

13 Fall, SA 102, 7h57

Madam Orleán,

It would be my honor to meet you then, and I will be sure to have prepared a comprehensive outline of the work I've done. I should hint, with a wink, that the information isn't precisely a *technology*—in fact, it's something that could be much more powerful. I hope that holds your interest!

Respectfully yours,
Aran Hawthorne
Associate Professor, Biogenomics
Sector Research Institute

18 Fall, SA 102, 18h28

Aran,

I have spent much of the day reflecting on the poor outcome of our meeting this morning. I wanted to send you a note of reconciliation. I am incredibly impressed by the research you and your assistant Elijah have been doing, and I am thrilled that you have chosen to include me in your considerations as we decide how to proceed with this information. That said, however, I regret that we do not agree on how the OAC and the Sector might best use this powerful tool. I would like to meet with you again at your earliest convenience, so that we might discuss more amicably how to proceed.

I also politely request, as your superior and supervisor, that you send me the DNA you have been attempting to decode, along with the information about the key you claim to have found.

Your friend,
Corine Orleán
Director, R&D
Okarian Agricultural Consortium

19 Fall, SA 102, 2h16
Madam Orleán,
You flatter me and underestimate me simultaneously. After our meeting today I am convinced that you have no interest in using this information for the good of the Sector. I, in turn, have no interest in providing you with the details of my research, and I certainly do not intend to provide you with the key to the encryption. I cannot allow this vital information to go to waste or worse, be destroyed, at your hands.

Regretfully,
Aran Hawthorne
Associate Professor, Biogenomics
Sector Research Institute

I have to bite back the urge to laugh bitterly at his sarcastic response. I can picture her cold anger as she read his last courriel: narrowed eyes, pursed lips, slight frown. Did her desire to possess this information drive her to murder? Was this why Hawthorne and seven innocent students died four days later?

I bury my head in my hands. In the blackness, I remind myself that it could be sheer coincidence. It is possible. It's possible that an Outsider terrorist just happened to target Hawthorne and his classroom four days after he and my mother argued about—whatever this was. It could be nothing more than a coincidence. I can't assign blame based on an email argument and one line— hearsay from Elijah and Remy, traitors to the Sector—from the mouth of a murderer. I have to keep looking.

I instruct the computer to do a system-wide search for Hawthorne, but not much else turns up. Only a few mentions of his public research projects, a bizarre black-and-white image file, and the obituary my mother wrote for him in which she called him a "martyr to the cause of Science." I do the same search for "Elijah Tawfiq," and this time two results come up: A correspondence between my mother and Evander Sun-Zi, within the last few months, and a map of the Okarian Sector and surrounding territory with a list of known sightings of Elijah. I recognize the map; it's my own. I made it to use in my board presentation for the mission. My mother has added her own touches: highlights and numerical references that don't mean anything to me. In the courriels with Evander, he asks my mother if she's made any progress on the encryption—is he referring to the same project that Hawthorne mentioned? And, in her response, she asks for any new information on Eli's last location. But why are they so interested in Elijah? And why is Evander involved? He doesn't have anything to do with pursuit of the Resistance, or with military affairs.

The only possible reason is Hawthorne's project. Is she tracking him so she can get more information? Is that why she was so eager to have me bring him in to the Capitol? Does this explain her disappointment when she heard that I returned, not with Elijah, but with Remy and Soren?

I do several searches to see if she's tracking any other members of the Resistance. There are a few hits for Dr. James Rhinehouse, but a quick check reveals that those have to do with assigning people to fill in his place in the research department. All professional business. Nothing on anyone else other than routine notes about people who have disappeared. No vested interest in tracking their movements, as far as I can tell.

Valerian: I can't leave without confirming or denying whether she was involved in Hawthorne's death, but I don't know where to look.

Demeter: Search her research files for the information she and Hawthorne discussed in their courriels and in the meeting that went awry.

She's right. If my mother has a copy of whatever Hawthorne was working on, then she's most likely complicit. She could only have obtained the information if she were willing to kill to get it. My face goes hot at the thought, and my breath comes up short. I pray that I won't find it, but I have to look. I have to know.

A few quick searches for "DNA", "old world," and "technology" turn up hundreds of hits, but they all look like legitimate projects my mother is working on or supervising. I search again for "Elijah" and "Eli" and "Tawfiq" but nothing comes up. I search for keywords included her courriels with Hawthorne, such as "powerful tool" and "for the good of the Sector", but those just direct me back to the correspondence. I run a search on Hawthorne again, but all it brings up is the obituary, the image file, and the courriels. I open the obituary and read it again. Nothing interesting—my mother singing Hawthorne's praises as a scientist and saying how tragic it was that he was murdered by the Outsiders. I open up the image file. It looks like a sunflower, but it's in black and white, and when I zoom in it appears to be made up entirely of dots. I try to zoom in further, but then, strangely, a passcode prompt appears.

Valerian: Can you hack it?
Demeter: The password is not contained online. I cannot access a passcode for this file.

That's fascinating. I've never heard of that happening. I don't even know how that technology would work. I type in a few quick ideas. "Sunflower," "Hawthorne," "Elijah," "old world," and "DNA" are all busts. I jot off a half dozen more, to no avail. I punch in my mother's birthday, her wedding date, "Okaria", "Resistance", "Philip". Nothing. In a fit of frustration I try my own name in about ten different incarnations—first, last, initials. I try my birthday. I want to punch the computer. I lean back in her chair, exhausted and irritable. I rub my eyes and stare at the sunflower image.

Then it hits me. What has she hid behind in this whole situation? What is her shield? I type in "Outsiders" and the passcode prompt disappears. My stomach does a flip. I attempt to zoom in further, and I realize that this time I can manipulate the image: It's not 2D, it's 3D. I can spin it and look at it from different angles. I select a spot and hone in on a line in the sunflower and notice that the dots aren't disconnected from each other. They're connected by a thin filament that weaves around the shape of the sunflower. I select one of the dots and a little symbol "AT" pops up next to the dot. My heart is pounding so hard I'm wonder if it will break through my ribcage. I force myself to breathe and I select a string of dots. "AT-GC-CG-AT-GC-TA-AT," it reads, and the symbols appear on the side of the screen. I zoom out, struggling to control my breath, my sweating, and I see a message pop up on the corner of the screen from Demeter, but I ignore it. She whispers determinedly into my ear:

"Vale, you're breathing too fast. You're going to hyperventilate. You need to calm down."

I try to relax, but I can't stop twirling the sunflower. I zoom in on it and select a string of hundreds of dots, and the base pairs line up both on the image and in a dialogue box at the bottom of the glass panel. This must be what Hawthorne was working on. There's no reason why she would hide this as an image file, encrypt it, and use the word "Outsiders" as her passphrase. Unless she wanted to be absolutely sure that no one but herself ever saw it.

Valerian: This is it.
Demeter: So it would appear.

17 — REMY

The drugged haze eventually faded from my mind, and Soren was kind enough to inform me that I may have put our lives in far more danger than they already were. I remember the shifting, dancing shapes in front of me, the almost hallucinatory revelation that came from being able to see the shape so vividly in my mind. I remember watching, almost as though the transformation was beyond my control, the sunflower broaden, expand, shift into the lotus. And I remember coming down out of that euphoria to hear Soren calmly inform me that I'd probably destroyed everything.

Thanks, Soren.

He's right, though. Now that my eyes are working again, I can see the cameras up in the corner of the room, recording everything we do or say. If we thought our project was a secret, it certainly isn't anymore. And if Corine is after the key to the DNA, she'll know we have it, too.

Fortunately—or unfortunately, depending on how I look at it—no one seems to have noticed. We're still being ignored, driven to insanity by our hunger, thirst, real sleep deprivation and uncomfortable position. My sense of time has disappeared altogether, but even I can recognize that it's been many hours since our encounter with Vale and the old man with the scars. I asked Soren why he was so afraid of the old man, but all he would tell me is that he's a general in the Sector Defense Forces, and his name is Falke Aulion. I pressed him, but he wouldn't say more in front of the cameras.

Since then, I've been drifting in and out of sleep, trying to dream that I do not in fact have to pee. Just when I've finally convinced myself that I don't, the door opens, and at the prospect of getting let out, I suddenly have to pee so much worse. The stream of bright light hurts my eyes and my heart lurches. I try to focus. It's not General Aulion or Vale; that fact alone sets my heartbeat at a steadier tempo. It's just a guard, carrying what looks to be a tray heaped with food.

"Breakfast! Eat up, kiddos." I scowl at him and can only imagine the look the kid's getting from Soren. He kneels down and, with a smirk, places the food just out of reach. "The best and the brightest, huh. Maybe you can figure out how to eat with your feet." Then he leaves.

The rage is hard to contain, and the hunger overwhelming.

"They're goading us," I say.

"Assholes." Soren curses in agreement, but we can do nothing but wait and seethe. The smell wafts towards me, and after so long without food, my stomach is twisting into nauseated coils. I simultaneously want to vomit and devour the entire tray. I close my eyes and force myself to relax.

Something like an hour later, the door opens again, revealing the same freshly scrubbed, pink-faced guard.

"I thought you'd be hungry by now! Guess not." He picks up the tray and leaves, but the door remains open, and after a quick, hushed conversation, Aulion strides in. Soren tenses, and my heart pounds in time with the clicks of his boots.

He stops a few strides away, feet planted firmly, hands clasped behind his back. I look up and study his face. A large scar runs down the left cheek, matching his crooked nose and burned neck. He'd clearly been through hell at some point. He has small, snake-like nostrils and prominent lips enhanced by finely trimmed white facial hair. His well-groomed and starchy composure overcompensate for what I decide is a bitter and astonishingly ugly man. I can't help but wonder how Vale can tolerate working with him.

"Remy Alexander," he says, turning his unblinking, gargoyle-like stare on me. "We have not been properly introduced. My name is Falke Aulion." He turns to Soren, and his lips twist in a capricious sneer. "Soren. I apologize for giving you such a fright last night. I thought a fully grown man like you would have learned not to be afraid of monsters in the dark anymore." Behind me, I feel Soren shiver. Who *is* this man, and what has he done to make Soren so afraid?

His eyes dart back to me, and he just barely shakes his head, frowns, and looks me up and down. Not leering, simply looking, as if I were a specimen under observation. He speaks abruptly: "You both have appointments to keep now." My heartbeat quickens and I start salivating, wondering for a half second if they're going to feed us, bathe us, let us pee. Aulion turns on his heel and walks out. The door remains open, though, and four guards enter the room. Two walk to Soren and the others toward me. One of the guards slaps a wet cloth firmly over my nose and mouth and holds it. I panic and tense up, struggle, try not to breathe, but after a moment, I gasp and instantly feel a wave of relaxation—euphoria, almost—flood through me, and I feel like I do when I've had one too many of Eli and Firestone's home brews. It's a happy drunk and I can feel a silly smile tugging at my lips. As the two guards detach my bindings from the pole in the center of the room and pull me to my feet, I grin stupidly as my knees wobble and the world twirls around me. The guards have to steady me, hands under my arms. I'm overwhelmed with the desire to turn toward Soren, try to talk to him, tell him I don't really hate him as much as I pretend to, that, in fact, we could be friends, maybe better than friends since Vale ... but I don't want to think about Vale. *I will not think about Vale!*

I glance at Soren and see that he's biting his lip so hard a bead of blood rests against his white teeth. My legs don't work right, and I nearly crumple to the floor, but the guards hold me up by my armpits and lead me out into the hallway right behind Soren. I fight to keep my head up but find I lack the strength, and my chin lolls down to my collarbone. I close my eyes and allow myself to be dragged. It feels like my whole body, inside and out, has been stretched to its limit and then left to sag in the languid sun. My eyes flutter open and closed, open and closed, my legs move forward only because I'm being half-propped, half-dragged down the hall.

We arrive at a door, and one of the guards moves around me to key it open. We enter and the guards deposit me in a deep, comfortable leather chair facing an empty desk, behind which sits another elegant chair. Clarity slowly returns to my mind, but I find I still can't operate my limbs the way I would normally. Something stinks. I strain to look around, focus and stretch out my neck muscles, and then I realize my pants are wet. *Oh fuck,* I think. *I've pissed myself.* The smell, coming off of the relaxant, is nauseating. But there's nothing I can do about that now. Where is Soren? The guards bind my hands, but nothing else. It doesn't matter. I couldn't make a run for it no matter how hard I tried. My legs might as well be made of jelly rather than bone and muscle.

The room is expansive, luxurious, but strangely empty. Only the two chairs and the desk decorate it. It's as though someone prepared this empty office especially for me. Maybe someone did. There are no windows. The walls are decorated only by maps of various parts of the Sector—a map of the city, right down to the neighborhoods and streets, of all of the locations of the Farms and factory towns, and of open land that the Sector has claimed and guards carefully from the Outsiders. There is nothing on the desk except a plasma, which is dark right now.

I start to fully register Soren's absence. Where is he? They haven't brought him in yet. Wasn't he just behind me? Or was he in front of me?

I hear the door open behind me, try to crane my body to see who it is, but I'm not quite functional enough for that complex action. But when the man walks around the desk, my heart stops.

Chancellor Philip Orleán. Vale's father. The most powerful man in the Sector.

Memories come rushing back. The first time I met him, at a formal event celebrating my father's designation as Poet Laureate of the Sector, long before Vale and I became friends. Shaking his hand and thinking how nice he was. How genuine. The first time I visited Vale at the chancellor's manor, when he offered me a ginger beer and a plate of fresh figs. How did he know my favorite foods before he knew anything about me? He always liked me, I thought. Philip always seemed happy that Vale and I had become friends.

Now, I'm not a guest at his dinner table, talking with him about his art collection. I'm a political prisoner working for an organization that opposes everything he believes in, trying to bring down the government he represents. My heart is thumping, thick in the back of my throat. I feel like I am betraying him as much as he betrayed me. I wonder if he agrees.

He sits down at the desk opposite me with a slight smile. "Remy," he says, somewhat fondly. Distantly, as though he too is awash in memories.

I feel the muscle relaxant wearing off and the energy return to me, gradually. I nod my head in some pathetic half-greeting, half-acknowledgment. He shakes off the reminiscence and glances at the plasma on his desk, then sits back in his chair. He interlocks his fingers, setting his hands on the empty space in front of him. As he stares at me, takes in my haggard appearance, his smile quickly fades into concern, or something like it.

"I'm so sorry that you are here," he begins. "I'm sorry it's come to this." He sounds genuinely contrite.

"What is *this*?" I ask hesitantly.

"I believe there's an unnecessary chasm between us, an unfortunate misunderstanding. I know you've grown and matured, but to me you'll always be Vale's friend, the girl who had a love affair with fresh figs." He smiles sadly.

"Is this the way you treat Vale's friends? Leaving them handcuffed to a pole and sitting on the cold floor for—I don't even know how long I've been here."

"Ah, I'm sorry about that. You should know I only want the best for you." His eyes are full of compassion, and I wonder if it's real. I grind my teeth and try to keep the sarcasm out of my voice, to stay as deadpan as possible.

"The best, huh? So that explains the luxurious accommodations and delicious meals." His gaze hardens as I continue. The compassion disappears, replaced by coldness. "And the injections, very nice, thank you for sharing. Thank you for providing only the best for me."

"Remy, I know Vale cared for you at one time. For months all he talked about was 'Remy this' and 'Remy that' until he practically drove us crazy. Vale had never talked about another girl like that, and we thought at one time that the two of you might have a future together."

The coppery taste of blood fills my mouth as I bite into my cheek to keep from crying. His words pierce me like a volley of arrows slicing through a paper target, and I wonder if it's true—if Vale really talked about me. If he really cared.

"But I'm much more than a father. My responsibilities go far beyond you and me, and even Vale. As chancellor, I am sworn to protect all the people of The Okarian Sector, and you have chosen a path that is dangerous to the safety and security of those people. I wish we were meeting under happier circumstances, but that was your choice to make, not mine. And I'm sorry that you're here, because it means we're enemies. I wish that was not the case."

I push Vale to the back of my mind and lean forward. "You know what I wish wasn't the case? I wish Tai wasn't dead. I wish I had my older sister back. But I can't get her back, not ever," I say, fighting to keep my voice calm. "Your wife was responsible for her death, and you sit here and say it was my choice to make?"

Philip looks down at his hands, and an expression of pain and sadness crosses his face. When Tai was murdered, he cried at her cremation ceremony. I remember watching him brush the tears out of his eyes with his leather gloves, trying to avoid being caught on camera. I wonder for a second if he's grieving again for Tai's death, and I am almost touched. But then he looks up again and responds, and his voice is hard:

"Remy, your sister's death was avenged. The Outsiders who perpetrated the crime were destroyed. Your accusation against Corine is ludicrous, and the fact that you're willing to say such things pains me. I'm afraid we're going to have to move on."

I am so stunned by his willful ignorance that I have nothing to say. No words form in my mind or come to my lips.

Philip continues: "Remy, perhaps you don't realize the danger the Resistances poses. If left unchecked, it will lead to disaster. A return to famine and violence. We won't risk the future of the entire Sector for the simplistic and idealistic beliefs of your leaders. Now you have to choose between your fellow citizens of the Okarian sector or the backwards beliefs of the Resistance. It's up to you." Here he takes a deep breath and looks at me very seriously, leaning forward. "I know you're a good kid. I watched you grow up. I worked side by side with your parents for years. You know I don't want anything bad to happen to you." He pauses, maybe for dramatic tension.

At this point, I'm awash in desperation and cynicism. How can he be so deluded?

"But I also need you to understand that the choices you've made in the last three years have consequences."

He settles back in his chair slightly and relaxes when I say nothing. Maybe he was expecting more of a fight. "You've been brought to see me for a reason, Remy. I can help you. We need information, and once you've provided it, we'll be happy to feed you, give you access to the showers, give you real beds to sleep on."

"Where's Soren?" I demand. "I'm not giving you any information until I know at least that."

Philip seems to consider this question, deciding whether or not to answer me. "Soren is currently meeting with General Aulion."

I shudder, imagining the pain and horror Soren's in, being locked up in a room alone with that man.

"Classic 'divide and conquer,' then?" I say, working up a grin, trying to put on a brave face. This is what Soren would do if he were in my place. Be as bold and uncooperative as possible. I shrug and look around, pretending to examine my surroundings. "Well, at least it's a change of pace."

Philip glares at me. "Now is not the time for attitude, Remy."

"Oh, I'm sorry. Why don't you let me know when would be a better time, when you can fit 'attitude' in on your calendar? I'll have my people contact your people," I growl back. He holds my gaze and for a second looks like he might let a trace of anger show on his face. But after a few seconds, something in his face softens and melts. He sighs and stares up at the ceiling.

"I know you're in pain. I know you despise me right now, that you think I'm the bad guy. But whatever you think of me, I really do only want the best for you. I don't want you to suffer any longer. Talk to me. I just want to help you. When you help me, I can give you everything you need."

My stomach is empty and my body feels like it might start to devour itself soon. The hunger is already making me lightheaded and dizzy, and I struggle to prevent my thoughts from tripping over themselves. I *need* food. Something, anything. I let my face crumple. *I can play-act at regret and sadness too, Philip.* I look down at my hands.

"I'm really hungry," I say softly. "They haven't fed us since we got in here." I peek up through my eyelashes and see Philip lean forward eagerly as I start to give in. How could I have ever thought he was genuine and kind?

"We can feed you, Remy," he says. "The information we need is simple. Names and places. Just answer my questions."

"What do you want to know?" I ask, praying that Soren isn't going to give us up either. But I know he's not. Aulion and a few puny hours without food won't break him. Philip's mouth twitches upward in one corner, and he glances briefly behind me, presumably at the guards, who I assume are still in the room.

"What's the name of the person you call the Director?" Philip asks.

"I don't know his name. I've only ever heard his voice." The Director is a woman. Her quarters are down the hall from mine. I squeeze my eyes shut, trying to bring up tears of regret. My "betrayal" has to feel real.

"Where is your base? Where are you located?"

"Just feed me, please, Philip, I'm starving," I sob. It's a good one, almost genuine. "I can't betray my friends!"

"Then I can't help you, Remy." He looks at me with tragedy written all over his face. "Think of the lives you'll save by helping us. We're either going to kill them when we find them without your help, or we'll offer them a deal, a surrender, amnesty maybe, if you help us." He suddenly reaches out his hand across the desk, as though offering to comfort me. Like Vale, at the mission site, reaching out his hand, offering to take me to a safe place, to help me. There might still be hope for Vale. The way he looked when I told him about Tai—his shock, his panic, the way he stared at me as though he might dare to believe me—but there's no hope for Philip. I stare at his outstretched hand across the table. "You didn't make the choice to leave, Remy. Remember that. Your parents made that choice. Now you can make a different choice."

I drop my head and try to fight off the tears. He's making it so easy for me to maintain the act. "Okay, okay," I manage. "We work out of an abandoned industrial area."

"What's the name of it?" Philip continues, his voice calm, insistent, encouraging.

"I don't know."

"I'm not an idiot, Remy."

"Hartford," I gasp, staring fixedly at my knees, looking as embarrassed and contrite as possible. Truth is, Hartford is a ruins. We tried to scavenge there, but the place had been blown to smithereens.

"Hartford," he repeats, again looking over my shoulder. "Why Hartford?"

"I don't know. I didn't pick the base."

"But there had to be a reason … what did they manufacture there?"

Hartford, Hartford … what do I know about Hartford? We tried to scavenge there once, but it was useless, an abandoned, overgrown mess. But the Director said that they used to be known for … what? "Fuel cells. Those old-fashioned fuel cells."

"Ah, that's right. If I remember correctly, Hartford's on a river. Out in the Wilds. Can you show me on the map where it is?" He points at one of the maps, a rough sketch of what the Wilds to the south of the Sector look like. Their maps aren't very good, I notice. We have better ones. I can throw them off. I nod. One of the guards releases my cuffs behind me and I stand up, then collapse back into my chair. The guard starts to help me, but then Philip abruptly stands up and darts around the desk, putting his hands under my arms to help me. His touch is abhorrent. An enormous shudder runs up my spine, and I desperately hope he'll think it's because of the hunger and not my revulsion at the fact that his skin is touching mine. I want to be sick, to throw up everything left in my body all over him. Instead I offer him a weak smile.

He helps me limp over to the wall where the map is displayed. I scan it quickly and find the location where I seem to remember Hartford actually is. I hope I'm right. I point and look at him nervously, my lip trembling. He smiles magnanimously at me.

"Thank you, Remy." He helps me back to my seat, and I cringe with relief when he lets me go.

"Are your parents with you?"

"No."

"Where are they? They're the ones who betrayed the Sector. They're the ones we want. If you help us find them, I'll personally make sure they're treated well."

Over my dead body. At least this question I can answer honestly. "I don't know. They've never told me."

"What do they do?"

"Set up communications systems for other bases." They pose as modern-day troubadours, an itinerate healer and a musician who travel to the Farms and factory towns offering alternative medicine and nutrition information and evangelizing for the Resistance. Their job is incredibly dangerous, and I'll be damned if I'm going to lead Philip anywhere near them.

"Where are the other bases?" His expression is blank.

"I don't know. We're not allowed to know where the other bases are specifically for this reason." I wipe the tears from my eyes. Of course I know where the other bases are, but they're much smaller than mine, well hidden, and I'm pretty sure there's no way in hell the Sector has gotten wind of their locations.

"Do you know where Dr. James Rhinehouse is?"

"I know what base he works at...." I sniffle.

"Which one?" He leans forward, betraying his eagerness.

"Base Five. I don't know where it is." Shit. That was stupid. I wish I'd come up with a cleverer name. In reality, the bases are named after some of the greatest battles or strongholds of ancient resistance fighters—Normandy, Antietam, Yorktown, Bannockburn, Teutoburg, and our main base, Thermopylae.

"What does Rhinehouse do for the Resistance?"

"I don't know. The Director doesn't tell me anything," I whisper. At least that part is true. For once, I thank the stars that I'm low in the pecking order. "I've never met him. All I know is where he's stationed."

Philip sits back in his chair. Does he know I'm lying? I try to read his face but his expression is emotionless. I know they could use the truth serum and lie detector machines, but Philip obviously wants me to come over to his side of my own accord. Before we left for the mission, Rhinehouse gave us truth serum antidotes in case we were captured. Standard procedure for all risky raids. They biodegrade after a few days, though, so if we're stuck here and they shoot us up with the serum, we could be in trouble.

"Why don't you tell us what were you after at the Carbon Seed Bank?" *Is this a question about the DNA? I wonder. Do they know about what I said this morning? Does Philip know about the DNA, too?*

"Why don't you give me something to eat?" I say, avoiding the question. "I've answered your questions. Please," I put on my most pitiful stare, appealing desperately to whatever traces of kindness might linger within his perverted being. "I'm starving."

"You can eat when you've answered all my questions, Remy. What were you looking for at the Seed Bank?" My mind races. What can I tell him? I don't want to tell him anything that resembles the truth. What else are they well known for having at Carbon that I can pretend we were looking for?

"Technology," I whisper. It's the best I can do. "Charge multipliers, faster cloning devices, more efficient DNA sequencers, proton couplers."

"Is that all?"

"Yes."

"Why are you lying to me, Remy?" He asks. I stare at him. Was it really that obvious? Or is he playing with me?

"I'm not," I say determinedly. He leans back, studies me, and I think back to everything I was ever taught about lying. Hold his gaze. Relax. Don't fidget. Believe the lie. I believe it. My life and the lives of all my friends depend on it. Finally, he sighs and waves at one of the guards.

"Remy, Vale has done his homework. We know for a fact that Dr. Rhinehouse works with you at the base you call Thermopylae, that Hartford is nothing but a shell, and that your parents do not in fact set up communications networks. We know that Thermopylae is located in the middle of an old world city, not some abandoned industrial scrap. And we know that the Director is, in fact, a woman."

I keep a straight face, but my heart might very well be bleeding out my toes right now.

He looks at me again, sadly. "I really thought better of you, Remy. I thought you would be able to recognize truth when you saw it. I thought you would be willing to help your parents and your friends escape a devastating fate."

Suddenly one of the guards is at my side. I start in surprise, but then he quickly lashes each of my wrists to the armchair. The second guard pulls my shirt apart at the collarbone and slaps on a few charge multipliers. He looks down at me and makes eye contact for a second, but then I realize what he's doing and he averts his eyes and turns away.

"No—what, you can't, this is—" I start to fight, throwing myself back and forth, wriggling fiercely, but my hands are bound, and now my feet, too, to the chair.

"You're obviously not willing to help yourself, so I'm going to provide another incentive. Remember, this was your choice."

"Philip, no—this is torture, this is—" I cry out but he pays me no heed.

"Just answer the questions, Remy, and this will all be over," Philip says to me in a reassuring, almost comforting tone.

"Fuck you," I spit. "This is insane." Pain lances through my back, shoulders, temples, a vicious throng of spasms, ripping my muscles to shreds. I cry out, but it's over in a heartbeat. I gasp for breath and fall limply back against chair, panting.

Then again, it rips through me like shards of glass, and my muscles torque uncontrollably, twisting and curling viciously around my bones. The pain blinds me, deafens me, to everything but the screams echoing in my ears and the blood pounding through my skull.

It seems to last an eternity, this time, but then it's gone. Just an echo resounding over and over again through my body. Philip nods at the guards, who start to strip off the charge magnifiers.

"Does Vale know you're doing this?" I sputter, gulping air like a drowning victim. Philip regards me thoughtfully.

"Yes," he says after a moment. "He's the one who authorized it."

"You're lying." He cocks an eyebrow at me, and I conjure up an enormous quantity of saliva and spit it across the desk in a move that would have impressed Eli.

He doesn't even flinch. "No, I'm not. But I'm sure Vale will be thrilled to hear that you thought so highly of him."

"So you admit that what you're doing is despicable."

"Remy, I am willing to do whatever is necessary to keep my people safe. After years of experience, I've realized that sometimes that means doing things that I don't like or enjoy. This is one of those times. I regret that you've put yourself in this position, but I've offered you a way out and you've refused. Now, I'm going to send you back to your cell, and you and I will try again in a few more hours. And," he gives me a slight, conciliatory smile, "when you give us what we want, I'll personally hand you a bucket of fresh figs, just like I used to." He stands, waves to one of the guards, and walks out of the room as a hand from behind me presses a cloth back over my nose and mouth. In a second I'm euphoric again, wobbly, giggling like a happy little child, all the pain forgotten.

Ten minutes later, I'm tied to the pole again, back to back with Soren, who looks awful. The euphoria has already faded and the pain and trauma have returned tenfold.

"Did they shock you, too?" Soren asks hoarsely when the guards have left. Not that it matters. The red lights of the corner cameras are still winking at us.

"Yeah," I mutter. "What happened to your voice?"

"I don't want to talk about it," he whispers, barely audibly. I suspect his encounter with Aulion went about ten times worse than mine with Philip. I change the subject.

"Did they ask you about the you-know-what?" A shudder runs through my spine as the memory of my revelation returns, and I try to quell it. I lean my head back against the pole and close my eyes.

"No," he says. "You?"

"No. Maybe they don't know what I was talking about. Maybe they thought I was just a crazy person on drugs." Normally I would expect a scoffing noise from Soren right about now, but either he's too tired to bother or he actually thinks I might be right.

"Either way," he sighs. "Get some rest. I'm sure they'll be back for more later."

I nod in agreement and let the sweet memory of electric shocks, starvation, and Philip's promise of figs lull me to sleep.

18 — VALE

The silence is stifling. It's just after 02h00 and I've spent the last six hours looking through research documents, genetic codes, compiled programs, and more, trying to find out what was so important about the DNA that my mother was willing to kill for it. I now know Aran Hawthorne's biography better than he did. I've looked through every detail of his life story, searching for clues as to why he took such an interest in the DNA and how he found it. *What was so valuable that my mother was willing to have a man killed to keep it under her control?* I've found nothing. I'm exhausted, and I know it's time to go. Demeter wipes clean any trace of our activity on my mother's computer, and I log off and shut everything down.

I slip my pack over my shoulders, my grappling hook and military-grade rope still safely inside. Thankfully, there won't be any dashing heroics tonight. Just as well—I don't think I can take any more surprises. I make my way back down through my mother's private meeting rooms toward the door to the main hallway, hoping that I can take the service elevator down, slip out into the alley and make it safely and unobtrusively back to Assembly Hall, where my Sarus is waiting.

I open the door and start to step into the hall. Then I get the surprise of my life: Someone in a sleek, tailored tunic is standing with her back to me, long brown hair washing over her shoulders.

It's my mother.

Every muscle in my body is frozen, except my heart which slams against my ribcage like a piston. *What is she doing here? She was supposed to be at a seed bank, hours away!*

"I am at your service, Madam." The man's voice is familiar, but I can barely hear it. It's low and muffled, and he must be standing around the corner because I can't see him from my vantage point. My brain is screaming at me to move, to shut the door and find some other way out—or somewhere to hide—but I can't. My curiosity has me pinned to the spot, waiting, listening.

"Of course you know about the two members of the Resistance my son brought back from the raid." Her voice is urgent and demanding, not at all the calm confidence I am used to hearing from her. Remy and Soren. *She's talking about Remy and Soren.* "The surveillance camera in their holding cell showed us clear evidence that they are in possession of dangerous information. If what I fear is true, and this information were to be used by the Resistance, our food supplies could be contaminated, our way of life destroyed. They must not be allowed to share that information with anyone—ever. Do I make myself clear?"

He says something I can't make out, and I have to stop myself from opening the door wider.

My mother's back straightens, and she rolls forward on her the balls of her feet as if she's about to launch. She is obviously not in a pleasant mood. "Disappearing them into the Wilds is not good enough." Her voice is harsh.

"With all due respect…" the voice trails off.

"No!" She is angry now. "I need a permanent solution. They are dangerous and must be eliminated. Now, this morning. Before my son has an opportunity to see them again."

She's asking him to kill Remy and Soren.

"Move, Vale, move!" comes Demeter's urging in my ear. Is she frantic? I think so. That probably means I should be frantic, too. Hell, if a computer is … but I have to hear, I can't leave yet.

"Yes, Madam. I will remove them within the hour." *Whose voice is that?*

"Make it look like suicide. I'll tell Aulion that I want to see them in the OAC interrogation room at 05h00. His guards will discover them."

My knees are shaking, and I'm numb with disbelief. Is it possible what I just heard? My mother commanding, without trial, the deaths of two Sector citizens? Is this why she came back? What did she see on that camera that earned Remy and Soren a death sentence?

What have I done by bringing them here?

"When your task is complete, you'll have to disappear. Hide in the Wilds and I'll get a signal to you as soon as it's safe for me to bring you back under my wing." My mother sounds almost nurturing now. *Who is she talking to?*

I can't wait to find out. I pull the door shut as quietly as I can and run back toward the lab. I have to get out of here. She's undoubtedly heading towards the office, and who knows what she'll do if she catches me here. I don't have much time. I glance around, pausing to catch my breath, to reconsider my escape. *Think, Vale!* I berate myself.

"Pull up the building's schematics and get me out of here," I whisper to Demeter, so quietly I wonder if she can hear me—I'm terrified of being caught by the room's security recordings.

Not three seconds later: "There's a dumbwaiter in the southwest corner of the meeting room."

Of course. I forgot about the dumbwaiter—my mother hates it when people interrupt her when she's working, so she has the Dieticians zoom all her food directly up to her. No wonder. I wouldn't want anyone walking in on me while I was plotting murder, either.

The dumbwaiter is in the corner of the formal meeting room next to a credenza full of fine wines and expensive liquors. I examine the buttons hesitantly, but realize that triggering the dumbwaiter will no doubt alert someone in security that I'm here. I'm going to have to crawl down the hatch. The mysterious voice said he'd kill them within the hour. *That's not enough time.*

I try to slide open the dumbwaiter door. It won't budge. It must only open when it's called, and I can't do that without logging my presence into the security system. Panic starts to set in. I look around to see if there's something I can pry it open with. Nothing. The room is a vision of my mother's penchant for sparse, utilitarian design. And then it hits me. *I have a grappling hook.* I pull it out of my pack and pry one hook into the corner, hoping it doesn't leave scratch marks on the burnished metal. I wedge the door apart and peer down into the tiny darkness. I'm not claustrophobic, and I'm not afraid of heights, but crawling down forty stories of narrow, pitch-black space isn't exactly appealing. I pull my magnetic gloves on and slap on the charge so the magnetizer activates. I hear a beeping outside, and my eyes flash to the door. *Shit!* No choice but to jump in now. I climb in and try to slide the panel door closed behind me. It slides almost closed, but where the hook bent the metal in the corner, it sticks. Damn. Someone's going to notice eventually.

With just a sliver of light from a crack in the panel door, I start to crawl down into the darkness. I cling tightly to the cable, inching slowly as my hands stick to the metal, and try not to think about the black abyss and hard stop that awaits me if I should slip. In a way, the smallness of this particular elevator passage is an advantage, as it makes it easier to support myself as I descend. Several times, there's a break in the width of the chamber, probably doors to other conference and meeting rooms. But I want to get as far down as possible before I climb out.

Suddenly my feet hit a barrier. I've run into the dumbwaiter itself. I push on it, but it doesn't budge. I'll have to crawl back up to the nearest door stop and pry my way out the same way I pried my way in. It's probably another eight meters back up to the last space I felt. That's far from impossible, but not terribly enticing, either. I brace my back with my hands and start pulling myself hand-over-hand back up the metal cable.

Soon my muscles are aching as I have to overcome the magnetic field to forcefully pull each hand off the cable. Within minutes I feel the break in the space and I know I've hit a door. I first try to slide it open from the inside, then push it with my feet, and then, finally, I fumble to get out my grappling hook and pry it open. I crawl out as quickly as I can. Never in my life have I been so happy to see a desk chair. I don't know whose office this is, but it's empty, and that's the only thing I care about.

Out of the dark space, I take a breather to assess my situation. I catch a glimpse of myself in the window. I'm covered in dust and dirt and my hair is all mussed up. And I lost my hat, so my disguise is gone.

Just then, the door starts to beep. Someone is keying in. I don't even have time to think about hiding or taking cover before the door slides open. It's a janitor wearing headphones, and my response is instinctive and thoughtless. I take a running leap at him and just as he looks up with a stunned expression, slam my hand down on the back of his neck like a knife. He collapses, toppling over face-first. He's out cold but probably won't be for long. I drag him out of the doorway and leave him face-down on the floor. I don't have time to worry about him. He'll come to with a headache, but with any luck, he won't have any memory of me.

I head out of the office and dart for the stairwell. Even taking them two at a time, it still feels like the stairs are endless. I reach the ground floor, wind my way to the back service entrance, and slam my body against the door, bursting through to the alley.

Outside, I don't even bother to stop for breath. The PODS isn't running now and it's already taken me twenty minutes to get outside. The man in the hallway said he would take care of Remy and Soren within the hour. I tear down the alley, this time making no attempt at secrecy, counting only on the cover of night and Aulion's mandatory ten-kilometer-per-day morning run to get me where I need to be. *And to get me there in time.*

Just as I round the corner, a noise as loud as a thunderclap and as high-pitched as screeching metal on metal assaults my ears. I turn to look behind me and see flashing red and white lights. The security alarm.

"Find out what's going on," I tell Demeter, fearing the worst. Fearing I've been discovered.

"The janitor keyed in the alarm code. I'm waiting for him to upload further details to see if he identified you."

Shit! I head toward the PODS tracks, the straightest line back to the Complex, and pound out the run as hard and as fast as I can, checking the time constantly.

"It looks like he didn't ID you, but OAC Security is broadcasting his description. They're looking for you, Vale." By the time I reach the Military Complex, Demeter announces that it's 02h47. There may still be time.

I enter the overnight passcode and palm in through the same door I'd gone out hours earlier. I push through the stairwell doors and bound down the steps two, three at a time, almost ricocheting off the landing walls. Remy and Soren are on B Level 3, Holding Cell 28. I'm almost there, when I round a corner and run face-first into—

"Sir?"

"Chan-Yu?"

"I've been looking for you everywhere, sir. There's a..." He stops and stares at my mussed hair, dirty skin, and all-black getup. "Are you all right?

"I'm fine, but you'll have to excuse me," I say, far more confidently than I feel. "I have an urgent matter to attend to." I push past him and start down the hall, when a strange thought stops me in my tracks. *It was him.* It was his voice I heard talking to my mother. That's why he's here—he's on his way to kill Remy and Soren. *Or did he already do it?* Desperation floods through me like a fever. My heart thuds and then stops. I spin around and without a thought, I grab Chan-Yu's collar and slam him against the wall. I stare down at him, and he meets my gaze, unafraid. There's no fear or panic in his eyes—no emotion, really. He almost looks unsurprised. Though I can feel every muscle in his body tense, he makes no move to resist.

"Did you do it?" I demand. His breath is hot against my face.

"Do what?" His eyes are unreadable, his face innocent, his voice perfectly calm.

"Did you kill them?" The corner of his mouth turns up in the faintest hint of a smile.

"No, sir. I have not." I take a deep breath and let him go, releasing my death grip on his collar. My knuckles are white, my hands shaking. I take a step back, but he remains precisely where he was, his back pressed against the wall, watching me. He's always watching me. Waiting. What is he waiting for?

"Chan-Yu, you are under my command, correct?"

"Yes, sir."

"You have taken an oath."

"I have, sir." The man is stoic and impassive. His voice belies nothing.

"Then if I command you to answer me truthfully, will you do so?" His eyes narrow almost imperceptibly, but he responds as usual.

"I will."

"To whom are you loyal?"

"To you, sir."

"Above all others?"

"No, sir."

"Who holds your true allegiance?" I shout at him, once again afraid. The grim possibility settles on me that I may have to kill him to save Remy and Soren. *But can I kill him?* He's as good a soldier as I am, probably better. "Who are you?"

He says nothing.

"Are you one of my mother's men? Do you carry out her orders?"

"I am not one of Corine Orleán's tools." He doesn't flinch, but this time there is a hint of contempt in his voice. *Who is he, if not my mother's man?*

"I know it was you," I say. "At OAC headquarters. With her." In response, Chan-Yu looks me up and down. Something on his face changes then, as if a window has opened and he has made a decision. He opens his mouth, and words spill out that I never expected to hear.

"My allegiance lies outside the Sector, Vale—" that's the first time he's ever addressed me by name "—but that is not a matter to discuss now. My loyalty to Madam Orleán ended tonight, and I am ready to move to the next stage in my task." I stare at him, confused. I have no idea what he's talking about. "Time is short. You have one last command to give me, I believe," he says, as though challenging me. This is the moment, I realize. This is what he's been waiting for. This is why he's been watching me, judging me. He wants to know where I stand.

"Get them out of here," I say. The corners of his mouth turn up in a grim smile, the first real expression I've ever seen on his face. He nods.

"Yes, sir. It is best that you not be here. That you return to your flat. Aulion will be expecting you bright and early. And he will not be happy."

I start to turn away, but he pulls my elbow, turning me back to him. He puts his hand to his neck and tugs at a something—a little chain I've never noticed before. It comes free in his hand, and he holds it out to me. I open my palm and he drops it in.

"If you should ever find yourself lost in the woods," he says, "this may help."

It's a pendant, a charm in the shape of an acorn, enameled in green and gold. The symbol of the Outsiders. Is he working for them? Is that what he meant by "my allegiance lies outside the Sector"? Who is he really? There are a thousand questions in my mind, but when I look up to ask them, Chan-Yu is nowhere to be seen.

19 — REMY

I awake from a sleep that at last brought some semblance of peace. I look around groggily to try to find whatever disturbance stirred me from my rest. My left leg has fallen entirely asleep—ah, that must be it. I shift my thigh slightly against the cold, hard floor and thump my leg a few times, rousing it from numbness. The pins and needles set in and I grit my teeth, waiting for them to fade. When they finally do, I lean my head against Soren's shoulder.

"Remy," he croaks. "Are you awake?"

"Yeah," I whisper back. He is silent for a moment. I wonder what time it is. I lost all sense of time when I passed out on the mission and then woke up on a gurney in a doctor's office, strapped to the bed. It could have been two hours or two days since I was sitting across that desk from Philip, and I wouldn't know the difference.

"Why didn't they ask us about the you-know-what? I can't stop thinking about that."

"Maybe Eli was wrong. Maybe Corine doesn't have it. Maybe nobody in the Sector knows about it."

"But then why would she have ordered Hawthorne killed?" I ponder this.

"He didn't know Eli had downloaded a copy, right? So maybe he kept it hidden—just like my granddad did. Maybe she couldn't find it," I respond.

Soren forgets to spit back his usual derisive expression. I guess being held hostage, starved, and tortured does something to bring people together.

"It doesn't make sense," he says finally. "Corine's too smart to let something she desperately wants slip her notice just because Hawthorne hid it well. I don't buy it. I think it's Philip and Aulion who are in the dark. They don't know about it."

"But why would Corine hide something that important from Philip?"

Soren is silent.

"He's not just the chancellor—he's her husband, too."

After a few minutes, he takes a deep breath. "I don't know."

We sit in silence for a while, the mystery and confusion mingling with the sleep deprivation and hunger to create a chaos in my mind. The bleak, white walls of the room are starting to press in on my brain, and I notice that the room is starting to smell rank and foul. I wish they'd let us wash. I notice the goosebumps on my skin. It's cold, and I wonder how long they'll keep us in here. How long before they'll feed us.

"Remy," Soren croaks again. "Do you think they're coming for us?"

"Corine and Philip?" I close my eyes. Yes. But that's not the question—the question is what they're going to do with us.

"No, Eli. Rhinehouse. Your parents."

"Well they're sure as shit not going to let us rot in here." If there's one thing I know about Eli, he'll go through hell to get us back. He'll fly in here with Firestone and blow the roof off the building if that's what it comes to, the Director and all her plans be damned.

Suddenly, at the thought of Eli and his lopsided smile, his ridiculous antics, I feel my breath short and I can't quite catch it back. The force of recent memories rocks me. Everything that's happened. The mission, Vale's interrogation, Aulion's drugs, the needle piercing my shoulder, the hallucinations. I close my eyes and press my head back against the pole, trying to calm myself. I can't seem to relax. Philip, Vale's dad, looking on casually while his guards electrocute me. Claiming Vale authorized the torture. Is it true? True or not, it's too much to bear. My breath catches in my throat and I feel like the air is being pressed from my lungs. I pull in a wheezy breath and shut my eyes against the world.

"Remy, it's okay," Soren mutters, his voice soothing, calling me back. "We didn't break. What they did to us was bad, yes, but it wasn't that bad. More surprising than anything. No permanent damage, no long-term pain. They did it to scare us, to shake us up. But we didn't break, Remy. We didn't give anything away. You hear me?" He bumps his shoulder into mine, and the touch comforts me. I straighten up and draw in clean air. "We might be starving and exhausted, but we're still alive. Okay? There's still hope. Eli might be on his way with a team right now."

He leans his head back against mine and I find myself relaxing. It strikes me that I'm glad we're here together. And then I think back to how we've always been at each other's throats, and I can't help but laugh.

"What?" he says. "What's so funny?"

"I was just thinking."

"Thinking what?"

"That I'm glad you're here with me. Can you believe it?"

He laughs hoarsely. "Jahnu and Kenzie would be proud of our newfound friendship. But seriously, Remy, they're not really trying to kill us. What would that get them? They're just trying to scare information out of us. But we're not going to let them. Right?"

"Yeah." He *is* right. I can see the logic now. What would they gain from killing us? Nothing. Of course, it's what they're willing to do to us in the meantime that worries me.

Just when I'm starting to contemplate that happy possibility, I hear a dim clicking from somewhere.

"Soren. Shh. Did you hear that?"

"Yeah," he says. "You probably can't see it from your angle, but one of the cameras just moved."

"Shit," I swear.

"No, it's okay," he whispers. "I don't know why, but it's pointing up towards the ceiling now." I hear the same clicking again, this time from a different location, and I look up to see one of the cameras in my field of vision swerving slowly up towards the ceiling.

"What's going on?" I muse.

"This is either really good or really bad," Soren says tersely. Then there's a click to my left and I look up to see the door swing open. My heart jump-starts and my breath quickens again. But it's not Aulion, or Philip, or Vale—it's the soldier who was with Vale. He has a stack of clothes in one arm and two backpacks draped over the other. He drops one pack each in front of us, separates the pile of clothing into two identical stacks and drops one at my feet, one at Soren's. He pulls out a bolt cutter and, in about five seconds, cuts through the bindings around our feet and hands. His movements are clean, efficient, and precise.

"Get up," he says, and Soren and I scramble to our feet, motivated by his tone of command. My leg is still stiff and sore, and since I'm not drugged at the moment, I feel the pull of my stitches. And I'm so hungry that I'm woozy.

"What the—" Soren starts, rubbing his freed wrists, but the man cuts him off.

"I'll explain later. If you want to get out, do as I say." He picks up the uniform at my feet and hands it to me. It's a food-service uniform by the look of it. The clean laundry scent wafting from the clothes reminds me of fresh air, childhood, and freedom. "Change now. We have maybe five minutes, tops."

Soren and I exchange glances, worried, awed, and confused. *Can we trust him?*

"Now!" the soldier snaps, startling me into action. I stop worrying and start obeying.

We jump to do his bidding. Without a thought about privacy, I slip my ragged, destroyed, dried-pee pants off and pull my shirt off. It's a relief to have those dank clothes off. I try not to look at Soren as he strips, too, but my eyes keep tugging in his direction. I turn away. Shivering and cold, I pull my uniformed pants and shirt on as quickly as possible. The uniform fits me perfectly, and I notice Soren's is equally well-tailored. How observant is this man?

"Stuff your ruined clothes in the backpack," he says, and we quickly obey. He hands each of us a cap, and we put them on. "We don't want to leave evidence that someone helped you out of here. Don't worry about shoes. I've got boots for each of you in your packs, but right now we don't have time. Follow me." Wordlessly, we shoulder our packs and obey.

He leads us out of our cell, beyond the room with the two-way mirror, and into a long hallway. The lights are off and the halls are lit only by low green lights on the floors, so I assume it must be nighttime. It's hard to see, and I wish for my infrared contacts, but the doctors took those out. I follow our mysterious rescuer by the sound of his footsteps, and Soren takes up the rear. My stomach burns from emptiness, and my body feels like it might implode. Standing up and walking of my own accord is a lot harder than I thought it would be. My stitches threaten to rip apart, and I grit my teeth with every step. I distract myself by wondering who this man is. But I keep my questions buttoned up inside my mind and pad softly through the darkness in my strange uniform.

We come to a door, and the soldier punches in a code and scans his palm print. The door opens, revealing a flight of twisting stairs going in only one direction: up. I shudder a little. So they were keeping us in the basement—the dungeon. Just like the stories my dad used to tell me when I was little. I wonder if there's a dragon outside, and then think: Yes, there is. Her name is Corine Orleán.

Inside the stairwell, the lighting is a little better. We trot up the twisting stairs, barefoot, and the metal is cold on my feet. I pray the man has done as good a job guessing my shoe size as he has with my clothes. After a few twists of the stairwell, we alight on a different floor and the man palms and codes this door open as well. The halls here are dim and green as well, but I can see a hallway up ahead with brighter lighting. We push through wide swinging doors and find ourselves in an enormous industrial kitchen filled with 3-D printers, and I feel horribly exposed. Someone's going to recognize me or Soren—after all, his mother was chancellor years ago, so he had his moment in the spotlight. But everything is quiet and empty. Even in the kitchen, the lights are dimmer than they would be during the day, and the shadows we cast are ominous and dark. It's almost creepier than it would be if it were pitch-black.

We zig-zag around printers and packaging machines and come to another door. Our rescuer—if indeed he is rescuing us—pushes it open. There is a gentle *whoosh*, and I feel a breath of fresh, cool air on my face. It's an exit, I realize, and the man holds the door open for me.

Just then, the room erupts in throbbing high-pitched noises. *The alarms!* Did we trigger them just now? No, not possible, they would have gone off immediately after he opened the door....

"Aulion must have found your empty cell," the man says, appearing unconcerned. An automatic voice comes over the loudspeaker system.

"All available Sector military personnel to guard stations. Code Red, Code Red. All available Sector military personnel to guard stations. Initiating building lockdown in ten seconds."

"Get outside," the soldier says. "We need to get to the PODS." Soren and I jump out the door and now my feet are freezing. Fortunately, there's a POD glistening not fifty meters away.

Before we can make a dash for it, though, the man throws a hand out to stop me from running. He points up slowly—far too slowly, given our predicament—at a camera trained broadly around the exit. He pulls out a handheld Bolt and takes careful aim, fires. The blue light flashes around the camera and when it dissipates, the light on the camera is off.

"Now we run." The three of us sprint to the POD, and the man punches in an emergency override code. They're not supposed to be running at this hour, but apparently our rescuer has a way around that. The POD door slides open and starts to shimmer, indicating that it is active and receiving passengers. We slide in and the door shuts, and the POD starts to roll us through the capital, to an unknown destination. Soren and I sit down side by side, and the man sits across from us.

"You'll find your boots in the bags, along with several spare pairs of socks. I recommend putting them on now, because we'll need to move quickly once we arrive at the end of this line." He pulls his own pack off his shoulders and digs through it. He pulls out some antiseptic wipes and bends over me. "You'll need to pull off your pants for a minute. I need to check on your stitches."

"I can do it perfectly well," I respond curtly. The idea of getting naked yet again in this tiny enclosed space does not appeal to me. He looks up at me and shrugs. He hands me the wipes, and I start to roll my pants down exactly as much as is necessary for me to see all the various places where they've stitched up my thigh. I unroll one of the wipes and start to gently massage the dried blood off my skin. It stings, but it's nothing compared to the pain of the electroshocks from earlier. Once I've finished and the wounds are tingly clean, he takes the used cloths, douses them in rubbing alcohol, and pulls out a lighter. In the corner of the POD, he lights them on fire, and they incinerate.

"No DNA evidence this way," he says. I nod, looking at the little scorch mark on the POD.

"I didn't have time to get much food, but this should do for now," the man says, handing each of us a little round sticky fruit ball and some preserved meat. Soren and I eye the food lustily, but we don't dare take it. Who knows what the Sector could have put in it?

"It's okay," he says, with a trace of a smile. "I have my own personal supply of food, untainted by the Sector Dieticians."

"How is that possible?" Soren asks, grabbing the fruit bar and stuffing it in his mouth.

"Who are you?" I demand.

"That's not relevant now." I stare at him. I should feel grateful that he just rescued us, that he is risking his life to get us out of the Sector's hands, that he's done so much for us, but all I feel is a frustration at our helplessness. Why won't he tell us anything?

"We've put our lives in your hands—" Soren says with an edge to his voice. I'm glad he's on my side.

"You're not safe yet," the man interrupts.

"Maybe not, but the least you can do is tell us who we should thank for getting us out of that cell."

"Chan-Yu," he says, softly. "Chan-Yu Hayashi. That's my name."

20 — VALE

Jeremiah sits opposite me, eyes closed, head back, chair tipped up on two legs against the wall. I've been briefing him on everything I found at my mother's lab—about Hawthorne, the DNA, and the massacre. I haven't even mentioned Remy and Soren yet. Now he's quiet, still, and I know he's deep in thought. Usually he's a blur of movement, always tapping his fingers or his feet to some unknown or nonexistent rhythm. It's only when he's quietly contemplating something that he stops moving. It's as if all the energy in his body flows directly to his brain, and everything else stops. I can't even see him breathing. I can't help holding my breath myself—will he believe me?

When I left Chan-Yu in the hallway and headed up to the rooftop flight deck where my Sarus was parked, I had every intention of going home like he said. I even had Demeter program the flight path. But going home didn't feel right. All I could think of was whether or not I made the right choice. I left Remy and Soren's lives in Chan-Yu's hands, but how could I know I'd done the right thing by trusting him? He'd been my aide for all these months, and yet I didn't know anything about him. Did he lie to my mother or did he lie to me? He could have killed Remy and Soren and then disappeared, just like my mother commanded. But then I heard the Code Red alarm, and I knew he had been true to his word. I gripped the Outsider pendant in my hand and instructed Deme to change the flight path. I needed to talk to the one person in the Sector I knew I could trust.

Jeremiah was furious when I showed up at his door, and no wonder, given that it was just after three in the morning. But he caught on to the urgency in my voice and let me in. I mixed him up a cup of the Dieticians' brew for alertness and sat him down to tell him everything I'd just learned.

I'm the restless one now. I tap my fingers, stare anxiously around the room, and shift my weight in my chair. Finally, unhappily, Jeremiah raises his head and his chair slams down on all four legs. Then his foot starts tapping again.

"Okay."

"What do you mean, 'Okay'?" I exclaim. I was expecting more than that.

"I don't know what else to say, Vale. I'm terrified, frankly, now that I know all this. I believe you, every word you've said. There's no reason for you to lie to incriminate your mother, so I can only assume you're telling the truth. But you've put my life in danger by telling me this. What will Corine do if she finds out I know about her crimes? She certainly won't think twice about my well-being."

I stare at him. I hadn't thought of that. She was willing to have Remy and Soren secretly murdered because of something they said on camera—she would almost certainly be willing to kill Jeremiah to protect her secret. *My mother, the murderer.* I think I'm going to be sick. How many other atrocities have been committed at her behest? Does my father know about this? He can't—he can't know. *But does he?*

The biggest question looming in my mind is: Why? Why did she want them dead? What did she hear or see them talking about on the security cameras that necessitated an act of murder? For that matter, what about that DNA was so important that Hawthorne had to die? Are Remy and Soren connected to him somehow? To the DNA?

"I had to tell someone," I say, embarrassed. "I thought I could trust you." There's a slight edge to my voice, a feeling of betrayal. *I can't lose Jeremiah, too.*

"You can." He laughs, almost barking, an awkward, uncomfortable laugh. "It's not like I'm going to tell anyone. I'm not about to throw away my life like that. I'm just worried about what happens next."

"Next. Shit. I don't know. I can barely process what's happening now, let alone think about what happens next." I stare at him, conscious of the fact that I still haven't told him the full story. He doesn't know about the Resistance, the raid, Remy and Soren, or the fact that my mother almost had them killed, too. I haven't gotten that far yet. Technically, Jeremiah only has first-level security clearance for his engineering work, so he's not supposed to even know about the existence of the Resistance. I know word's gotten around a little bit among some of the Sector workers, but Jeremiah has never mentioned them to me, and I know I've never spoken about them openly in front of him.

Damn the security clearances.

"Look, Miah, there's something I haven't been telling you, because under Sector security authorizations, I'm not allowed to." He looks up at me curiously from across the desk. "But you need to know, because there's a piece of the story I'm leaving out. There's a group of, shall we say, rebels, former high-ups in the—"

"Are you talking about the Resistance?" he interrupts sharply.

"I—what?" I sputter. "How did you know?"

He laughs bitterly. "I think my father is one of them. He left his job in Ellas about six months ago when one of his friends was killed in a freak accident. He didn't think it was an accident and he couldn't get any answers he liked. So he sent me a note and disappeared."

"He sent you a note and said he was joining the Resistance?" I ask, incredulous.

"No, of course not. He didn't say anything about why he was leaving, just that now that I'm a grown man, I need to make my own choices—and watch my back."

"Damn," I whisper.

"I hadn't seen him in a long time anyway, only a couple of times since I came to the Academy, so it wasn't a huge loss. My parents divorced a long time ago, and we were never very close. But I put my ear to the ground and asked the right questions, and I found out about the Resistance."

I stare at him, speechless. Once again, I realize, I have underestimated my friend. I've relied too much on my mother's judgment. But how will he react to what I have to tell him next? I clear my throat nervously.

"Okay. You know about the Resistance. Did you know that the Seed Bank Protection Project was just a cover-up? It should be called, 'The Resistance Annihilation Project,'" I say with a forced, desperate laugh.

"No way," he whispers, leaning forward. "So that's why you've been spending so much time at the Military Complex with good old Aulion. You're preparing to take on the Resistance."

"Yeah," I say, looking down at my shoes. "Something like that." There is a long pause as I weigh the things I've done over the last year, in my training and preparation for my new position, and the steps I've taken recently as a commander. "So, anyway. The reason I have to tell you about this is—" I take a deep breath "—I recently led my team on a raid interception. It was a hostage-capture mission at one of our seed banks we had reason to believe the Resistance was interested in." Jeremiah's eyes go wide as he listens, whether with awe and intrigue or disgust, I can't quite tell.

"We were supposed to nab Elijah Tawfiq—you remember him, brilliant researcher, one of the smartest people I've ever met. Long story, but he was a perfect target. He was slippery, though, and too quick for us. But we came back with Soren Skaarsgard and Remy Alexander."

Jeremiah lets out a low whistle. He stares at me, sizing me up. I force myself to hold his gaze and accept whatever judgment he may pass.

"My former best friend. And your former girlfriend."

"She was never my girlfriend—" I protest, but he lets out a low chuckle and a smile creases his bearded face. I know then that he doesn't hate me, that he's not going to judge me.

"She may not have been your girlfriend, but you can't deny you were in love with her for a long time. Maybe *still* in love with her." He tosses me a grin. "What a strange coincidence that she should have made it back to the capital with you."

"You think I did it for love? Oh, that's hilarious. Let me tell you about how my mother almost had my 'girlfriend' and your best friend killed."

I run him quickly through my disastrous interrogation, Aulion's injections, and Remy's words about her sister. I explain that she was the one who inspired me to go hunt down the real reason for the attack on Professor Hawthorne's classroom, and how when I started to leave my mother's lab, I overheard my mother telling Chan-Yu to kill Remy and Soren, cover it up, and disappear. Jeremiah's eyes light up when I tell him how I had to sneak out of the building using the dumbwaiter shaft. When I get to the part where I ran into Chan-Yu and realized it was him my mother had been speaking to, he gasps perfectly.

"Did you kill him?" he asks.

"No!" The thought sounds absurd now, even though I had been prepared to do it—or die trying—when I confronted him in the hallway. "No, here's where the story gets even more bizarre, if that's possible. It turns out he's an Outsider, and he had no plans of obeying my mother anyway. He said, 'My allegiance lies outside the Sector,' and I had no idea what he meant until he gave me this." I pull the pendant out from my pocket and hand it over. Jeremiah picks it up and twirls it admiringly.

"I've never seen one of these before." He turns it over in his hand.

"I hadn't either. 'If you should ever find yourself lost in the woods, this may help,' he said."

"What the hell does that mean?" Jeremiah holds the pendant up to the light, examining it from all angles. "Is it some miniature Outsider food printer or something? A grizzly bear vaporizer? Does it blow up into an airship?" I laugh. He passes it back to me

"Who knows? Anyway, Chan-Yu told me to go home, to get ready for work, and to show up on time, like it was a regular work day. At first I had no idea whether I'd made a mistake and had left Remy and Soren in their cell to die, but when I heard the Code Red alarm, I knew he'd gotten them out. I don't know how safe they are, but I have a feeling Chan-Yu will take care of them. He's the stealthiest person I've ever met. He's practically invisible. And if he's with the Outsiders...."

"Why didn't you get them out yourself?" Jeremiah demands.

"I went down there to save them, but I had no real plan ... and then Chan-Yu ... I'd have been recognized at every turn. Everyone would realize I was doing something crazy. No. It wouldn't have worked. I'd have drawn way too much attention to them—and to myself. It's better this way."

Jeremiah stares at the ground for a minute, processing all of this. He goes still again, and I know he's thinking. I stare off into the corner of the room as the weight of everything that's happened starts to bear down on me. My mother, a killer, ordering assassinations in the secrecy of night. My father, possibly complicit. Me, a traitor to the Sector, aiding the cause of the Resistance and freeing government hostages. I rewind slowly, see myself aboard the airship flying to the site of the seed bank for the mission. See Remy injured, Soren trying to protect her, Eli on the roof. How surreal it all feels now, how strange and ridiculous, that I should ever have thought it was a good idea to bring anyone *into our possession.*

"Vale, your mom—"

"I know." I take a deep breath as the shame rips through me like a rusty razor. "You don't have to tell me. I can barely think about it."

Jeremiah looks at me with wide-eyed pity, and I look away, unable to hold his gaze. I'm ashamed. Ashamed of what I am, who I am, what I thought I was. I want to defend myself. How could I have known what they were doing? But I should have been more aware. If the others found out, if they saw through the lies, through the façade, how could I not? And when they all disappeared, one by one, why did I not bother to investigate? And Remy ... oh, god. When she disappeared, I was disappointed—no, I was mad because it hurt when she turned her back on me. No wonder she hates me. *Does she hate me?* She has every reason to. I was ignorant, and I chose to remain that way. Regret smolders in my gut like white hot coals, but I can't change the past.

"Listen," Jeremiah says abruptly, jolting me from my personal hell. "We have to figure out the next step. What do we do now?"

I contemplate the question. I can't turn my mother in. I don't know what she'll do to me, but it doesn't matter—no one will believe me. They'll say I've gone insane. I don't have any proof, anyway; it's all locked up on my mother's computer. Besides, the very thought of testifying in front of a court about the things she's done makes me sick, especially since I now know what Eli went through. I could tell my father, but there's always the risk that he's already privy to the gruesome details, that he's just as guilty as she is. And even if he doesn't know, who would he believe—his wife or his son? I could confront them both. As the thought occurs to me, I realize I owe my mother a chance to explain herself.

"I have to talk to them."

"To—to who?" Jeremiah looks at me, startled.

"To my parents. I have to give them an opportunity to justify what they did. Maybe there's something we don't know. Some missing piece of the puzzle."

"Vale—" Jeremiah's expression is shocked and dismayed "—there is nothing that justifies cold-blooded murder."

"I agree, Miah, but they're my parents. I have to give them a chance."

Jeremiah leans back in his chair. He's staring off into a corner of the room above my head, as though he doesn't want to meet my gaze. There's another long pause as he furtively dodges my eyes, though I'm trying to pin him down. He's shifting so much in his chair that I wonder if his pants aren't being invaded by a large army of fire ants. Finally, he responds, though his eyes are still firmly trained on the upper-right corner of the room.

"Fine. You talk to them. But we need a backup plan, because I highly doubt they're going to have a good enough justification for the murder of a classroom full of students and the attempted murder of two of our former friends that will make us want to stick around."

"Are you suggesting we run?" As the concept rolls off my tongue I contemplate it, visualize it, try to imagine myself fleeing everything I've ever known. I've already made myself a traitor to the Sector. Even by breaking into my mother's lab I've committed crimes that would result in exile to the Wilds. My eyes linger on the Outsider pendant sitting on Miah's table, and I wonder if that will come in handy sooner rather than later.

"Yes," Miah responds definitively. "I'm not planning on sitting around and waiting for your mom to find out I know she's a killer. I've never been high on her list anyway. This puts both me and Moriana in danger—if your mom finds out I know, she'll wonder if Moriana knows too." He sighs. "This is deep, Vale. I don't think we can fight it from the inside. Maybe you can, but I'm hardly in a position of power—and at some point, they're going to figure you out and take you out of the equation. Remember what happened to Soren's parents?"

"No, what happened to them?" I sit up, shocked. I met Soren's parents a few times at official government functions back when Soren's mother was chancellor, and once or twice after that when Soren and I were at piano competitions together. But after a certain point they stopped showing up, and I never saw them again.

"You didn't know? Well, I don't really know either. I always thought they went sort of off their rockers—that's what the official documents said. You know his mom, Cara, was chancellor when SSD201 went raging through the wheat and corn crops and destroyed a quarter of the food supply. That was in '95, and there was a mini famine. Lots of people starved. Of course no one in Okaria knew the full extent. We had food rationing, but it didn't hit in the capital as hard as it did the Farms and factory towns. Anyway, the Corporate Assembly gave her a vote of no confidence. She was removed, and an interim head was appointed before your dad took office."

"I know, I know all this stuff. I just thought that was the end of it. What happened after that?"

"Well, Cara and Odin kept to themselves after that. They went back to their research, and, in public, just focused on Soren. But they kept publishing papers and making little jabs at the OAC's research, detailing all the negative side effects of the drugs being used on animals and, in some cases, on humans. They also wrote occasional journalistic pieces about the practices used on the Farms. Nothing revolutionary, but I guess the Sector didn't like it, and...." He pauses.

"And, what?"

"Sorry. I just feel kind of weird telling you all this. Soren never really liked you, you know—"

"No, really?" I say sarcastically. "You think he didn't like me back then, just imagine how he feels about me now."

"It was always complicated, Vale," Miah says, sounding vaguely parental, as though explaining a concept way over my head. "Anyway, Soren said his parents went off for a vacation one weekend, and when they came back, they were just ... different. 'Flat,' was what he said. Barely paid attention to anything he said or did after that, never criticized him, never responded when he was angry or upset. They were emotionless." Jeremiah glances around the room, looking everywhere but at me.

"His parents were formally removed from their research positions after that and demoted to lab techs, essentially. The OAC reports said that they were demoted because the trauma of losing power in the government made them biased and unable to conduct objective research. Soren never said anything outright, but now that I think about it, it seems pretty clear that he suspected foul play."

I stare at Jeremiah for a few seconds, trying to process this new information. Soren's parents, drugged? Tortured? Lobotomized? Hundreds of ideas, each one more brutal than the last, flow through my head, and I feel like a hundred pounds have been dropped onto each of my shoulders, bowing me down, crushing me.

"You knew all this?"

"What do you mean? Yeah, I knew all this. Soren told me some parts of the story, and some parts I looked into myself. "

"And you never told me? You never thought about it? Never thought that maybe there *was* foul play?"

"Oh, and you're one to talk?" Jeremiah glares at me. "The older sister of the girl you were in love with was killed in an 'Outsider attack' and then her entire family disappeared, and you never thought to ask questions?"

"I did ask questions! I talked to my parents, I talked to my professors, I talked to Moriana, I..." There's a pause.

"You didn't ever do any actual *research* until tonight, though, did you?"

"Well, you did, and you didn't do anything about it!" I say, too accusingly. I try to bite my anger back into my throat. "You actually had cause to suspect, and you just turned away?"

"What was I supposed to do? Go to the Watchmen? The OAC? My parents? With a couple of court transcripts and Soren's word against the whole Sector?" He's standing now, leaning across the table toward me. "You think it was any of my business, Vale? Hacking into my best friend's parents' mental health records and reading through old Corporate Assembly transcripts when I was fifteen?"

He's shouting now, and I want to tell him to keep his voice down, but I can't get the words in—

"I didn't know what to think, so I kept quiet and kept my head down. And then Soren disappeared, and I had no idea where he went or how to find him or even if he was still alive. So tell me, Vale, what would you have done? Run to your parents?" he says disdainfully.

I freeze. Jeremiah, too, suddenly stops talking or moving, his mouth half open, his eyes narrowed accusingly at me. I can't seem to think. My mind has gone blank. The contempt melts off Miah's face as he realizes what he's said, and he drops his eyes to the floor.

"I'm sorry, that wasn't—" but he doesn't finish his sentence.

There's a long silence as Jeremiah stares at his hands on the table, and I stare at him. The buoyancy that normally decorates his face is gone, and I get a glimpse of what he might look like in twenty, thirty years. My mind swirls as I watch him, immobile, both of us stuck for a moment in time that we want to erase, but cannot. Now, Jeremiah is replaced by images flashing before my eyes: photos of Tai in the autopsy room, her eyes as clear and glassy and dead as water stones; Remy's amber-eyed stare, angry and questioning, as she turned away from me before slamming the door in my face; my mother sitting me down in our house, telling me in her gentle dulcet tones that the Alexander family had disappeared.

"Sorry, I shouldn't—" Miah begins again, snapping me out of my memories.

"No, no, stop," I say abruptly, cutting him off. "You're right. I was just as blind, if not more, and I—" I stop. Demeter has a message for me from General Aulion. I hold up a finger to tell Jeremiah to wait, and I listen carefully as she relays the words in her calm, low voice, and I'm grateful she's the messenger and not Aulion himself. She could have just played his recording, of course, but she knows I'd rather hear her voice than Aulion's. Especially now.

"Valerian Augustus Orleán, the Resistance prisoners, Remy Alexander and Soren Skaarsgard, have escaped. Despite lockdown and emergency high-security measures, they have disappeared. You keyed out of Sector Headquarters at 0302 hours, just prior to a Code Red lockdown. Because of this you are being temporarily relieved of your duties as director of the Seed Bank Protection Project pending further investigation into your role in the prisoners' disappearance. Report receipt of this message and your location immediately. If you do not report within five minutes, we will issue a warrant for your arrest as an accessory to the traitors' escape."

Well, that was fast.

I mutter to Jeremiah something about my boss wanting to talk to me, and I give Demeter the message to send back: "Valerian Orleán reporting from Jeremiah Sayyid's flat, Unit 244, Building 25 in the Old Quarter. I had no role in the hostages' escape." Demeter sends the message off, and not ten seconds later she announces that Aulion would like to speak to me directly. I tell her to ignore the call. "I'll call him in the morning. Repeat that I had no involvement in the hostages' escape, and I am currently occupied with other urgent matters." Demeter actually laughs at this.

"What could be so urgent that you would want to ignore General Aulion?" she asks and then sends off the message.

"So, big news," I say with a mirthless smile. "I've been demoted. 'Relieved of my duties.'"

"Really?" He looks unsure of whether this is good or bad.

"Pending further investigation into my role in the escape.'" I frown. It's okay, I tell myself. Better that I come under investigation than that Chan-Yu be thrust into the line of fire. "At least this way I'm not helping the Sector anymore. I don't think I could in good conscience continue to do my job anyway."

"Well, lucky you, then. A most opportune time to be fired."

I nod.

"So, when are you going to talk to your parents?" I think about that, but I don't have a good answer. I'll have to work up the courage, and that might take a while. I might not even get the opportunity for several days, what with dealing with the fallout from Remy and Soren's escape.

"I don't know. But if you're serious about leaving, I'll come with you. I may not have a choice with Aulion on my tail. Just let me talk to my parents first."

"And Vale—we can't take Moriana," Jeremiah blurts out. "We can't tell her."

"What? Why not?"

"I'm not going to endanger her life like that. She's got a good thing going here and she needs to make her own choices. Just like my dad told me. And if we tell her, we'll be putting her in as much danger as you and I are now. It's better if she doesn't know."

I frown, but I know he's right.

"Okay," he says, speaking more easily now, "if we're really doing this, then we should be ready to leave at the drop of a hat. You have no idea how they're going to react, how far they'll go to hide the truth."

"I don't think they'll hurt me." Miah cocks an eyebrow at me, skeptical. "But you're right. Let's get our stuff together tomorrow so we can be ready to move whenever we need to."

Jeremiah grabs his plasma and starts making a list. "Imagine we're going camping," he says. "My dad took me a few times when I was little. We're going to need extra clothes, rain gear, good boots, something to hunt with in case we run out of food—oh, and a good supply of our Mealpaks—and probably a few weapons, too. I'll count on you to commandeer those for us. It's not like I've got a ready supply of Bolts hanging around."

I have to resist the urge to laugh. Leave it to Jeremiah to create some comedy from this whole thing.

"And we'll probably want to take your Sarus, if possible—it's not bugged, is it?" I shake my head, hoping I'm right. "Great. So we'll take the Sarus, and we'll want some blankets and rope, and...."

As Miah rattles on about the list, I sit back and think about what leaving really means—and the impending conversation I must have with my parents. I owe it to them, I know. But what will I learn? Is my mother really the cold-hearted killer I overheard two hours ago ordering the deaths of two Sector citizens? Or will she emerge from all this with her characteristic political silkiness, somehow justifying her actions? The very thought of confronting them, of judging them and demanding they account for themselves, brings a lump to my throat like I've swallowed an old chunk of coal. I blink back the tears and lean in. Like Miah said, it's time to plan for what comes next.

21 — REMY

Across the POD, Soren and I stare at the man called Chan-Yu, thankful but uncertain of where we stand or who he really is. Soren and I both open our mouths to start peppering him with questions, but he holds his hand up to shush us, and we clamp them shut. I look around, fearing that someone has seen us, that someone is after us, but no one is there, and the streets of the capital are quiet and dark. It's a little surreal, looking outside the window during the quiet night and watching the city I once called home slide by. It feels hostile and threatening, and I keep looking around for angry eyes to turn us into the Sector authorities.

The POD moves with smooth efficiency as Chan-Yu looks out the window, and I look at Chan-Yu. He has the kind of face you wouldn't notice unless he called attention to himself. He has narrow eyes, a square jaw, and high cheeckbones, vaguely reminiscent of Asian heritage. He's not attractive, but he's not unattractive either, just sort of nondescript, the kind of man who could easily fade into a crowd without notice. I try to gauge his age and guess he must be about twenty-five or twenty-six. He's compact, shorter than Soren, but he radiates quiet strength and confidence, like the unnerving calm before a summer storm. A million scenarios swirl in my head, and it's all I can do to keep quiet. I glance over at Soren. His leg is vibrating up and down like it's on a spring, and it's clear he's about to jump out of his skin if we doesn't get answers soon.

Without warning, Chan-Yu reaches out and pushes the emergency STOP button, and Soren and I are thrown forward as the POD lurches to a halt. The door slides open silently and Chan-Yu stands up and shoulders his pack. We do the same and follow him as he jumps down onto the rail path. I wince as my leg wobbles when I hit the ground. He punches in a code, and we watch as the POD starts moving again, continuing its way down the line.

"That was just a way to get us out of the headquarters quadrant fast. Sector drones and soldiers will be searching the PODS line, so we have to move. I know you're tired, but I hope you have enough in you for a short run." Soren and I nod brusquely—what choice do we have? I grit my teeth against the ache in my leg and follow our rescuer as he takes off at a lope toward a darkened side street.

We're outside the city center and running through neighborhoods full of apartments, shops, and restaurants. It's been so long since I've seen the city that everything strikes me as opulent. Soren and I are haggard, exhausted from trying to keep up with Chan-Yu's relentless pace. Just when I think I can't keep up this pace, after at least twenty minutes of jogging punctuated with an occasional sprint between open spaces, Chan-Yu comes to an abrupt stop under a storefront awning.

"Wait here." He rounds a corner and disappears.

"Fuck," Soren swears, bending over with his hands on his knees. "I'm beat." I nod my silent agreement—I don't have enough wind left in me to actually speak—and hope the running is over.

We stand in the shadows of the enormous apartment building, gripping our packs and looking around nervously, catching our breath as we wait for Chan-Yu to return. My heart is beating so loudly I'm surprised Soren can't hear it, and I try to calm myself, to tell myself that Chan-Yu is in control of the situation. But I've never liked putting my fate in anyone else's hands, much less a stranger's.

After a few minutes, I hear the telltale low hum of a hovercar, and I grab Soren and we duck into the shadows as a supply truck with Chan-Yu riding shotgun rounds the corner. The official Sector sunflower emblem is painted on the side, and beneath it reads: OKARIAN SECTOR FARM SUPPLY DETAIL. The driver is a mousy woman with her hair pulled back in a ponytail. She doesn't look at us but instead seems to be peering into the rearview mirror as if she has something in her eye. Chan-Yu pushes a button on the dash and then hops out as the back door rolls open. He motions us in, and we climb up and find seats on a pile of boxes. Before Chan-Yu joins us, he looks up into the sky and a look of alarm crosses his face. My heart stops. He quickly hops in with us and slams the door down.

"We're being tracked," he says. "Drones."

"Do they know we're in the truck?" I demand.

"We'll find out soon enough," Chan-Yu responds. I contemplate this grisly possibility and wonder how short-lived our escape will be. A wave of molten fear courses through me at the thought of facing Philip and Aulion again. A light comes on above us, and Chan-Yu smiles.

"Sela is very thoughtful," he says, presumably referring to the driver.

"Who is she?" Soren asks.

"A friend," he responds. "I hope we'll have a few minutes of quiet now, so you should rest," he says casually, as though we were out for a pleasant afternoon jaunt.

"Where are we going?" Soren asks.

"I recognize you from when Vale interrogated us," I say.

"If you're Sector military, why are you helping us?" Soren adds, gesturing at Chan-Yu's uniform.

"I have my reasons."

"We deserve to know what's going on, where you're taking us, and why," Soren says.

"Is that so?" Chan-Yu turns his narrow, unsmiling eyes onto Soren. "You *deserve* to know? And what have you done, Soren Skaarsgard, to earn the right to know everything that goes on around you? What gives you the right to know the thoughts and decisions of others?" He shakes his head at Soren, who looks subdued, though unrepentant. "Not everything is within your control, and there is nothing in this world that gives you the *right* to know how all things have come to be."

Soren opens his mouth like he's about to spit out a response, but he stops halfway through and thinks better of it.

"What is important is that your lives are in danger. You have something very valuable, and Corine Orleán knows you have it," he says, shifting his gaze from Soren to me. *Does he know about the DNA?* "Make no mistake, she wants you dead. She believes fervently that if you should return to the Resistance and give them what knowledge you have, the control she has worked for years to obtain will be nothing. The OAC's power will be diminished—*her* power will be diminished."

My mind is racing. Corine must have seen me on camera, just as Soren feared. She can't risk anyone else learning about the key, so she ordered us killed, and somehow Chan-Yu found out. But he was with Vale during the interrogation. *Does that mean Vale knows?*

"What about Vale...?" I can't finish the sentence.

"I have been working for him at Corine Orleán's directive, and—"

"Wait," I stop him. "You worked for Vale or Corine?"

He looks at me calmly and without blinking says, "In the Sector, everyone works for Corine Orleán."

I pull up short, considering the implications of his words. *Does she have that much power?*

"You wear a Sector uniform and yet, by all accounts, you just committed a treasonous act by freeing us," Soren interjects.

"Yes, I wear a Sector uniform. As far as the Orleáns or anyone else in the Sector knows, I was a TREE scholar who opted to forego the Academy to join the Military Youth Training Program. I was ultimately recruited, along with several other promising candidates, by Corine. So, formally, I am attached to the OAC Security Directorate."

At this, Soren and I glance at each other, wondering again whether we can really trust this man. In the Resistance, the OAC Security Directorate is nicknamed Corine's Black Ops. They're an elite team of soldiers who are selected for their intelligence, physical fitness, and dedication to the OAC's cause. And, rumor has it they are paid very well for their loyalty.

The TREE Program is a scholarship program for kids from the outer quadrants. Every child in the Sector has to take standardized evaluations each year from the time we first enter formal schooling at age three. By the time we're fourteen, most of us know what school, if any, we're headed for. For the brightest in Okaria and the children of the privileged, it's the Academy, but most of the kids in the quadrants attend local schools until age sixteen and then are apprenticed out to work in the factory towns or on the Farms. But every year, one student from each quadrant, the kid with the highest score on the Level Eleven standardized test, hits the jackpot and earns a free ticket to the Academy. Those are the TREE Scholars—it stands for Talent Revival and Education Enterprise. It's how Eli made it to the Academy.

"You said, 'As far as the Orleáns or anyone else in the Sector knows, you were a TREE Scholar; does that mean you weren't actually in the program?" I ask.

"No. Outsiders don't send their children to Sector schools," he says, with what I swear is almost a twinkle in his eyes.

"You're an Outsider?" Soren says, stunned. "How did you get registered in the Sector? Human Registry is impossible to breach!" Sector Human Registry is the database that keeps track of everyone's identity. It involves DNA testing as an infant, and then constant, weekly monitoring of growth, emotional and intellectual intelligence, hormone levels, personality tests—basically everything that's possible to know about an individual. The Dieticians use the information to create personalized diets, tailored to the individual and his or her educational pathway and profession.

"Obviously it's not impossible, because here I am," he smiles, this time a real, genuine smile, and I can see he takes pride in the fact that the Outsiders have, in at least one way, outsmarted the Sector. "The Outsiders have connections on the inside," he says, without a trace of irony. "Sela, our driver, for instance. We have found, over the years, that it's helpful to keep an eye on what's happening here." His eyes darken and turn stormy as he looks past us, beyond us. "They have a tendency to blame their more heinous crimes on us, and their retaliation is swift and deadly."

He's talking about Tai, I realize, and I wonder how many innocent people were murdered in the name of avenging the classroom massacre that was so conveniently blamed on an "Outsider terrorist." I close my eyes and shudder at the thought.

"How does Vale figure in all this?" Soren asks the question on my lips. "Does he know about this information we have? If you worked for him, does he know you're helping us?"

"He is aware of the situation." I notice he didn't answer Soren's first question. *He knows we've escaped.* But what does that mean? Did he want Chan-Yu to help us or did he know and was just unable to stop him? I'm afraid to ask. For a few moments, we are silent, lost in our thoughts as the truck glides through the darkness.

Finally, I can't stand it any longer.

"Chan-Yu?" He looks at me as if he knows what I'm going to ask.

"Does Vale know Corine wants us dead? Did he *want* you to help us or—"

Suddenly the hovercar lurches and starts to slow, and my heart pounds. Chan-Yu notices the fear in my eyes and says simply, "Checkpoint."

"Where are we going?" Soren asks again.

"The port. There's a supply ship that leaves across the lake at six in the morning. They should currently be occupied loading the cargo onto the ship, so it won't be easy for us to get on." Not to mention that soldiers and drones will no doubt be thoroughly searching every corner of the boat for the escaped Resistance fugitives.

"But—the Code Red, won't they search—" I start, but Chan-Yu shakes his head.

"Not now." I sigh in relief, but it's short-lived. "There's another checkpoint before we reach the port. That's where they'll search the truck." My heart sinks. "But don't worry, we're getting out before then," he says. "The hard part will be getting on the boat, and once we're on the other side of the lake, there are no guarantees. Hold on. We'll be there soon, so be ready to move." Soren and I sling our packs over our shoulders and hold our breath.

❀

We get through the checkpoint and pick up speed for a while. Then the light above us flickers once, twice, and the truck starts to slow again. This appears to be some kind of signal, as Chan-Yu stands and pulls the door open about halfway. "She's not going to stop, only slow down, so we have to be quick. Sit on the edge and jump out. Then get off the road immediately."

Soren and I plop down on the back of the truck and push ourselves out, landing on soft dirt near an unpaved path to the port. We squat beside the road and wait for Chan-Yu. The city has faded into the background, giving way to sparse trees and shrubs as the land slopes down to the lake. In the distance, I can see the glow of dim lights from the port and then stark, empty darkness—the lake.

Chan-Yu lands gracefully as the door thuds shut behind him and the truck continues on its way. He motions for us to follow him, and we head down a barely visible path, taking refuge in the tall grass spreading across the otherwise empty field. The port is on a spit of land that stretches out into the enormous lake, leaving ample space for ships to dock and load. We can hear voices carry over the water, dockworkers shouting to each other. The port isn't huge—it can only handle about ten ships at a time—and most of the loading and unloading is done using airborne robots, so there usually aren't too many people around. I'd been down to the port a couple of times when Mom and Dad had gone on tours of the area quadrants after Dad was named Poet Laureate. They usually took airships, but once in a while, they'd go by boat. I thought it was old-fashioned and kind of romantic and always begged to go with them. They only let me go a few times because they didn't want me missing so much school. The last time I traveled across the lake was when we stowed away, when we left the Sector and our old lives behind us.

We find ourselves crouching behind some sort of shed, peering around the edges to look over the ship, which is docked about a hundred meters from us. A small device on Chan-Yu's wrist starts to flash a dull blue light, and he looks up at the sky.

"Get down!" he whispers urgently, dragging us down onto our bellies under a bush. "Drones," he says, so softly I can barely hear him. "They must be canvassing the whole city." Fear clutches my stomach and wraps tightly around my lungs, squeezing the breath out of me. After all this, to get caught now would be such a waste. Chan-Yu fusses with his pack and then pulls out some sort of blanket and covers us with it. It must be a temperature cloaking device to hide us from the drones' heat sensors. We lie in silence for several moments, huddled together on the ground, waiting for—what? After a few seconds, the drone sensor on his wrist stops flashing. Chan-Yu indicates to us that we should stay where we are, but he stands up and disappears.

"I wish he'd stop doing that," Soren mutters.

"I wish I were back with Eli at base," I hiss back. "But that's not going to get me anywhere, now is it?"

I feel a tapping on my shoulder and I push the blanket over my head to see Chan-Yu staring at me, motioning us up. We climb to our feet and brush ourselves off.

"We have less than an hour to get on board. Drones and a small detachment of soldiers are surveying the area and searching the ship. We can't board until they've finished and cleared it for departure, but we can't stay here, either. Human soldiers and drones combined will find us with or without heat shields."

I stare at him hopelessly.

"So what do we do?"

He gives us a look like *Are you ready for this?* "I hope both of you know how to swim."

Chan-Yu leads us along a roundabout path down to the waterfront, far from the bustle of the docks. I'm shivering already, just thinking about how cold the water must be at this time of year. Once we're as close to the sandy beach as we dare, he hands Soren a small glass vial containing a crystal-clear liquid. Soren and I glance hesitantly at each other. The thought flashes through my mind that he's going to kill us now—poison us and then trick us into the water, where our bodies will never be found. When I ask what it is he doesn't respond at first, but just glances at me as though I were a child speaking out of turn in class. He's busy occupying himself with something in his pack, and after a few seconds he pulls out a wide jar. He hands the jar to me and then nods at me expectantly. I stare at him, dumbfounded.

"You've never used heat gel before?" he asks. Soren and I both shake our heads no. "It's infused with nanoparticles that have thermotunneling capacity. You rub it on your skin and the particles use the differential between your body temperature and the air or water temperature to produce heat. It's insoluble in water so it will cling to your skin, but it's not as good as a wetsuit, and doesn't last forever." When neither Soren nor I move, he looks at us with a hint of anger in his eyes. "Hurry. We don't have much time."

Soren and I each scoop out a handful, and I turn my back to him and drop my pants. As I rub the gel on my legs, I immediately feel the particles activate. The boost in heat on my skin is undeniable, and I lift my shirt and rub the stuff all over myself.

"Boots and clothes will be useless," Chan-Yu says and starts to strip. "You'll want them dry when we get to the other side, so stuff them in your packs. They're waterproof."

Lovely. The thought of being naked in front of Chan-Yu and Soren doesn't bother me. At base we all share the shower room, so we're comfortable with nudity—to a point. I personally have never seen Rhinehouse naked, but Kenzie's shared her horror stories more than once. But the thought of being caught stark naked by Sector soldiers is a whole different story. *Oh well, what the hell.* I pull off my shirt and start to rub the gel all over my skin.

As I undress, I can't help but sneak a sidelong glance at Soren as he, too, peels off his clothes. Of course I've seen him naked before, coming out of the showers, but after everything that we've been through, somehow this time it feels more intimate even though we're standing out in the open. Back at base, it was a casual thing, something that could happen any day. It meant nothing. But here, to me, it seems to be one more thing, one more shared experience, that brings us closer.

"Drink the liquid in the vial, too," Chan-Yu says pointedly. "Two swallows each." Neither of us makes a move to open the small glass bottle. We're standing in the middle of nowhere, half-naked with drones swarming overhead, and now we balk when asked to drink from the little vial? Still, I frown and shake my head.

"What's in it?" I can't shake the image of my purple and bloated body washing up on shore weeks from now.

"Another warming concoction. This one works from the inside out. It slows your heart rate, allowing you to conserve energy, but it will also dilate your capillaries, allowing more blood to reach your skin cells in the cold. You won't be able to swim as fast, so don't push yourself, but you'll be able to stay in the water for longer."

"Why do you just happen to have this stuff in your pack?" Soren demands.

Chan-Yu just shrugs. "It's winter," he says matter-of-factly. I guess the cold weather is as good a reason as any to have a stash of heat-providing substances.

Especially if you're planning on escaping into the Wilds at the drop of a hat.

"Is it all Outsider-made?" I ask. "I've never heard of these things."

"The gel is an OAC product." *Great*, I think. *We're supporting Corine Orleán's business enterprise.* "We—" I presume he means *We Outsiders* "—don't have the capacity to produce nanotech. The liquid in the vial is plant-derived. That is Outsider-made."

Once Soren and I have finished slathering our bodies with the strange gel, the jar is almost empty, and I have to wonder how Chan-Yu will survive without it. Soren and I look at each other anxiously before he unscrews the top of his vial and chugs the liquid inside, two swallows. I do the same. It's like doing shots at home with Eli and Firestone. It's sweet, and it tastes *tingly* somehow, like bubbles of sparkling wine on the back of my tongue. When I don't immediately start convulsing and turning purple, I breathe a deep sigh of relief.

"Okay," Chan-Yu says, grabbing the vial and tipping it back for his own dose. "Move. Stay under as much as possible," he says. "Even with the heat protections, we only have so long before the cold water turns deadly." He nods at us, and we move.

I pull my pack over my shoulders and we dart down to the beach, trying to spend as little time as possible running naked out in the open. Soren's at my heels, and we wade in. It's frigid but doesn't seem to affect me. I wonder how long we can stay alive, even with Chan-Yu's concoctions. Hypothermia seems the most likely outcome of this little adventure—that is, if the drones don't get us first. I go in gently, trying not to splash, immersing myself in the water. I take a deep breath and dive under, relishing the way it flows over my face but seems not to touch it, how chill and refreshing it is but not cold. It soothes and buoys me, and I come up for air smiling.

"Remy?" Soren whispers.

"I'm here."

"I can't see you. It's too dark."

"Good. But I can see you. Your hair."

"Shit," he says, bringing a hand up to muss his bright, blonde hair.

"It's like a beacon," I whisper. "You need to stay under." He ducks under and swims out further, as far out as feels safe. I follow him, feeling the current he's making. I feel something at my side and squirm, suddenly afraid—what is in these dark waters, after all? But it's only Chan-Yu. "Head for the ship. Swim slowly to save energy. We have time."

I swim back towards the light of the port, staying a comfortable distance from shore and swimming underwater as often as possible. I breaststroke slowly and easily, as I remember how much I loved swimming when I was younger. I feel as though I could do this all night long. I can feel my skin tingle from the cold, but I keep moving to stay warm. Soren's head flashes up now and then, his hair reflecting the light from the dock, and I pray we won't be discovered.

Slowly, we paddle the three hundred or so meters to the ship. I pull up about thirty meters away and tread water, counting on my dark skin and hair to keep me shrouded from view in the black of night. On the ship ahead of us, I can see lights coursing up and down—looking for the fugitives? I keep my eyes low and hiss at Soren whenever he pops his head up. Chan-Yu is as invisible as I am, his black hair inconspicuous against the dark water. Occasionally I look up and see the flashing metal of a drone, but either they haven't been directed to investigate the water or they don't think it's possible that we're hiding here, because they don't venture far from shore. I can see lights patrolling the spot where we first hid, and a few moments later, where we were stopped when we slathered ourselves with Chan-Yu's miracle heat gel. But no one has thought to search the water.

The cold is seeping into my skin, slowly but surely. I try to dive down, to move, to keep my body in motion without using too much energy or creating strange water patterns, but the cold is getting to me. My muscles are stiffening and I wonder what time it is. But still the lights patrol the boat. Will we ever get aboard? How long will we have to shiver here in the cold winter water? How long can we survive? I'm thankful that the lake isn't frozen. Some years the ice is two meters thick; other years the lake doesn't freeze at all. You never can tell.

Finally, the lights on the boat disappear and I can hear the drones resume hauling cargo. By this point my bones are sore, and the pack on my back feels like it weighs a thousand pounds. The next time Soren comes up for breath, I tap him and point at the boat. He nods and ducks back under, and together we swim towards the ship. By the time the hull looms large in my vision, I can see the ladder towards the stern. I angle in that direction. I'm freezing and shivering, my teeth are chattering, and I know we have to get out soon or risk hypothermia. Not to mention that my euphoria at being in the water has completely faded, and now I'm exhausted, hungry, *and* frozen. There's a faint buzzing above me, but I can't see anything, and I assume it's just an insect. I'm five meters from the ladder, thinking joyfully of the dry clothes that await me once we get to a safe hiding space, and then—

A hand slaps over my mouth. A leg clamps around mine and a strong body pulls me under. I try to gasp and thrash but I can't breathe, I can barely move. I kick my legs out and fight, wriggling, throwing my weight around, but he drags me down further, pinning my arms to my side. My body is slippery from the heat gel and my attacker loses his grip on me, but before I can pull up for air his arms are strong around me again, dragging me back down. I'm suffocating, I can't breathe, *I'm drowning*. I thrash and bite and kick but I'm losing energy, I'm sinking, I'm....

Suddenly he lets go. I feel his arms and legs release me and I kick hard for the surface. I come up gasping, almost crying, exultant from the rush of oxygen and traumatized from the attack. I spin around, searching for my assailant; he can't be far. I see Chan-Yu rise to the surface next to me. He, too, draws in an enormous breath. Anger pounds at my chest. Why did I ever think I could trust him? I dive at him, aiming for his throat, but he throws out his hands to hold me at bay, his eyes flashing in the dim light from the port.

"Drones." As he holds out his arms, I see the drone detector on his wrist flashing a faint, luminescent blue. "You couldn't see them. Your head was above the surface of the water. They would have caught you." He's panting, catching his breath, too. "I'm sorry, but there was no way to warn you."

I glare at him. *I almost died!* I want to scream. But after a few seconds of clear breath, rational thought kicks in: We were only underwater for about thirty seconds, and I was fine once I got a breath of air. His actions probably saved me from death at the hands of a drone—or worse, Corine and Philip. But still, the pressure in my chest, the pain in my lungs, and the panic of being unable to draw breath, of helplessly kicking and clawing my way through the black lingers, and the rage is hard to shake.

"You can head for the ladder now," Chan-Yu says quietly, wearily. He, too, starts meandering in that direction. I can see Soren's head bob to the surface— did he know about the drones? Maybe he caught a glimpse of the flashing blue light and knew to stay below. We glide towards the ladder, and Chan-Yu gets there first. I remember he didn't have much of the gel on him, and it occurs to me that he must be even colder than I am. He pulls himself soundlessly out of the water, and holds himself for a moment to let the excess drip off of him. He's covered in goose flesh, and my anger dissipates as I realize he's probably freezing. I watch him ascend to the top of the ladder, where he peers about for a moment. It's only now, looking up at him from below that I realize exactly how fit he is. He's thin, but in the dim light, his body shines and I can see the contour of every muscle. I almost wish I could draw him, poised at the top of the ladder. He gestures for us to follow, and it occurs to me that I should let

Soren go before me.

"You first," I say to him.

He grins. "Not a chance in hell, Remy."

Damn.

In the open air, the world is even colder than it was in the water, and my entire body is shaking. I can't think of anything but finding heat. I suck in a deep breath and try to keep my teeth chattering to a minimum. Chan-Yu hops over the rail and I poke my head up to watch. He moves quickly, quietly and surely, and then hops over the edge to where the lifeboat is waiting. I glance around to make sure no one is watching, and then follow suit. My feet are numb to the bone as I patter along the metal flooring. I clutch my arms to my chest for warmth and hop over the railing, joining Chan-Yu in a narrow, angular little lifeboat that sways with my weight. Quivering uncontrollably, I try to open the water seal on my pack to pull out my clothes. My hands are shaking too hard, and it takes me four tries before I can pop the seal and open the bag. By that time, Soren has joined me, and he immediately puts his arm around me and hugs me close for warmth.

"Stop it. You're getting me wet."

Soren lets me go to pull his clothes over his shuddering body, but as soon as he is fully clothed again, he pulls me back against him, and I close my eyes with relief and fatigue. We shiver together and I can hear his teeth rattling, too. His body, nearly twice my size, is just as cold as mine, but somehow comforting. I almost hope body heat isn't the only reason he's pulled me into his arms.

Chan-Yu, as cold as he must be, somehow seems unchanged. He is still and calm, and he breaks the seal on his pack and pulls his dry uniform back on.

"We don't have long before the ship departs. And the sun will be up soon, so I suggest you get some rest now."

Soren and I need no encouragement. We settle ourselves in on the floor of the lifeboat, and he throws his arm over me, nestling his head into my shoulder without a thought. Within seconds, he's sound asleep. I can feel the warmth of his breath on my shoulder, and I curl up against his body, thinking *I could get used to this.* As I drift off, my eyes linger on Chan-Yu, who is staring off into the distance without a trace of fatigue. I wonder at how different our situation was three hours ago, and my last thought as I fall asleep, even while curled up against Soren, is that Chan-Yu never got a chance to answer my question. Did Vale try to stop Chan-Yu and fail, or did he want Chan-Yu to help us escape? With all my heart, I hope it is the latter, but, if so, what price will he pay for our freedom?

A pale light glimmers through my eyelids and I breathe in, conscious of the cold air and the warm body next to me. Soren. His arms are wrapped around me, and I squeeze my eyes shut against reality, hoping I can ward off the daylight. Maybe then we will wake up peacefully together and find ourselves back at base. Back home. But then a breeze tickles my shoulder, teasing me, and I can't help but open my eyes. The sky is dimly blue and purple, and a pink edge is materializing to my left. I can feel our little lifeboat swaying gently. We're moving.

I open my eyes fully and squint around. Chan-Yu is sitting exactly where we left him, his eyes closed and his arms crossed around his body, presumably to keep himself warm. Is he sleeping? His chest rises and falls regularly, but I can't tell.

Suddenly I realize how exposed we are in the rising sunlight, and I shudder and start to push Soren's arms from around me. He groans in protest but gives way when I move him. I sit up and the wind rustles around my ears. We must be moving fast.

"Chan-Yu," I hiss. The man doesn't stir. "Chan-Yu!" I whisper, louder, more urgently, and I stretch my booted toe out to poke him in the shin. His eyes flutter open and come to focus on me. He looks at me expectantly. I still can't tell if he was really asleep or not—he doesn't look groggy or disoriented.

"Were you asleep?" I mouth silently, suddenly too curious to let it pass.

He shakes his head and responds at a normal vocal level. "Meditating."

I wince as though his voice has hurt me. "Not so loud!" I whisper, barely audible over the rushing wind around us. He shakes his head again.

"It doesn't matter," he responds, and again his voice is normal. "They can't hear us. The wind is too loud, and everyone will be below deck anyway."

"We won't get caught?" I ask, hushed.

"They don't usually come out and peer in the lifeboats, if that's what you mean. Especially not after soldiers and drones have swarmed the ship. Typically crewmen on a cargo ship like this will stay below deck for the voyage. If they do come up, they won't be able to hear us."

Soren has begun to stir next to me, and he opens his eyes at Chan-Yu's words. "We moving?" he asks groggily.

"Yeah," I respond, as loudly as I dare. "How long 'till we're there?" I ask.

Chan-Yu gives me a faint smile. "Not long. Probably an hour yet. You can go back to sleep if you want; I'll wake you when it's time." But now that I'm awake and sitting up, the cold wind against my face and the open lake around us, I don't want to sleep. I haul myself up to the edge of the lifeboat and peer out as the water glides endlessly by. Soren rolls over and curls into himself, closing his eyes again. Chan-Yu resumes his quiet meditation, and I pass the rest of the trip in silence. I wrap my arms around myself and tuck my legs up against my chest, but already I can feel the air warming. I remember once when the lake froze solid, and my father took me and Tai out to explore the ice. It was a strange, mystical landscape: white, jagged, and bleak, but somehow promising. I remember skidding around between pillars of frozen waves like monsters from a nightmare, foamy fingers clawing at us. Tai and I laughed and played for hours. Three weeks later the ice was gone, and Okaria hasn't seen a storm like that since. I close my eyes and try to remember what the world looked like, frozen in place, perfectly still.

When the light is full bright over us and the sun's rays are sparkling across the wintry lake, Chan-Yu stirs again. He twists around so he's facing the front of the boat, and then turns back and announces we're almost there.

"Wake up your friend," he says to me. "We have to swim to shore." I stare at him, aghast. *Swim? To shore?* Didn't we just finish getting warm? Chan-Yu pulls out another glass vial, like the one he gave us last night. He nods down at Soren. "Wake him," he says again. I crouch down next to him and gently shake his shoulders. He rolls over and groans again, but when he sees me his mouth turns up in a smile. An odd feeling of supreme happiness wells up in my stomach when his blue eyes alight on me, and I have the most peculiar urge to lean over and kiss him. But instead of doing that, I say: "Wake up, stupid. We're almost there."

He grins at me and shrugs himself up, and I back off. Chan-Yu is watching. Or so I thought. He's actually fishing something out of his pack—yet again—

and when I look closely I realize it's a v-scroll. He hands it to me, and I take it from him, my hands still stiff from the cold.

"What is this?"

"Coordinates," he responds. I wait for more, but he doesn't bother to offer any information as to what those coordinates mean or why they might be important.

"What do I do with it?" I ask.

"Put it in your pack and seal it up. Don't lose it."

"What do these 'coordinates' have to do with anything?" I demand impatiently. He turns what I by now recognize as his "disapproving" face to me and responds slowly and deliberately.

"Coordinates typically indicate a destination. I suggest that when we disembark and find land, you and Soren find your way to the location marked by those coordinates as quickly as possible." He hands me the vial. "Drink." I chug my two swallows and pass the vial off to Soren. Soren looks lost in the horizon, squinting at something as though he can't quite see. After a few minutes, he takes his sips, and then caps the bottle and hands it back to Chan-Yu. But then he points beyond the prow of the boat.

"Shoreline," he says. "Not far off." I follow his finger and see the trees arising out of the misty morning, and I can dimly make out the hovercraft waiting to cart the goods the rest of the way by land.

"Why do we have to swim?" I ask, miffed and not enthusiastic about the idea of getting back into the frigid water.

"Would you rather walk down the loading bay?" Chan-Yu asks without even looking at me. I frown. I don't want to admit it, but he's right. There's no way for us to get off the boat without the crewmembers noticing us, especially now that it's broad daylight. I avert my eyes out to the sea, glaring at nothing. The idea of getting wet and cold all over again is not appealing, but we don't have a choice. I strip off my clothes and stuff them in my pack like last time, and in minutes Soren and I are naked—again—and ready to go.

"Now," Chan-Yu says, "it's time." Then he abruptly stands up off the edge of the lifeboat and hops up and into the air, over the side of the boat. Soren and I rush to the side, watching as Chan-Yu drops soundlessly into the water. There's a moment of silence between us as we contemplate this.

"What the fuck? Do I have to do that, too?" Chan-Yu's head bobs to the surface, and he waves at us to follow him in.

"Looks like," Soren responds.

"Why can't we take the damn ladder?" I grump.

"Because then we'd have to get back on the deck, Remy," Soren says condescendingly. "Would you like to alert the crewmembers to our presence? It's broad daylight. They'd catch us in an instant."

Shit.

"You go first," Soren says. "That way I can push you if you need an extra incentive."

"Oh, please," I sniff putting every ounce of disdain I can muster into that *please.* "I don't need a push." But inside my heart is pounding so fast I wonder if I'm going to go into cardiac arrest. I probably will when I hit the water. It's got to be at least a ten-meter drop. I've never jumped from anything nearly this high without a parachute or a magnetic line in my hands. The waves are roiling and foamy, and I'm feeling sick to my stomach just thinking about it. I shoulder my pack ferociously, determined not to be a coward in front of Soren and Chan-Yu. I stand on the edge of the lifeboat and take a deep breath, trying not to think about how high up we are, how strong the wind is, or how cold the water will be. Would Tai have been able to do this? I wonder. *Tai was always adventurous. She would have loved it. She would have done it in a second.* I close my eyes. *Could Vale do it? Can I do it?*

"Oh, for God's sake, Remy," Soren swears exasperatedly. I feel a light push in the small of my back and I yelp as I lose my balance and fall off. Everything in the world comes to an abrupt halt as I try to right myself, to make sure I don't fall flat against the surface of the water. I flip over in the air and narrow myself into a dive. The water approaches slowly at first and then faster and faster, too fast and then finally with a sharp *pop* everything is icy and dark.

I could have killed him.

When he came up for air, I wanted to drown him, but he was laughing so hard he got a stitch in his side, and I actually had to swim over to him to prevent him from drowning. So instead of killing him, I guess I saved him, but we decided to call it even.

We followed Chan-Yu as we swam towards the beach, but then all hell broke loose. The sirens on the ship started blaring and the emergency lights started flashing. We weren't sure if they had spotted us or if something else went wrong, but either way we panicked. Chan-Yu shouted something at us about the coordinates, but we couldn't hear him over the waves and the sirens. He took off swimming towards the shoreline, and neither Soren nor

I could keep up with him. We watched helplessly as he sprinted towards the port, knowing we couldn't—and shouldn't—follow him in that direction. He disappeared from view and we haven't seen him since.

Now, I can barely feel my feet, my fingers are numb, and I can't stop shivering. But I'm warming up as we move, running in a half crouch, trying to make ourselves less visible in the light of day. We stopped long enough to slip on our clothes, and then took off again. Our black clothes were helpful last night, but now we stick out against the dense vegetation and patches of sand. We don't know if they're following us or not, but there's enough commotion in the distance that we know we can't stop moving. We keep running, tracking along the water's edge, hoping the waves will wash away our footprints. The beach is littered with driftwood and the detritus of abandoned boats that have washed ashore over the years. Keeping the beaches clean isn't a priority on this side of the lake. Besides the few harbors near the factory towns and Farms, it's been a no-man's land for a hundred years.

We hear yelling carrying over the water, and a dog barks in the distance. A boom echoes out, and we drop to the ground, panicked. Quiet. Breathing hard. The dog barks again, and we look at each other.

"Chan-Yu?" I whisper.

He stares into the distance. "If it is, we can't help him."

I grab his arm. "Maybe he's helping us."

He scrambles to his knees and then crouches in the sand. "If he's buying us time, then we better not disappoint. You ready to run?"

"Yeah. But where do we go?" I whisper. The whining sirens are still audible in the distance—we're not far enough away. Who knows when they will come upon us and drag us back to the capital, to Corine's waiting arms and Philip's instruments of torture? Or will they just execute us on the spot?

"The coordinates," Soren responds. "Whatever they are, they sound important. Get out the v-scroll."

I pull out the small, thin filament paper and unroll it. It's blank. I stare at it for a few seconds as Soren and I lie in the mud and wait to see if something will happen. When nothing changes and the paper remains stubbornly empty, I swear.

"Why couldn't he have just told us the damn coordinates?" I mutter, but as the words slip out my mouth, the scroll animates and the nanoparticles begin rearranging themselves, dispersing throughout the paper in a seemingly random pattern. It must have been voice activated, I realize, and I wonder how Chan-Yu got a sample of my vocal pattern to code to the v-scroll. After a few seconds, the picture comes into focus. Chan-Yu's "coordinates" don't look anything like coordinates at all. It's a map. There's the port behind us, along with the lakeshore, a sketch of the forest terrain at our side, what appears to be a river, and a spot along the river marked by the word OSPREY, whatever that means. The name sounds ominous. But it's the only definitive marking on the map, aside from the port, and it looks like our destination.

"Is that where we need to go?" Soren asks.

"I guess. Looks like it's our only choice. We need to get moving before they send drones up and down the coastline." Soren nods his assent. I scan the v-scroll quickly to make sure I know where we're going, and then roll it up and stuff it back into my pack. I seal it up and together we head down along the coast in the direction of the Osprey.

✿

Several kilometers later, we arrive at the mouth of a river. We'd long since given up running, as the fatigue from the night before came back with a fury and the adrenaline of the chase dissipated. The noises of pursuit have faded completely. If Chan-Yu helped to provide a diversion, he'd done his job well. There's no way to tell if we're being followed by drones, but I suppose if we were, we'd already be dead.

According to the map, the Osprey site is downriver a ways, and if the map is at all to scale, it's probably at least fifteen kilometers further. My heart sinks. I'm starving, and Soren looks equally downtrodden. We haven't eaten anything but Chan-Yu's nut bars in close to three days now.

"We have to eat something," he says quietly.

"Know how to fish?" I mutter. An idea suddenly occurs to me. I shrug my pack off my back and break the watertight seal, checking to see if Chan-Yu put any food in there for us. There's two more nut bars, several full water bottles, and a small pocketknife, but much to my dismay, that's all there is. Soren's pack is similarly equipped. With a sinking heart, I unwrap the bars and devour them both in seconds. I crack open one of the water bottles and drain half of it as Soren does the same. It feels amazing to have something in my stomach, but when I'm done, I realize how ravenous I really am.

"Didn't he know how hungry we'd be?" I grumble.

"Maybe he only had so much Outsider food, and he knew we wouldn't eat anything from the Sector. He probably gave us all he had."

That thought doesn't make me any happier—or less hungry.

"Maybe there'll be food waiting at the Osprey?" Soren says hopefully.

Maybe someone's waiting to kill us at the Osprey, I think, but I recognize that thought as irrational and push it away. "I wish you had your knife." The hunger is overpowering.

"Even if I did, we can't make a fire here; we're still too close to the port. So we couldn't eat anything I killed. We need to keep going. Let's find out what's at the Osprey."

The bars give us enough energy to keep moving, and we trudge along in silence, chilly but grateful for the sun's warmth. I keep my eyes on the ground, looking for anything that might be edible but finding nothing worthwhile.

I find myself stumbling, hazy-eyed, aimlessly following Soren's lead. The minutes slide by in a fog, slowly turning into hours. Every step is like lifting a fifty-kilo weight attached to my feet, and by the time the sun is high in the sky, I might as well be delirious. I hope I don't start hallucinating again. That last time didn't turn out so well for us. But then again, maybe it did—after all, if Corine didn't want us dead, Chan-Yu might never have rescued us and we might still be stuck in that cell, starving and at the mercy of Philip and that ugly, old general. If we were still there, though, maybe they would have fed us by now.

"Remy." Soren's voice jolts me back to the present. "I think this is it." He's staring at the v-scroll—I don't remember giving it to him—and looking up and around every few seconds. I survey the little patch of river we're in. "This looks like the notch in the river the map indicates. There are three sharp bends before the Osprey site, and we've passed three bends." He's been counting? I come over to his side, and he holds the v-scroll down a little lower so I can see it. Standing at his side, it surprises me how tall he is. "I think this is where we are." He taps the map where the Osprey site is.

"Okay. So what's here?" He shrugs.

"I don't know. Let's have a look around; see if we can find anything."

He starts walking away from the river a bit, squinting at things on the ground and looking up into the trees. I have no idea what he's looking for, but I follow suit, peering around and exploring the spot. I examine various pieces of driftwood, the lapping water against the riverbank, and the stones that litter the water's edge. I pace downstream a bit, squinting at the trees, when something out of place catches my eye. It's grey and stony and blends in perfectly with the rock that it's perched on, but it looks more like paper. I edge closer and look at it hesitantly, afraid to touch it in case it triggers a bomb or something. It's nothing like the color of a normal v-scroll, but the fibers look the same, and it's certainly too thin and too regular to be anything found in nature. Tiny flecks of red dot the filament—blood?

"Hey, Soren," I shout. "Check this out." He's at my side in seconds, and together we examine the strange paper. "Should we touch it?" I ask nervously.

"Why not?" he says, and lifts the rock that's tamping it down, preventing it from blowing away. As he does, just like with Chan-Yu's v-scroll, the fibers and filaments come to life. This time words, not images, materialize on the map.

To the Resistance fugitives,

I'm sorry I couldn't meet you in person. Chan-Yu instructed me to prepare the next stage for your journey, and though I hoped to be able to do that personally, that is not to be. The boat I had planned to bring for you is more than a day's journey by foot downriver, but now you have no choice. Follow the river and you'll find the boat. Once you're there, the river will lead you safely down in the direction of the nearest Resistance base. There's a more-detailed map on the boat that will help you navigate there. The best I've been able to do for you is leave a tent and a bow in the hopes that one will provide shelter and the other food.

I'm sorry I wasn't able to do more.

Best of luck. I hope we may meet sometime in the future.

Osprey

"What kind of a name is Osprey?"

Is that *really* Soren's first thought? "Who cares?" I hiss. "Let's find the bow." Food is all I can think about.

We start to canvass the area, but this time the search is easy. A little ways up, hidden behind an enormous tree, is a small pack containing the tent and a few pears. Leaning against the tree next to it is a beautiful wood-carved bow, a magnificent thing that I hope desperately Soren can use. I've only ever used the composite ones we practiced with back at base, and those look completely different. There are only three arrows, so we'll have to be careful not to lose them.

Soren suggests we keep tracking downriver so we don't waste time finding this boat. My thoughts are on food, and I insist we try to at least kill something before we continue.

"No. We don't have time. Let's eat these and keep going; we don't have time to hang out and hunt."

I am silent. He's right. But I'm hungry.

Soren hands me a pear. I bite into it hungrily; it is perfectly ripe and juice spurts out and trickles down my wrist. After one particularly noisy slurp, I briefly avert my attention from my own fruit and turn to look at him. He has juice all over his chin and mouth and it's dripping down onto his jaw. I can't help but break out into laughter.

"What?" he demands.

"You look ridiculous. You're covered in pear juice. There's even a seed stuck to your chin," I laugh, and reach to flick it off. He recoils at first from the unexpected gesture, but I get my fingertips to the seed and gently wipe it off. He looks at me with an expression so peculiar that I worry I've offended him.

"Sorry," I say quickly.

"No, it's fine." He looks like he wants to say something else, but instead he bites into the second pear, more cautiously this time, staring at me. I keep eating, but his eyes are relentless. When he finishes, he wipes his face off on his shirtsleeve.

"Remy, I—" He stops and stares morosely at the ground.

"What?" Suddenly my heart is pounding. Why?

"I don't know, I just—fuck." He stands up and glances around, looking everywhere but at me. "We need to move. It's already almost high noon. We need to get as far away from here as possible by nightfall. I don't want to be exposed to any drones while we're sleeping." I stare at him as he paces.

He grabs the bow and the few arrows and stalks off, and I am left wondering what on earth he was about to say. I decide it's best not to worry about it now. I jump up and stuff the tent into my pack—it's practically featherweight so there's plenty of room—and follow his footsteps into the forest.

We track through the woods slowly and quietly, keeping the sounds of the river close to our left as we head south. Soren leads, bow at the ready, looking for something to shoot at, but it's clear neither of us are any good at this. Our footsteps crackle through the underbrush every few seconds, and anything big enough to shoot probably has the good sense to stay far away from us. I'm not convinced we'll be able to do anything with the bow at all. I've never been hunting before, and even though I know Soren's been out on a few excursions back at base, I have no idea whether he's ever killed anything or not. I probably would have heard about it if he had.

With dark thoughts of starvation echoing through my mind, Soren and I shuffle along through the day without much in the way of words. He stops at one point and holds his fingers to his lips, staring at something I can't quite see. He points wordlessly through the trees, and I see it—a small deer, frozen in place. Behind me I can hear the river rushing, but otherwise everything is perfectly quiet. I don't dare to breathe. Soren silently pulls back the bow and takes aim, and I watch him, tensing every muscle in my body, hoping he will make the shot. He stretches the bow a little father and then releases the arrow. I hear the *zing* as the arrow whistles off the bowstring and my eyes jump to the animal—which is bounding away into the woods, unharmed.

I swear silently and heave a deep breath. Soren heads off dejectedly to find his arrow, and then we track back to the water.

The rest of the day passes uneventfully, and we see no more animals worth shooting at. My stomach starts to grumble more and more as we walk along. Daylight is short this time of year, and dusk settles in quickly. As the sun sinks below the treetops to our right, we know we have to stop. We're exhausted, anyway, from the lack of sleep over the last few days and the emptiness in our bellies. We don't want to risk being exposed to drones from the air or being eaten by wild animals in the forest, so we opt for a site just away from the riverbank, shaded by trees and tucked behind some big rocks. Soren immediately starts gathering firewood.

"What are you doing?" I demand.

"Fire, Remy. For heat."

"You want to alert anyone in the area to our presence?"

"There's no one around. It'll be fine. We need to stay warm."

I shake my head vigorously.

"No. That tent will be well-insulated and there are heating packs and blankets in our packs." I am firm and defiant. "If we had something that needed cooking, that would be a different matter, but we're not going to risk bringing unfriendly eyes down on us just for a little comfort."

Soren narrows his eyes at me, frowning. After a few seconds he turns back into the forest, maybe for a last shot at finding something worth shooting at.

I finish setting up the tent—which is so simply and elegantly designed it almost pops up out of the air without any assistance—and it turns out my warnings against fire were well-justified. The tent isn't just insulated; it also has heating fibers woven throughout. Little fibers that use thermotunneling technology, the same way Chan-Yu's heat gel did. Not long after the tent is up, Soren and I are snuggling together again, warm and toasty, and the sky outside is plastered with stars.

Soren does a strange thing then—before he closes his eyes and rolls over, he gives me a little kiss on the forehead and says, "Goodnight, Remy," leaving me feeling as baffled as I did this morning when I woke him up. My wonderment doesn't last long, though. I'm asleep in seconds.

I wake up the next morning to a dim yellow light trickling through my eyelids. The air in my nose is humid but clean and crisp, and as I realize that Soren's body is pressed against mine, one arm slung across my chest, an odd feeling washes over me, a brightness and an energy that takes me a few minutes to place because it's been so long since I felt it: happiness. The rejuvenation that's come from getting a good night's worth of warm, undisturbed sleep is overwhelming, and I can't resist the urge to start moving. I crawl out from under Soren's enormous body and stretch. I open the tent flap and feel a burst of chilly air across my face, refreshing me. The light is pale in the distance but yellow, and my mood brightens even further at the prospect of another sunny day.

"Soren," I call. He stirs inside the tent. "Soren, it's beautiful out here. Let's go. We need to find that boat."

My stomach is growling, but Soren is equally energetic when he gets moving, and we pop the tent back down into its place and pack it up. We head down along the riverbank, energized from sleep and not bothering to hunt today—we're hoping we'll find the boat sooner rather than later. But as high noon approaches and we still haven't found it, we're starting to get nervous. My belly feels like a sinkhole. I'm surprised it hasn't started to devour the rest of my body yet. I imagine eating the leaves on the trees or trying to grab a fish out of the river with my bare hands when the dark thought occurs to me that we might have somehow missed the boat.

"What if someone else took it?" I mutter anxiously to Soren as I brush against his side, briefly outpacing him. "What if we never find it?"

"It'll be there, Remy," he says in his calm way, as though he's looked into the future and seen that the boat will be waiting for us.

"What if it isn't?"

"It will be." His tone says *hush*. I continue in silence, dark thoughts seeping into my brain again like ink spilling across paper.

But then I trip abruptly and am pitched forward into a pillow of muck. Soren bursts out into laughter when I come up, covered in mud and no doubt looking like a bog monster, until he sees what it was I tripped on: some sort of rope lying on the ground, half-buried in the mud. He stares at it for a minute and then looks out at the water, and I follow his eyes. Something about the reflection of the water doesn't quite look right, as though there's a piece of the river missing. Instead of offering a hand to help me up, Soren stoops over next to me and grabs the rope, and as he picks it up, the missing piece of the river shifts and changes, and a boat materializes as if out of thin air.

"Cloaking," Soren whispers, awed. "Deactivated by touching the fibers of the rope. Otherwise, perfectly hidden." It's a little thing, not much bigger than six meters end-to-end, but there's a roof over the top and a pretty little deck, and it looks to be in pristine condition. There's even a name painted on the side: *The Zephyr.*

I pull myself to my feet and head to the water's edge, splashing my face and wiping the muck off my clothes. Soren, meanwhile, hauls on the rope, pulling the boat in closer to shore. "The anchor must weigh fifty kilos," he complains, and I catch myself admiring the contours and shadows of his body as he works. Soon, I hear the soft scrape of the hull against the sandy river bank.

On board, we find more than we could have hoped for. A bed, a stove for cooking, filtered water. A proper toilet and an actual tiny shower. Cured meats, jars of jam, dried fruits and vegetables, cheese, even a stale loaf of bread that Soren and I tear into and smother with raspberry preserves. We declare ourselves in heaven. In fact, we eat an entire round of cheese between the two of us. There's also a much more sophisticated map on another V-scroll. This one is in 3D; it shows us exactly where to disembark along the river and how to navigate through the woods to get to the nearest Resistance base. The only thing they didn't think to include was some sort of communications device. I wish for anything we had a radio of some sort, something to get through to the Director and Eli and my parents and just let them know we're alive. But there's nothing. I wonder how they could have forgotten such a key item. Or why they chose not to provide it.

Then I see it, another note from Osprey. This one, too, is bloodstained, though this time the droplets are much bigger and more obvious.

Hope this helps. No comm. devices for fear of alerting S drones. Keep to the riverbanks & keep cloaking on when possible. —Osprey

The bloodstains are worrying. I can only hope this Osprey person is still alive. But there's nothing we can do but to take advantage of what he's left for us.

Soren and I immediately set about trying to figure out how to work the ship, which runs on a computerized system neither of us has ever encountered before. Instead of having an interface to talk to or give commands, there's a slew of dials, knobs, and levers that seem to do things that have to be turned or twisted or flipped in a certain order. Soren figures out fairly quickly how to set the engines in motion and how to reel in the anchor, and we head off downriver. The rest of the controls remain a mystery, though. Eventually I realize that a few of them regulate the internal temperature of the boat. We can't figure out which ones control the cloaking device, which is troubling. Besides the engines, that's probably the most important thing. But there will be time for that later. Meantime, Soren cranks on the water heater, and in a half an hour I'm standing in a steaming hot shower and washing all the grime off of me from the last week—the sweat, the torture, the cold, the misery—and when I come out of the shower, I feel like a whole new person.

23 — VALE

I shrug my dinner jacket on over my shoulders and look at myself in the mirror. I'm in my bedroom—not at my flat, but at my parents' house, the chancellor's estate. My hair is still sticking out over my ears, so I drag a comb through the brambles to try to tame it. The picture of composure, elegance, and confidence. Marvelously deceptive. How fortunate I am that no one can see what thoughts lay beneath my pressed evening wear and calm visage.

I put my hand into my jacket pocket to check that it's still there. The compass. I found it earlier this morning when I was going through my room to see if there was anything else I wanted to take. Tucked away in a box I hadn't opened in years. It was Tai's; before that, her grandfather's. Tai used to carry it around like a talisman, and I always admired it. It's a beautiful old thing, definitely pre-Famine craftsmanship. Just like Soren's knife. It's encased in gold, and the initials engraved on the bottom are elegant and stately. Remy gave it to me after Tai died, since I had been friends with Tai as well. She insisted Tai would have wanted me to have it, even though I protested. Of course, all that was before Remy decided she hated me. *For good reason.*

"Valerian?"

I start and turn around sharply, shoving the compass back into my pocket. My mother stands in the doorway, looking at me with an odd, furrowed expression on her face. I don't want her to see the compass. When the Alexanders disappeared and public opinion turned against them, I knew my mother wouldn't like it if I had an old heirloom of theirs hanging around. That's when I hid it. And I certainly don't want her to know I've got it in my pocket now.

"Are you all right?" she asks.

"Yeah, of course," I say. I want to ask them about—about everything, but I'm not going to confront them until we get into the airship. That way, if things go to hell, I can get out and dodge through the throng of people at the Solstice Celebration.

I look her over—she is dressed in a floor-length, deep purple evening gown with diamonds sewn into the v-neck. Even at forty-five, she's beautiful. I smile falsely and look into her dark brown eyes, her heavy lashes, and wonder how many crimes those lashes have batted away in the last twenty years.

"You look beautiful tonight," I say, though I doubt she picks up on the sarcasm in my voice.

"Why, thank you, dear," she says, coming over to kiss me on the cheek and straighten my collar. "The airship is ready."

I look back at the mirror one last time. "I'm ready, too."

I am ready, but my mother has no idea what I mean by that. Stashed inside my Sarus are two lightweight, waterproof backpacks with several sets of spare clothes, a week's worth of food, a water purification bottle, our Bolts, a two-person tent, a month's supply of mission-ready contact lenses, a Geiger counter, several lengths of thin, lightweight rope, and a hunting knife. And, of course, I've also got Soren's knife, the one I took from him during the raid. Together, Miah and I have enough supplies for a week in the Wilds. With any luck, the celebrations, the speeches, the hashish, the alcohol, and the subsequent hangovers will give us at least eight hours to get as far away from the city as we can. We have no plans, no destination, and nowhere to go except out. Jeremiah wants to head for the nearest Resistance base, but I've been lobbying for tracking down an Outsider encampment. Either way, it doesn't really matter. After tonight, we'll be hunted. Traitors. Just like Remy and Soren.

My mother smiles and turns to leave, and I give my unruly hair one last pat-down before I follow her out. I take a deep breath. *Can I do this?*

I trace her steps, walking behind her as we head out the back door to where the airship bay is. My heart is pounding, and I wonder if I'll be able to bring myself to ask the questions I need to ask. Or to talk to them at all. At this point, I'm not even sure I can look them both in the eyes.

Outside the night is chilly and crisp, but golden lights atop the buildings have already begun to glow, marking the solstice. At midnight, hundreds of thousands of candles will be lit outside of individual homes, illuminating the whole city as a tribute to the Blackout that set off the tailspin of destruction that almost wiped humans off the planet. That night, almost two hundred years ago, neighbors and small communities banded together to support each other and lit candles for light on a night of global darkness. We call it the "Blackout." They called it the "Apocalypse." Now, we memorialize it with candles, golden lights, and an enormous party.

I step into the chancellor's official airship and follow my mother to the lounge. My heart catches in my throat as my father glances over and smiles at me. My palms are sweaty, and I'm sure my cheeks are flushed. My father either doesn't notice or chooses not to mention it. Instead, he just clasps my arm and says, "Looking sharp, Vale."

I give him a shaky smile in return and sit down across from him. He beckons my mother to sit next to him, and I try to keep my smile plastered on, even as it threatens to dissolve and run off my face like water.

Neither of them have mentioned my temporary removal from duty two nights ago, although I was reinstated as director of the Seed Bank Protection Project once Aulion was satisfied there was nothing linking me to Remy and Soren's escape. Despite my few mishaps getting out of the OAC building and my suspicious exit of Sector HQ during a Code Red, no one has yet managed to connect me to the security breaches. Reluctantly, Aulion reported to my father that there was no evidence of my involvement. When my father first learned the two prisoners had escaped, he was enraged. I've never seen him so furious. He demanded I conduct a full investigation into their disappearance and that we dispatch soldiers and drones to every corner of the Sector to search for them. His rage was bearable. It's my mother's silence that eats at me. She hasn't said a word on the subject since I heard her speaking to Chan-Yu. Aside from Jeremiah, only my mother and I know that Chan-Yu was supposed to kill Remy and Soren that night. Only we know how thorough his betrayal of the Sector was. And no one—yet—knows that I was complicit as well.

But that's about to change.

I don't have much time. It's only a few kilometers from the chancellor's estate to the Solstice Ball, and it will only take a few minutes for the airship to make the trip. I clear my throat nervously, and my father's happy smile changes to one of mild concern.

"Are you okay, Vale? Your face is flushed," he says, leaning forward to get a better look at me. "You don't have a fever, do you? Hell of a night to get sick." My mother instinctively reaches out to feel my forehead as if I were a toddler.

"No, I'm fine." Some part of me wants to brush her hand away, but another wants to hold it, press it against my cheek one last time. The airship's engines thrum beneath me, and a few seconds later we lift off. I close my eyes briefly, and Demeter whispers soothingly in my ear.

"You owe them this, Vale." I nod, trying not to grimace. I wish I could have her by my side as Jeremiah and I make our own escape tonight, but her networking capabilities won't work once we get outside the Sector. And since she's just a tool to link to the OAC database, for all intents and purposes, she doesn't exist without networking. I'm keeping the earpiece with me though, just in case. Maybe just for nostalgia's sake.

"Mom," I say, my eyes still closed, forcing the words bodily out of my chest. "I was the one who broke into OAC headquarters the other night." I open my eyes. My parents are staring at me dully, as though without recognition. "I overheard your conversation with Chan-Yu." I can't bring myself to say the second part: *when you ordered him to kill Remy and Soren.* Suddenly my mother's face is frozen, too still, too stony. "And ... I know about Tai, too." I think of the compass pressing against my chest, tucked into my jacket. "And Hawthorne." I turn to look at my father. "Were you a part of all this, Dad?"

A vague, uncomfortable smile surfaces on his face briefly, and his eyes flit back and forth between me and my mother. "A part of what, son?"

"A part of the plan to kill—"

"Stop!" Her voice is low and hot, her body is tense, her hands wrapped so tightly around each other that her knuckles are bone white. Her face, normally so serene and beautiful, is knotted and afraid. But her next words come out in a whisper: "Don't tell him."

I gape at her. No words come to me. The smile has fallen off of my father's face. He squeezes my mother's knee a little too tightly, and his jaw clenches.

"What are you talking about?"

"I'm sorry, Mom," I respond quietly, meeting her eyes. But I say no more, because nothing more has to be said. She knows. She knows what I've done and why. Sadness is scrawled across her pale face, her eyes are downcast, and tiny beads of sweat dot her lip. She sets her mouth in a firm, unhappy line and nods at me slightly. It's an acknowledgment, maybe, that we've found ourselves on opposite sides of a bitter decision. But to her left, my father's eyes are narrowed. They are a window to a brewing storm and for the first time in my life I recognize the steely, grey anger that makes people cower before him, that makes people afraid. He pulls his hand away from her knee as she squeezes her eyes shut, and tears sparkle beneath her lashes. She won't look at him. *He doesn't know.*

My father leans back and casually stretches his arm out behind my mother's shoulders. His voice is calm but with a harsh edge. "One of you is going to tell me exactly what you're talking about." The threat attached to that statement goes unspoken. But I'm not going to further incriminate my mother—she's done that well enough herself.

Below us, the airship extends its landing gear, and I know the door will soon open. I summon up another smile from the depths and think *maybe this will save her.* "Dad, we can talk about it tomorrow, after the party. I'm sorry I brought it up." The airship settles down, and I hear the engines shut off. "Forget it," I say. "Let's just have a good time."

"Too late." He stands, straightens his tie, holds his hand out for my mother, and with a twisted look on his face, says: "Everyone smile for the cameras."

The door whooshes open, and I step down off the airship into the cool winter air and let the flashbulbs drown my senses. I pose, laughing, answering idiotic questions, as my mother steps out delicately from the ship and I offer my hand to her, the tears gone already, wiped away, replaced by the cool confidence she always shows the cameras. I kiss her on the cheek and everyone wants a recording, microphones are shoved into our faces, careless eyes and dull people, and it seems as though maybe sound has disappeared from the world and we are living in a vacuum. My mother speaks less than usual and her mask falters once or twice, her lips quiver, her eyelashes blink away liquid that shouldn't be there, but then the chancellor steps out of his airship, and all eyes turn to him. My mother leans in and whispers in my ear, so quietly I almost don't hear, "I'm sorry, Vale, but it had to be done."

There is nothing to say to that. I turn and leave them behind. I stalk away from the cameras, the photographers, the politicians who are now swarming the dock waiting to greet the chancellor and the director general. I'm sure the photographers will be confused about my abrupt departure, but I don't care. I turn away from it all and head into the party, looking for sympathetic faces, searching for people who don't believe that murder is the only answer.

For the governors of the Okarian Sector, high-level researchers and administrators at the OAC, and the very, very wealthy citizens, the Solstice Celebration is held every year at a building called Kingsland. It's an ancient building that managed to survive the Religious Wars and even the Famine Years, despite that it had already been over three centuries old on the day of the Blackout. In our history classes, we learn that Kingsland is actually where the Okarian Sector was properly born. The soldiers and the governors who fought for unity in the Sector and established an aggressive plan to colonize and develop farms in the surrounding areas held their meetings here. Eventually, it became the temporary home for the new government, but it was too small to last for long. Now, restored using modern and recovered technology, we use it for weddings, celebrations, inaugurations, and the like.

Inside, the ballroom is beautiful. Polished black-and-white marble floors are complemented by glowing chandeliers that appear to be floating. The dome is an enormous blue and green stained-glass window, and during the day the sunlight dances through it, shimmering in a way reminiscent of the sunlight playing off of the Great Sea to the east of us. The solemn austerity of the place is offset by thousands of colorful bouquets, all arranged with a bright sunflower in the center.

A waiter approaches with a plate of fresh oysters and scallops in tiny glasses, but I have no appetite tonight. I wave her away and scan the room looking for Jeremiah. I spot him off to one side of the dance floor, talking to Moriana. I'm just heading off in his direction when I'm cornered by a reporter waving his camera in his hands.

"Valerian! Could I get a photo?" He grins at me wildly, flashing two rows of absurdly perfect teeth. I give him a thin-lipped smile and turn towards him, knowing that I am already being watched. Any suspicious activity on my part will make it impossible for me and Jeremiah to get away. The light flashes several times, and then he leans around the side of it. "So, Vale, how do you like your directorship?" This must be one of those rogue photographers, some no-name working for a low-budget publication, trying to get gossip on the politics and celebrities of the Sector.

"It's great. Really great." I stare around the room, stretching up on my tiptoes, looking for someone to pull me away from this event.

"Any big plans for the future?"

Does getting away from you as fast possible count?

He ducks behind his camera again and the flash almost blinds me.

"Oh, yes, but I'm sorry, I can't talk about it. It's all classified information." I head off to the left, but he's back in my face in seconds.

"Do you feel like you're living up to your parents' expectations for you, Vale?"

"Meeting and exceeding," I say breezily, trying to dodge past him. Suddenly, I get an unexpected blessing: To the right of the reporter, I spot Linnea Heilmann, dressed in a marvelous blue floor-length gown, watching us with a faint, almost hopeful smile on her lips. Thinking fast, I give a broad smile to the reporter.

"I'm so sorry, err—buddy—but I've just spotted my girlfriend. Would you like to get some photos of us together?" As the reporter's mouth drops open, no doubt thinking of what price he could get for breaking the story that Valerian Orleán has a mysterious girlfriend, I push past him and boldly stride towards Linnea, smiling at her brightly. She looks just as surprised by my enthusiasm as the reporter, but hers shows only in slightly arched eyebrows and an upward curl of her lip. She stands stock-still, watching me as I approach, and half the guests I pass on my way turn to get a glimpse as well. I reach out to take

Linnea's hand and I bring it delicately to my lips, wondering what this will cost me. She accepts and smiles at me, wiping all traces of surprise from her face. After all, she must have known that I couldn't hold out against her charms for too long. Indeed, how could I not? I'm sure she's just wondering why it took me so long.

"Linnea, you are without a doubt the most beautiful woman in the Okarian Sector tonight," I say, surprised to find that I mean those words sincerely. I rest my hand on the small of her back, and a quick glance around confirms there are at least a dozen onlookers. The flash on the reporter's camera is going off over and over again. Linnea always was a media darling.

"Thank you, Vale," she says, giving me a seductive smile. "You look quite dashing yourself." I wonder how long it will take my mother to find out I'm "dating" Linnea, and if that will make her think I've somehow forgiven her for her crimes. Remembering Linnea's connection to Corine helps remind me who I'm dealing with. Linnea's hardly trustworthy in this game.

"I'm sure everyone in here is looking forward to finally seeing us together," I say, out of the corner of my mouth. I can't quite keep the sarcasm out of my voice, and Linnea looks up at me sharply and her smile fades a little. She's not an idiot. I feel bad using her as a distraction, but I'm committed to this ruse now, and she's going to figure out what I'm up to sooner rather than later.

A few minutes later, Linnea and I have fended off several reporters, and I have steered her to the dance floor for our first "formal dance as a couple," as she put it to one of the reporters. The chilly edge in her voice told me she knew something else was up. As the music begins and I lead her river of blond hair around the other couples, her piercing blue eyes slice my façade to pieces. She sighs enormously, and I almost laugh—she always did have a flair for the dramatic.

"Okay, as happy as I was when I thought you might actually want to spend the evening in my company, I can see now that you want something from me."

Guilt resurfaces in my gut. Am I legitimately hurting her? Am I no better than my parents, manipulating people to suit my needs? I put my hand on her hip and try to conjure up a look of sincerity and concern. Out of the corner of my eye, I see Jeremiah and Moriana staring at us, obviously disturbed by this turn of events.

"I do want to spend the night in your company, Linnea. But bigger things are happening than you and me tonight." Her eyebrows arch and her eyes widen. "I'm sorry if you think I'm using you, so I'm going to be completely frank. I need a favor." Her face settles into a cold, judgmental stare.

"What makes you think I have any interest in helping you?"

"Maybe you don't. But I can give you something in return."

"It had better be worth my while."

"It'll more than compensate for the tragedy of letting Valerian Orleán slip through your fingers tonight," I respond, maybe too harshly. I'm not happy about the possibility that, to her, I really am, as Moriana said, *just a few rungs from the top of the power ladder*, and Linnea is using me just as much as I'm using her. We are pawns in each other's games. "You were asking about Elijah Tawfiq...."

She stops moving. Still as a statue, eyes as wide as the sea. *Does she really care about him that much?* If she does, I'll feel a lot less guilty about not going along with her romantic whims. "I can tell you where he is, but in return, you have to provide a diversion for me tonight."

"Eli?" She shakes herself back into action, and I can see her mask slide back into place after that brief moment of astonishment. "And what, precisely, would I do with that information?"

I shrug. I know she's already gone for it. I don't have to persuade her.

"What do I care? Use it to track him down, if you're still in love with him." Her mouth purses ever so slightly. "Or sell it to an interested buyer. You're a clever girl. I'm sure you can put valuable information like that to good use. If you cover for me—and don't even pretend that lying would be difficult for you—"

"What are you doing tonight," she interrupts, "that's so desperate you're willing to sell me highly classified information?"

"I can't tell you that, Linnea. I just need you to cover for me." Her eyes narrow. But when she responds, I know I've sold her.

"How do I know you'll follow through on your end of the bargain?" I pause. Good question. I haven't thought this through yet. Then again, I haven't thought any of it through. I'm playing this game moment by moment.

"You don't," I say. "You'll just have to trust me. But I'll give you something else. I don't want you to give some throwaway diversion—I want you to tell everyone we spent tonight together. That we slept together. That way you get both the big conquest and Eli's whereabouts, and if I don't follow through, at least you'll have the first part."

I feel her eyes flicker over my face. I'm sure she's wondering what on earth has driven me to this point. Of course, what she doesn't know is that neither of the things I'm offering mean anything to me anymore.

"Okay," she acquiesces, casually tossing her blonde hair over her shoulder.

"I'll do it. But I want you to prepare the message right now. Instruct your C-Link to send me a message at 0600 hours in the morning with all the available information on Eli's whereabouts." When I hesitate, she snaps. "Now, Vale!" I can see why she and my mother get along so well.

"Demeter," I say cautiously, looking around to make sure no one is eavesdropping. "Prepare a message to auto-send to Linnea Heilmann at 0600 hours in the morning. Include in the message all the information about the whereabouts of Elijah Tawfiq—" of course, she doesn't know that we don't know *exactly* where Elijah is, but I guess she'll find out in the morning, "—including last sightings, verified location, and association with the Resistance." I pause and look Linnea in the eyes, still speaking to Demeter. "Make the courriel untraceable. And make its release conditional upon Linnea's release of a public statement tonight between eleven and midnight saying that she's going home with me."

"Done," Demeter responds. "You've gone insane, haven't you?" I bite back a laugh. Strange how I will miss an AI program more than almost anyone else I know.

Linnea smiles at me with a trace of real happiness. She's won her prize. For a moment I almost allow myself to forget the game we're playing. She is beautiful, especially when she smiles. I find myself wishing that circumstances were different, that I really could spend the night with her, that we could genuinely enjoy each other's company. But I remind myself that if circumstances were different, I might not be about to run away from everything I've ever known. My mother might not be a murderer; Remy might still be here; Tai might still be alive. So many things could be different. So I smile back at Linnea and take the earliest opportunity to duck off the dance floor and find Jeremiah and Moriana, desperate to get away from this tragicomic masquerade.

When I find them, Jeremiah grabs my shoulder and glares at me. "What the hell are you doing?"

"You are so not going to go out with *her* … are you?" Moriana asks.

"I don't know; maybe I've decided I need a diversion." I look at Jeremiah. "After all, I think this is going to be a long night and declaring my undying love for Linnea might just be the thing I need to get everyone off my back." Jeremiah stares at me, his brows furrowed, mouth terse, his face creased in suspicion.

"Okay, I get it," he says finally.

Moriana punches him in the arm. "You can't seriously think it's okay for him to be hanging out with her?"

"No, I don't think that, but I do think it's time everyone stops telling Vale what to do."

"Well, she's bad news, and don't expect *me* to stop telling you that anytime soon."

I reach out and give her a hug. "You don't need to worry about me spending time with Linnea."

A pang of regret rolls through me. Moriana is my oldest friend. I hate deceiving her, and I hate leaving her behind. Miah and I debated whether or not we should tell Moriana, but ultimately we decided against it. First of all, she'd want to come with us, but Moriana Anderson in the Wilds? She'd hate it after day two. And second, she idolizes my mother. If Moriana continues working in Mom's lab, there's a chance she could learn something that would be valuable to us later. But only if she's not under any suspicion. Only if my mother is convinced that Moriana knows nothing about our disappearance. And that means we can't tell her. It almost broke Miah's heart to know that he'd be breaking hers. But it's the only answer, the only way to keep her safe.

"Now stop worrying about my love life. You two need to go have fun. Get out on the dance floor or find a dark corner. The evening will be over before you know it."

Moriana looks at me and then at Jeremiah whose face is set in a grim smile. "I'm not an idiot. What is going on with you two?"

He pulls her close and kisses the top of her head. "Nothing's going on except that I'm with the most beautiful, most intelligent, most amazing, most—"

"Okay, okay," Moriana laughs. "You've already told me that about a dozen times tonight." She pulls Miah toward the dance floor, and I watch them go and wonder what tomorrow will bring for all of us.

Left to wander the floor until my father gives the celebration address, I schmooze with politicians, ask researchers and professors for details on their work, and even do a few more photo ops with Linnea just to boost my alibi and keep her happy. I determinedly avoid being in my mother's presence, even in her line of sight. She makes no effort to find me, whether out of shame or fear of another confrontation. A few times I catch my father trying to corner me, but each time I manage to drag Linnea into the spotlight again, in front of the cameras, or to find some bigwig to talk to, making it impossible for him to confront me. But for the most part, he's too preoccupied to find me. There's too much else going on tonight.

In some small, superficial way, Linnea and I actually manage to enjoy each other's company, telling little jokes about General Aulion and Evander Sun-Zi, admiring the decorations, and commenting sarcastically on the absurd fashion pieces the partygoers have chosen for the evening. At one point she catches my eye and gives me a small, narrow smile, and I wonder if maybe I've misjudged her. Maybe we have more in common than I thought.

❀

About two hours later, I lean tiredly against one of the columns bordering the dance floor. The pianist picks out a slow song, and all I can think of is how his timing and rhythm is off—he's tripping over the harmony on the left hand, and while it doesn't sound awful, both Soren and I could play this song asleep.

I see Jeremiah and Moriana dancing together, her head against his shoulder. She barely comes up to his chin, and she looks tiny in his arms, like a fawn in a grizzly's embrace. His eyes are closed, and I can see his hand playing in her hair, coiling slender tendrils around his fingers. It hits me—for the first time, it truly hits me—that we're leaving. Maybe forever. And if not, whatever we come back to, it won't be the same. *We* won't be the same. I feel weak, hollowed out as if everything I've ever thought about myself has crumbled and wafted away like dust. I steady myself against the column behind me, leaning my head back and staring up at the ceiling. Flashes of memories dart through my mind like silver fish, strange and unfamiliar as though viewed through a distorted lens. Everything looks different now that I am leaving it all behind. But I can't stay. That much is clear. Not after what I've done. Not after what I've learned.

Suddenly the song is over, and a new song, excited, anticipatory, begins. It's the announcement that my father is about to begin his speech. The crowd turns towards the podium, set up at the very front of the great hall, and a spotlight trains on him as he ascends the dais, smiling and waving. He stands for a few seconds, grinning for the cameras before he begins. I wonder what it's costing him to keep his composure now.

"Friends, fellow citizens of Okaria," he starts at last, "We've gathered here tonight to celebrate another important milestone in the history of our Sector. Tonight is the one hundred and sixth Winter Solstice Celebration since the formal incorporation of the Okarian Sector, and tonight marks the beginning of a new year!" There are cheers and applause, loud, raucous noise, and as I look up at my father's strong, handsome face, I wonder who it really was who raised me to believe in the right thing, to treat people decently and fairly, and to believe in myself. What is in store for him and my mother? Will he feel just as betrayed as I do? Or is he guilty of crimes as terrible as hers?

"We are gathered here tonight for a ritual and a celebration. The solstice marks the beginning of a new growing season, and this year, that has a special significance: Thanks to the dedication of the Farm workers and the OAC scientists, this annum marks seven full years since the Sector has seen a death from starvation!" Huge roars of approval meet with ringing cheers at my father's triumphant announcement—after all, that's something that is definitely worthy of celebration.

"After the Religious Wars destroyed the old world, and the Famine Years consumed vast swaths of human civilization, we who have fought with our parents and our grandparents—and now our children—recognize how powerful a victory that is. And fought we have." Philip's expression turns grave and his eyes cloudy, as if remembering the battles himself. I fight the urge to roll my eyes. His acting skills clearly haven't been compromised, despite his anger and confusion from earlier. "We have fought to unify the Sector—to bring the northeastern quadrant together under a combined, cohesive system of government, so that we may work together to protect ourselves from threats from the outside and from starvation on the inside. We have fought every year to plant and grow enough food to feed every single citizen of this nation. We have fought to increase crop production and nutrient production through the dedicated work of our scientists." A smattering of applause.

I feel a light touch on my shoulder and turn to see Jeremiah.

"Now's the time. She's in the bathroom."

"—as we celebrate the solstice, we must remember the violent, tormented history that shadows our society and do everything in our power to prevent a—"

I close my eyes and shut out my father's words.

"Vale. Let's go," Jeremiah says. His jaw is set, his eyes steady and determined. "If we wait, we're going to miss our opportunity."

"You first," I mutter. "Take off your jacket and go out the service door." We'd both studied the Kingsland blueprints before packing today, just in case we had to dodge security staff or escape through a side route. "I'll tell Demeter to bring up the Sarus, and I'll meet you up there. But first, I'm going to put on a show with Linnea, and I don't want her to see the two of us together."

He nods and mutters a gruff *okay* and then disappears through the crowd.

"—never forget the deaths, the disease, the terror and the bloodshed behind us, and fight against those who would return us to those days—"

I catch Philip's subtle jab at the Resistance. *What would you think if you knew what I'm doing tonight, Father? Would you try me for treason? Starve and imprison me the way you did—the way we did—Remy and Soren?*

I catch Linnea and sweep her up for one final romantic kiss before I smile at her and whisper that she had damn well better uphold her end of the bargain. She pretends to look shocked at what I'm saying and then titters nervously. I hope everyone thinks I've invited her back to my flat tonight. How many layers of lies will I paint on my face? What would Remy think if she heard I'm sleeping with Linnea? She probably wouldn't care. I depart just as the crowd begins clapping at whatever charming statement the chancellor has just made. I slip out the service door, and as best as I can tell, everyone is too focused on watching and listening to my father's speech to pay any attention to me. I hear the door swing shut behind me and my father's words, the murmur of the crowded hall, and my former life fades behind me like a dissipating dream.

24 — VALE

We find the back staircase up to the airship bay and wind our way up to where Demeter has programmed the Sarus to land. While we wait, Jeremiah taps his feet nervously and glances anxiously around us, his eyes darting this way and that. For my part, I lean up against a metal pillar and wait calmly. Anxiety has left me. Everything I needed to do has been done, and now all that's left to do is leave.

"Did you talk to your parents, Vale?" Miah asks, making conversation as his eyes flit around.

"I did."

"What happened?"

"I don't really know." I close my eyes and pause before responding more completely. I don't want to talk about it, but I know Jeremiah deserves a response. I take a deep breath and then finish. "My dad didn't seem to know what I was talking about. But my mother—Corine—as good as admitted everything."

He stops looking around frenetically and stares at me. "But that means Philip could be innocent," he says. "Isn't that a good thing?"

I sigh. Now that we've escaped the noise and commotion of the ballroom, I feel like my mind has gone blank. Everything just is and I can't analyze why or how right now.

"I don't know. I'm not assuming anything. I was afraid of him, for a minute, in the airship." *All I know is that we need to get out.* Jeremiah nods brusquely and doesn't push me any further.

A few minutes pass in silence before I hear the thrum and the slightly tense air that indicates the Sarus is above us. She lands delicately, and as always, I can't help but smile when I see her. This morning, I flew to Jeremiah's apartment, and together we coursed the entire ship looking for tracking devices of any kind. Thank goodness for his engineering skills. He ran a diagnostic program on the ship's controls to make sure we could disable the navigation feature, by extension making it impossible for the ship to report our location to any Sector monitors or passing drones. Of course, that also means we'll have to pilot her manually. But we figured a minor traffic infraction would be no big deal in the heap of charges that will be leveled at us if we get caught.

I palm open the door and we climb in. Jeremiah scrolls through and initiates the necessary programs to deactivate the connection to the Sector navigation system.

"Excited?" I ask, mustering up a grin. I feel anything but excited, but I know he's looking forward to being able to fly. I ceded the controls to him earlier today. I start looking at the map of the city on the nav panel. "We should head west, I think," I say, offhand. We'd talked about which direction to head but hadn't made a decision.

"Why west?" Miah asks, glancing over his shoulder at me. I shrug.

"It's the fastest way out of Sector territory." I don't say the rest. *The Resistance is that way. The Outsiders are there.* "We'll figure it out. Let's just get out of the city first." Again, Miah doesn't push.

"Demeter," I say quietly, touching my fingertip to my C-Link. I've talked to her in front of Miah before, but it still feels weird. Jeremiah is determinedly not paying attention to me, as though he's giving me privacy.

"Yes, Vale?"

"I'll have to turn off my C-Link now so no one can track me. I don't know when I'll get to talk to you again. But I'm keeping the earpiece with me, in case I ever get to a place where I can bring you back."

"I know," she says, soothingly, lightly. "You'll be fine."

"It's not me I'm worried about," I say.

"Vale," she says, almost laughing at me. "I'm a part of the cloud. I'm just a series of electrical processes. They can't do anything to me." *Aren't we all just a series of electrical processes?*

"Okay. I'll talk to you when I can."

"Until then," she says, "be safe." I nod, trying not to acknowledge the absurdity of saying goodbye to a nonexistent being. I reach up and touch my ear, deactivating the device. *I'll get her back someday,* I think. Jeremiah settles into the seat to me and quickly powers up the ship to get us in the air. The Sarus starts to lift off the bay, accelerating past the Kingsland building, where the ballroom's enormous windows glimmer one last time before disappearing behind us.

"So," he asks, his tone falsely bright, "what's out there in the Wilds?" It's a good question. Even I'm not sure. I've spent precious little time outside our borders, and though I've read some reports on the state of the surrounding areas, the government has always seemed surprisingly unconcerned about the rest of the world.

"I don't really know. The western-most Okarian establishment is Windy Pines, a factory town. If I remember correctly, they specialize in nanotech. In the Wilds, I'm less sure. Most of the areas outside of the Farms and Sector borders have returned to their natural state. And I know Outsiders live out there, but I have no idea where, or how." Jeremiah gives me a sideways look as we cruise past Assembly Hall. "And, of course, the Resistance."

"You know, for being so high up in the government, you're surprisingly useless," he says, smirking.

"It's amazing, isn't it? Why they ever let me into a position of power...." I touch one of the controls to lower the opacity of the ship's exterior. The skin of the Sarus becomes translucent and we can see all around us as we fly.

"No wonder Aulion was constantly on your case."

"The man is truly wise," I say, trying to conjure up a laugh. But my heart isn't really in the joke, and I return my attention to the city brushing by us. The city we may never see again.

Tonight is a perfect night to be flying over the capital. All the streets are lit up by hundreds of thousands of individual candles, and from above it looks like a shifting, flickering ocean of light. We fly past pillars of light, buildings that have been allowed to leave on the electricity for the parties and celebrations. The city looks spectacular. It makes me think about what waits for us outside Okaria.

The lake is visible off in the distance, quiet and dark. I realize that out there, over the lake, is where the Resistance is located and where most of the Outsider sightings have been.

As if reading my thoughts, Jeremiah asks, "What's on the other side of the lake?"

"There's a factory town across, if you track northwest a little ways along the lakeshore. And two Farms, about fifty kilometers from the shore."

"We need to decide where we're going," he says, somewhat sharply.

"Let's just get outside the Sector first," I respond, not meeting his eyes. "Then we can check our maps, eat a bite of food, change clothes, and decide what's next." He nods silently, but I don't think he's happy about my indecision.

We fly westward in silence for a while. I presume Jeremiah is just as preoccupied with his thoughts as I am with mine. The lights from the city dim and diminish slowly, fading into the black background of night. Above us the stars are brilliant, illuminating the pathway of the sky just as the candles did in the city. The world suddenly seems much more expansive as the white-pink dome of stars becomes the defining feature of the landscape. Whether that's threatening or promising, I can't tell.

It's too dark to see much on the ground, but we can watch the landscape change through the ship's radar imaging. We watch the rolling, hilly fields below us give way to trees and marsh, and I realize we're already well outside the Sector's administration area—the onset of forest means the land isn't maintained or used by the Sector in any way. There are no real defined borders or lines drawn in the sand to mark the end of the Sector and the beginning of the Wilds. Instead, drones and soldiers will patrol the areas around the cities, towns, and Farms. In between, though, is mostly no-man's land. There are some hovercraft paths to follow, but in most cases, it's just wilderness. We're probably already past Windy Pines, I realize, so we're definitely beyond the normal reach of the drones. Miah's been quiet as we fly, piloting the Sarus with all the grace of the bird she was named after.

"We're definitely beyond the Sector's reach for now."

"I thought so," he says, his eyes on the controls.

"So, you want to set her down? We can get out the maps and take a look at the area." My stomach is growling. After all, I never did eat at the party. I check the clock on the screens. It's already past one in the morning. No wonder I'm hungry. "We're far enough out that we should figure out where we want to go. Specifically," I say, though the words come out reluctantly because I have no idea where I want to go.

Jeremiah nods and starts to bring us down to a clear landing space, a little meadow along the side of a river. He sets her down gently and powers off the engines.

"Actually, Vale, we might need to stay here overnight. She doesn't have a lot of energy right now. There wasn't a ton of sunlight today and she needs to repower. We could just fly on the reactor for a while, but I think we're far enough out that we can stay safely for the night."

I check the energy meters. He's right—the solar cells are low. They're only at about fifteen percent capacity right now, which will be enough to keep the heating and cloaking on through the evening. We'll be warm and invisible to passing drones, if there are any. If we push her further, though, we might end up sleeping in the cold. We prepared for all weather types, but I wasn't planning on breaking into our camping gear already.

"I think so. We should have at least until mid-morning or early afternoon before they realize we're gone, anyway. We can rest here for tonight and set out again early in the morning."

Miah stands up to stretch. I can tell he's tense. I'm sure leaving Moriana behind without so much as a hint of an explanation is weighing on him, and neither of us is happy about leaving our old lives behind.

"You okay?" I ask.

"Yeah," he says, eyeing me somewhat warily. "You?"

"Fine." He cocks a questioning eyebrow at me. I meet his gaze, undeterred. He looks away, satisfied, at least temporarily, that I am sane and functioning. "I'm going to get out of this tux."

"I'll change when you're done," I say. I step out of the cockpit and head to my pack. I pull out the plasma I stashed and load the map I saved onto the hard drive. I set it on the ship's UMIT, the universal magnetic information transfer module, and a three-dimensional, topographical map comes up in the center of the tiny lounge area. Jeremiah, meanwhile, has started pulling his clothes off, and when he's done and looking like regular old Miah again, he starts pulling food out of the ship's tiny built-in fridge.

"Here," he says, tossing me a Mealpak labeled VALERIAN ORLEÁN. We made sure to bring as much food from the Dieticians as we could. After all, we don't want to lose our edge, intellectually or physically. I catch it and peel open the packaging, but something nags. Then I remember Soren's words from the interrogation room: *You and your friends dine on lavish meals juiced up with customized cocktails designed to amp up your cognitive abilities so you can laugh and philosophize about art and culture and science ...* Now I realize why I wasn't keen on eating at the party. I hesitate, and when I look up, Jeremiah's watching me, half his Mealpak already gone.

"What?" he asks.

"Nothing," I respond, and I pick up a bamboo fork and start to dig in. I don't have a choice. It's the only food I have. Eat or starve. I pick up the little dumplings that have evidently been prescribed for me. The label says *beef, rice flour, watercress, leek, turnip, apple*, and on the back there's a comprehensive list of every vitamin, amino acid, hormone, and protein the Dieticians have included. I wonder what this particular concoction is designed to do to me.

Jeremiah sits on the small bench next to the hologram, stabbing at his food, and starts to play with the map.

"It's pretty accurate around Sector territory, like towns and Farms, because drones are constantly patrolling and taking aerial photos," I comment, and then stuff two dumplings in my mouth. "Buh ih geds aachy ah you go earth er out." Jeremiah is piling food in his mouth, looking at me incomprehensibly.

"Wha 'oo say?" he demands.

I swallow. "I said it gets patchy as you go further out. See, we're probably around here," —I point to a location and use my hands to zoom in on the area of woodlands I think we've found— "which has pretty good mapping because it's not far from Windy Pines. But if you go further out, the detail isn't nearly as good."

Jeremiah starts to play with it a little bit, zooming way out over the continent and then back in on the Sector and the surrounding area.

"Where do you think we'll find the Resistance?" I glance at him, hesitating. Is he really ready to commit to their cause so quickly?

"Is that where you want to go?" I ask. I put the rest of my dumplings aside. We've had this conversation before, but now we have to make a decision.

"It seems like our best option. I don't know where else we'd go. Take up with the Outsiders?" My hand instinctively goes to the acorn pendant hanging around my neck. Thoughts of Chan-Yu, Remy, and Soren fly through my mind, but I shut them back down. Jeremiah notices the gesture. "Is that what you want to do? Go live in the Wilds with the Outsiders?"

I shrug. "I don't know. I don't know what's right or wrong right now, and the Outsiders seem to be neutral players. Hiding out in neutral territory doesn't sound like a bad idea."

Jeremiah scrutinizes me. He's usually a lot more eager to voice his own opinions, but he's been remarkably quiet tonight. I wonder what he's watching me for. Hesitation? Fear? Signs of a nervous breakdown? I clear my throat awkwardly, and he looks away.

"Either way," I say, breaking the pregnant silence, "we want to go south tomorrow, over the lake. No one really knows where the Outsiders are, because they move around so much. But as far as we can tell, they operate primarily south of the Sector. And the Resistance is southwest of here. We think their main base is south of Lake Ayrie." I zoom in on the map on a blur of an old, ruined town. "This is the nearest base we've been able to locate. We think it's really small, though—no more than ten people. And we're not even positive it's the Resistance. Could be Outsiders or just stragglers, nomads. But if you really want to join up with them, that's the closest place with identifiable ties to the Resistance."

"I don't know about 'join up with them,'" Jeremiah says. "But I think we should definitely consider going there. There will be people we know there.

People who are familiar with us."

"I know," I mutter. "That's what I'm afraid of."

"I get that you think they'll hate you, but you can't hide out with the Outsiders forever. Maybe for a few days, a few weeks at most. But no one—not the Resistance, not your parents, not the Outsiders—will let you stay out there forever. You're too important, too dangerous. You'll get sucked back into this conflict eventually. And the Resistance needs us." His eyes light up a little bit, and he's staring at me dead on. "We could fight back, Vale."

I know he's right. I know what I should do. But I don't know if I can bring myself to do it.

"I don't think they want me on their side, Miah," I say, rubbing my fingers against my temples. I look back at the map. "Who I am, who my parents are … I don't think they want an Orleán with them." In fact, I'm pretty worried they might just shoot me on sight.

"Are you kidding?" He leans forward, his elbows on his knees. "Vale, you'd be the most important person to join them. Think of what you could do. How you could help them." I know I could. The things I know about the Sector, the things I could tell them. "Think of the morale you'd bring over from the other side. The son of the chancellor, defected to the Resistance? They would love that."

Yeah, but would they trust me? I wonder. *I'd also be fighting against my parents every step of the way.* Can I do that? I let out my breath and lean back against the wall.

"Let me sleep on it, will you? I can't process all this right now. I can't make heads or tails of any of it."

Jeremiah leans back in his chair. I can't meet his gaze, so I keep playing with the map, zooming in and out on the locations of other possible Resistance bases, and then swinging upwards to where our drones have spotted Outsider encampments. It could be so peaceful, so simple, with them. I could get away from this whole mess and never have to deal with it again. *But what would Remy think of me?*

After a few minutes, Jeremiah reaches over to his pack and pulls out a blanket.

"Okay, we'll talk about it more in the morning. I'm tired; I'm sure you are, too." His weak smile looks like he dragged it forcibly onto his face. "Just think about it, okay? Think about it seriously." He heads back up to the cockpit and settles into one of the chairs, reclining and draping the blanket over his shoulders.

I think about it.

What it would mean to go join the Resistance. I lean my head back against the wall and contemplate the possibility. They would hate me at first, of course. They might suspect me of being a spy, or they might just throw me into prison. I reflect briefly on the irony of possibly finding myself in the same situation that Remy and Soren did. As soon as we surrendered ourselves to them, I would be at their mercy. Would they kill me? Starve, torture, and execute me like we did—almost did—to Remy and Soren? Try to drag as much information out of me as possible? Gruesome scenes fly through my head. My breath quickens and my heart pounds. Jeremiah, at least, has an in. His father is already with them. I have nothing. Worse than nothing. I represent the enemy of the Resistance. *I am the enemy of the Resistance.*

And what if they did let me join? What then? If they let me fight for them, could I do it? I trained alongside a number of soldiers who will no doubt continue to work for Aulion and my parents. They're good men and women, no matter which side they're fighting for. Could I fight against them? Killing Aulion would be no trouble, I think, reflecting on his coldness, his brutal nature. But my parents.... *No.* I can't even think about that.

As I'm contemplating the impossibilities of turning on the Sector, of fighting against everything I've ever known, it feels like something is missing from this puzzle, and it takes me a few minutes to figure out what it is.

Remy.

And Soren. I feel like I owe them a debt. Helping them out of captivity in the face of certain death wasn't enough to make up for the fact that I got them there in the first place. And now I don't even know where they are. They could be dead, I realize suddenly, and the thought is accompanied by the claustrophobic feeling that the air is compressing around me, suffocating me. If they're alive, I owe it to them to do whatever I can to help them. At the most basic level, I owe it to them to make sure they're okay.

And if the Resistance does decide to do to me what I did to Remy and Soren, haven't I earned it?

Winter 2, Sector Annum 106 05h45
Gregorian Calendar: December 22

The air is freezing and thick with moisture. I can see my breath with every exhale, and I clutch the blanket tighter around my shoulders and wrap my arms around my knees to keep warm. It's still pitch dark outside, but I know we're close to dawn. Today, I think our spell of sunny weather will be over. Rain portends.

"We'll take turns sleeping," Soren said last night. We still couldn't figure out how to activate the boat's cloaking, so we were both paranoid about being spotted by drones as we meander down the river. "I'll take first watch," he told me.

I shiver underneath the blanket as I stare out into the misty, impenetrable darkness of the pre-dawn forest. I'm on watch now, though it doesn't do much good, as I can't see anything through the mist. Drones, soldiers, Outsiders, wild animals—I wouldn't have a clue if any or all of them were watching us right now.

After Soren told me he would take the first watch, I collapsed into the narrow, single-man bunk and sank into the kind of deep, restful sleep that can only come from a feeling of safety and peace. For once, we weren't in any immediate danger. I let myself go. I don't even know if Soren tried to wake me up for my watch. All I know is that a few hours ago, I woke up to darkness and closeness and found myself latched around him, limbs entwined like lovers. Somehow it was different this time than the last two nights, when we'd slept curled up together for warmth. That was out of necessity. This was something more. But as I attempted to extract myself without waking him, I realized he wasn't moving. His mouth was slack, his face pale, his skin cold and clammy. I thought he was dead.

I panicked.

I shook him, grabbing his shoulders frantically, hollering and crying like a mother who'd lost her firstborn, until he opened his eyes in alarm. Once the confusion fell from my face and I realized he was alive, I stopped panicking, and an enormous smile drowned his blue eyes and he reached up and kissed me. His arms wrapped around me and I collapsed into him. He pulled me against his full length with an urgency that both startled and drew me closer and … and….

And now everything is different.

We came together with a passion that bordered on insanity. His teeth tore at my lips and neck, and I ran my hands through his blond hair and pressed every inch of my body against his. He rolled on top of me and pulled my shirt open, attacking my shoulders like a starving man eating meat off the bone. I pushed myself up, leaning against my elbows so I could get to him better, to caress his face with my own, and then I made the fatal mistake of trying to roll over on top of him. That's when we fell off the bunk.

In the awkward silence that ensued, Soren sat up and pushed his hair out of his eyes. He looked at me wordlessly and stretched out to try to kiss me again, but I was mortified. I told him I needed water, that I would be back, and I walked out. But I didn't go back. I didn't know what to say or do. So I've been sitting out here, keeping watch in the bleak, freezing morning air ever since.

Nothing's happened, so I stand up to check on him. I don't know how I feel. A part of me wants to go back and kiss him awake, curl up into his arms, and find that spark again. To have him devour my skin like a hungry animal, to feel his body connected deeply to mine. To finally let myself put aside the past and embrace the here and now. But something holds me back. I step inside the heated interior and shiver at the warmth. I crack the door to the miniscule sleeping area and peek in. Soren is passed out, his chest rising and falling regularly. Now that I'm gone he's taken over the entire bed, a mess of arms and legs draped over the thin mattress. I shut the door, satisfied that he's content and resting, and tiptoe back outside.

The cold air cuts at my eyes, but there's a tiny bit of light in the world now. The sky is dark and blue, the river and the trees around us a deep, dusky grey. I hear a *splish* off to the side and wonder if the fish are waking up, too. But then I hear it again. *Splash.* I peer around the bow of the boat, but I see nothing. I check over the sides, but there's nothing there. Satisfied but still nervous, I settle back down in my chair and watch the world drift by as we meander downriver. I feel the air change somehow and notice raindrops pattering on the deck, on the roof over my head. Maybe that's the noise I heard. Raindrops. I stare off into the distance and am thankful that this looks like a nice, gentle rain. If the weather turned ominous and one of those devastating winter storms hit us, Soren and I, on this little boat in the middle of this river, could be in dire straits.

Is anyone searching for us? We haven't heard any drones or seen any airships since the beach. It's as if we're the last people on earth. We've seen precious little but dull brown trees and water since we boarded, and certainly no people. Once we felt as though we were being watched, but it lasted for only a few moments and then dissipated as we headed around a bend and left whoever or whatever it was behind us.

I think about how long we've been gone. What day did we leave for the raid again? I do some quick math in my head and realize that yesterday was the solstice. Today is a new year. I think of the parties they'll be holding in the capital and wonder what the Resistance is doing. Celebrating? Looking for us? Mounting a rescue attempt? A new year means one hundred and six years have passed since the founding of the Okarian Sector. Three years since Tai died. Four days since I was captured. Three since I last saw Vale. Two since Soren and I were tortured. Three hours since Soren and I kissed. How strangely relative time is. Enough has happened each day recently to fill the space of months or years.

I wrap the blanket tightly around my shoulders again, listening to the music of wind in the trees and rain on the tarp, the deck, and the water. I'm so stiff and chilled I can barely move, which is unfortunate because I hear the splash again, and this time my heart flutters, and I know something's wrong.

There's a knock against the side of the boat. I feel the deck beneath me rock slightly, dipping to one side as if something's pulling at it. Instantly alert, my heart thuds in my chest and blood surges through my body like the opening of a dam. I don't have a weapon, so I grab the first thing I can put my hands on, which turns out to be an old wooden crate. I crouch in the shadow of my hiding place. What *is* it? What's happening? Before I can find an answer, I see the hand. Pale knuckles gleam as it grips the side of the boat, disembodied and foul. Then the leg, pants sopping wet, the long skinny foot with a dark slick coating of mud between the white toes, swings over the gunwale. The shapes are visible more as outlines than as actual tangible things, like phantoms stealing up from another world, monstrosities from the deep.

Indecision and fear paralyzes me. To scream will alert it—whoever or whatever it is—to my presence. Can I kill him myself? Or will I die quiet and alone? Still hidden, I see the rest of the man's body land on the deck with a soft *thud*. He stands, turns, and bends over the side to help haul up a companion. The second man, who lands on his feet with hardly a sound, is much smaller.

Who are they? Outsiders? Corine's Black Ops sent to kill us in the night? I tense, tighten my grip on the wooden crate, and get ready to fight.

"Kill whatever moves," the smaller man says quietly, and I can barely hear his voice over the wind and rain. His hand disappears under his shirt and reappears with the glint of a blade in it. "It'll be easy. They're probably sound asleep." The big man grunts and starts for the cabin door.

Almost without permission, my body surges into action.

"Soren! Soren!" I scream like a battle cry. I launch myself at the man with the crate and swing it into his head like a cudgel.

"Shit!" the big one gasps as my crate connects with his face and sends him backward, stumbling into the smaller man, blood pouring from his nose and face. Still holding the crate, I try to whirl it around and bring it down onto the smaller man as well, but he's too fast. He ducks away and then tackles me, his knife hand ready. I grab his wrist, forcing it up and away from my belly, and bite, sinking my teeth deep into the flesh. I swear I can feel bone. He howls in pain and drops the knife, which I promptly dive after, but it slides out of reach. I scramble after it, lose my footing on the rain-slick deck, and fall. My butt slams into the deck hard, and I twist to try to get up, get my feet under me. As I roll, I feel the thick handle of the man's knife dig into my hip, and I thrust my arm underneath my body to pull it out. The smaller man throws himself at me, pushing me back, trying to reach under me to grab the knife. I scream for Soren again and see the big man look back and forth between me and the cabin as the light of understanding—there's someone else in there—dawns on him. He puts his hand on the doorknob and turns.

Just as soon as I see the glint of silver appear in the larger man's hand, I manage to bring my knee up hard, a violent thrust into the little man's crotch, and feel his *ooof* of pain as he rolls off me. I twist aside, grab the knife from beneath me, and without thinking, rear back and throw it with a hard flick of the wrist. I'm hoping for a distracting flesh wound, something that will keep the big man from opening the cabin door, from walking right in and murdering Soren in his sleep. What I get is a direct hit to the jugular.

Everything stops.

The dying man's eyes widen in surprise, and he drops his own knife as his hands fly to his neck. He grabs the hilt of the weapon and pulls it free.

"Sam!" the little man cries, agonized. He dashes to the dead man's side as his knees buckle beneath him, and he slumps against the door. Soren appears at the window and begins to push against it, sliding the man's body across the deck. He slumps further down, legs spread out before him, blood pumping from his neck like a hose. The deck is stained a wet, rainy red.

Then it hits me. The dying man—Sam—still has his knife in his hand. I dive towards him, shoving the smaller man out of the way. I grab the knife and pull it from the big man's hand just as he dies, the light in his eyes extinguished as abruptly as if someone had pinched out a candle flame.

I did that.

I killed him.

I scramble backwards and stand, panting, trying not to look at those lifeless eyes. I hold the knife at the ready. The smaller man crawls to his companion. He clutches his sleeve around his bleeding wrist and cradles the dead man's big head against his chest as Soren pushes against the door, cracking it just enough to open it.

"You killed him." The little man's voice is quiet, despairing and exhausted. He doesn't look at me. He takes his friend's dead hand in his own and holds it tightly.

"You would have done the same to us," I say, my voice shaking, though my hand, holding the knife ready to throw, is still. The man doesn't seem to be a threat anymore. He makes no attempt to move.

Soren steps over the two men and comes to me, enveloping me in his arms. "Give me the knife," he says, as he pries it from my hand, which is gripping the hilt so hard he has to unwrap my clenched fingers. My hands, my whole body, won't obey the signals my brain is sending. I feel like I've been turned into a stony statue, frozen in time, forever immortalizing the moment when I first took a human life. Soren's voice is the only anchor I have to the idea that I'm still alive, that things might someday be okay even though a man is dead at my feet. At my hands.

"Who are you?" Soren asks calmly, as the man huddles over his friend's body.

"No one," he responds, and his voice is muffled, lost. Is he crying?

Soren releases me from his arms and walks slowly over to the pathetic, shivering form. He turns his head to Soren's advancing figure. Soren crouches down in front of him and points the knife at his throat very deliberately. He speaks, calmly and quietly.

"This weapon is proof that you were going to kill us. You boarded our boat and were going to murder us in our sleep. Your friend is dead, and you are lucky to be alive. But if you don't answer our questions, you won't be for very much longer."

The man then turns and gently lays his companion's head on the deck. The gesture is tender, soft. The full force of what I've done hits me, and salty tears and rainwater course down my cheeks. I close my eyes and lean my head back, wishing the rain would just dissolve me and carry me with it, with the blood and sweat and bones down into the river to be diluted and purified. When that doesn't happen, I open my eyes again and fall back into my chair, watching as the man kneels over his companion and pulls his lids down, erasing the surprised, wide-eyed expression forever. He smoothes back the dead man's hair and whispers something. A prayer, maybe. Or a pledge.

Then he grabs hold of the railing and starts to pull himself to his feet.

"Not so fast," Soren says, standing up abruptly and waving the knife in front of him. "Keep your hands visible."

He holds his hands up in the air and looks at Soren wearily.

"Can I stand now?" he asks bitterly. Soren glances back at me, and then beckons him to stand up. He grabs a piece of rope from the deck of the ship and uses it to lash the boy's hands behind his back. His wrist is still bleeding where I bit deep into his skin. That's what he is, I realize. A boy. I knew he was small, but standing in front of us now, it's clear he's even smaller than I thought. He's closer to my size than Soren's. He can't be any older than fifteen or sixteen, but the expression in his eyes makes him look like he's closer to a hundred.

Soren drags the boy inside to the tiny kitchen area and sits him down at a little table just behind the helm. I follow reluctantly, not eager to face the child whose friend I have murdered. But it's warm inside, and I'm cold, wet, and maybe in shock. I need to warm up. I sit down at the controls, a little apart from them. Soren starts heating up some water, and I watch blankly.

"I know who you are," the boy says. "You're Soren Skaarsgard."

Shit. I turn my head to the boy and stare at him. *He's recognized us.* Soren and I lock eyes briefly, and the flicker of understanding that passes between us means we don't tell him anything. Not until we know more about him. Soren goes back to preparing tea.

"Who?" he asks nonchalantly.

"I saw you years ago. You were visiting our Farm with your mother when she was chancellor. You played the piano for us. Some piece called Chopping," he says, and I almost laugh out loud. I choke it back and turn it into a cough, but he looks at me somewhat indignantly.

"What?"

"Chopin," Soren corrects gently, more tactfully.

"So you are Soren!" he exclaims, his eyes lighting up.

"Just because I know what Chopin is doesn't mean I'm this Skaarsgard person. You're from a Farm?" he asks, handing me a mug of tea as he sits down across the table from the boy.

"I know you're him, so stop pretending you're not. And *you're* Remy Alexander," he says, nodding purposefully at me. Soren and I look at each other again as we realize the charade is up.

"How do you know her?" Soren asks, speaking for me, since my throat still doesn't seem to be working.

"You're famous," he says simply. "You were all over the official Sector broadcasts. But I know *you*," he says, nodding at me with a glint of anger in his eyes, "because of Sam. When the massacre at the SRI was on the télé, we all heard about it. Sam couldn't get enough of it. It hit him hard, the deaths of all those students, and especially ... your sister."

I think back to those months after the killings. The endless broadcasts, the analysis of the killer's psychology, the speculation about why he did it, the photos of all the students' faces shown over and over again on the Sector programs. They made the students into martyrs and the Outsiders into murderers.

"*'Elle était si belle,'* he always said."

She was so beautiful, I translate, remembering how strong the old French influence is on the dialects outside of the capital.

"He adored her. He just couldn't get over it. And so we watched the broadcasts, and they always showed photos of you. You've grown up, but not so much that I wouldn't savvy you anywhere." He takes a deep breath. "Sam hated the Outsiders after that, and was always talking about how if he ever met any, he would kill them. That's what we thought you were, when we saw the boat on the river. Outsiders."

I look away. *Sam, the one you killed ... your sister ... he adored her.* So this is what I am. The killer. The girl who killed a man who adored my sister, who grieved for her, who wanted to avenge her. Just like I do. *They would have killed us first*, I remind myself. They would have stabbed us to death in our sleep. But that argument rings hollow in my head. I didn't have to kill him. I could have stopped them some other way. *I didn't have to kill him to keep myself safe.*

I don't know who I am right now.

"So you know us," Soren says, returning to the questions, "but we still don't know who you are or why you and your friend saw fit to board our boat and try to kill us."

"Like I said, we thought you were Outsiders. We saw your boat and thought there might be food and a fast way out. We were just trying to stay alive." He talks like he wasn't doing anything wrong by sneaking onto a boat and plotting to murder the people on it.

"By killing other people?" Soren demands.

"We didn't have a choice. There's a bounty on our heads, and we needed an escape."

Soren glances at me, his eyes raised, nervous. Why were they being hunted?

"What's your name?"

"Bear."

"Bear?"

"I'm registered as Antoine Baier. But apparently I was a difficult child. My wet nurse complained that when I was hungry, I cried so loud and thrashed so wildly, I sounded like a bear charging through the woods. So, Antoine Baier became just Bear."

"Okay, Bear. Tell us why there's a bounty on your heads."

"Because of Sam. His real name was Samuel, but everyone in the camp called him Samson on account of how big he was. He is—was my best friend." His head bows momentarily and he stops talking. When he resumes speaking, his voice is thick and gritty. "He … was a few years older but for some reason got it in his head that I was smart and funny. He liked me. One of the few who ever did." His eyes are downcast, and he swallows like he's fighting back tears. My stomach churns and I look away.

"Anyway, he'd always been a bit of a troublemaker, but he was so strong—he could do the work of three men easily—so Boss put up with it. Until after the Alexanders disappeared." I look up at the mention of my name. The boy is shivering, and Soren takes pity on him and pours him a mug of tea as well and puts it on the table in front of him. Bear clutches it between his palms and lets it warm him. He takes an awkward, slow sip with his bound hands and then sets it back down.

"What does my family have to do with you and Sam?" I ask.

"Sam got the idea in his head that not everything was the way we'd been told. He started asking questions. Like, 'Where did Tai's family go?' and 'How come they never held any hearings about the killings?' and 'How come nobody ever hears about the Skaarsgards anymore?' He started telling the rest of us workers that the government hired the Outsiders to kill them. Then he stopped eating the food, saying he wouldn't eat anything given to him by murderers. Finally, last summer, they put him on silo duty."

"Wait," Soren interrupts. "Who's *they*?"

"They're called the Enforcers, but we all just call them Boss. They're the guards and the administrators at the Farms. They're in charge of assigning tasks and passing out the Dieticians' food and stuff like that."

"So what's a silo, and what do you do in one?" I ask.

Bear leans back. "There's these tall structures, silos, where the grain is stored. When the grain is moist, it'll start decomposing, and it starts to clump up and gets pretty nasty. We go in and break up the clumps."

"Why are clumps bad?" I ask.

"Makes it hard to get out of the silo and into trucks for transport, I suppose. Maybe causes problems for processing, I don't know. We just grow the crops. After it's trucked away, I have no idea what happens to it."

"Okay, so what happened in the silo?" Soren asks.

"I don't know in his case. Sometimes a sinkhole forms and the grain turns into a giant funnel, sucking everything down. If you don't have your harness on, you go down too and drown in the grain. Or if you're walking on the top level, scraping clumps off the sides of the bin, the whole pile can collapse on you and one minute you're breathing air and the next minute you're ten feet under, breathing corn. Probably Sam's weight collapsed a load of grain around him—everyone knew he was too big for the silos. That's why it was so crazy when Boss put him up for silo duty. Anyway, if the harness don't hold or your partner don't pull you up, *tu seras mort*."

"But obviously Sam didn't die," Soren says.

"No, the harness held. Me and a couple of friends managed to pull him up. But he was so heavy, it took us longer than it should've. He was under too long. Never was quite right after it. Brain damage, the doctors said. They wanted to euthanize him. But then the chief Boss figured it didn't take too much brains to do what Sam did. Since he was dumber than a box of rocks now, at least he wouldn't cause more trouble. So they fixed him up and put him back to work.

"Problem was, after that they worked him like an animal. Well, after that, he was an animal. Just a big dumb ox, a work horse that toiled from sunup to sundown without ever saying a word." Bear stops, his eyes cloudy with memories. He sniffs and wipes his face on his sleeve.

"So you left," Soren prods, gently.

"Yeah. About month ago. They were gonna work him to death. And he'd looked after me, so I decided to look after him. We snuck out one night when some of the uppity-ups from Okaria were doing a visit. There was a big fête and all the Bosses was so busy kissing ass that they didn't savvy when we just walked out through the unlocked front gate. It was unreal. We've been habitating out here since, trying to make our way west. There are others out here, too. Some of 'em will give you a helping hand. We met up with a healer who tried to help Sam, but there wasn't nothin' she could do for him. Damage was already done. But she was nice. And her husband … he was a poet, sang songs and such."

He stops and studies my face as I hold my breath. *Is he talking about my parents?* They travel in disguise, but could he have recognized them? But then he shakes his head and goes on. "But some...." He stops and is quiet for a while. Neither Soren nor I press him.

"Did you … like living at the Farm?" I ask, my voice quiet, trembling.

"Like it?" he asks, looking up with a perplexed expression, as though he's never quite thought about this question. "I didn't know anything different, 'till I got out to the Wilds. I guess I liked it well enough. It sure was a lot easier than being out here. But I liked that out here we could do what we wanted." He thinks about this for a minute. "So much for my brains Sam thought so much of, huh?" he jokes weakly, with a pathetic, weepy smile. He takes a deep breath and shudders visibly. "'Stead of saving Sam, I got him killed.

"So, Remy Alexander and Soren Skaarsgard, you going to kill me now? I really wouldn't mind. Just do it quick." He looks at Soren, and then his eyes flick back and settle on me. I don't like the way he's looking at me. Cold, unflinching. "You do it. A flick of the wrist. That's the way I want to go. Just like Sam."

I'm listening to Jeremiah snore quietly as I load up the map again. I didn't sleep well, so I've found myself in need of a distraction. My stomach growls, but I resist the temptation to open another Mealpak. The food will only last so long—I can't go stuffing my face at every opportunity. I start tracing a path from our current location to the nearest sighted Outsider camp, due west about a hundred kilometers. If we go there, will we find anyone? Will Chan-Yu be with them? *Will Remy?* I realize that the odds of finding the Outsiders with just a rumor and a few photos to go off of are pretty slim. We'd have to do a lot of flying, checking back and forth, crosshatching over the land. And even then, there's no guarantee. Our drones haven't had much luck photographing them, so we know they're evasive. What's to say we'll succeed where the drones haven't?

It's a dismal, grey day outside, but it doesn't look like it's raining. The light is bright enough to illuminate the interior of the airship, but not much more than that. I wish I'd thought to dim the panels again so we could sleep longer, but now I'm awake. Nothing will change that.

I can't stop reliving my conversation with my parents last night. I still don't understand—none of it makes sense. *I'm sorry, Vale,* she said, *but it had to be done.* Why? What did Remy and Soren do that made my mother believe they were such a threat and a danger that she had to have them killed?

I check the distance to the Resistance base I pointed out to Miah last night. It's farther away, at least two hundred kilometers. Only an hour by airship, though. Apprehension sets in as soon as I begin virtually navigating to the abandoned town on the blurry, pixilated map. Who will be there, and what will they do to me?

I turn back to find Jeremiah stirring, stretching his arms and rubbing his eyes.

"Morning," I call casually. I toss a canister of water at him, which, much to my surprise, he reaches out and catches instinctively. "Nice reactions," I add.

"Thanks," he says groggily. He pops the top on the canister and starts drinking as he sits up.

"Sleep well?"

"About as well as I could have in these chairs. I half wish we'd set up the tent outside for a little more space."

"As if," I laugh. "We'd have been sleeping on top of each other. I like you, Miah, but not that much."

"What's the point of a tent if you can't sleep in it?" he grumbles.

"Miah," I say, cutting to the chase, "I think we should go find the Outsiders." I wait for his inevitable argument, but none comes. I search for his eyes with my own, but he's stretching, checking the controls on the Sarus, pulling his boots back on over his pants. When it becomes clear he's not going to respond, I fill the silence. "I think Chan-Yu will have found a way to get back to them. Even if Remy and Soren aren't with him, we can find out from him whether or not they're safe and decide what to do from there."

Jeremiah just nods.

"No argument?" I ask, prodding him. His silence is unnerving. Usually so comic and quick to respond, his dull, quiet manner is peculiar. Maybe he's just groggy, I tell myself. He swivels slowly in his chair and looks, not at me, but past me.

"I just think you're postponing the inevitable because you're afraid." His eyes finally settle on me.

"Well," I admit, "I am. I'm terrified. I saw what happened to Remy and Soren, and to be perfectly honest, I'm afraid of being treated the same way my parents treated them. I don't feel like walking into a death trap." I take a breath.

"Okay." He shrugs, conceding. "I get it. I don't think they're going to kill you, but you know more about them than I do. If you think that's a possibility, let's steer clear. Let's go find the Outsiders." A twinge of the classic Jeremiah Sayyid grin crosses his face, and he turns back to the controls. "I bet the horse riders are surprised when we show up in this swank ride."

"Yeah, they definitely don't have the same kind of flight capabilities we do. I don't even know if they have any airships. None have ever been sighted."

"As usual, you're taking everything I say too seriously. I meant we should buzz the treetops when we find them."

"Oh, right, because that's definitely the easiest way to win their hearts and convince them to let us band together with them," I say. "Great plan, Miah."

"Thank you," he says with a grin.

We fly due south across the lake, and Jeremiah and I spend the next few hours flying aimlessly between the sites on the map that look like Outsider camps. The terrain is beautiful but rugged with mountains in the distance and bare rock outcroppings sticking up from the wide expanses of green and brown like fierce, grey sentinels. Most of the area is covered by tall grasses, shrubs, or, at the higher elevations, pine and fir trees, but occasionally we come across blackened open spaces where even the skeletons of trees that have obviously been burned recently—maybe forest fires?—are few and far between. Once we see a spot that looks like it might have been recently occupied, where the shrub has been beaten back slightly and the wild grass trampled underfoot. But there's nothing else, and no signs indicating where they might have gone.

We're halfway to the next site when the communication feed goes insane. It starts flashing blue and red, and even when I turn the volume down, the message keeps playing.

"Valerian Orleán, please report, Valerian Orleán, indicate location and status," the feed says over and over again, crackling with static. There's no visual, no hologram, just audio. Then the interface starts going crazy, and the ship banks steeply to the right and begins to pick up speed.

"Override the route!" Miah yells. "Somehow they've taken over the ship!"

I power down the guidance system, and the ship levels off. I breathe a sigh of relief—at least we're not flying back towards Sector territory. Only problem is, now we don't have a route programmed. "Looks like we've got to fly this thing the old-fashioned way." I slide up the control panel and it disappears soundlessly into the nose of the ship, exposing an antique interface complete with dials, switches, and what they used to call "joysticks." This will allow me to pilot the Sarus manually. Most airships don't have a system like this because, if you get into trouble, Sector air traffic control just overrides your system and brings you down safely. But Dad taught himself to fly on an old plane he and some friends rebuilt back when they were at the Academy, and he always said that if you're going to be a pilot, you need to know how to keep your bird aloft and land her safely even when all your systems fail. Trouble is, I never really saw the need, and I've only ever used the system on a simulator and only then because Dad insisted.

"We must have missed something in the code," I say, as I fiddle with levers and dials, trying to remember how the old-fashioned system works.

"Yeah, but what?" he looks over at me, obviously worried. "We went through it line by line."

"I don't know, but—" We're thrown sideways as the Sarus tips to the right again. I grab hold of the joystick and push it left to get us back on track, headed away from the Sector. Nothing happens. I push it harder. Still nothing.

"We're going to have to power everything down." Miah growls.

"What do you mean 'everything'?"

"Everything except internal controls." He starts scanning the old dials, pushing buttons and flipping switches. "I'm turning off all electrical systems so drones trying to track us can't pick up any signals. All we've got now is our cloaking and your flying skills."

"Great." I'm gripping my joystick so hard my knuckles are white, but the Sarus keeps accelerating, keeps heading back east until suddenly I feel her start to respond. Miah must have pushed the right combination of buttons to regain control of the ship. I push the joystick left and her nose lifts and we tilt back and away.

"Valerian Orleán, please report, Valerian Orleán, indicate location and status," continues to repeat, and I think of Aulion and what waits back home if the Sarus betrays us and flies us straight back to the Sector.

"What the fuck?" Miah yells and grips his seat as the ship banks right again.

"You're gonna have to get into the electronics," I say. "Pull the circuit breakers one at a time and find out what the hell is going on."

Miah drops to the floor and pulls up the hatch, sticking his head down into the tight space that contains the humming boxes for all the ship's systems. He reaches in and starts sliding the symbols on the touch screen to break the circuits. "Shit!"

"What?"

"How'd we miss this?"

"What? How'd we miss what?" I demand.

"An active beacon transmitter," he cranes his neck to look up at me.

"But we scanned the ship for transmitters."

"Apparently we missed it. But that's not all." He sticks his head back down in the hole. "You want the good news or the bad news?"

"Good news first."

"I think we can regain partial control of the ship if we reactivate all but the autopilot systems and fly below the radar. As long as we stay low, they can't see us even if something goes wrong with our cloaking."

"Okay. What's the bad news?"

"The auto-stabilization controls are on the same circuit breaker. As soon as I pull it, we're going to be flying disabled, and every little move you make with that joystick of yours will be amplified."

I think back to the simulation and the warnings about pilot-induced oscillation. "You don't get motion sick, do you?" I ask, remembering the feeling of flying chaotically in the simulation module.

"I hope not," he croaks out a laugh. "You ready? I'm going to pull it."

"Ready," I say and grip the joystick with both hands. I hold my body still, poised and wary of any sudden movement. The ship is still accelerating and heading back toward Sector airspace. I need to turn us back south and get us out of here, but I have to do it gently, delicately.

Miah struggles back into his seat and shows me the transmitter as if it's a prize. I hold the joystick steady as sweat rolls down my back. Small moves, I think. Small moves. I nudge the joystick left and the ship responds. Okay. I can do this. I nudge it again and we begin to track back north and west. This isn't so hard. I glance over at Miah and he's smiling. I reach up with one hand to wipe my forehead and the joystick moves left and forward and this time the ship dives, sending us into a roll and lifting us out of our seats. "Fuck!" I yell and grab for the harness that I've never used before. I pull right, trying to ease us out of the roll, but my knee knocks into the joystick and we're tumbling, and all I can hear is Jeremiah yelling: "Pull back, pull back. We're going to hit the trees!"

"I see the trees!" I shout as we careen towards them while I try to sort out the controls. I flick my eyes back and forth between the fast-approaching treetops and the joystick, which I grab with both hands, pulling it ever so slightly back to lift the nose. That works—enough to pull us out of the rolling dive and bring us around and level, away from sudden death via impalement by fir tree.

"WATCH OUT!" Miah screams, just as I see the massive cliff face looming ahead of us.

"Okay, okay!" I pull steadily back and to the right, and instead of crashing into the cliff, we arc gracefully along its face like a hawk in the wind. I exhale and scan the distance for anything else I need to avoid.

"Well that was fun," I say finally.

"Valerian Orleán, please report, Valerian Orleán, indicate location and status."

"We need to get out of here," Jeremiah says.

"You think?"

"But we may not have to rely on your expert flying skills anymore—which turned out to be a massive disappointment, by the way—because I might be able to re-activate our guidance system. Now that I've taken out the transmitter beacon, we should be able to set the system up again so you don't have to fly with that damn joystick." I breathe an enormous sigh of relief.

"What do you need?"

"Well, I have no idea if it will work, and I'm going to have to power up just to find out. If we're lucky, I'll just have to drop in some code. They'll be able to see us for as long as that takes and then we'll go dark again. You want to fly with that stick or chance it that I can pull this programming trick off?"

"Do your magic, my friend." He taps away on the control screen and the lights flash back on as I reach up and slide the main interface panel back down. He pulls up a hologram of the ship and zooms in on the areas that are flashing red, indicating disruptions in normal functionality.

I pull up the ship's wave sensors, trying to see what they're pinging us with. A list of recent incoming signals with frequencies and wavelengths appears. *K-Band microwave – 15 GHz.* Standard drone network communication frequency. So there are drones on our tail.

"Valerian Orleán, please report, Valeri—" Jeremiah slams his fist down on the comm feed and, miraculously, it shuts off. We both stare at the glass pane for a moment in astonishment.

"I didn't know you could do that."

"Me either," he responds.

"Look," I call his attention back to the wave sensors. "Drones. Anywhere from fifty to a hundred kilometers away. That's how they're getting a signal through to screw with the interfaces."

He shakes his head. "We can go dark for long enough to get out of here, but they're going to find us eventually."

"There's no way to block the incoming signals? Even if we fly with the old interface, with that damned joystick?"

"Not since they've already homed in on our general location. A military grade Sarus might have more cloaking features on her, but this model wasn't designed to hide." He pulls up the shield monitor. "See, there's radar deflection and visual camouflage but nothing to block sensors operating on other wavelengths."

My heart sinks. "We have to abandon ship, then."

"Yes. If they've already got a reading on us, we're dead. They'll trace us anywhere we go."

"I guess we'll get to use that tent after all," I respond drily. He looks over at me and starts laughing.

"Looking forward to snuggling later?" He reaches over and rubs my cheek with the back of his hand, grinning. I slap his hand away.

"In your dreams, Jeremiah Sayyid."

"More like nightmares."

Searching for a place to land, we spot crumbling smokestacks in the distance. Drawing nearer, I recognize an old, wasted coal plant from the history books, a remnant of a time when burning fossil fuels was an acceptable thing to do. Decorated with rundown buildings and an overgrown forest, it's a perfect place to hide the Sarus. Not to mention that if we ever want to find it again, it'll be easy enough. Jeremiah follows a bend in the river that runs alongside the old plant and brings the ship in for a landing among the ruins. We're eager to get off, now that we know we're being tracked. Before we go, I put in a pair of my mission-ready contacts, just in case. We grab our bags, stuff them with our Mealpaks, and head out with barely a backwards, mournful glance at the Sarus. I feel like she betrayed me somehow, and I have no regrets about leaving her behind. We head south, in the same direction we were originally headed. It's raining here, small light drops bursting with aplomb on our waterproof jackets. The world is brown, rough, and craggy; leafless trees and dull green shrubs litter the horizon. Within minutes, both Jeremiah and I are shivering, and we quickly realize we're going to have to layer up on clothing to stay warm.

After we've taken a few minutes to strip and add more layers of sweaters, gloves, and hats, we continue on. I wonder how far we'll get, if we're on a fool's errand, and if it might just be safer to head towards the Resistance. At least we have a confirmed location on them. The Outsiders are nebulous and invisible. If our drones can't find them, how will two inexperienced woodsmen? I think back to my training in emergency situations, survival in the wilderness, when we learned the basics of hunting, building fires, tracking and trapping. I hope I won't have to use those skills; our instructions were rudimentary at best. No one's ever gotten stuck in the Wilds before—at least, no one who wanted to return.

After about an hour's worth of walking, we're both starving, so we decide to take a break to eat and check that we're headed the right way. We're halfway through a meal when I suddenly realize I have no idea what time it is.

"Jeremiah," I blurt, "did you bring a watch?" He pulls up short.

"No, I don't think I did." He starts rummaging through a side pocket in his enormous bag. After a few seconds of browsing, he zips the pocket back up. "Nothing."

"Shit."

"Not like it really matters out here, does it?"

"No," I respond, realizing he's right. "I guess it doesn't. Just wondering how much more daylight we've got."

"We left the Sarus around eleven. I think we've got at least four or five more hours."

We finish our meals in silence, check the map, and shoulder our packs. The sound of rain hitting the damp, decaying leaves beneath our feet mingles occasionally with bird calls, though those are few and far between. Mostly it's quiet. Every out-of-place noise sets me on edge as I listen intently for drones, passing airships, or followers on foot. Do the Outsiders know we're here? Have the drones found us yet? What will happen if—or when—they do?

Sometime in the afternoon, we come across a clearing that has obviously seen recent use. There's a fire pit with blackened, ashy logs, and Jeremiah points out faded boot prints in the grass and mud. I hold my hand over the ashes, checking the temperature, but it's cold.

"I wonder who was here?" he asks, poking around in the grass.

"Looks like no more than one or two people. It's a small site." An idea flashes in front of me. "I wonder if it was Chan-Yu."

Jeremiah rolls his eyes dramatically. "The odds of that are astronomical, Vale."

"Are they? How many other people are running around in the Wilds in small groups? We're looking for the Outsiders; they're looking for the Outsiders."

"Probably a fair few. You're the one who admitted that we know next to nothing about the Outsiders or anyone else who lives in the Wilds. What's to say these woods aren't crawling with people? Or that the reason the Sector has a hard time tracking the Outsiders is that they split up and travel in groups of two or three? You're letting your hopes of finding Remy and Soren cloud your judgment."

I have no response to that. Instead, I start examining the footprints, checking out the exterior of the camp. "Zoom," I say and my contacts zero in on bent blades of grass and crushed leaves as I try to remember what they taught us in our day-long seminar on tracking last year when I first started my military training. *Look for any sign of disturbance*, they said. *A snapped twig or a bent branch can give your quarry away.* I stop when I notice a scraggly bush. A few winter berries have been plucked off; I see the stem that's left where the fruit was plucked. "Identify," I say, and HUCKLEBERRY – EDIBLE appears by the bush. Someone knows what they're doing. At least more than I do. I look ahead, out of the clearing and into the forest. I take a few steps forward, bent over, staring at the ground. A few crushed leaves indicate a striking heel. A stick crushed into the ground here. I follow the path, looking up from the ground every few minutes. It seems well-worn; the underbrush is clearer here than along the rest of the forest floor. Every few feet there's another broken twig or crushed leaf pile, so I'm confident I'm following someone's—or something's—tracks. It's natural and easy to follow. So natural I don't notice the silence around me, and when I turn around to call Jeremiah, I realize he's nowhere to be seen.

"Miah?"

No response.

I look around. I didn't realize how far I'd come. I can't even see the clearing behind me.

"Jeremiah?" I call again, being careful not to raise my voice. I look around, to either side of me, wondering if he wandered off in some other direction. I squint into the distance.

Suddenly a chill runs up my spine, and I feel a cold cylindrical object pressed to the base of my skull. I freeze.

"Put your hands on top of your head, Valerian." The voice is low but dangerous, and somehow familiar. *How did the Sector catch up to us that quickly?* Every muscle in my body is tense, coiled. I raise my hands slowly and place them on my head. *Who is that?* Someone pulls my hands roughly behind my back and binds them together.

"Do not speak," the voice says. *I know him,* I think, but who is it? I decide to follow his advice and keep my mouth shut. Hands shove me forward, and I stumble, walking back towards the clearing where I last saw Jeremiah. "Walk." I obey, treading gingerly. I keep my eyes peeled, not daring to turn around. I can hear the crunch of dead leaves underfoot behind me, the noises of people who don't care if they're being followed or not. *They can't be Outsiders,* I think. *I know that voice.* My heart plummets to my boots as I imagine facing my parents again, this time as a traitor and a fugitive. I stumble back into the clearing and find Jeremiah standing, facing me, his hands similarly bound, and a Bolt similarly aimed at his head. Somehow, that doesn't surprise me.

What does surprise me is that the hand holding the Bolt belongs to Elijah Tawfiq.

27 — REMY

After Bear begged me to kill him, I just walked into the bunk room and lay down for a few hours, immobile and numb. I tried to think about everything that had happened, but nothing would process. *I killed a man,* I kept hearing over and over again in my head, an echo accompanied by the image of the dead man's eyes staring unblinking into mine. Only instead of irises and pupils, they contained coins, small golden coins with the numeral *one* emblazoned on them. I might have been dreaming. I don't really know. At one point Soren came in and tried to talk to me, but I didn't respond. I didn't even move. Finally, with a sigh, he simply lay down beside me and put his arms around me. This time, I didn't protest against his embrace. Instead, I turned into his shoulder and buried my head there, like a turtle hiding in its shell. I wanted to cry, but nothing came.

"Bear?" I croaked. I wanted to say something more, but the words stuck in my throat. Soren knew what I meant.

"He'll be fine. But we have to bury the body soon." I nodded, my nose smushed up against his collarbone.

In the comfort of Soren's arms, I fell asleep, and when I woke up again, he was gone. I stirred, confused and worried about his absence. My fears coaxed me out of bed as dark scenarios flew through my mind—Bear committing suicide or murdering Soren; Sector soldiers attacking the boat and killing us all—but they were unfounded. The two of them were sitting at the table in the kitchen area, Soren regaling Bear with stories of the glamorous life in the capital while they shared a block of cheese.

Now, Bear and I are sitting in silence while Soren checks the ship's controls.

"What was he like?" I ask suddenly, looking at the boy curiously. He's about the same age I was when Tai was killed, I'd guess. Bear doesn't look at me, and it takes him a minute to respond.

"Always moving. Full of energy. He wasn't the smartest guy in the world, but he could hold his own in a conversation. Thought for himself, even if they weren't always the right thoughts."

"How old was he?"

"Year older than me. Like I said, he took a liking to me. Kinda took me under his wing. Didn't let the Boss give me shit ever."

"Did they? Before you got to be friends?"

"They weren't the nicest people in the world," he says, but he doesn't sound angry. "Never did nothing so bad to me as what they did to him, so I guess I can't complain." I think of the coins in Sam's eyes from my dreams, glinting dead and metallic.

"So where are you all going?" Bear asks after a few minutes of silence. My eyes flit to the back of Soren's head, but he's engrossed in checking the map and the controls.

"Home," I say simply. He doesn't press the issue.

We don't say much for a while. Finally Soren turns back to us.

"We need to clean the deck and bury Sam. It's about three in the afternoon. We should do it before it gets dark." Soren stands up, business-like. "I think there's a good spot ahead. It looks like there's an old industrial site up ahead—I saw some smokestacks a little ways downriver." He nods pointedly at Bear. "It would be a good spot to memorialize him. That way if you ever want to come back, you'll know where to find him."

Quietly, timidly, Bear responds: "Yeah. Okay. Don't know if I'll ever make it back here, but that'd be nice." He gives Soren a small, hesitant smile. "He woulda liked being by the river."

I nod my agreement. Giving Sam a proper burial is probably the best thing I can do right now—both for him and for me. I stand and follow Soren out the door, preparing myself to look at the man I killed. I'm determined to face my fears. Someone—Soren or Bear, or maybe both—has lain Sam out and crossed his arms in a sort of final salute and set his knife on his chest, the blade pointing down towards his feet. He looks both peaceful and warlike, somehow. The boat is already drifting to the eastern bank of the river, slowing and coming to a halt. Soren hops out into the water and pulls the boat into shore as far as possible. This way we'll be landing on the beach, not in the water. He looks at me, his eyebrows raised, as though asking, *Are you ready?*

I'm ready.

Sam is bigger than Soren, which is saying something. He's too big for Soren to carry alone. It'll take both of us. And I'm not going to ask Bear to help us carry the body of his best friend, the man I murdered.

I cross the deck to where the dead man's body is lying and I bend down to lift his feet. There's something sickening about holding, touching a dead body, but I quell my revulsion and do my job. Soren lifts his shoulders, and together we heave Sam's enormous weight over the deck and dump him unceremoniously over the gunwale. The body falls in a heap onto the sandy beach, and we scramble over, righting Sam's body and carrying him awkwardly a little ways off the beach. I make sure to pick up the man's knife and tuck it back under his arms. Bear follows us, hopping off the boat, moving with slow, reluctant motions. We prop the body up against a tree and start scouting a good burial site.

It occurs to me that we don't have a shovel. When I mention this to Soren, he doesn't seem bothered.

"It's healthier to let him decompose naturally anyway," he whispers back to me, out of Bear's earshot.

"Healthier? He's dead."

"You know what I mean." He shoots me a scowl. "We'll cover him with some underbrush and let nature take over from there."

I suppress a shudder.

We let Bear select the burial site. He points out a spot under a giant honey locust tree. "They're beautiful in the fall," he whispers. The decrepit smokestacks are visible above the treetops, towering over the skeletal remains of the old buildings. Soren and I dutifully move the body over to the indicated spot and start gathering leaves and branches with which to cover him.

"I'm sorry," I whisper to Sam's closed eyes as I throw leaves over his face.

Finally, after the body has been covered, Soren, Bear, and I stand back so Bear can say a few words.

"I'm sorry I brought you out here, Sam. I thought we could find something good." He's quiet for a moment. "They're nice," he says finally. "You woulda liked them." I contemplate Bear's words. He's not implicating me or angry at all. On an impulse I reach out and grab his hand, feeling his rough, calloused palms, hardened from a lifetime of physical labor. I squeeze it tightly and look at him sideways. He looks up at me and gives me a weak, bleary-eyed smile: *I forgive you.* I nod back at him. *I forgive you, too.*

"Sam, I'm gonna miss you," he continues, still holding my hand. "You looked after me when no one else did, and I tried to do the same for you. I'm sorry I wasn't as good at it as you were. I hope you've found peace, and I'll do everything I can to get back at the Boss and all them people who hurt you. I'm gonna go fight with the Resistance, Sam," he says, and Soren and I exchange suddenly worried glances. "I'm gonna make up for what they did to you, you'll see." He wipes his eyes with his free hand and lets go of mine.

"I'll miss you, buddy. Goodbye, Sam." He turns away, and Soren and I are left together, staring down at the patch of leaves and brambles that mark another lost life.

I look up at Soren.

"What did he mean," I whisper, "he's 'gonna go fight with the Resistance'? He's too young."

"Why?" Soren shrugs. "That's about how old you were. He doesn't have anywhere else to go. We might as well take him along."

But I'm not looking at Soren anymore. I'm looking past him, beyond the trees to a shimmering patch in the distance that doesn't look normal. It's … glistening, I realize, and not just from the rain. It's *glistening* in an unnatural, almost magical way. The trees are shimmering like a mirage in the desert. I look back at Soren to check to make sure it's not me, that my eyes aren't malfunctioning. No, Soren looks perfectly normal, although he's looking at me like I might be sparkling, too.

"Are you okay?" he asks.

"Yeah," I respond slowly, shifting my focus back to the shimmering trees. I walk past Soren, in the direction of a little clearing, and here the shimmering is more distinct, so strong now that sections of the trees appear to shift, out of place, or to blur in with the background. I walk towards the shiniest spot I can see. It's hovering in midair, like a window to another world. I reach out to touch it when I bang my head against something—something hard.

"Ow!" I exclaim loudly, clutching my forehead. I look above me, but there's nothing there, just more shimmering. I put my hand up and feel something metal, smooth and cold, dripping with raindrops. I use my hand to trace along it gingerly.

"Remy, what are you doing?" Soren demands, staring at me from a distance. "You look like a crazy person right now."

"Can't you see it?" I call back. "There's something here. Cloaked. Can't you see the shimmering?" I realize I probably sound like a crazy person, too. I look back at him and see him squinting at the air above my head.

"Well … maybe," he concedes, and starts walking in my direction.

"Keep your head down," I implore. "If I could hit my head on whatever this is, you'll probably be decapitated." He nods and ducks down, walking idiotically through the woods with his knees half-bent.

"It gets stronger the closer you get," he acknowledges. "I can see it now.

Kind of like the air is shining, right?"

"Iridescent, almost," I add, tracing along the smooth metal paneling with my hands. I arrive at something rounded, like the belly of a whale, and I put both of my hands against the metal. My fingers are cold, but I keep following the paneling, searching for any gaps, any openings, any distinction that might tell me what I'm holding onto. Soren's doing the same, padding his palms along the invisible metal in the opposite direction from me.

Suddenly, one of us hits the trigger spot, because the cloaking disappears and the metal stops shining and materializes before us. We're staring at one of the most beautiful airships I've ever seen.

"It looks like a bird," Soren whispers, awed.

"It's magnificent," I agree.

We hear crunching leaves behind us and both of us jerk around, panicked. It's just Bear. His eyes are on his feet, but when he looks up at us, his jaw drops.

"Whoa."

"I know," I laugh, feeling an odd warmth and excitement spread throughout my body. I bounce up on the balls of my feet. "Look at this!"

Soren walks over to the door and puts his palm on the small outline that appears to be a palm reader. The machine beeps.

"Palm print denied." The words seem to emanate from the whole ship. My excitement dissipates almost immediately.

"What are we going to do with a ship we can't get into?" I ask mournfully. Soren shakes his head.

"Figure out a way in. This treasure is too good to leave behind." He starts tracing the ship, checking underneath it and examining the metal casing. "Remy, go check back on the boat and see if there are any tools—bring whatever you can find." I nod and dart off as Soren's voice fades into the distance: "Bear, do you know anything about airships?"

An hour later, darkness is falling, and Soren is prying a metal panel off of the exterior of the airship as Bear and I watch over his shoulder anxiously. Bear, it was no surprise, knew nothing about airships, and I was only able to find a laser knife, a screwdriver, a wrench and a pair of tweezers on the boat. Soren's face fell when he saw my haul, but he set to work trying to find a way into the ship's circuitry. The perfectly smooth paneling makes it hard to identify where any critical systems might be, and it's not like any of us are engineers. I think of Eli and wish desperately that he were here. He'd have us in the airship in minutes.

We all breathe a sigh of relief when Soren pulls off the paneling around the scanner without any alarms going off. Inside is a clear glass pane lit up with blue, red, and green lights that create a complex web of shapes, concentric circles, and connecting lines.

"Great," Soren whispers. "It's all nano-circuitry. This will be harder than I thought."

I sigh and wonder if we're going to be forced to return to our humble water-locked abode once again. Soren starts moving shapes and colors around on the glass panel, rearranging things in various combinations, moving lines and shapes and colors.

"What are you doing?" I ask.

"Circuits like this work via combinatorics. What the palm scanner does is read the arrangement of lines and heat on the palm that's being scanned and maps them to the 'correct' image stored in the system's memory. On a circuit board like this, that will display as having found the optimum combination of shapes and lines to solve the problem of 'matching' the palm's pattern to the stored image." I nod and visualize a load of formulas flying at high-velocity over my head.

"So right now, you're just moving things around trying to find that optimum combination?" Bear asks. I look at him in admiration. Did he really understand that?

"Yes."

"How long will that take?" he asks.

"I don't know. Anywhere from five minutes to five years."

Bear and I look at each other, and I shrug helplessly.

"Is there any other possible way to open the lock?" I ask.

"Unless you somehow manage to figure out whose ship this is and get a digital read of his or her palm print, then no, there's not." Soren's entering his I'm-working-in-a-state-of-Zen-concentration mode, which is usually closely correlated with him being a sarcastic asshole. I walk off and let him work.

I head back to the ship to grab some food, seeing as how I've barely eaten anything all day. I cut a few pieces of cured meat and bite in with relish, savoring the salty, earthy flavor. The energy burst is immediate. I grab some cheese and the rest of the hunk of meat and wrap it in a towel to take back to Soren and Bear. No doubt they're hungry.

When I emerge, it's too dark to see, so I rummage through the packs Chan-

Yu left for us and find two bio-powered torches and bring those with me. When I get back to the airship, I find Soren still staring at the glass circuits, moving things around with his fingers, changing the alignments and combinations. Bear is sitting on a moldy old log, and I join him. His lanky legs are tucked up beneath his jacket to stay warm.

"Has he even moved?" I ask, offering him some meat.

"No," he answers, taking a bite. "Hasn't hardly even looked away mor'n once."

I cut a big slice of the meat off and walk over to Soren. "Need a light?" I hold out the torch.

"No thanks, I can see fine," he responds without looking at me or making any effort to take the lamp from me.

"I brought you some food from the ship, are you hungry?"

"No, thanks." When I see that nothing more is forthcoming, I shrug and head back to Bear.

"He gets like this when he's working on something," I say to him. "When he was playing music or working on a math problem, or even playing chess, he would dive in and wouldn't come up for hours."

"Maybe one of us should keep watch on him, and the other should keep an eye on the boat?" he suggests nervously. It's a good idea. We shouldn't leave the ship alone, and Soren's obviously deadly focused on one thing only.

"You want the boat or Soren?"

"I want Soren," he says. I don't blame him. He's lost his only friend in the world today and probably doesn't want to be alone right now—even if his only companion is an enormous blond robot.

"Holler if something's wrong, okay?" I instruct him. "We're not far away from each other. I'll come running if I hear you." He nods. I hand him the spare torch. It's odd, feeling like the leader. I'm so used to being led, looking up to other people, following orders. For once, someone else is looking up to *me*.

"You do the same," he says, setting his mouth in a fierce line.

I head back to the boat and settle down in the same position I was resting in this morning, at the crack of dawn, when Bear and Sam snuck up on us. I keep the torch on next to me, the slanting beam flickering off the river, staring out into the darkness just like this morning.

I keep watch over the boat for what must be several hours. Impatience comes and goes, and I stand up and pace every now and then, checking our packs for anything I might have missed, something that would help us break into the airship—anything at all, really. I'm not tired, even though it's getting late and I've been mostly awake since the crack of dawn. The numbness from earlier has worn off completely, and now I'm restless. I want to be home, I think. I *just want everyone to know I'm all right. I want to tell my parents, tell Eli, that I'm alive.* I fight the urge to tell Soren to stop working on the airship, that we need to keep moving, but I know if we can break in it will save so much time, so many days of walking through the woods, through unknown, potentially hostile land—

"REMY!"

It's Bear. In an instant I'm off, leaping the gunwale like a hurdle in Eli's training drills, clutching the pocketknife from Chan-Yu's pack, and tearing through the woods towards the clearing.

"He did it!" Bear shouts enthusiastically at me, materializing out of nowhere and startling me so much that my first instinct is to slap my hand over his mouth from behind and hold him still for a second. My blade is uncomfortably close to his face, but I don't care.

"Not so fucking loud," I swear, my voice a low growl. "Do you want to get us killed?"

Bear's eyes are wide and full of surprise as he shakes his head vigorously *no.* I release him.

"Sorry," he says, rubbing his cheek and glaring at me, half awed, half indignant. "What are you so afraid of?"

"Everything," I spit back, furious. I spin off and head into the clearing with the airship.

Soren, meanwhile, is nowhere to be seen, but the hatch of the door to the airship is open, so I bound over and hop inside. He's sitting in one of the two pilot's seats, his back to me. The basic interior lights are already on, and the glass control panel is lit up with a few pulsating lights, but I can tell by the silence that the engines aren't running yet.

"How'd you do it?" is my first question. I know he'll want to brag about how he cracked it. Sure enough, he swings around in the chair with a triumphant grin on his face.

"It was just like a Rubik's cube, all I had to—"

"A what?"

"A—it's this puzzle where you have to—oh, never mind, it won't make any sense unless I show you. Bottom line is it was just a puzzle, where anytime I moved anything, something else changed, but all I had to do was figure out the parameters and which movements would affect the rest of the puzzle and how. It's all about optimization. So, for instance, if I expanded a pair of concentric circles, the green lines would change to blue, and if I contracted them—"

"Spare me," I cut in, sitting down eagerly at the copilot's seat and running my hands along the smooth glass panes of the control panel. "Congratulations, but I don't have a clue what you're talking about. Soren," I say, turning to him with a smile lining my face, "we can go home in this!" I feel like a beacon of hope has descended upon us.

"That's the plan," he says, grinning just as enthusiastically. "Do you know how to fly?"

My beacon flickers.

"No ... don't you?" I ask. The smile slides off his face.

"No."

The beacon dies.

"Are you shitting me?" The anger I felt with Bear just moments ago quickly resurfaces.

"We spent five hours trying to break into this damn airship only to find out that neither of us can fly it?" The beacon of hope is devolving into a maelstrom of rage.

"Remy, calm down. We're intelligent people. We can figure it out," Soren says matter-of-factly, and his tone is so condescending that it actually does calm me. It's like we're back at home, at the Resistance base, going at each other over totally stupid things again. It's comforting, in a way. Soren turns back to the controls and starts touching things on the glass panel, which right now is dark.

"Maybe there's an instruction booklet," Bear pipes up from behind us, who has evidently joined us on the ship. I fight the urge to laugh.

"Okay. I'm calm. Sorry." I find my smile again.

"Even when we were in the Sector I never flew a plane," Soren mutters. "They were always on the city-wide nav system."

"And Firestone does all our flying for us now."

"Yeah." He's running his hands all over the glass, touching all the lights, looking for anything that will power up the ship. There's a small pulsating green light across from him, and I reach over him and press that one out of curiosity. The interior lights come on and I can hear the soft hum of the energy cells activating. Soren glares at me and turns back to the panel.

"Hey, nice," Bear says.

"Bear, do us a favor and go get all the food from the boat, as well as our packs and anything you need, and bring it all over here." Without so much as a grumble or a complaint at being ordered around, Bear hops outside and disappears. Soren and I exchange surprised glances, and I shrug.

"I guess he's used to being ordered around a lot," I offer.

"And doing heavy labor," Soren adds.

It takes us about fifteen minutes to figure out how to get all the control panels and display systems operating, but by the time Bear has schlepped everything into the airship, we think we're ready to give this flying thing a try. As soon as Soren closes the pod door, though, a message starts beeping on the communications feed.

"Valerian Orleán, please report. Valerian Orleán, indicate location and status."

My heart goes stiff and cold and every cell in my body seems to be frozen in confusion and agony. Soren, too, is totally immobile, his face tense, and both of us stare at the comm feed. The voice is rough and full of static, but audible.

"Why's the ship talking about Valerian Orleán?" Bear demands.

"What the hell?" Soren swears under his breath.

I can't even speak.

28 — VALE

The familiar voice behind me turns out to belong to Jahnu Nair, Moriana's cousin, and it's no wonder I couldn't place it. I haven't heard his voice in three years, and since then, it's dropped at least an octave. Last time I saw him, he was an awkward, plump kid that Moriana was always babysitting. Turns out, he's not plump or awkward anymore. And I recognize Kenzie Oban—I remember her as a tall, fit girl with startlingly red hair. She, Eli, and Jahnu are all together, along with someone I don't recognize, a man with dark black curls and a lazy, slouching expression, and they look none too happy to see us.

"What are you—" The metal of the Bolt is pushed harder against my head and I stop talking.

"Keep your mouth shut, pretty boy," Eli interrupts me.

I'm hoping Eli doesn't have the authority to kill me, but I'm not going to test his limits. Jahnu sits me down on a log and Eli does the same for Jeremiah. Miah gives me the once-over, presumably making sure I'm okay. His eyes are narrowed and his mouth set in a tense line.

"Okay," Eli begins. "First things first. Where are Remy and Soren?"

"I don't know," I respond honestly.

"See, here's the thing. That doesn't make me happy," Eli says casually, easily, staring out into the sky as though talking to the moon. "Because the last time I saw you, you were carting them off in your airship. And I assumed, naturally, since you are a man of great integrity, that you would be taking personal responsibility for their welfare. So, if it turns out I was wrong and you have somehow allowed them to be injured—or worse—then I will have no qualms about shooting you." He muses on this for a second. "They might not be too happy back at base, but frankly, I don't give a damn what they think."

Okay. Eli's a loose cannon, and I'm directly in his line of fire. Great. I need to diffuse this situation.

"Look," I respond, keeping my voice quiet and steady, though Jahnu's

Bolt pointing at my head makes rational thought a little difficult. "Remy and Soren escaped from the capital almost three full days ago. A soldier under my command helped them, and they've been fugitives since." For some reason, I don't want them to know Chan-Yu is an Outsider. I'm not sure whether it will lend credibility to my story or if it will sound even more farfetched. I'm not sure what sort of relationship the Resistance has, if any, with the Outsiders. "Jeremiah and I voluntarily left the Sector yesterday, and we abandoned our airship because we were being tracked. I have no idea whether Remy and Soren have been recaptured, but I'm willing to bet my parents are a lot more worried about finding me than they are about Remy and Soren."

"Is that so?"

"Yes, that's so."

"Tell me, Valerian, why would they be worried about finding you?" Eli asks. "Have you gone missing?"

"Something like that," Jeremiah mutters, and I see him wince as Kenzie raises her Bolt. Eli turns and considers him.

"Something like that, huh?" Eli says. "And what are you doing out in the woods with an Orleán, Sayyid?"

"He doesn't have anything to do with Remy and Soren," I interject. The last thing I want is for Eli to take out his anger on Miah.

"If he doesn't have anything to do with Remy and Soren, why is he out here tramping through the woods with you?"

"Listen, we're not here on the Sector's authority. We fled. Just like you did three years ago."

I notice Kenzi's eyes flick over toward Jahnu's, but Eli's never leave my own.

"That's funny," he says, "because just last night I was watching a Sector broadcast about everyone's favorite celebrity. Valerian Orleán. The handsome son of the chancellor was bragging about his wonderful job and his new love affair with Linnea Heilmann. And now here you are! Out in the Wilds with nary a security detail in sight." He peers up through the trees as if Sector troops are going to start dropping through the branches at any moment. "So, you say you left just like I did three years ago."

"Yes, we left last night after the—"

"And did you leave the girl you loved laying in a pool of blood? Or your mentor crumpled in a headless heap, his brain sprayed against the back wall? Or a whole team of former colleagues testifying that you'd gone crazy? Or maybe you left because suddenly your parents disappeared off the face of the earth—poof, gone, just like that. Is that how you left just like I did?"

I don't know how to respond to that. Fortunately, Eli spares me the trouble. "Let's try this again. Where are Remy and Soren?"

"I told you," I say. "They escaped with the help of a soldier under my command and—"

In about a half second Eli's got a knife at my throat and I can already feel the tiny droplets of blood being pulled from my skin. "You expect us to believe that? That you helped them escape?" He spits the word derisively.

"Yes," I choke out, trying not to move. "I told him to get Remy and Soren the hell out of there. Otherwise, my mother would have had them killed. It was the only way to keep them alive."

Eli continues to stare at me for another few seconds while I hold my breath and hope that this time I've said the right thing. Finally, he lets me go.

"Why?"

"I don't know, exactly. She was afraid they had some really important information. Information that my mother—Corine—couldn't risk getting back to you guys, to the Resistance." At this, Eli's eyes flick to Kenzie's and Jahnu's. *Do they know what my mother was after?*

"Tell me everything you know about Remy and Soren's whereabouts," Eli says calmly, again staring out at the darkening sky.

"I already have. Their lives were in danger, so I asked one of the men in my command, a man I had just learned was ready to disappear as well, to help them escape."

"And how did you know this man was 'ready to disappear'?"

"Look, their lives were in immediate danger. I believed this man could help them. And I know he got them out of the building. That much I'm sure of."

For several seconds Eli is silent. Then: "So you said you abandoned your airship because you were being tracked. Where did you leave it?"

"We landed close to the river, by that old power plant. We've been walking ever since. We thought we'd figured out how to disable any tracking capabilities, but someone in the Sector took control of the airship and started flying us home." I glance at Jeremiah. "It wasn't pretty."

"Yeah. We watched you lose your cloaking and almost run in to a cliff."

"You saw that?"

"That was when we started tracking you."

"But we were able to reengage the cloaking."

"Sure, you were. There's this little thing called echolocation; you know, acoustic locators, sonar? Once we knew your general vicinity, we were able to follow you pretty easily."

"So you saw what we were up against. You saw us trying to get control of the airship."

"Or maybe you're both just really shitty pilots," the man with black curls pipes up.

"We're telling the truth, Eli," I insist. "Remy and Soren escaped with one of my men. And then we left. Now, we have no idea where they are. All I know is that they're probably not in the Sector."

"'Probably'?"

"Probably. If they've been recaptured in the last eighteen hours, they could be back in Okaria. But I doubt that's happened. I've trained with this soldier for the last two years, and I have no doubt he can take care of himself—and Remy and Soren, too. Besides, as much as the Sector will want to find the escaped prisoners, I'm willing to bet my parents are more focused on finding me." But is that really true? If my mother was willing to kill Remy and Soren because of the information they had, I doubt she's stopped looking for them just because I've disappeared.

Eli's immobile for a few more minutes. Everyone is looking to him for some sort of decision—everyone, that is, except the man with the mop of black hair, who seems way more preoccupied with Jeremiah. He's staring at him intently, scrutinizing him, as though trying to place him. Finally he speaks up.

"You related to Zeke Sayyid?" All eyes spin to the black-haired man, and then back to Jeremiah.

"I'm his son."

"Who's that?" Jahnu demands.

"He's with us," the dark-haired man responds. "Works at Waterloo. We're from the same factory town. You're Jeremiah, right?" Jeremiah nods. "You were a TREE scholar?" Miah nods again. I always forget that Jeremiah's not from the capital—he took to the high-flying city life so easily you'd never know he was originally from a small town. "What're you tagging along with an Orleán for?"

"He's my best friend," Miah says simply, and for some reason that admission makes me so happy I could float into the air on the bubble swelling in my chest. "We left together after we figured out what was going on."

The black-haired man watches the two of us for a few seconds, and then addresses Jeremiah again:

"You tryin' to find your dad?"

"I'd like to see him again, but that's not why I'm here."

"Well, he's nary at our base, but we can take you to him," the man says, and

I wonder how Jeremiah managed to lose his country accent so thoroughly.

"We're not doing anything of the sort until we find Remy and Soren," Eli snaps at him. The black-haired man shrugs.

"Elijah, if you don't report to the Director immediately that we've found Valerian Orleán running around in the woods, she's gonna throw your ass in the lake."

Jeremiah and I keep our mouths shut. I don't know which option sounds less appealing—being stuck with Eli while he's on the warpath, or facing down the Resistance's infamous Director in a few hours.

Eli swears and tells Kenzie to go radio in that they've taken me hostage. Kenzie runs off into the woods somewhere, and I wonder if they've got an airship in the vicinity. *What a surprising turn of events.* Despite my best efforts to stay away from the Resistance, Jeremiah was right. Sooner or later, they'd find me. It just turned out to be a lot sooner than I expected.

After a few tense moments, Kenzie comes running back with instructions to return with the hostages immediately. Eli spits and swears at the black-haired man, who looks perfectly unperturbed. He and Eli grab our heavy packs and head through the woods. Jeremiah and I are instructed to follow them, and though I can no longer feel the cold gunmetal pressed against my head, Jahnu and Kenzie are right on our heels. They don't trust us. I don't blame them.

Half an hour later, we're in their airship, a fat, clunky old thing that, from the smell of it, seems to run off of fossil fuel. *It still has propellers!* Jeremiah mouthed at me as it came into view. But once inside, I realize the ship is powered entirely by a micro fusion generator and that the control panel is almost as sophisticated as the Sarus's. The propellers must just be for backup— like my dad's archaic control system.

The black-haired man sits down opposite us. He throws his arm up over the back of the seat and leans back, obviously not nearly as threatened by us as everyone else seems to be.

"What's your name?" Jeremiah asks.

"Firestone."

"You worked in Ellas with my father?"

"True enough," he says simply.

"Did you leave first, or did he?"

"I did. Tried to convince him to come with me, but he wasn't for it at the time. He was one of the ones who thought about stuff, more than just the average person. I think something finally tipped him over the edge, but he never did tell me what. Just showed up at the Thermopylae base about six months ago."

"What's he do for the Resistance?" Jeremiah asks eagerly.

"Firestone," Eli calls from the front, warningly. "Get up here and fly the damn ship." Firestone winks at us.

"Guess you'll just have to find out."

Their ship isn't nearly as smooth as the Sarus—maybe because of the drag from the old propellers— but we're in the air without a hitch after a few minutes. They ignore us for the most part, though Jahnu steps into the holding area for a moment to ask me about his cousin.

"How's Moriana?" He sits across from us.

"She's …" I look at Jeremiah. "Well, she's great. She's working for Corine. With the OAC." I know Jahnu won't be proud of this. True to form, he sighs and looks up at the ceiling.

"We watched the graduation. I heard her placement announcement." He looks at Jeremiah. "Have I been reading the broadcasts right? Were you going out with her?" Jeremiah looks flustered, which is unlike him. His cheeks are going red, and he's determinedly ignoring Jahnu's eyes.

"Yeah."

"Is she … is she okay? Happy?"

"Yeah, she's happy. She loves her research." Jeremiah is now staring intently at a spot on the floor. I know how guilty he feels about leaving her without an explanation.

"Did she know you were leaving?" There's a long pause before Miah responds.

"We didn't tell her." Jahnu nods, and there is a long, awkward silence before he stands to head up to the cockpit where his team members are sitting. Before he rejoins them, though, he turns back to us.

"Comfortable? Hungry? Thirsty?"

"You're really concerned?" I ask.

"We're not going to starve you," he responds, and a pang of guilt throbs through me.

"I could eat." Jeremiah perks up. "We've got Mealpaks in our bags."

"Really?" A suspicious frown crosses Jahnu's face, and I remember Soren's sneering comments about my ignorance of the Dieticians' manipulations.

"Yeah, we took as much as we could carry," Jeremiah responds nonchalantly, though suddenly everyone in the airship is looking at us. "Why? What's so weird about that?"

But Kenzie and Jahnu have started opening our bags and going through them, pulling out our Mealpaks, opening them and dumping the contents into a compost hatch.

"What are you doing?!" Jeremiah shouts. "We need that!" I should have known they would do this. Soren's anger should have clued me in to the fact that the Resistance wouldn't let Sector food anywhere near them. At my side, Jeremiah is panic-stricken, but all I can think is, *maybe it's for the best.*

"No, you don't." Eli's voice is cold. "So long as you're with us you won't eat anything from the Sector." He turns to us, unsmiling. "You might even get to find out who you really are after a few days."

"What's that supposed to mean?" Jeremiahs demand. Eli ignores him.

"They've been manipulating you," Jahnu explains patiently. "Everything the Dieticians put into the food is designed to control you, to shape your brain and your body into whoever or whatever they want you to be."

"Sounds pretty damn good to me," Jeremiah interrupts. "I *like* that they feed me stuff that makes me better able to do my job. You don't?"

"Maybe you're just not naturally as intelligent as I am," Jahnu responds with a smile, which shuts Jeremiah up for a while.

The rest of the trip passes in tense—and hungry—silence. The strangeness of meeting a group of people in the Wilds who used to be my classmates and friends, now as something like enemies, hangs over us all. I keep catching Jahnu and Kenzie sneaking glances at us, as though looking at an illusion they can't quite figure out. I don't mind—it gives me an opportunity to watch them, too. They've undoubtedly seen a fair few Sector broadcasts with my face plastered all over the displays, and Jeremiah has probably made an appearance or two as well. But aside from the raid under the cover of night, I haven't seen any of them in three years.

When we finally touch down, Kenzie and Jahnu tie black kerchiefs around our eyes and then lead off the ship. I try to make use of my other senses while blind—the ground beneath my feet is paved, and the air crisp and moist. We suspect the Resistance base is located somewhere in one of the old world cities, but nothing around me gives any indication as to where the base is within the city. We start to descend, though, and I realize we're going underground. *Of course.* They wouldn't have built their facilities on the surface where our drones would be able to photograph them.

We make a few sharp turns and finally are sat down somewhere. Here the air is stale and recycled. It's clammy and cold, and I'm sure Miah's not happy about any of this. He's claustrophobic. Someone pulls off my blindfold and I open my eyes, expecting to be blinded by bright lights. But the lights here are dim and luminescent, probably to save energy. I blink a few times, refocusing my eyes, and Eli's face swims before me. I look around and see that I'm in a tiny holding room, and Jeremiah has disappeared.

"Where's Miah?" I demand.

"You're being separated so we can corroborate your stories independently." Eli's cutting the ties binding my hands behind me. When he's finished, I rub my wrists together, trying to get rid of the red marks. Eli steps out of the tiny room without another word and closes the door behind him. I can hear a series of locks click into place.

I wait patiently, expecting something to happen soon. Surely they'll want to talk to me immediately, right? I steel myself for the impending interrogation, and my mind flits anxiously back to the condition that Remy and Soren were in when I first saw them in the capital. I can only hope I won't meet a similar fate. *Karmic retribution,* I think bitterly.

But even after half an hour, nothing has happened. I lie down on the wooden bench in the small room and try to relax. I'm expecting someone to walk in the door at any minute. But still no one does.

I realize it's entirely possible they have more important things to do than talk to me immediately. After all, they're a small group of people. Just because Valerian Orleán walks into their midst, I shouldn't expect them to drop everything to hear my story or exact their revenge. Somehow that calms me.

With that in mind, I quickly relax and drop off into a light sleep.

Some time later, the sound of the metal locks clicking in the door wakes me. I stir and sit up, my spine stiff and sore from sleeping on the rough wooden bench. The door creaks open and Eli stares at me, incredulously, as I rub my eyes.

"Were you *sleeping?*" he asks.

"Maybe," I respond defensively.

"Doctor Rhinehouse wants to talk to you." He ties the kerchief around my eyes again and everything goes black. He walks me out blindly through the stuffy corridors and dumps me in a chair. This time when the blindfold is removed, bright purple lights shine down at me, the rays stabbing into my eyes, and for a moment I am almost as blind as I was before. After my pupils adjust, I see an old man with an eye patch sitting on the other side of the table, watching me cautiously. His face looks more like it is covered by a thick protective bark, rough and creased, than by skin. Only the slate-colored beard stubble and the glistening, attentive eye give him away as human rather than tree.

"Good evening, Valerian," he says, somewhat cordially. "Eli—out." Eli turns on his heel and stalks out, slamming the door behind him. He always did have a problem with authority. I'm sure he doesn't like responding to Rhinehouse's commands any more than I did to Aulion's.

"Dr. Rhinehouse," I nod in his direction. "Pleasure to finally meet you. Is Jeremiah all right?"

He stares at me stonily. "You're not in a position to be asking questions like that, Valerian."

"You can do whatever you want to me, but Jeremiah's here in good faith. Is he okay?"

"He's fine." Rhinehouse's good eye is deadly focused on me. "Firestone is feeding him some soup. He said he was hungry." There's a note of humor in his voice, but his face is blank, unsmiling, neutral.

"He's always hungry, so I hope you have a lot of soup." I was hoping for a trace of a smile, but the scowl doesn't change.

"The Director wants to talk to you, but I told her I didn't think you were trustworthy. Tell me why I'm wrong." It's a challenge.

"Because Remy and Soren are out in the Wilds somewhere, free, at my command." Rhinehouse stares at me, expressionless. When he doesn't speak, I continue. "Three nights ago, I overheard my mother command a soldier in my employ to kill Remy and Soren. When I confronted him, I discovered he had no intention of carrying out her orders. I asked him to help them escape. After that, I knew I couldn't stay."

"Tell me why Corine did this. And why that prompted such a sudden change of heart."

I briefly explain, as simply as possible, what Remy told me during the interrogation about Tai's death, and how I hacked into my mother's computer to find out if what she said was true. I tell him about the conversation I overheard between my mother and Chan-Yu, and explain how I dashed back to Sector Headquarters only to find him preparing to spring them free anyway. I don't mention my conversation with my parents. I tell him only that when I told Jeremiah the whole story, we agreed we couldn't stay and decided to leave under the cover of the Solstice Celebration.

"And yet last night, for all the world to see, you were so eager to espouse the virtues of the Sector," he states calmly.

"It's easy to do when you're not planning on sticking around."

When I fall silent, he finally looks away, dropping his one-eyed gaze from my face. The room is so still I can hear him breathe. Finally, after several moments of heavy silence, he says, without looking at me:

"I would think your story was an elaborate construction if not for the fact that it's so similar to my own." He stops here and takes in a laborious breath. "Your very identity makes it hard to believe you, but the transformation you claim to have undergone is the same one that brought everyone in the Resistance here." There is a brief silence. He looks up at me as though contemplating a chess board. Maybe this is a game of chess to him, and I am a knight or a bishop, and he's trying to decide where to move me. The game is made more complicated by the fact that I could be playing for either black or white, and he has to guess which side I take orders from.

"You say Remy and Soren are out of the Sector's hands." He raps his knuckles on the table in front of him. "But you don't have any idea where they are?"

"Not a clue. I couldn't have gotten personally involved without drawing attention to their escape. I left them in Chan-Yu's hands."

"And you trust this Chan-Yu?"

"I didn't really have a choice."

"That's not helpful, Vale."

"I would have trusted him with my own life. More helpful, now?"

"Maybe if you kept your sarcasm to yourself," he snaps. I drop my eyes. I probably deserved that.

"Sorry." There's another pause as we both stare across the table, sizing each other up.

"So, do you know why your mother wanted to kill Remy and Soren?"

"She said they had some information that was a threat to the Sector. Something that could destroy the Sector and the OAC. I don't see how anything could be so dangerous that it was worth murder."

Rhinehouse muses over this for a minute. "Yes, we have that in common, Vale," he says, almost absentmindedly. "I think I know what Corine was referring to, but how did Remy and Soren find the solution?" I can't tell if he's posing me the question or talking to himself.

Just then, the lights flicker overhead, and a red light in the corner of the room starts flashing.

"Orange alert. Orange alert. Sector airship detected entering radar space. Prepare for possible conflict. Raid teams on high alert."

"Damn it," Rhinehouse swears at me, slamming his fist down on the table. "Did you lead them here?" he shouts. On the defensive, I throw my hands up, palms out.

"I have no idea what this is about," I protest. "You can strip me bare—there are no tracers on either me or Jeremiah." Cursing, he stands up and spits something incomprehensible at Eli, who dashes in, pulls my hands behind my back and binds my wrists again. He hauls me up and out of the room as we follow Rhinehouse. I guess speed is important now, since they don't bother to blindfold me.

Rhinehouse stalks down the hallways, and Eli and I follow. Eli's got his Bolt out again, and though it's not pressed to the back of my head, it's clear he's ready to shoot. After a series of turns through the winding hallways, we're in some sort of control room. Rhinehouse shoves a technician out of the way and touches one of the screens, pulling up a hologram of the incoming ship.

"Defensive positions, Eli," he says and Eli turns on his heel and takes off running. Then Rhinehouse turns to me. "What is this?" he demands. I take a few steps closer, staring at the hologram.

"Holy shit," I whisper.

It's my Sarus.

Winter 2, Sector Annum 106, 21h37
Gregorian Calendar: December 22

Soren tries to get the constantly repeating message to shut off, but there doesn't seem to be a way to disable it or even to turn the volume down.

"What do we do?" I ask nervously. "Do you think Vale is out here?"

"Did they finally catch up to us?" Soren asks, fear in his voice.

"Why is the ship ordering him to check in? Was this his ship?" There are a million unanswered questions racing through my mind right now, and I can tell by the way Soren's fingers are flying across the glass panel that he's in a similar state.

"Why would this ship just be here, though?" Soren asks, and that seems to be the most perplexing question of them all. Why was this ship here? "Did they plant it as a trap?" We discovered this miraculous, beautiful airship, left mysteriously out in the woods as though for us to find. It's almost like one of the Outsiders planted it for us, just like the *Zephyr*. But then why is it calling Vale's name? Why is it demanding he report in?

"What's going on?" Bear asks. "Why would Valerian Orleán be setting a trap for you?"

Soren and I look at each other, trying to figure out what to tell him and what to do next. We haven't fully explained to Bear what we're doing out here. He's figured out we're with the Resistance, but he might not realize how much attention he's drawing to himself by tagging along with us. And furthermore, after all that effort, all that time spent breaking into the airship, getting everything ready—have we walked into a trap? Can we continue in this ship?

I take a deep breath and turn around, locking eyes with the young man behind me.

"Bear, there's something we haven't told you. You said earlier there was a bounty on your head. Well, there's a lot more than a bounty on our heads." I wait for him to ask, to inquire further, but he doesn't, and the ship interrupts us again.

"Valerian Orleán , please report, Valerian Orleán...."

"We're running from the Sector. We just escaped from the capital a few days ago. They were going to kill us," I say, looking hard at Bear, trying to impress upon him the gravity of the situation. "Valerian Orleán was the one who captured us in the first place."

"Whoa," he says.

"Jackass," Soren mutters. I can't agree or disagree either way. I still can't get over the look in Vale's eyes when I was shouting at him about Tai. I want to believe he knew something was wrong, but I just don't know.

"Do we at least have enough fuel to get home?" I ask.

"Looks like we're at full capacity," Soren says. "It's partially solar-powered, and the panels are fully charged."

"Well, listen," Bear says practically, "'less you two want to head back to the river or go by foot, I say we don't have much choice but to fly this ship out of here."

He's got a point.

"Do you think they'll track us?" I ask Soren nervously.

"We're taking a calculated risk either way," he responds. "We could wander out in the Wilds for days, starving and cold, or we can take the ship now. This will save us days of travel time."

"Maybe ..." I start. "Maybe we could land it a ways outside of base. Then even if the Sector is tracking us, they still won't know exactly where the base is."

Soren nods. "If we stay out in the Wilds, we could get lost or the drones might find us. But if we take the ship, we could lead them directly to us. If we land outside the city, though, I think we'll be okay. We might even draw their attention away from main base."

"Better that than going by foot for another few days," Bear offers.

Soren seems to acknowledge this and moves a few dials on the control pad. We are pressed ever so slightly into the ground as the ship lifts into the air, carrying us above the treetops and forward. We've made our decision.

"Wait," I interrupt, though we're already flying. "Do we know where we're going?"

Soren shakes his head. "If we can at least get to the outpost we were originally instructed to walk to, then from there I think we can figure out how to get back home. We still have Osprey's map. Pull it out. That should help us get to the first outpost."

"Shouldn't a ship like this have a navigation system?" I ask, as I rummage around for the map. Not that I don't trust Soren. I just don't want to take any chances flying around in the middle of nowhere.

"We can't activate it without alerting the entire Sector to our presence."

I sigh. I guess Soren's navigational skills and a rough map on a v-scroll will have to be enough to go by.

"Besides, once we find the lake, we'll be fine," Soren points out. That's true. If we follow the lakeshore, we'll make it home. But if we over- or under-shoot, we could end up deep in the Wilds, completely lost, without any way of communicating with the Resistance. I close my eyes and hope like hell we can find our way.

As it turns out, though, Soren's navigational skills are less useful than my visual skills when it comes to following the map on the v-scroll. Because it's now dark out, we're viewing everything on the ship's infrared and deep-radar sensors. Soren keeps getting confused about the markers, wondering where we are along the path, but for me, matching the images on the ship's sensors to the images in the map is easy. It's just like drawing. So I'm appointed the unofficial navigator, and surprisingly, I manage to track us to the lake in less than an hour.

Once Soren and I had managed to get the control panels up and running, everything was intuitive. In fact, the computer guides us through almost the whole process of flight. There's a diagram of the airship that can be expanded into a hologram if necessary, showing exactly where and how to turn, ascend, descend, and lift up or down. The computer makes recommendations based on the objects, wind, and air pressure in the immediate area, and all we have to do is follow those recommendations by doing simple things on the control panel.

Now the one thing we all agree on is that flying is an adrenalin blast. It's beyond exhilarating. None of us have ever been so thoroughly in control of an object capable of moving at such high speeds, and if it weren't for the trauma we've all gone through in the last few days, it would be downright fun. Even though it's dark out, the swooping feeling I get in my stomach when we take her up high and then drop her down, plummeting back to earth, is delightful. We fly high up over the trees and swoop down low, cooing over the beautiful motions the airship makes and the way we always seem to pull out of the dive right before a deadly crash. We head south first, to the trail Osprey originally marked on our map for us to follow by foot. We follow that path for a while, until we feel confident swerving west to try to find the lake. Once we hit the lake, we track the shoreline instead of flying over water so we don't miss the city by going either too far north or south.

But all the while, in the background, the communications feed is barking, *"Valerian Orleán, Valerian Orleán ..."* and I can't get it out of my mind that danger lurks, that we're being followed, that something threatening is looming over us like a storm cloud, pregnant with thunder.

Finally, after an hour of following the lakeshore, the distant grey hulking shells of ruined buildings tell us that the city is approaching. *Home*, I think, so happy I could cry. I envision Eli's crooked grin and try to picture the life-or-death hug coming my way. I wonder if my parents have been recalled from their mission because I was taken hostage; maybe I'll get to see them again, for the first time in a year. And Jahnu, his broad, irrepressible smile; Kenzie, her eagerness, excitement, and innocence. I'm even looking forward to seeing Rhinehouse again. He'll probably scold us for not coming home sooner, or not bringing onions with us, or something similarly ridiculous.

And, I realize, something I haven't thought of in a long time: the DNA. Have they cracked the code in our absence? Unlikely. Even though it feels like a lifetime, it's only been five days. We'll bring the solution with us. I smile, thinking of how pleased Rhinehouse and Eli will be. Of course, we don't know for sure, yet, if *Lotus* is the correct keyword. We still have to test it to see if I'm right. But I'm positive I am.

"There's a good clearing over there," I say, pointing to a relatively flat spot ahead. "We can land there and hike in. You should slow the ship down."

"That's a beautiful spot, Remy," Soren says, a note of desperation in his voice, "but I can't figure out how to land the airship. I can't even figure out how to get the landing gear out."

"Oh," I say. "Shit." Visions of the ship tumbling nose-over-tail through a copse of trees until we burst into a fiery inferno, or screeching along pavement, tearing into the reactor and causing an explosion suddenly fill my mind. That would not be optimal, as Eli would say.

"I can't even figure out how to hover, Remy. I can go forward, backwards, and sideways, but how do I bring the airship to a full stop without powering down completely? We'll drop out of the fucking sky."

"Well," I say, too confidently, as we blow past the spot I had originally sighted, "we'll figure it out." I give him a reassuring smile. "We can loop around and come back to that spot." Soren starts to angle the ship in a wide circle over the lake, but his face is tense and worried. He's trying every combination of slides, buttons, and flashing lights, but nothing seems to be happening.

"Soren," I reprimand, "punching every button on the panel isn't going to help."

"Let me know when you have a better idea!" he snaps as we pass the landing spot a second time. He starts to loop back around again.

I start searching around on the panels for any indication of the landing gear that was out when we first found the plane. Nothing obvious stands out at me. I can't even remember pulling the tripods *in* let alone trying to get them back out.

"Maybe the ship does it automatically?" I ask, perplexed. "When you descend?"

"We can't take that chance," Soren responds. "I don't think we can land in a clearing," he says, as we pass our intended spot a third time. "We need a runway of some sort."

"Shit." I check around the area on the ship's sensors, but there's nowhere long and clear enough to land the old-fashioned way. "Should we head to the city, then?"

"It's that or a crash landing. Damn it," Soren swears. "If there are drones on our tail, we'll bring them with us."

Bear hasn't piped up for a while, and when I check behind us, I find him passed out in the tiny lounge area. Small wonder. The kid's probably exhausted, physically and emotionally.

"At least if we all die, he'll go peacefully," I mumble.

"What?" Soren's still screwing with the controls.

"Nothing." I pull up a model of the airship's hull and scan it, trying to figure out if I can instruct the computer to pull out the landing gear that way. I peer at the hologram, looking under the ship's belly where I know the tripods to be, but there's nothing that indicates a way to release them. "We could just land without the gear. What do we need landing gear for?"

"I still haven't figured out how to hover!" Soren snaps.

"Just cut the velocity to zero and keep the upwards lift on," I say, reaching over him to try to demonstrate. He slaps my hand away.

"What are you doing? We're going a hundred and fifty kilometers per hour! You can't cut our speed when we're not even into the city yet!"

"Oh," I mutter, cowed, my hand shrinking back to my side of the cockpit. "Right."

"This is the problem with modern computing," Soren mutters. "If everything were controlled by levers and dials, we'd have figured it out in a second."

"Really?" I challenge. "Yeah, we'd have just stepped into this ship and instantly known which levers and dials did what, is that it?"

But as we fly in and over the city, it quickly becomes apparent that the ship isn't going to let us cut our velocity to zero. We try a few test runs, cutting our speed and declining in altitude, but each time we get close to a landing a voice beeps at us that *parts of the ship are not functioning at full capacity*. Neither of us has a clue what that means, except that we can't hover down to the ground and we can't figure out how to get the landing gear out. We're getting closer and closer to base, and it's obvious that our original plan has been shot to hell. It's my screeching at Soren as we come within twenty meters of the pavement that finally wakes Bear up behind us.

"Slow the ship down!" I'm shouting wildly as we press every button in sight, trying to figure out how to get the landing gear out as we career past crumbling high-rises and abandoned factories. I can see where our base is—we're so close to home!—but we blow past it, still unable to bring the craft to a hover and too afraid to descend to the ground for fear of tearing the whole thing to pieces.

"I'm trying!" Soren shouts back at me. "We better hope they don't shoot us down."

"What's going on?" Bear pops up behind us.

I'm panicking. I'm pressing every button I can see. None of them are helping.

"What do we do?" Soren shouts helplessly. Just as flustered as I am, he goes to hit a button and accidentally slides the elevation control down by about ten meters.

"ENGAGE THE FUCKING LANDING GEAR!" I scream at the top of my lungs.

"*Landing gear engaging.*" The ship's computerized voice is complacent. On the status hologram, three tripods emerge from the airship's belly, and our velocity drops almost instantly from the air resistance. "*Landing gear engaged,*" the peaceful female voice confirms for me. Soren looks at me, his mouth slightly open, his eyes wide.

"How'd you do that?"

I stare at the glass panel, at a loss for an answer.

"I guess I just told it what to do," I shrug. "I didn't know we could do that."

"Shit."

Soren kills the velocity further, drops the airship to the ground, and we settle in rather nicely, almost as if we actually knew what we were doing.

"Phew," Soren says. It's an absurd thing to say, considering that we were seconds away from death. I close my eyes, let my breath out, and sink deep into the pilot's chair. My mind has gone blank. I stare at the green and black behind my eyelids for several seconds before Bear pipes up behind me.

"Great save, Remy. You guys wanna get out now?"

I can't bring myself to move quite yet. Even after that miraculous save, something feels wrong. I sit up and open my eyes, but it takes a minute to realize what it is. The ship's comm feed isn't asking about Valerian Orleán anymore. The message is gone.

I nod in response to Bear, trying to pretend that wasn't the most harrowing thing we've experienced throughout this whole disaster. I still haven't gotten my breath back, and my heart is pounding in my chest.

Soren pops open the hatch and Bear glances out and around.

"Kind of a dump," he says. "You guys live here?" Soren and I exchange rueful looks. If Bear wants to join the Resistance, he's going to have to get used to living in a ruin.

"We don't live in it. We live underground," Soren corrects. Bear wrinkles his nose and glares down at the streets. He hops out and disappears from view.

"Well, Remy Alexander," Soren says, smiling at me. "It's been a pleasure." I laugh.

"I wouldn't go that far," I respond, and suddenly I want nothing more than to be in his arms again. He leans into me, like he did this morning, only this time I don't recoil. Hesitantly at first, he stretches his hand behind my head and leans in to kiss me. I can feel my face flushing and warmth spreading up through my body. A smile paints itself across my face, and I can hardly breathe. I want to kiss him back, to wrap myself inside of him and bury everything that's happened in his tender blue-eyed smile. But instead he pulls back and grins at me.

"There will be time," he whispers in a voice full of promise. He stands up. I sigh, somewhat dismayed despite everything, but allow him to pull me to my feet and lead me, hand in hand, out the hatch. I hop down onto the pavement and scan the dark streets. We're about three blocks past the southernmost entrance to the Resistance tunnels. Bear's looking at us expectantly, and Soren and I turn and start walking towards the tunnels. But out of the shadows figures materialize, and I abruptly find myself staring into the lidless eyes of about ten Bolts, a phalanx of Resistance members running towards us in formation. I freeze. This is the exact opposite thing I was hoping for.

"Well, I wasn't expecting a parade, but this is a little much," Soren whispers, at my side.

Suddenly I find myself knocked backwards, arms around me tightly in what feels like a death grip. I yelp in surprise and try to wrestle free, unsure who's hugging me.

"Remy, you dumb shit, it's me!" *I know that voice.* The arms pull back for a second. I look up to see narrow, offended green eyes staring at me through a haze of brown hair. Eli.

"What's with the warm reception?" I demand, though the guns have been lowered and everyone is looking at us, confused.

"You're the ones who flew a damn Sector airship here!" Eli shouts, but he's smiling, almost as if the whole thing is a joke. He grabs me and wraps his arms around me protectively. This time I reciprocate the hug. I allow myself to relax into his arms and take a deep breath, and the exhaustion finally hits me. The feeling of being back among friendly faces is overwhelming. "You okay, little bird?" he asks, and I nod. I try to shake off the shock of almost being attacked by my friends. *It's okay,* I tell myself, but when Eli lets me go I find my hand reaching out for Soren's, a grounding point. He laces his fingers into mine and squeezes.

"Remy!" I hear another familiar voice shout dimly, as though from a great distance, or underwater. I peer past Eli and see my mother and father running up behind him, and in an instant I'm drowning in more bodies. I start shaking, sobs catching in my throat as I am buried in my parents' embrace. "Oh, Remy, thank the fates you're alive, we were so worried." I can hear my mother's voice more through her rib cage than through the air.

"Tried to send a squad out to rescue you—" my father's operatic voice is trembling with emotion. I'm suffocating slightly under the weight of the limbs and torsos around me.

"Yeah," I say, my voice catching in my throat, "But right now I can't really breathe, so can you stop hugging me for just a second?" They pull back, their faces bright and shining with tears and happiness. I offer them a pathetic, floppy smile, and my father leans over and kisses me on the forehead. He wipes the tears from his cheeks, and I wonder if there's even a word for the combination of confusion, relief, and fatigue that I'm feeling right now. Soren is embracing Jahnu, Kenzie, and Eli, and Bear is standing at Soren's side, unsure of his place in the crowd.

With my parents, we break through the ranks of the Resistance soldiers, who stare at us as though we are some sort of returning heroes. Behind me, I can hear Soren introducing Bear to the rest of our friends, and once again I'm glad Soren's with me so that I don't have to explain, don't have to talk. We start to walk down the streets, and I'm so tired I'm stumbling, though my father holds me up and supports me at the elbow. I glance around at the buildings and realize it's still a few blocks back to the entrance to our base, and the blocks seem to grow and stretch into kilometers of distance. I tremble and cling to my parents' arms. I glance behind me and realize that the soldiers who were prepared to shoot us just minutes ago have now formed up as a sort of honor guard around us.

A vague humming, as though from a bee buzzing around my ear, suddenly strikes me as wrong, somehow *incorrect*, and I look up and around for the source of the noise.

"We should go," I say. What is that noise? The buzzing continues, growing in intensity. "*Now.*"

The distant hum turns into a much more persistent thrum as airships come into view over the treetops and buildings, and my world explodes into fireworks of blue light. Bolts, firing with abandon around us, from the airships overhead, drown the streets in electricity. I hear a dull thump behind me, the unmistakable sound of a body hitting the pavement. I turn numbly. A man I didn't know well, whose name I cannot recall, has collapsed on the ground. Soren locks eyes with me and I can tell he's thinking the same thing that's blazing through my mind at a thousand kilometers a second.

We brought them here.

"Run!" Soren shouts behind me, and with my parents at my elbows, none of us armed, we need no further urging.

30 — VALE

I watch as Remy and Soren and a third person I don't recognize descend from my airship, as Eli hits Remy with a hug and she tries to fight him off. I watch as her parents, Gabriel and Brinn, run up behind her and comfort her and lead her back down the street towards the entrance to the Resistance tunnels. I am confused but thankful—I have no idea how they found my ship, but of all the people who could have hijacked it, better them than an Outsider, or worse, Sector soldiers. The Resistance members around me are celebrating, and even Rhinehouse wears a weary smile. Everyone seems to have forgotten about me. I breathe a sigh and rest up against the wall and watch the homecoming parade through the cameras.

On the display screen I see Remy and her parents look up at the sky, confused. As one of the Resistance members beside them collapses in a flash of blue. I watch, horrified, as Remy and her parents, unarmed, sprint down the street. As Soren and the teenage boy duck into an abandoned building for cover. As Eli, Jahnu, Kenzie, and the armed team members drop to their knees and fire up into the sky at targets that the street-side defensive cameras cannot angle high enough for me to see.

I watch as Remy's mother, Brinn, takes a shot in the back and falls to the gritty pavement face-first. As Remy opens her mouth in a soundless scream and falls to her knees at her mother's side.

I am running. I somersault through the halls and come up with my bound hands in front of me. A move I never practiced but somehow intuited through a combination of desperation, guilt, and anger. My combat contacts zero in on a man with a Bolt in his hands, looking confused, as though at a loss for what to do next. I grab the gun from his hands and keep moving.

"Hey!" he shouts at me, but his cry is already echoing through the halls behind me.

I was blindfolded when I came through here but I distantly remember the turns and twists I made with Eli at my side. I do it backwards, cradling the Bolt in my arms like a firstborn child, always choosing the path that leads uphill. I follow the scent of fresh air and miraculously find myself outside in just a few moments. I scan the streets, looking for Remy. "Zoom," I command, and my contacts zoom in on a group of people two blocks down. I run flat out in their direction, past hulking shells of buildings, abandoned, rusted vehicles, and skyscraping trees that have sprouted in the ruined city. There. My contacts zoom in on Remy's figure, kneeling next to Brinn's prone body. REMY ALEXANDER, my contacts say. WANTED – TREASON. Similar names and wanted listings pop up for her father, who is cradling Brinn's head in his lap. They are prime targets, motionless on the ground. The Resistance team has largely taken defensive cover from the Bolt fire overhead, but Remy and Gabriel are too distracted to seek shelter from the onslaught.

I drop the Bolt and bash my wrists on an automobile door, hanging limp and broken from its hinges. The cuffs around my wrists don't break, so I do it again, and again with all the strength I can muster. Four, five, six times until the cuffs finally snap and my hands are free, my wrists bleeding from the abrasion. I barely notice. I pick the Bolt up again and sprint to Brinn's side, whose breaths are shallow and hoarse but audible. I look across her body at Remy and her father, who haven't quite noticed me yet. Remy is clutching her mother's hand, her face ashen and tear-streaked.

I sight up into the charcoal skies, past the hulking, decaying buildings above us. My contacts immediately highlight the humming ships in the air, which have passed over us and are preparing for a second assault. A note pops in my vision that identifies the airships: EAGLE 2F. Ships designed for precision and assault. Two soldiers in black helmets emblazoned with the OAC's wheat-stalk symbol. OAC Security Forces. My mother's black ops.

They're here to finish Chan-Yu's job.

This is my fault.

They must have tracked my Sarus here when Remy and Soren hijacked it. Now they're swinging back into range, so I don't have time to waste. Remy and Gabriel are too vulnerable here, out in the open. I bend down to Brinn's side, whose face is pale and drained as she draws in short, desperate breaths. A metallic stench fills my nose and I look down to see blood pooling around my boots. There is a gaping hole in Brinn's back, just barely visible from where I am, and her clothes are torn and soaked with sweat and blood. Remy finally looks up at me now, as though seeing the outside world for the first time since her mother collapsed.

"Vale." Her voice is so tormented it sounds as though her heart is being ripped physically from her body.

"We have to move," I say, looking back and forth between Remy and her father, whose face is contorted and full of grief. "You'll die if you stay here." The world explodes in blue and I turn my face to the sky. The black ops are back.

"I don't care," she whispers, and turns her eyes back to her mother. Her words are sharp enough to flay the skin from my bones. But Gabriel nods at me, acknowledging the truth in my words. Without speaking he moves next to me and puts his arms under his wife's back and shoulders, lifting her from the ground. Brinn gives me a weak smile.

"Thank you," she says, so softly I am reading her lips rather than hearing her words. I jog along with them, keeping my Bolt trained at the sky, trying to provide cover as Gabriel carries Brinn into a darkened old storefront whose windows and doors have long since been broken or rotted through. There's still a part of a roof over it, which is what matters. From the sky, the black ops won't be able to touch them. Remy follows him into the little old store and watches as Gabriel lays Brinn's body down on the moldy floor, littered with detritus. She kneels next to her and I turn, guarding the threshold to the building. From there, I watch as the Eagles swing around for another pass.

This time, they're not using Bolts. I watch as sonic and explosive grenades blossom like flowers in the bleak streets. The sonic grenades are invisible, but I can hear the *whump* and feel the bursts in my chest like a hollow drum, and I can see the buildings avalanche to the ground. The explosives are much more violent. They leave craters in their wake, and I can tell that the black ops aren't aiming those at the buildings. They're trying to blow through the streets into the tunnels below. They know there are more Resistance members underground.

The base is lost. We have to get out of the city before hundreds of people die. I turn back to Remy and her father just in time to see Remy charging at me with her fists forward. I barely have time to throw my Bolt up in self-defense, but she gets her second hand solidly into my rib cage and I stagger back.

"Remy!" I gasp, but she's coming back for more.

She spins and lands a foot in my chest that would have impressed even my hand-to-hand combat instructor. I stagger backwards, the wind gone from my lungs, but then she grabs a shard of glass off the floor and launches it at me. I drop to my knees to avoid having my throat sliced by flying glass.

"What are you doing?" I sputter. "I didn't bring them here!" But she's deaf to my words. Her feral expression never changes. She charges at me again, and I catch her around the legs and knock her to the ground. But she's kicking at me, at my shoulders and my face, and this fight doesn't even make sense anymore, it never did, it's me against a wild animal, cornered and desperate. I cling more tightly to her legs so she can't get away, and I reach a hand up and pin it around her abdomen. She flings her fists, small but powerful, at me and then suddenly pulls a knee up into my stomach. I groan and roll off of her, but she's on me in a second, a blade in her hands and at my throat.

But before I can close my eyes and pray that she kills me quickly, she's gone, standing up, dragged away from me. I look up to find Gabriel pulling her back, pulling her close, whispering something to her that I cannot hear or understand. Words that saved me from the unflinching justice of her hands. I push myself up on my elbows and watch as Remy glares at me, murder in her eyes, but she does not move. I glance up at the table, where Brinn lies motionless.

"I'm sorry." That's all I can say. I watch the two of them for a minute before Gabriel nods at me and says simply:

"Go."

I stand up and grab my Bolt. I watch as Remy and Gabriel turn back to Brinn's side and kneel over her, like penitent worshipers at an old world temple. I want to mourn with them, to comfort Remy and tell her how sorry I am, but instead I do as Gabriel commanded and stand up and turn away. Outside, the battle is raging. I may be able to redeem myself there. I need to give Remy and her father their peace.

An explosion rattles the frame of the building. I turn on my heel and survey the streets from the threshold of the crumbling storefront. The Resistance is scattered, and there are enormous holes in the pavement where sonar and explosive grenades have fallen. My contacts point out the Resistance fighters around the dark battleground, identifying them and their various crimes against the Sector. The word TREASON pops up above many of them. I can see Eli and Soren from here, but I don't recognize any other names. The words THEFT AND MURDER hover in red lines above Eli's head. The Resistance leaders must still be underground. We have to get them out.

The other Resistance members are firing up at the ships, but their Bolts are useless against the Eagles' shields. The blue electricity flashes harmlessly on the hulls, dissipating across the metal. But I know where the shield generators are. I know the structural deficiencies of every military airship currently in use by the Sector. When General Aulion was quizzing me on the minutiae of the blueprints, I doubt he anticipated that one day I'd use that knowledge not to defend our ships but to shoot them out of the sky. Is he up in one of these ships? Is my mother?

"Ship schematics," I say and blink twice as my contacts outline the airships in light red lines. I switch the Bolt's voltage to maximum and sprint from the threshold to another old vehicle, this one upturned in the street. I can use it as a barricade. Looking to the skies, I kneel behind it. I sight up along the line of the Bolt and take careful aim at a small point at the tip of the wing where the shield generators are located. If you hit them at the right angle, you can destroy the circuitry and take out the shields on one side of the ship. I watch carefully and wait for the perfect moment when the wing will dip slightly to the ground and I'll have a direct shot. I wait. Blue flashes twenty meters from me, and there—the wing dips.

I fire. I hold my breath and wait for my Bolt to recharge. There's no real way to tell whether I was successful or not. Not until I fire again. The capacitor glows blue, indicating it's loaded, and I take aim again and squeeze the trigger, this time at the belly of the ship. Orange sparks fly, and I know I've done damage. The shields are down—on this side, at least. I fire again and again, as quickly as the Bolt's capacitor will reload. After four direct hits and one that clipped the tail, the Eagle is smoking and spinning out of control. I watch as black shapes drop out of the ship and realize we have to prepare for a ground assault. As dangerous as they are from the air, the OAC black ops are even more deadly on the ground.

There's a lull in the explosions. Maybe they're watching the Eagle go down, wondering who knew where the shields were located and how to take them out.

"Vale!" I hear a voice shouting in the distance. "Valerian, is that you?" I don't call back. I can't identify the voice and I don't want to confirm my identity in case it's one of the black ops soldiers. I stare dimly into the streets, and my contacts pick up a shape moving at me quickly, keeping to the shadows. The facial recognition software kicks in and identifies Elijah. I hold my gun ready, just in case. Out of the corner of my eye, I watch the airship I shot down spiral and crash into a ruined high-rise in the distance. The sound of the impact of metal on metal squeals through the city, but there is no explosion. The engines must not have been hit.

"Did you just take that ship down?" Eli shouts at me from not ten meters away. He finally comes to a halt next to me, his face streaked with sweat and creased with worry.

"Yeah, that was me," I respond, but before he can continue, I go on. "There are at least ten men on each of those airships, and I counted seven. No way you have enough soldiers to counter that assault."

"No," he agrees, crestfallen. "We'll have to evacuate the base. How'd you take the ship down? We might be able to hold them off for a while longer if we can take out a few more."

"I'll show you." I realize that this will be harder for Eli, who doesn't have the mission contacts I have. I point up to the sky at one of the ships nearest to us, flying out in a wide circle around the city. "See the very tip of the wing, there, where there's a white light glowing? That's where the shield generators are. If you hit it with a straight shot, you'll blow the circuitry. But you have to do it when the wing dips towards you; otherwise your shot will be deflected by the shields. It's a matter of timing." I take aim and wait. When the Eagle starts to angle back our way, I pull the trigger.

"How do you know you've hit it?" Eli asks.

"You don't until you take another shot. Try now."

Eli sights up in to the sky and fires at the ship. When I see the sparks fly, I know my aim was true and the shields are down. Together we fire until the ship stops turning, listing in the sky in a slow descent to the ground.

Eli nods, by way of acknowledgement. He looks at me hesitantly. "They must have tracked that ship Remy and Soren flew here in." An explosion rocks the ground at our feet, and in the distance I can see the fires leaping from where the Eagle nose-dived into the ground.

"They did," I respond. "It's my ship. We abandoned it because they started tracking us. But Remy and Soren couldn't have known that. Anyway, we've got to move. I'm not going to be responsible for any more dead today. Brinn's gone." Eli stares at me for a second, and then his eyes harden and narrow. I take a step back. Is he going to jump at me, too? But then he looks away from me, staring up at the hovering airships as the explosions bloom around us. I guess my willingness to shoot down a Sector airship was proof enough that I'm trustworthy. For now.

He is silent. When he speaks again, his voice is low and cold.

"Two of our soldiers are down, too."

"Who?" I ask, even though I don't want to know.

"You wouldn't know them." I breathe a sigh of relief. Their anonymity makes it easier for me to bear, but not by much. At least it's not Jahnu or Kenzie— people I would have once called friends.

"Eli," I put my hand tentatively on his shoulder, "we can—"

He slaps my hand away.

"Don't," he says, without looking at me. "We need to evacuate. We don't have a hope in hell of winning this battle."

"Tell me what I can do," I say. "I know the Defense Forces better than anyone here. I can help you." Eli glances at me warily.

"Remy and Gabriel—are they alright?"

"They're unhurt," I say, which is only partly true.

"Okay. Let's move. I'll call our team off the streets and meet you in the tunnels. Get Remy and Gabriel and bring as many ships down as you can."

He nods at me and I meet him eye to eye. A look of understanding passes across his face. Five days ago he was screaming at me from the rooftops of a Sector seed bank as I took two of his friends and comrades hostage. Today we find ourselves fighting for the same thing, even if we're doing it for different reasons.

"The closest entrance to the tunnels is two blocks south of here. You can't miss it."

"I think that's how I got up here."

"Oh." He looks at me as though suddenly confused. "I was wondering how you got up here." I hold out my wrists, which are still bleeding.

"It wasn't easy."

"That's nothing," he says. "Just wait 'till Rhinehouse gets hold of you." His tone is wry and he gives me the barest twinge of a smile. But then it slips off his face so quickly I wonder if I imagined it. "Get Remy and Gabriel. Meet in the tunnels." He takes off back in the direction he came, jogging easily with his Bolt in his arms, checking around him. I don't relish the thought of facing Remy and her father again, but I run back to the building they're hiding in and rap on the threshold to announce my presence. I don't want to startle them. Both of them look up at me, their faces tear-streaked and grimy. Gabriel has his arm around Remy, and they have closed Brinn's eyes and are gripping her hands with white knuckles.

"I know I'm the last person you want to see right now, but we have to move. OAC black ops are landing. We have to get out of here."

"Why should we trust you?" Remy chokes the words out.

"You don't have a choice. Follow me or stay here and die." I look her in the eyes. "You'll have to leave her. I'm sorry." Remy lets loose a guttural sob and buries her head in her mother's chest. But Gabriel nods wordlessly at me and takes Remy by the hand.

"Let's go, little bird."

The injustice of losing both a mother and a sister hits me as solidly and surely as Remy's fists ever could. I swallow my own tears and turn, waiting for Remy and Gabriel to lead the way out.

Remy stays close to her father's side, and together we make our way slowly out to the streets. I blink to clear my eyes. Focus, Vale. I can hear shouting in the distance and see the blue flashes that indicate Bolt fire. I keep careful watch, ready to fire at a moment's notice, but for now the battle is beyond my vision. I lead Remy and Gabriel through the dead city, keeping to the shadows. A sonic grenade explodes to our left and a building starts to topple into the street.

"RUN!" I shout, and I grab Remy's arm and pull her forward in a sprint, and her father follows. Old stones and concrete fall into the street, littering the pavement with chunks of rock. Another grenade, this one a traditional explosive, goes off thirty meters in front of us, blowing a crater in the street five meters deep. Have they spotted us, or were those grenades thrown randomly? Remy and I stare at the crater and I push her over to the side, under an old tattered awning, for cover. Her father follows her and they huddle together. A few meters away, I kneel behind some of the fallen rock and stare up into the sky, searching for the Eagle responsible for these latest grenades.

I catch sight of a wing tip and my contacts light up, outlining the ship. I don't bother to aim—I fire as rapidly as the capacitor will charge, launching blue streaks into the sky and giving away my position. As the ship's Bolts are turned on me, I duck behind the crumbled wall I've chosen for cover. I wait for the Bolts from above to stop, hoping I've hit the shield generators. After a few seconds, I turn my fire onto the main hull. Telltale orange and red sparks fly like falling stars. We can't wait to check to see if I've done enough damage to get it off our backs. I gesture to Remy and Gabriel to follow me. It's only one more block to the tunnels. I close my eyes briefly and hope we can make it.

The airship plagues us no more. A half block from the entrance to the tunnels, I hear shouts behind me.

"Remy!" I turn and my contacts identify Jahnu, Soren, Kenzie, Eli, and the man called Firestone, moving low to the ground in formation, as a team. Soren is shadowed by a smaller figure, who I recognize as the boy from the Sarus. Behind them, another group, is also moving in formation. Another Resistance team. Soren breaks formation and runs up to Remy, throwing his arms around her and hugging her tightly, his lips pressing into her hair. She clings to him and jealousy sears through me. *She hates me, but she's found room for Soren.* I quell my anger and turn away, checking the skies above us. Eli comes up to me, his expression grim.

"Black ops are scattered throughout the area, headed this way. Almost all the ships have unloaded their men. They'll have us surrounded in minutes. Everyone who was aboveground when Remy and Soren landed has been accounted for, dead or alive."

"I don't know how far the Sector is willing to go," I tell him. "I want to believe they won't annihilate everyone, but …" Eli nods.

"Understood. We'll act on the assumption that they're taking no prisoners." He relays this information through his earpiece and then addresses everyone surrounding him. Soren has his arm around Remy, comforting her as I wish I could.

Just then I see a moving shadow out of the corner of my eye. I turn to my right and my contacts outline a soldier in red, stealing a glance around the corner from an alleyway. I duck and pull up my gun at the ready, but not before he pops off a shot. It whizzes by me, but I hear someone cry in pain. I aim and fire, and the man collapses.

"Tunnels!" Eli shouts, suddenly aware of the danger. "Move!" The Bolt hit one of the Resistance fighters in the leg. He's limping but alive. Jahnu and I cover for Remy, Gabriel, Soren, and Soren's younger shadow, none of whom are armed, while Eli, Kenzie, and Firestone fan out across the rest of the street, walking backwards as everyone else jogs towards the tunnels. But when Bolt fire starts erupting from the alleyway, I know we've been found.

We return fire, but they duck back behind the corner. They're impossible to hit in the darkness, and I'm fairly certain I'm the only one in the Resistance group with combat contacts in. We fire ceaselessly at the alleyway, but quickly realize that they're approaching us from more than one direction. One by one we duck into the entrance to the tunnels. Finally Eli is the last one in, and Jahnu and I cover for him on either side as he sidesteps down the incline. We turn and sprint down the rest of the way, and as we descend we pass an enormous set of metal doors that Eli and Jahnu slam and latch from the inside.

"They won't have brought a battering ram," Jahnu grins.

"Who needs a battering ram when you've got explosives?" Eli responds, rolling his eyes. Everything around us is chaos. The lights are flickering and have gone off in sections of the tunnel, and in the distance I can see one hallway has collapsed. We're isolated here for now—everyone seems to have already abandoned the facility.

"Listen up," Eli says, addressing the motley crew of people, tired and haggard, from aboveground. "We're going to Code Evac. Teams will go to their pre-assigned rendezvous destinations outside the city, just like in the drills.

Disable all communications devices—they'll be able to track you by the signals they emit. You'll be disconnected for a few hours, but it'll be better than being shot down from above."

I realize then that I'm forgetting something incredibly, terribly, overwhelmingly valuable.

"Where's Jeremiah?"

Eli gapes at me, realizing he has made the same mistake. Then he puts his finger to his ear, listens, and turns as someone I don't recognize stands. "Good luck. We'll see you at the rendezvous point," Eli says to her. They must have gotten a message from the Director. They shake hands and the woman and her team—including Remy's father—stand. I watch as Remy and Gabriel hold each other. Though Remy is still crying, tears streaking down her cheeks, her father's face is set in grim determination. He bends down and whispers something in her ear, and she nods. Then he kisses the top of her head, turns on his heel and follows the rest of his team out the door.

"They're going to help Rhinehouse destroy his lab before we they leave," Eli says, by way of explanation. Then he scans my face and turns to Soren. "Soren and Vale, go get Jeremiah. He's in the first holding room in the west hall. Kenzie, come with me—I need to get my hard drive. It has the backup of the DNA on it. Jahnu, Firestone, Remy, and you"—he points to the boy with Remy and Soren—"head to the mess hall. We'll all meet there in ten minutes."

Soren raises his eyes to me for the first time since we faced each other in the capital. I can tell it's all he can do not to rip my throat out with his teeth. His eyes aren't quite as murderous as Remy's were, but they're full of rage and bitterness. It's just then I realize his knife is in the pack that Eli and his team confiscated from me when they brought us here.

"Jahnu," I whisper. "Where'd you guys put my stuff?"

"I'll take you there," he says. "It's on the way to the mess hall. We can all go together." He squeezes Kenzie's hand and she gives him a reassuring smile. They must be together. I wonder if Moriana would be happy for her cousin. Just then, there's an explosion somewhere above us and the lights go out. Dust falls from the ceiling and I duck, covering my head with my arms, just in case. I hold my breath, but nothing major collapses around us.

A torch light comes on.

"Everyone okay?" It's Jahnu. His light flashes around and everyone appears unhurt, though uncertain and afraid.

"We're fine," Kenzie returns, her own light coming on. "Let's move. We need to get out of here." Everyone except Soren, Remy, and I have torches, and as we move to split up, Firestone tosses his torch to Soren. He and I form the rear guard behind Remy and the boy as Jahnu and Firestone lead the way down the dark, oppressive halls. Soren matches his stride to mine as we pace tersely through the corridors, measuring ourselves against each other.

Jahnu points out to me where he has to turn to get to the mess hall and to the little alcove where my pack was stored. I jog forward and rifle through my backpack. I don't bother with any of the rest of our supplies—they'll just weigh me down. I pull Soren's knife out of the pack and turn back to him, holding it in my palm. I can't find the words to express the guilt I feel at having been responsible for his experiences the last few days. So I open my palm to him soundlessly.

Soren takes the knife and tucks it into his belt without looking at me. Without a word, he turns away and continues down the halls. I sigh and remind myself that making peace will take time. I follow him, keeping my footsteps light and my ears tuned for any sign that we're being pursued, any hint of an explosion above that will bring the world down around us. But aside from our footfalls, silence abounds.

At a certain point I start hearing muffled shouts through the halls, and I quickly identify the voice as Jeremiah's. My stomach does a flip. Soren shoots a backwards glance at me, presumably thinking the same thing, and darts off in a jog. The shouts grow louder, but they're still unintelligible. I can hear him pounding on the door. Is this corridor so deserted that no one's heard him and thought to let him out? I anxiously follow Soren until he stops abruptly, throws the locks on the door and pulls it open. On the other side, Jeremiah's mouth is open and his eyes wide in fear and anger. But when he looks up and sees Soren, his expression morphs into one of surprise and even happiness. A grin spreads easily over his bearded face, the first real smile I've seen in days. Soren's eyes are similarly alight, and it occurs to me that Jeremiah and Soren were once just as close as Miah and I are now.

"Soren Skaarsgard. Well," Miah looks Soren up and down, "I see you haven't taken a bath since I last saw you."

Soren's smile is so wide it looks like it might take over his whole face, and he throws his arms around Jeremiah in an embrace that might knock another man down. But Jeremiah matches Soren kilo for kilo, and they clap each other on the back and pound for so long I'm about ready to warn them these tunnels could collapse on us at any minute when they finally pull apart.

"I knew you'd come around eventually," Soren says to Jeremiah.

"Well, when Vale told me you'd been back to the capital and hadn't bothered to come say hello, I had to track you down to exact my revenge."

Soren's expression dims for a moment, but the smile flares back to his face and he claps Miah on the shoulder one last time.

"Let's get you out of here," he says and steps aside, letting Miah out of his tiny holding room.

"Yeah, it took you two assholes long enough." Jeremiah suddenly glares at me in mock anger and I roll my eyes.

"There was a lot going on," I respond. "Let's go, we need to move. Soren, you know these tunnels—lead the way." I'm trying to be deferential, but maybe anything from my mouth sounds like a command. Soren's eyes narrow and I think he's about to spit at me. He thinks better of it, though, and turns, heading back the way we came and in the direction of the mess hall.

"Seriously, though, Vale," Miah mutters to me as we jog, "what's going on up there?"

I fill him in quickly on the events of the last hour, and Jeremiah's face falls when he hears about Brinn.

"I never knew her, but Moriana said she was one of the Sector's best scientists. And now Remy...."

The halls are tomb-like and skeletal without light or people. When we turn into the mess hall, Remy's eyes are dead and cold, and she doesn't even acknowledge me. Soren quickly sits down next to her and throws an arm around her, and Jeremiah shoots me a questioning look. *What's going on?* his eyes seem to say. When Remy doesn't seem to notice Soren either, a grim, bitter smile briefly flutters onto my face. A distant explosion rocks the foundations, though, wiping away all traces of jealousy and bringing me back to the danger of the moment.

"Everything's deserted. We're just waiting for Eli and Kenzie," Firestone says in his lazy drawl. He's the only one who seems unperturbed by the fact that the Resistance base is being decimated.

A dim flash of blue light down the hall alerts us all to danger, and pounding feet and shouting echo through the halls. Remy is suddenly on her feet, flame in her eyes. I can see her chest heaving, even in the shadowy torchlight. Jahnu, Firestone, and I pull our Bolts up and at the ready, and Soren's knife glints in the light.

"Eli!" I recognize Kenzie's voice, breathless, and there's another flash of blue down the corridor. My heart thuds to a stop, but around me, everyone is moving. Jahnu and the boy are physically restraining Remy, pulling her back, away from the fight. Soren's got his arm thrown out against Jeremiah's chest, telling him not to move. I realize only three of us are armed, and I leap into action, running to the hallway where Kenzie and Eli are coming from. Firestone is somehow at my side. We kneel together and sight down the halls, where I can see Kenzie running frantically, pulling Eli by the hand, who's stumbling and looks dazed. I blink twice and my contacts outline the distant soldiers in red, and I know they'll have similar sights on Kenzie and Eli. I aim and prepare to fire, but before I can even get a shot off, Firestone has casually loosed three low-energy warning shots down the hall. The men duck behind a corner or into a door and disappear. I glance over at him, surprised.

"Well, we don't want to kill 'em if we don't have to," he says easily in response to my inquisitive look. Kenzie and Eli dash past us into the mess hall, and we quickly turn and follow them. Firestone shuts and bolts the door behind us.

"Go!" Kenzie shouts at Jahnu, who has been waiting tensely for orders. Without a word he turns, dragging Remy by the elbow, and leads the team out through a separate passage. Firestone and I take up the rear, but there's not much time to check behind us. We're all sprinting through the base, the last remnants of the fleeing, defeated Resistance.

The sun is risen now, pinkish yellow in the sky as rays feather out through the treetops. I clutch my knees to my body, pulling them in tight for warmth like I did when I was a child. The forest around the boulder I've chosen for my perch is brown and wintergreen, and the chill air nips me playfully, smiling at me, beckoning me to its games. I do not smile back. I see my mother's face in the treetops and the clouds, everywhere. I wish we'd burned her, but maybe the Sector's grenades will have done that for me. Maybe the explosives started an inferno that consumed her body and will distribute the carbon remnants of her soul through the world to start something new. I hope that's what happened. The thought of her body rotting, desolate, in the bleak and empty streets of our twice-abandoned city is enough to steal the blood from my heart.

This is our rendezvous point, an old factory about a hundred and fifty kilometers away from the main base. It's long since crumbled and been retaken by the surrounding forest, beaten back for so many years and now returned with a vengeance. My dad's team was supposed to rendezvous here, too, but they still haven't shown up. I wonder if they couldn't get to their vehicle, or if they had to walk, or if....

My team made it here last night at around one in the morning, a long blurry trek that is already fading from memory. The tunnels were funereal and empty. The second home I've had to put behind me was easier than the first. We were dogged for a while by the black ops, but we lost them in the maze of underground tunnels. Jahnu and Kenzie led us up above ground, to our emergency escape vehicle hidden in some old garage. It was a small thing, a modified hovercar that was nearly impossible to cram eight people in. Bear had to ride stuffed on the floor, clutching nervously to the seat as Firestone zipped us out of the city, swearing at every shadow and cloud.

I didn't look at Vale, and though I felt his eyes on me a few times, he never tried to speak to me, to my great relief. Just kept quiet. I know he didn't bring the airships down on us. It wasn't his fault. Soren and I should have guessed we would be tracked back to base—but we didn't have much choice. I still don't trust Vale, but Eli told me not to worry about him now.

I keep thinking of Dad, whether he's okay, whether they'll make it to the rendezvous point. Soren told me not to think about those things. "They'll be here," he said last night, when I was trying to sleep. "They'll come." He showed me how to practice breathing, calming exercises that he said would help me sleep. "Count your breaths and watch as you breathe in and out. Count them one to ten. And then do it again. If you start to think about your parents, or Tai, or anything else that's bothering you, that's okay. Just let the thought happen, and then let it go and return to your breathing." And then he held my hand while I closed my eyes and tried for a few minutes. It helped, but not much.

At the rendezvous point, everyone except Eli was surprised to find a well-stocked little house, ready for visitors. Ten sleeping bags with extra blankets. Dried fruit, meat, and purified water. A little communications station and even a two-dimensional computing display. Eli either knew all this was waiting for us at the rendezvous or was too dazed to know what was going on. We couldn't quite figure it out. Kenzie thinks he got a concussion when the soldiers in the tunnel first started firing at them. "He dived to dodge a Bolt, and I think he hit his head on the tunnel wall," she said. Once he heard that, Vale stepped in and took over. Apparently part of his training in military command was basic first aid and medical knowledge, so he volunteered to keep watch over Eli and make sure he didn't fall asleep and drank plenty of water. I didn't like the idea of placing Eli's life in Vale's hands, but when Soren and I protested, Kenzie said Eli wanted us to work with him. "For now," she said, her voice at a whisper.

Jeremiah, I barely remember from the Academy. He was Vale and Soren's year, so I didn't interact with him much. I don't like the fact that he came here with Vale. He and Soren spent a lot of time talking—or maybe it would be better said that they spent a lot of time eating. The two of them wolfed down more food than the rest of us combined. It was only at Soren's encouragement that Jeremiah would touch it, but once he started, he couldn't stop.

"Man, this cheese is great," Jeremiah kept saying. He speared something on the plate and his eyes went wide. "What is this?"

Soren grinned at him. "It's a tomato. A real one."

"Where do you get this stuff?"

"We make it or grow it," he said, to which Jeremiah nearly spat out his food.

"You *make* it? Why? That's what the Farms are for!" Bear, nearby, took offense at that.

"Maybe if more people grew their own food, I coulda lived in the capital, too. Maybe I coulda gone to the Academy."

"You're from one of the Farms?" Jermiah asked, eyebrows arched in surprise.

"Yeah," Bear said, puffing his chest out. "I found Remy and Soren out … in the Wilds," he says. His next words are quieter. "Maybe if more people grew their own food, Sam would still be here." Soren's smile slipped off his face at the memory and I turned away, the numbness seeping back through my limbs. So many dead these last few days.

When it was finally time to sleep, Vale said he'd take the first watch so he could keep Eli awake at the same time. But all I could think about was how easy it would be for Vale to murder Eli while the rest of us were sleeping, so I said I would do it. I knew I wouldn't be sleeping much anyway.

"Are you sure?" Vale said, as though doubting my ability to stay awake the whole night. "Shouldn't you—"

"Fuck off," I told him. He shut up after that.

Soren offered to stay awake with me and Eli, but I told him I'd be fine. I made him go to bed. But he wouldn't before he gave me his knife and a kiss on the forehead.

"Use it to kill Vale if you need to. Or anyone. Who knows who's out there?" So I tucked the knife into my belt and sat next to Eli outside in the starry darkness. Jahnu came and sat next to us, putting his arms around me, claiming he couldn't sleep either.

"Where's Kenzie?" I whispered, making sure she wouldn't miss him.

"Sound asleep," he responded kindly. "But I couldn't. I thought, if I'm going to be awake all night, I might as well keep watch with you. And I know neither of you should be alone right now." We didn't say much after that, none of us. The three of us pulled blankets around our shoulders and sat outside for the rest of the night, watching for Team Blue, my dad's team, or Corine's black ops, or airships raining fire from above, Eli's head in my lap as I played with his curly hair to keep him awake. And when Soren's breathing exercises didn't work and I couldn't stop remembering my mother and sister and I couldn't stop worrying about my father, Eli held my head against his chest while I cried.

Eventually, towards the creeping dawn, Eli fell asleep, and Jahnu said it was okay. I told him I needed to take a walk, so I left them there and wandered off, which is how I came upon this boulder in a little copse in the woods where I am sitting now. Counting from one to ten over and over and over again. Losing count and losing myself. Finding myself again. Finding my breath again. Counting from one to ten.

"Remy." The voice startles me and I whirl, Soren's knife drawn and ready in the span of a hummingbird's wing beat. It's Vale. His hands are up, defensively. A quick scan tells me he's unarmed. Well at least he doesn't have anything in his hands. I exhale. His presence is comforting, in a way. With him, I can let my grief give way to anger.

"Go away." I don't trust him enough to turn my back on him.

"No," he says, which surprises me. I raise my eyebrows at him, and his face is haggard, his eyes tired with dark circles under them, his sea-green irises dimmed to a hollow grey. He hasn't slept either.

"What do you want?"

"I know you wish it were me instead of your mother." He takes a step closer, but I recoil, and he stops. "You wish it had been me."

"Yes," I respond savagely.

"Two lives I owe you now." I glare at him. "What do you want from me?" he asks.

"Nothing. Go."

"No. I owe you a debt and I won't—"

"What you owe me you can never pay back!" I shout at him, and the outburst surprises me, though Vale's expression never changes. As though he was expecting my hatred. I close my eyes and calm myself. "You're right. It should have been you and not my mother. Not Tai." Vale looks down at the knife in my trembling hand.

"You could settle the debt right now." I consider this. I try to imagine, to contemplate the physical possibility of putting a knife in Vale's heart, or across his throat. I feel the weight of the knife in my palm, its balance and length. His eyes going glassy, his body limp, falling to the mossy carpet of the forest floor. Just like Sam, I realize, and the memory of Sam falling to the deck of the boat with a knife hilt sticking from his throat chills me. I don't want that.

"You owe me two lives. Yours won't satisfy that debt," I say and stick the knife back in my belt.

Vale nods and lets his glance slink away to the ground.

"Here," he says, pulling something out of his pocket. "You gave this to me a long time ago. I think you should have it back." He holds out his hand, and I recognize my grandfather's old compass, the K.A.L. engraved in fine, elegant script on the bottom. Granddad used to take it with him when he went out exploring, and he gave it to Tai before he died. A compass, he said, is more than a navigational tool; it's a symbol of finding true north. A symbol of truth. I stare at it in Vale's palm, remembering the day I gave it to him, remembering that he and Tai had been friends once, and that he, too, had been devastated by her death. I reach out and take it wordlessly, my fingers lightly brushing his. In my hand, the metal is warm from his skin.

"I'm sorry, Remy."

"I don't want your apology." I turn away from him, staring back towards the east where the sun is flickering over the leafless skeleton trees, turning the worn, old compass over again and again in my hand. When Tai died, everyone told me how sorry they were, but words of pity and apology are useless. Words won't bring her back. They won't bring Mom back. I want justice. *I want vengeance.*

Behind me, I hear his slight footfalls in the crunching leaves, and I know he's gone. I sigh and let my muscles relax, feeling the jagged rock from the boulder digging into my skin uncomfortably, keeping me awake despite dogged exhaustion. I squeeze my eyes shut, my hand clenching involuntarily around the heirloom, a bitter reminder of all the members of my family I will never see again. I lean my head back, skyward, letting the wind and the rising sun keep me company where humans cannot.

<hr/>

The rendezvous is silent and peaceful—too peaceful. There's still no sign of Team Blue, and Soren keeps squeezing my hand, telling me that it'll be all right; we'll hear from them eventually. We're instructed to stay here for at least three days while we wait for everyone to regroup. There are no more airships hovering overhead, no more soldiers sneaking up on us in the darkness. When Eli wakes up he's fine, back to normal, and now he insists that Soren and I tell our story.

"How did this happen?" he keeps demanding. "How did you end up in Vale's airship over the Resistance base with a renegade from the Farms and Outsider gear?"

He's already heard Vale's story, apparently, which he relays to me and Soren quickly. He says that's why he trusts Vale. That and the fact that he shot a Sector airship out of the sky. I'm still not sure I trust Vale, but his offering from this morning makes me more inclined to believe him. I haven't told anyone about our conversation, and I assume he hasn't either.

When I tell Eli about my drugged, hallucinogenic vision of the lotus flower, his eyes darken.

"That's what Vale meant. He said yesterday that Corine was after you because you had valuable information. I thought it had to do with the DNA.

She must have realized you knew the transcription key, and she couldn't let you get back to base with it."

"We need to try it," I say. "To see if I'm right. If it really is the key." Eli nods. It takes him, Kenzie, and Firestone about a half an hour to get the computer station up and running.

"What's this DNA thing?" Firestone asks, once everything is connected, sounding bored. If you can't fix it or fly it, Firestone's not interested.

"You'll see," Eli responds shortly.

When Eli gets his hard drive connected to the UMIT, the information transfer module, he pulls up the DNA with pictures of all the chromosomes and the endless strings of base pairs.

"I've seen that before," Vale interrupts, suddenly hovering over my shoulder. I shrink back from him and he looks down at me, apologetic, but doesn't back away. "That's the DNA project Professor Hawthorne was working on." His expression is grim and dark. Eli glances at me, worried.

"How do you know this, Vale?" he asks.

"I hacked into my mother's computer a few days ago. I was looking into Tai's death," he nods at me, "and trying to find out what happened. Corine..." he hesitates at her name, "and Hawthorne exchanged a series of emails where she insisted he give her the DNA, and he refused. It's why..." He pauses. "It's why she had him killed."

"I knew it," Eli growls.

"That's where I saw those images," Vale says. "On her computer."

"So she has it," Jahnu muses. "It doesn't matter. Even if she knows the key, it doesn't matter. We have the key, too. We can unlock whatever information is stored in the DNA."

Jogged into action by that thought, Eli loads up a decryption program he wrote when we first started working on the code. He instructs the program to decrypt the first chromosome using the cipher L-O-T-U-S. Jeremiah and Bear have by this point joined the gathering crowd and are watching over Eli's shoulder as everyone waits. The air is tense.

"We'll see what happens if we use it on just this first chromosome," he says, and after a few minutes, the program responds that the decryption is finished, and would Elijah Tawfiq like to view the results? Eli enters yes, he would, and when he pulls it up, the DNA from that first chromosome has been perfectly translated into a file system with a listing that says GENETIC CODES FOR VARIETIES OF ONION. After staring dumbly at the screen for several seconds as we realize what we've done, Jahnu grins, and Kenzie and Eli break out into hesitant smiles.

"Fuck me," Eli whispers. "It's a seed database." He starts navigating through the files. There's a complete genome map for every seed varietal listed.

"If Rhinehouse finds out about this, we'll be eating onion soup for the next twenty years," Jahnu laughs.

Eli sets up the decoding program for the rest of the chromosomes, and we all watch in silence as hundreds of file directories pop up across the screen with names like POTATO, APPLE, NUT TREE, CITRUS TREE.

"*Spiraling towers hide sacred flowers,*" Eli mutters, awed. "Think of what we can do with these seeds!" Jahnu, Kenzie, and Soren are talking animatedly about how the Resistance can use these codes to make old world seeds, untainted by the OAC's modifications, and Eli is navigating through the whole database, checking to make sure the information is complete. "Remy, your grandfather was a genius," he sighs happily.

But tears are dripping down my cheeks, salty and reminiscent of the sea like Vale's eyes, decorating my face with tokens to the dead. Vale, at my side, puts his hand on my shoulder. This time, I don't pull away.

End *of* Book One *of the* Seeds Trilogy
~ COMING NEXT: THE REAPING ~

Acknowledgements

We'd like to thank everyone who has supported us by reading our drafts and giving us feedback, helping us understand the science we explore in the novel, working with us on our social media platform, agreeing to read and review, contributing amazing original artwork, or just giving us an encouraging word. Among those who've helped along the way include: Rachel Adler, Alex Augustyn, C. G. Ayling, Kenneth Barr, Ken Floro III, David Johnston, Zoe Maffitt, Jason Makansi, Pat Nolan, Elle Opitz, Prashant Parmar, Peter Samet, Sarah Sarber, Imran Siddiq, Kathy Smith, Rachael Spellman, John Sternberg, Matthew Steffen, Jamey Stegmaier, Sam Stragand, Aaron Till, Regina Till, and Kevin Weitzel.

Coming Next

The Reaping, Book Two of the Seeds Trilogy, is coming in 2014. We invite you to connect with us on Twitter and Facebook to get the latest updates. If you enjoyed *The Sowing,* we'd love to hear from you. You can leave a review on Goodreads, Amazon, or Barnes & Noble, or contact us directly online. You can find us at:

www.theseedstrilogy.com
www.facebook.com/TheSeedsTrilogy
Twitter:
@readwritenow - Kristy
@akmakansi - Amira
@Elena_Makansi - Elena

About the Author(s)

K. Makansi is the pen name for the mother-daughter writing team consisting of:

Kristina Blank Makansi

Born and raised in Southern Illinois, Kristina has a B.A. in Government from University of Texas at Austin and an M.A.T. from the College of New Jersey. In 2010, she a co-founded Blank Slate Press, an award-winning small press, and Treehouse Publishing Group, an author services partnership. She has also written *Oracles of Delphi*, an historical mystery set in ancient Greece.

Amira K. Makansi

Amira earned a BA in History from the University of Chicago. She has served as an assistant editor and has read and evaluated Blank Slate Press submissions since the press was founded. She is an avid reader and blogger with a passion for food, wine, and photography. She has worked at various wineries in Oregon and France and is approaching fluency in French. She reviews books and blogs about writing, food, and wine at The Z-Axis.

Elena K. Makansi

Elena attends Oberlin College where she is focusing on Environmental Studies especially as it relates to her passion–food justice. She's also studied studio art and drawing and has had her work featured in several college publications. While in high school, she won numerous writing and poetry awards, was awarded a scholarship to attend the Washington University Summer Writing Institute, and also attended the Iowa Young Writers Studio. She and Amira enjoy backpacking together and share a passion for cooking, baking–and, yes, eating. Elena maintains a Tumblr site and a personal blog, both of which focus on food, environmental activism, social justice, and art.

CPSIA information can be obtained
at www.ICGtesting.com
Printed in the USA
LVOW12s0733211216
518199LV00002B/159/P